MORE PRAISE FOR *FIRE IN THE ROCK*

"*Fire in the Rock* demonstrates, to a remarkable degree, one writer's determination to make sense of yesteryear's divided Dixie. . . . It shows how friendship can follow intricate paths through a landscape that demands straight roads be taken." —*The New York Times Book Review*

"Joe Martin knows everything about the South that Anne Rivers Siddons and Terry Kay and Rick Bragg know, yet he also knows those secret and subterranean things that Alice Walker and Dori Sanders have been telling us for years." —PAT CONROY

"*Fire in the Rock* is a southern novel par excellence—a marvelous creation. And it's also the kind of book—nuanced, witty, perceptive—that makes you hope its author has another book already on the way!" —JOSEPHINE HUMPHREYS

"*Fire in the Rock* tells who we were and how we lived in the South in the 1950s and '60s. It is photographically real, painfully and, at times, comically exact. The book is thrilling in its honesty, rich detail, memorable voices. Those times breathe again, live again, and—make no mistake—they are us." —ROBERT MORGAN

"A host of memorable characters round out the story. . . . Martin is an undeniable talent, a man who has brought his longtime commitment to justice to the printed page with lyrical grace." —*The Charlotte Observer*

"This is first-rate southern writing—a torrent of words and images that brings life and depth. . . . Martin shares keen observations about racism and the role religion can play both to liberate and oppress." —*Booklist*

FIRE in the ROCK

FIRE *in the* ROCK

JOE MARTIN

BALLANTINE BOOKS • NEW YORK

A Ballantine Book
Published by The Ballantine Publishing Group

Copyright © 2001 by Joe Martin
Reader's Guide copyright © 2003 by Joe Martin and The Ballantine Publishing Group, a division of Random House, Inc.

The original hardcover edition of this work was published in October 2001 by Novello Festival Press, an imprint of The Public Library of Charlotte and Mecklenburg County, North Carolina.

Quotations: from *Tarzan of the Apes*, copyright © 1914 by Edgar Rice Burroughs; from *Tarzan and the Jewels of Opar* by Edgar Rice Burroughs, copyright © 1918 by A. C. McClurg & Co.; from *The Souls of Black Folk* by W. E. B. DuBois, first published in the U.S. by A.C. McClurg & Company, 1903.

www.ballantinebooks.com/BRC/

Library of Congress Control Number: 2003090125

ISBN 0-345-45691-2

Cover design by Andy Carpenter

Cover photo © Yagi Studio/SuperStock

Manufactured in the United States of America

First Ballantine Books Edition: March 2003

2 4 6 8 10 9 7 5 3 1

For Joan

"So we beat on, boats against the current,
borne back ceaselessly into the past."

— F. Scott Fitzgerald,
The Great Gatsby

Chapter One

———■———

SISTER HOLY GHOST & THE FOURTH OF JULY

J ust about the time Sue Snoddy became a teenager, she decided
that her name didn't amount to much. So she changed it. From her
mythology lessons at the kudzu-covered house up by the turn-off from the
main road, she chose "Terpsi-chore, Goddess of Dance" as her new name,
and she was dead serious about it. "Terpsi" would have been a perfect nick-
name for her even then, but Miz Snoddy Senior had asserted a mother's
rights and surrendered the old name only to the full thing — "Terpsi-chore"
— or, for short, Cora. And Cora had stuck.

Years later, on the Fourth of July 1956, Cora at a very ripe thirty was back
in the side yard of her mother's house out at the end of Brickstore Road,
absentmindedly doing handkerchief calisthenics with a limp lace rag high as
she could reach up over her head — more of a pose, actually, than an activity. She looked like a too-delicate alabaster reproduction of the Statue of

Liberty with her torch wilted in the heat. Crape myrtles at the edge of the yard framed her in deep red starbursts like so many skyrockets, their thunder muffled by the thick noontime humidity. There was no breeze at all. Nothing moved. Cora's breasts, so clearly defined by a white cotton dress that clung like thin molten bronze to every moist curve and crevice, just as clearly did not seem to rise and fall. Her knees and bare ankles, bent in a near faint, did not buckle. Her skin glistened, but no sweat dropped. She was fixed in some strange dimension right there in front of us, bombs bursting in mid-air, Miss Liberty in mid-wilt. Cora had never looked lovelier.

As far as I could tell, Cora had not noticed us gathering in the shade of a one-sided tree like cattle from some mixed-breed herd: her daughter Mae Maude and me on the arms of a wooden lawn chair, our summer tans almost matching its natural oak finish, and Pollo ("rhymes with follow," he would say, always adding, "follow Pollo," although nobody really ever did) the bicycle boy from the store. Pollo, just turned sixteen, same age as us, was sitting on the ground with his bare chocolate-bronze back against the trunk of the tree. Then there was Cora's mother Miz Snoddy Senior and the Young Senator standing under straw hats at the edge of the shade, both of them with pale white skin apparently never exposed to the sun — except for Miz Snoddy's leathery hands, which looked like they belonged to somebody else — and finally Sister Holy Ghost, who stood black as an iron fencepost and just as ramrod straight at the end of an old wicker settee.

"You call her, Sister," said the Young Senator in his low and reassuring voice. Leadership came easy and often to him, even when it didn't work very well.

"Not me," Sister Holy Ghost said. "She'll just start it all up again."

"Okay," he said in his most thoughtfully sincere tone. "Miz Snoddy, you see if you can get her over here."

"Terpsi-chore!" she called. "Get out of the sun. Come over here and have some tea. It's got that sweet mint in it just like you like. Come on over here, Cora. It's cooler in this shade."

It was no surprise to anybody that Sister Holy Ghost was right about Cora starting it all up again. As soon as she moved toward us, the high nasal hum-singing began, in a tune we had heard many times: "Out of the ivory palaces, into a world of woe."

"Uhnt uhvunh unhvunhree puhnluhnciz, uhnto unh wuhnld uhnv woe—"

Cora sang "woe" in a dragged-out, pouty-mouthed way, like Marilyn Monroe trying to say something more than she was really saying. When Cora got to "woe," her eyes always locked in on somebody and then drifted off again as she went on. It was the loveliest, liltingest, sweetest sound I'd ever heard. When Cora sang, I could see Jesus floating down from his ivory palaces and landing smack in the middle of that world of woe where Cora lived so much of her life.

But it just made Sister Holy Ghost mad.

For one thing, she was used to better stuff. When she wanted music, she wanted it with punch. Rhythm. Energy. Bodies rocking and hands waving and clapping. I doubt they ever sang Cora's song at Sister's House of Prayer in town, but if they did, it would have started with a shout: "Out!(clap) of the I-(clap)-vor-y pa-(clap)-la-ces(clap clap), In!(clap)to a world(clap)of woe (clap clap clap)..."

And as for that fixed-eye stare, I had seen Sister Holy Ghost use it herself, at a frenzied House of Prayer Saturday service when I was twelve and I went to see Daddy Grace, "Sweet Daddy," just to see if it was true that people would throw money at him or pay him for his handkerchief after he blew his nose in it or any of the wild things white people said colored people did. The whole place was rocking, throbbing to the drums and brass band and swaying with crowded bodies, except for Daddy Grace, who sat motionless on a red velvet throne fixed steady in the middle of that swirling mass, smiling, with his long black hair combed perfectly around his shoulders. Two light-brown women in pure white dresses and white feathered hats mopped his brow with little cloths they then handed out to people in two jumping writhing lines that snaked to the drumbeat past buckets filling with money while the horns blew louder and louder. Then Sister Holy Ghost fixed that stare on me, and I knew that I was in the wrong place and the Spirit had taken everybody but me, and I was a sinner for coming just to look and not to believe, and Daddy Grace was probably going to bring the whole place down on my head. I wanted to shout "Sweet Daddy, I'm sorry!" but somebody would be sure to tell my mother, and I wanted to run away but I could never outrun those shouting bouncing frenzied people, and Sister Holy Ghost still had that stare on me and I couldn't even turn my eyes away, let alone my body. I was dead in sin, and I stood there paralyzed until things calmed down. I sneaked out while people were looking for their seats again, and I ran home, and nobody followed me except for that stare, and I knew that my sins had been seen, clean through. Sister Holy Ghost was really good.

Cora was just pathetic. Where Sister Holy Ghost drew sin right out of her victims, Cora seemed to be trying to explain something about her own self. Her stare didn't even interest us very much. When she fixed those woe-begone eyes on the Young Senator beneath our one-sided tree, we didn't even look back at her; we looked at him. The Young Senator, far from freezing, fidgeted. He looked down at the ground and at Sister Holy Ghost and up at the tree and took his handkerchief out of his hip pocket and wiped the side of his neck and across his mouth and dabbed at his forehead.

"Cora," he said, stuffing the handkerchief back in his pocket, "you know Sister."

Cora smiled and settled slow motion onto the end of the wicker settee like a human antimacassar, her body draped across the curved arm, her legs crossed at the ankles and hooked around the ball-and-claw foot of the settee, her fingertips and handkerchief coming to rest on the dusty ground. Sister Holy Ghost sat down beside her, as starched as Cora was limp. The two of them were about the same age, but they couldn't have been any more different if they had tried. Sister's sensible black lace-up shoes were properly together in front of her; her black-stockinged legs, just slightly darker than her skin color, were perfectly vertical. With white-gloved hands, she smoothed her straight black skirt and arranged the ruffled high neck of her fresh white blouse, then rested her hands in her lap. Without moving her body, she turned her head precisely to look at Cora through the veil of a black pill-box hat. Cora only rolled her head back toward the Young Senator.

"Sister says she can help," he said. "She's a counselor. A minister, really, with her people in town. And she likes us. Lined up a ton of votes for me, you know. Everybody says, Sister, you turned the tide." He winked and pointed at her with both hands, ignoring the fact that Sister's voting bloc had been transferred from the Old Senator — the Real Senator — to the son for reasons that had nothing to do with the son. "Anyhow, Cora, she even knows hip-no-tism. Honest to God. She can help you get over that bad dream. If you know what it is you're dreaming about, it'll go away."

"Come on, Cora, honey," said Sister. "There's no magic to it. We'll just talk about it." She took Cora's hand. "Come on, let's go to the house."

Cora exhaled and somehow rose to an upright stance as if somebody had lifted her by strings attached to her shoulders, with her feet the very last parts of her body to come into line. Sister Holy Ghost nodded to Miz Snoddy Senior and marched off to the house with Cora sliding along beside her, the handkerchief now flying from fingertips held at right angles to her arm and swinging opposite to the movement of her body, like a flag of resistance to any forward progress.

Nobody had to recount Cora's dream for us. Mae Maude and I had heard it direct from Cora, and we had told Pollo. Besides, Cora had told it everywhere: She would dream that her eyes were wide open, and she would see a brown slowly-swirling haze in front of her; she would try to wake up before it covered her, but she couldn't take her eyes off it; then she would see the head of her ex-husband rolling with his eyes open and fixed in a dead stare and his face sliding into the brown bog, and she would scream out. No matter who came to comfort her, she could not stop screaming, because she could still see the face sliding into the pool of excrement, ever so slowly drowning, as she put it, "in shit."

In spite of whatever he had done to her, Cora loved the man – men, actually, since it was never clear to us or to her which man in her life was sliding in any given dream into the dark deep. Cora was not somebody who lived life exactly in focus. She was bound to be as good a challenge for hypnotism as Sister Holy Ghost would ever get.

Still standing in the shade, the Young Senator put his arm around Miz Snoddy Senior. "Let's hope this works," he said. "I know her condition upsets you, but I think we can get Cora back to her old self."

Pollo and I knew exactly what was at stake for the Young Senator. We had followed on our bicycles when he drove Cora home from a political meeting in the settlement one night just a couple of weeks before, and we had watched in rapture as they made out in the back seat of his car. Rapture may not be exactly the right word, but we were more than just entertained; I tried my best to figure out what he was doing, from what little we could see, because whatever it was made Cora moan and writhe around and slip right out of her clothes like they were made out of wet paper that he could just peel away. His own clothes were something else. For that, he had to get completely out of the big Buick, taking off his suit and tie and cuff-links and sweat-soaked shirt and undershirt and wing-tip shoes and socks and garters.

The harder he worked, the more he sweated, but he had finally stripped down to his shorts when Cora stepped buck naked out of the car, took him by the hand, and led him to the side door of the house.

It took them an eternity to get to her room, but eventually the lamp went on beside her bed, and we had a perfect view through her open window. The Young Senator was on her in a flash, and in no time at all Cora was moaning and writhing around all over again.

Then the Young Senator made a big mistake. He stood up to take his shorts off and dropped them on the floor.

Cora took one look at him and screamed bloody murder. The Young Senator went limp, instantly limp, while the rest of his body went rigid. With Cora screaming at the top of her lungs and yelling about a man "sinking in shit," he just stood there wide-eyed in his pale white skin, probably wishing he could sink into the floor.

Pollo and I were transfixed, but when lights went on in other rooms of the house, the smiles that came to our faces could have warned the Young Senator of the real disaster he was about to sink into. In the nick of time, he came to, started toward the door, then went back toward Cora, then started toward the open window, then went back for his shorts, and ended up in Cora's closet — where he stayed for a long, long time while Miz Snoddy Senior and Mae Maude covered up Cora and stroked her hair and her hands, with her screaming the whole time.

Pollo and I couldn't breathe for trying not to laugh out loud, thought we'd die if we stayed, but weren't about to leave. We would straighten up long enough to gulp in some air, then look at each other and fall over again.

"How hot," Pollo half whispered and half blurted, "How hot...do you guess...guess it is...in that closet?"

"Hot as pure hell," I meant to whisper but sort of wheezed out.

Patience is sure a virtue, and what we saw after a while was clearly worth the wait. About a half hour after all the lights were out again in the house, the Young Senator emerged from the side door of the house and headed toward his car, stepping ever so tenderly over the driveway gravel in his bare feet, his pale body wrapped up in one of Cora's dresses, with the dripping sweat on his face and shoulders glistening in the moonlight. He stopped by the car just to put on his wing-tips, hopping first on one leg and then the other and holding onto Cora's dress, picked up the rest of his clothes and threw them in the car, then pushed the car halfway out the long drive, finally starting the motor and driving off with no headlights.

As for us, we ran with our bicycles until we were out of hearing from the house, then collapsed in loud sobbing laughter. We wondered where the Young Senator would stop to change clothes on the way home and what he would think when he discovered that his suit pants were missing and how he would ever get into his own house and how he would explain to his wife that he came home from a political meeting with two dresses and no pants.

Weeks later, waiting for Sister Holy Ghost out under the one-sided tree, Pollo and I still had trouble looking at each other with straight faces with the Young Senator around. The others must have wondered why we would suddenly grin and then look at the ground or up into the tree or just turn our backs on the group. Pollo picked up a long stalk of grass to chew, holding it with his hand covering his mouth. I took off my shirt in the heat and covered up my head in the pretense of wiping off sweat. Mae Maude looked at us like we were both crazy, but she hadn't known what we'd been laughing about ever since that night. It was probably another one of those times when she wondered why on earth she had been brought back to this place.

When Mae Maude's father left home, she and her mother had tried to make a go of it where they were in Louisiana, but there was really no reason to be there without the attachment to his job on the oil rigs. Cora's looks attracted any number of other men, but her screaming fits made it difficult to hold onto them. By that summer of 1956, they were back at Miz Snoddy Senior's house at the Rocks, a bleak and God-forsaken area surrounding an abandoned granite quarry. Cora had actually been back since Easter, but Mae Maude had stayed with friends in Louisiana to finish her junior year and arrived at the Rocks about the same time I did, in late May, dropping her father's name as her mother had already done and creating an unlikely household with three generations of Snoddy women: Senior, Junior and Mae Maude.

I met all three of them for the first time on my very first day out there, when I went by the country store to pick up supplies for lunch. I only went out to the Rocks then on Saturdays, hired by our church in town to keep an eye on an old farm where they were planning a camp. There wasn't much for me to do, except to keep track of construction supplies and log in the workmen who came on odd schedules, but I liked being out there. Once school was out, I went nearly every day. Occasionally my parents let me stay overnight at an old one-room schoolhouse at the entrance to the property. It had plumbing, and a primitive kitchen where I could plug in a hot plate cooker that I brought from home. I had to bring ice for a cooler that served as a refrigerator for Cokes and milk.

It was my first taste of real independence, even if it was fairly close to town, and that was way more important than the little bit of money they paid me. For a preacher's kid, it was a rare opportunity to act like a normal person and not have every move monitored by members of the congregation. And it was the first time I ever had a chance to hang around with people my mother didn't pick out. Or even know.

On the Fourth of July, Mae Maude was in no mood to hang around in the heat waiting for Sister Holy Ghost's magic. "Come on," she said, snatching the shirt off my head and heading toward the camp truck, "let's go get a Coke." By the time I climbed up behind the wheel, she was already perched sideways in her usual place in the corner of the seat, legs crossed under her, with one arm on the back of the seat and one in the open window. That way, she could talk to me or lean her head back, right out the window, and yell to Pollo in his place on the open flatbed behind us.

The seating arrangement was not something we had discussed, but it did let us travel together without much notice. There was room in the cab for all of us, but Pollo had jumped up on the back of the truck the first time the three of us went somewhere, leaving Mae Maude alone up front with me. That way, he didn't look like he thought he was one of us, but more like maybe we had hired him to do some work. It's funny sometimes how people just know the right way to do something. Everybody around the Rocks was used to seeing the three of us arranged in the truck like that, and nobody paid any attention when we pulled up at the brick store for a Coke.

Mr. Snoddy had opened the store in the '20s in an old brick house his father had built up by the main road before the quarry opened. In the '20s and early '30s, the area was full of people who worked the hard granite from underground into tombstones and building blocks. When the quarry company moved to a new site forty miles away, they took the skilled white workers with them. There was no need to take the colored help, since there were plenty of colored people already living around the new quarry. So the colored people who lived in the settlement at the old site, who had done the heavy work of the quarry and had no particular skills, just stayed put. With no hope of finding work anywhere else, they were better off to stay where they were and scratch out a living on the land owned by Mr. Snoddy. He allowed them to keep some of the crops they raised on his land, provided a market for what little surplus they had in their own small gardens, and extended credit at the store when cash ran behind their need for food and supplies. The store was the center of community life at the Rocks.

There was a distinguished looking colored man who was always at the store and who acted like he was in charge. It seemed unlikely to me, especially after he introduced himself as "Do-Boy" in his sonorous and dignified voice. Everybody called him "Do-Boy." Probably from Mr. Snoddy saying "do this, boy" so much, I figured. It was the most insulting thing I had ever heard anybody call a colored man — much worse than calling them "uncle" — and other colored people were now the ones calling him "Do-Boy." "Because that's his name," Pollo had said.

At any rate, Mr. Do-Boy, as I decided to call him with proper respect, stood behind the counter most of the day, even when there was nothing going on but talk, and operated the cash register or wrote in the credit book whenever somebody made an actual purchase. As a result, he was the best informed person in the community about anything that might be going on — or what had gone on in the past, there being a lot more of that to discuss. He was not pretentious or officious about it but really rather kind and gentle, his demeanor suggesting that he recognized his position at the center of the community.

Mr. Snoddy himself had apparently been a different kind of community center. From various people with little jokes or from remarks by Mr. Do-Boy, we had pieced together a picture of Mr. Snoddy taking women right out in the field behind the store or into the little room in the back to exact payment of their debts. There was always a woman from the settlement living at his house, in the bedroom right next to Miz Snoddy's room, and she knew all about it. One would get pregnant and go back to the settlement and another would come in her place. We called him "The Father of His County." I even said when we saw Pollo for the first time working on bicycles at the store that he might be Mae Maude's cousin, and I just said it as a joke, but she was really struck by it.

Mr. Snoddy had ruled the Rocks, and he did whatever he pleased until he disappeared, just before the war, a long time before we were there, while Cora was still a little girl. She didn't remember him at all. Mr. Do-Boy had continued to operate the store, just as if Mr. Snoddy was still around. A man named Douglas kept the books; I didn't see much of him, because he always went to the back room to work when I came into the store. Pollo said Douglas just didn't care much for white people.

The only other white person still in the area was Miss Delphine Templeton, an old woman who lived alone next to the brick store, separated from it by the road that ran from the main road down to the Snoddy place. The Snoddys were the only people on that road, and Mr. Snoddy had called it Brickstore Road, so that's what it was called. Miss Templeton had come to the Rocks in the boom years as a nurse with the quarry company, had stayed on, and had become something of a legend as midwife, medicine woman, and sage. She called me by name the first time I showed up on her porch with Pollo, even before I could introduce myself, and if anything was going on around the Rocks, or had gone on, she would know it inside out.

"Why do they call the man at the store 'Do-Boy?'" I had asked her.

"Because that's his name," she said. It sounded like she was in cahoots with Pollo.

"I mean his real name."

"That's it." Miss Templeton was not the kind of person to slight anyone, and I found it hard to believe that she bought this degrading reference for what seemed like a pretty sharp colored man.

"Doesn't he have another name?" I asked.

"Samuel," she said. I felt like I was playing some sort of a riddle game with her and she had just given me a clue. Miss Templeton often sounded like she was talking in riddles even when she didn't mean to be.

"Samuel Do-Boy," I said. I didn't get it at all.

"Yes," she said. "That's it." She didn't seem to be enjoying the game particularly, but neither did she seem likely to help me out. So I gave up. Every time I saw her after that, I thought she was wondering if I had cracked the riddle. I didn't bring it up again, but I decided that "Mr. Samuel Do-Boy" sounded a lot more respectful than "Do-Boy," no matter what everybody else called him.

Not bringing something up did not keep Miss Templeton from knowing the truth of it, of course. I knew she knew that I still didn't get it, and it was impossible to avoid her. Nothing at the Rocks escaped her attention; she was bound to have seen Mae Maude and me and Pollo jump out of the truck on the Fourth of July and go into the store.

When Mae Maude had suggested that we "get a Coke," all three of us knew that phrase was a code, the prelude to spending some time alone together in the quarry. We paid Mr. Samuel Do-Boy for our Cokes — he yelled to Douglas in the back room to write Pollo's "purchase" in the credit book he ordinarily kept under the counter — and we went back to the truck. We drove down the main road, honked at Miss Templeton as we went past her kudzu-covered house, and a mile or so later turned down the dirt road that ran through the settlement and into the old quarry. We had a favorite place, a ledge halfway up the side of the steep wall of the quarry and under of couple of pines that had somehow wedged roots into the dyna-mited crevices and leaned out over the dark blue pool that had formed in the granite basin. We kept a camp blanket there under an overhanging rock.

We were just settling onto the blanket, popping the caps off our Coke bottles on the sharp edges of the granite, when Mae Maude said the magic words.

"Young Senator," she said, as Pollo and I looked at each other and then concentrated hard on the bottle caps and tried not to laugh, "is sure set on getting Sister Holy Ghost to clear up that business of the scream dream."

The silence was so shaky it made the Cokes quiver in our hands. Pollo and I focused on the bottles like they might be about to speak to us, then looked at each other, and our laughter exploded like dynamite from the side of the quarry wall.

"Stop it, Bo," Mae Maude said as she jumped right flat onto my stomach. "Just stop it! If you're gonna laugh, I'm gonna give you something to laugh about," and she started digging into my ribs. I can't stand tickling and sure as hell couldn't hold the Coke bottle steady while she was doing that.

"Get her off me," I yelled at Pollo, "get her, get her off," with Coke splash-ing everywhere. He pulled her back into his lap and held her as tight as he could with one arm, but she was jabbing him with her elbows and kicking his shins with her shoes, and he was laughing hard and pouring Coke all over them. I grabbed her arms and just got my breath long enough to say, "Okay, stop it; we'll tell you."

"Promise?"

"Yeah. Let her go."

And we straightened ourselves up and she said, "You better talk."

So we told her the story of that night with Cora and the Young Senator, and she thought it was sort of funny, but the only thing that really made her laugh was him coming out of the closet in Cora's dress, because the rest of it with them messing around and then the scream and all that was pretty much standard stuff with Cora, as far as Mae Maude was concerned. But she liked it that we took the Young Senator's suit pants.

"Maybe he told his wife he was in some kind of a pageant," Mae Maude said.

"The sun god had a thing like that, too," said Pollo. Those were words that had their own kind of magic, because Mae Maude loved to hear Pollo tell the myths he had learned from Miss Templeton, and he loved to tell them. It worked for me, because Mae Maude usually ended up in my arms as we looked out over the pool of water or up into the stars while Pollo spun his tales.

"The sun god lost his pants?" I laughed.

"Nope," he said. "Lost his lover."

"Tell," Mae Maude said and lay back with her head in his lap and her legs across mine.

This was getting to be strange. Mae Maude and I had messed around some early in the summer, but I hadn't gotten very far, mainly because I didn't know what I was doing. Then we discovered Pollo working on bicycles at the store, and she became fascinated with his color and his eyes and hair and every little thing about him. She insisted that he go everywhere with us, and when we talked she would laugh at something and poke him or grab his arms or pat his hair like he was from Mars or something. Now here she was, with her legs stretched out across my lap, but with her head in his lap.

"Tell us," she said.

Pollo started in, looking up at the bright sky as if he could actually see the sun god in his golden chariot, then looking down and all around the ledge like he was looking over the whole earth and found the naked wood nymph Daphne — Pollo's gods hardly ever wore clothes — anyway, he found Daphne, daughter of the river god, right about where Mae Maude's shoulder was. He examined that shoulder the way he said Apollo looked at Daphne and said she was very pleasing to him. Mae Maude was reaching up to touch the Coke splotches on Pollo's chest and his skin would stick to her finger a little bit each time she lifted it back. I figured there was nothing really wrong with putting my hand on her ankle, even with Pollo there, and I felt her leg tighten and took both hands to see how really firm her calf muscles were. Pollo said the sun god thought Daphne was beautiful and loved her and wanted to have her, but she only loved the sport of the chase, is actually how he said it, and would never really let him do anything, but he really wanted her. I thought that above her knee would be softer, but not a lot, and I had never touched a girl above the bottom of her shorts. Pollo was saying that Daphne's heart was hard and she ran from the sun god, and he wanted to love her but her heart was hard and she ran and she turned into a tree by a pool of water. He said the sun god could still hear her heart beating in the tree and he traced the skin of its branches with his lips and tried to warm her heart with his kisses and he caressed the bark of the tree and looked for smooth places where he could still touch her body with the warmth of his tongue. I was not at all sure that Pollo was getting all this stuff from Miss Templeton, but it was all right with me. Mae Maude closed her eyes and took Pollo's hand from the side of her neck and held it up against his chest. He said there was nothing the sun god could do because her heart was hard and she would never let him love her and there are some things you just can't have but they can lead to beautiful thoughts, just the same. And I knew as soon as I said "Your legs are real sticky" that I should have shut up and let Pollo keep talking, because Mae Maude took my hand off her leg and stood up and said, "Last one in the water's a rotten egg."

Pollo looked at me and grinned. "I don't suppose you want to hear the rest," he said, "about the sun god riding back across the sky in his golden chariot."

Mae Maude ran down the narrow path that went between dynamited boulders of blue granite, dropping clothes all along the way. Her shoes came off right at the water's edge, and she dived in like one of Pollo's naked nymphs and swam out toward the middle before turning around to see if we were following. "Don't get your pants wet," she yelled, which is precisely what we had done all summer up to that afternoon.

"Pollo!" I was too late. He had already stripped off his blue jeans and undershorts and went right in from the ledge with a one-legged cannonball that sent up a huge plume of water and brought a loud laugh from Mae

Maude. When he came up, she splashed him with both hands and yelled up at me.

"Don't be an old prude. Come on in!"

I went down to the lower ledge, turned my back while I put my socks inside my shoes and folded my pants beside them and put my underwear inside the pants, then, while they were swimming off to the far side, I went in, with a stomach full of butterflies. They were laughing and splashing each other under a rock overhang when I swam up.

Pollo was singing a camp song that we had taught him and the sound was echoing off the quarry walls:

> I went to the rock to hide my face
> The rock cried out: No hiding place!
> There's no hiding place down here.

"What do you think you're doing?" I said. "If anybody finds us here, we're gonna be in real trouble." I knew Pollo would understand, even if Mae Maude didn't.

But Pollo took a deep breath, went under, grabbed my feet and pulled me under the water. Pollo! I hadn't meant to make him mad. I tried to loosen his grip, but he was too strong for me. As he came up for air, he tried to grab my waist and then my shoulders to keep me under, but I braced off his arms and got my head above the water. We were both gasping, but Pollo was laughing! He apparently didn't understand anything at all, but I couldn't help but laugh with him.

"The rock cried out...," he sang, and the two of us finished it together: "NO HIDING PLACE!"

I grabbed for his head but missed, and we both went under again. He swam away under water, and I tried to follow, but he was much too strong a swimmer. When we came up, I skimmed my hand across the surface and hit him with a solid sheet of water and my best Tarzan yell — "Ah-i-a-a-ah-i-ah-i-ah!" — then noticed Mae Maude swimming slowly back to the other side.

"Hey," I yelled. "Where are you going?"

"I'm getting out," she said. "We better go home."

When Pollo and I pulled up on the rock, Mae Maude was already headed up the path to the ledge, picking up her clothes as she went. I used my socks to dry off a little, then started to get into my pants. Pollo had to go on up to the ledge where he had left his.

Mae Maude stood in his way at the ledge, looking for all the world like a naked wood nymph. She held the blanket out in front of her with both hands and said to Pollo, "Dry me off."

Pollo did the coolest thing in the whole world. He leaned across the top of the blanket, caught a trickle of water with his tongue right above her nipple and traced it back up to its source behind her ear. It was wrong. It was really wrong. But it was really cool.

"Don't be silly," she said, holding the blanket up higher. "Use this."

"Better get your pants on, Pollo," I said as I walked up behind him, carrying my shoes and wet socks. "We've got to get out of here before you get into real trouble."

Mae Maude looked like she might hand the blanket to me, then turned her back, dried herself off with it and put on her clothes. Pollo looked at me without any expression at all in his face, then grabbed his shorts and blue jeans and stomped off into the woods before putting them on.

———

As soon as we were in the truck, I whispered to Mae Maude as harshly as I could: "What are you doing? You can't act like that with him," I said, nodding toward Pollo on the flatbed behind us. "You're way beyond asking for trouble. You're just plain crazy."

"Don't be such a preacher's boy," she whispered back. I couldn't help being my father's son, and I hated it when people used it against me. When they called me a "preacher's kid" or just a "P.K.," it meant they expected me to be bad. "Preacher's boy" was reserved for a goody-goody, which to my mind was much worse. Mae Maude was sitting with her body squared up and facing straight forward. "You're just jealous," she said. Jealous? Of a country girl and a colored boy? Not likely. She must have thought I was stupid. I knew she was just curious and that her curiosity would only go so far with a colored boy. But I also knew that curiosity killed the cat.

"I am not jealous," I said. "That's not the point."

"Then what?"

"It's wrong, that's what. And Pollo's dumb to let you do it. He's not about to tell, but if anybody ever knows you're messing around with him, he's the one who will pay hell for it." That was true even if I was jealous.

"Oh, shut up," she said, her whisper turning to raspy anger. "Who cares? I wouldn't really do it with him, anyway. You are so stupid."

"You don't care, do you? You know you can't act like that with colored people, but you really don't care."

"You can act any way you want to with them," she said. "Who are they gonna tell?" After I didn't say anything, she added, "So just shut up."

"Did you ever hear of Emmett Till, Mae Maude?" I said.

"The colored boy they killed last summer?"

"Right. He was the same age as us. And they didn't just kill him. They broke into his grandaddy's shack and dragged him away. They beat him. They gouged out one of his eyeballs. They bashed his head so hard they broke his skull. They shot him. Then they threw him in the river."

"So?" she said.

"Do you know what he did to deserve that, Mae Maude?" She was quiet, and it made me really mad and my voice was getting louder. "He spoke to a white woman. That's all he did. He didn't touch her. He didn't go swimming with her. He sure as hell didn't lick any water off her. He just said something to her. And somebody didn't like it. So they beat him and poked his eye out and shot him and dumped him in the river." Mae Maude was still looking straight ahead. "What do you think they would do to Pollo?" I said, pointing to him in the back of the truck. Mae Maude looked at me, and I could see tears gathering in her eyes.

"Emmett Till was hundreds of miles from here," she said.

"Emmett Till's just one body that washed up to the front page of the newspaper, Mae Maude. Nobody knows how many more there are at the bottom of some river. Or some quarry pool." I knew I had pushed the point too far. Mae Maude didn't say anything, and I couldn't say anything, so we were just quiet.

We stopped at the store for our bottle deposits, and Mr. Samuel Do-Boy gave us ours in cash and wrote down something in the credit book for Pollo, who then got on his bicycle without a word and headed off toward the settlement. Mae Maude and I sat on the porch at the store for a long time, not talking, just thinking.

I knew I had overdone the idea of Pollo as Emmett Till, but I was having a hard time getting over it anyway. They were very different, from what I had read about Till in the newspaper, but there were similarities, too. Emmett Till was street smart, trained in the arrogance of Chicago. He knew his way around the city. But when he went to Mississippi to spend the summer with his grandfather, he was oblivious to the dangers of the real world there. It was just natural for him to take the dare of his country cousins and show off his big-time Chicago bravado, smarting off to the woman at the store. But he had swaggered across the line between life and death, without any malice and without even knowing it. Just a fish out of water who ended up back on the bottom of the river.

Pollo was an odder fish. His personality was perfectly pleasant, without any swagger at all. But his bearings were in the classical era introduced to him by Delphine Templeton, in that and in the simple doting care lavished on him in the settlement. Mae Maude was impressed with his knowledge and with his manner, but his comfort in the world of the sun god and wood nymphs of mythology and in the sunshine and woodlands of the Rocks was as much a misfit with the world beyond the settlement as Emmett Till's Chicago was with Mississippi.

A siren in the distance provided the perfect background for my thoughts. As it came closer, I wondered if maybe it was headed for the settlement. There had been fires there earlier in the summer, but no trucks came. Nobody over there had a telephone to call in a report, and the rangers in the firetower would overlook a burning house in the settlement if it didn't threaten the woods. Anyway, there was no smoke that I could see over in that direction.

Miss Templeton came to her front steps about the time the sheriff's car screamed past her house and turned down Brickstore Road toward the Snoddy place. Mae Maude and I looked at each other, ran to the truck, and drove into the dust cloud that flew up behind the speeding sheriff.

When we pulled up at the house, the sheriff was already talking with the Young Senator under the one-sided tree. Cora and Sister Holy Ghost were sitting on the wicker settee, Cora snuggled under Sister's protecting arm. At the edge of the yard behind the house were four men with shovels, just standing there looking out toward the sheriff. Miz Snoddy must have been in the house. The sheriff walked off toward the men with the shovels before we heard any of the conversation.

"What's going on?" Mae Maude asked Cora.

"We think there might be a body buried under the old outhouse," said the Young Senator, still taking charge. Mae Maude looked at him like he was stupid.

"Whose body?" she said with a heavy dose of doubt in her voice.

"Well, we don't know, but Cora seems to think she may have seen a body in the pit before they closed it up. We're just going to dig in and see what we find."

Mae Maude and I walked over to watch the digging, saw them shovel up the first chunks of dark smelly gunk from below the red fill dirt, and retreated to the tree where the Young Senator still stood watching from that distance with his hands on his hips. Cora and Sister Holy Ghost didn't seem to take any interest.

The men who were digging worked their way completely below ground level, but we could see buckets of stuff being handed up. Occasionally, a broken piece of furniture would come up, along with the smaller bits of broken china and other household debris that people always discarded into privy pits and that we knew must be embedded in the rich, fertile, and repulsive stuff coming out. I had heard that people in Charleston, nice people, dig up old cesspits inherited from their families, searching through the remnants of domestic wreckage for clues about the history of their people — and perhaps, but only surreptitiously, searching for treasure. Out here at the Rocks, little treasure was likely. Instead, only the meager domestic history of the Snoddy family, broken and inconsequential, was resurrected as the men kept digging further into the pit. Then they climbed out of the hole and all of them stood looking into the pit, with the sheriff holding a handkerchief over his nose and mouth.

"I think we should get the ladies out of here," said the Young Senator. "Mae Maude, run get your grandmother. We'll take everybody up to the store."

Mae Maude came back from the house without finding Miz Snoddy, but we decided to get Cora and Sister away from there and then come back for her.

We found Miz Snoddy around midnight. Her body was lying proper as could be in a furrow in the field beyond the woods on the far side of the house, one arm sticking ridiculously up into a cotton plant. There was a pistol in her hand and a bullet hole in the side of her head.

In the house, we found a note beside her bed, confessing to the murder of her husband in 1939 and saying that she did not want to go to jail. She did not ask for forgiveness, but she did add at the bottom that she had done the best she could. When they cleaned up what remained of Mr. Snoddy, they found a bullet hole in his head, too, right in the middle of his face.

With Mae Maude and Cora at home and Sister and the Young Senator gone back to town, I went off to the settlement to tell Pollo what he had missed. It was nearly dawn, and there were a few people already out in the yards. Pollo was not there. Nobody there had seen him since the day before, they said. Mr. Samuel Do-Boy, still wearing his serious in-charge demeanor, came out to join the little group that had gathered around the truck and agreed that Pollo was not there.

I was dead tired. I went back to the schoolhouse, took a shower under the barrel of cold water by the back door, drove the truck back through the settlement to the quarry, and walked out to the ledge. Nobody. No sign of anybody. The blanket was still crumpled where Mae Maude had thrown it, so I folded it up and stuck it back under the rock to keep it dry.

———

The sun was completely up by the time I headed back toward the school-house. When I came to the Templeton place, I turned in and parked the truck in the front yard. Heavy garlands of kudzu created a darkened cave on the porch, and I didn't see anyone there at first. From the dark behind the vines, Miss Templeton could always see people coming before they could see that she was there. But there she was, so pale and white she was almost not there at all, and there was Pollo, sitting on the floor with his back against the porch railing.

"Pollo! You missed everything. Morning, Miss Templeton."

"I know," he said, kind of softly. "Miss Templeton just told me."

Miss Templeton didn't say anything to me. She hadn't put her teeth in yet and kept mushing her lips together as she rocked.

"Where in the world were you?" I said to Pollo. His answer stopped me cold.

"I heard the siren, and I thought you had called the sheriff from Miz Snoddy's house," he said. "So I hid." Then he added, "I heard you fussing at Mae Maude in the truck."

"Pollo," I said, struggling to get clear what I had just heard. "Pollo," I said. "Pollo." There was a long silence, as Pollo looked at me with cold clear eyes. While I was looking for him that morning, I had felt so comfortably close to him; now that I had found him, I felt a painful distance. The betrayal he must have felt when he heard the siren and saw the sheriff's car flowed over me, and I felt like I was being smothered or drowned in his unfounded fear. He looked at me until I breathed in like I had just come up for air from the bottom of the quarry pool.

"What did you see last night?" he asked in a tone that broke the silence but left the aching distance untouched.

The fear that he should never have felt now fell hard and heavy on me, dragging me down again, this time into the injustice of his accusation against me. The whole business of the Snoddys seemed trivial as I looked at Pollo and tried to match that face to the laughing kid who sang "No Hiding Place" with me at the quarry. I wanted to run off through the woods into clear air and yell and breathe and sing, but I was stuck on Miss Templeton's top step, with the two of them looking at me as if the most normal thing in the world was to go on with the story of what I had seen. And so I told them. I started softly, but my voice came back strong as I got interested in telling every tiny detail of my night at the Snoddy's.

"What I don't understand," I said at last, "is how Sister Holy Ghost hypnotized Cora into knowing where a body was buried."

"There was no hypnotism," said Miss Templeton.

"Ma'am?"

"Sister Holy Ghost just told Cora the truth."

Silence.

"Sister and Cora knew each other a long time ago," said Pollo. "They were friends when they were little."

"Does everybody know that?"

"Nope," said Pollo. "Only Miss Templeton. And me because she told me. And now you. Miz Snoddy didn't recognize Sister all grown up, and Cora didn't, either, at first. Young Senator doesn't know anything about it."

Silence again. I tried to think of the right question.

"Sister...grew up...in the settlement," Miss Templeton said. She was leaning back in the rocker with her eyes closed, smacking her lips between phrases. "Same age as little Sue...at the Snoddy place. When she was twelve...Sister's father took her down there...while he worked in the fields...to pay off his debts. She...began staying over...and Mr. Snoddy kept her in the bedroom...next to Mrs. Snoddy's room."

A long silence. I knew the right question this time but I wasn't about to ask it.

"Sister was sure that Miz Snoddy heard her screaming for help," Pollo said. "But she never came to stop him. It went on for a whole summer."

"And then one night...he took Sue...Cora...to that room with Sister...and Mrs. Snoddy couldn't stand...those screams."

"So then she blew his face away," Pollo said.

"Those little girls...helped her dump him...in the privy. The next morning...Cora saw the bloody face...below the seat...still sinking into the pit."

"Miz Snoddy tried to help the girls, but she couldn't, really, so she brought them up here," Pollo said.

"I took care of them...and taught them what I could...and delivered the babies." Pollo turned and looked at her.

"Babies?" he asked. "More than just me?"

"You and Mae Maude both...were born right in this house. Sister...ran away to town...and left you...for me to raise." She looked at me. "I gave him...the name of Apollo...because his mother...like Apollo's mother...had nowhere to have her baby. The next year...Cora ran off with a soldier...who was here...in the war training maneuvers. She convinced herself...that he was Mae Maude's father. She...could never remember anything... about that night...except for her dream."

"And Sister Holy Ghost," Pollo said, "could never forget anything about it. All those years, she kept having the nightmare of Miz Snoddy's silence as Mr. Snoddy attacked, and she would wake up crying again and again for help." He was quiet for a long moment. "Yesterday," he said, "she set it all free."

Pollo looked down at the floor. "I know how those people felt about Sister Holy Ghost," he said. "And I know how they — how you feel about me and everybody like me. That's why I thought you called the sheriff after we left the quarry."

"I'm sorry," I said. I wanted to call out to him across the distance, wanted to take his hand and wanted to hit him at the same time, wanted to set us free, wanted to sing I went to the rock to hide my face, but the porch and the whole world fell silent. "You want to go get a Coke?" I said.

There was such a long and total silence that my heartbeat sounded like one of those jungle drums in the movies when Tarzan is about to be attacked. Pollo looked at me coldly as his jaw clenched and unclenched. "Nanh," he said, looking off through the kudzu to the woods across the road. "I need sleep."

I turned toward the truck, hoping neither of them could see the redness I felt rising in my face or the wetness rising in my eyes. I knew I hadn't called the sheriff. Pollo knew it, too. I didn't do that. I wouldn't. I didn't do that. I didn't do that. And I didn't know then how fear can rise up from the primal pit where someone had it hidden, how in its rising it creates a new world of its own, how in that altered world good people can be estranged by some dread thing they cannot remember or do not even know. And I did not then and do not now know how to set it free.

I stepped into the truck, started the motor, and turned so that neither of them could see my face as I backed out toward the road.

"Maybe later," Pollo called from the porch.

"Maybe," I said.

Chapter Two

———◆———

Bubba's Coming

With Pollo keeping his distance, Mae Maude and I were mostly by ourselves again. The week following the funerals, I had driven down to the Snoddy place to ask if she wanted to go for a ride. I opened the door of the truck for her, and she looked at me funny but took my hand and stepped into the cab like some kind of a lady. When I climbed in from my side, I saw that there were tears in her eyes.

"You want to shift gears?" I said. Guys with the new automatic shift cars would never know the power of that line with a girl. I put my arm up on the back of the seat, and Mae Maude slid over beside me so she could grab the wobbly stick shift with both hands. The truck lurched forward. It was the smoothest move of my life.

I could not have explained the excitement of Mae Maude's body close to me in the heat of that late afternoon. I hardly understood it myself. As we drove along, she would shift gears whenever I said "now" and then rest her hands in her lap. Once, she put her left hand down on my leg and traced the edge of my Bermuda shorts with her finger. I encouraged her with a squeeze around the shoulders when she did that, and that became the way we shifted gears. The first time, I was afraid she might not do it again, and I drove almost all the way into town so I wouldn't have to stop and she wouldn't have to move her hand back to the stick. After I knew there was a pattern, I could call for a gear shift any time I just wanted her hand to settle onto a different place. We drove around for quite a while without talking, except for me saying "now" and her moving her hand and putting it back and me squeezing her around the shoulders and imagining what she was thinking as her spirits improved. She was not crying anymore, but I was wrong about what she was thinking.

"Bubba's coming," she said.

"The guy from Louisiana?"

"Football starts next month and he wants to bring his stuff up to the university," she said. She looked at me and added, "He doesn't know anything about my grandparents."

"He won't have to," I reassured her. I knew Bubba was a stickler about social standing. He would never keep seeing a girl with a family history like Mae Maude's, let alone marry her, even if they did have a lot of property.

Mae Maude had told me all about Bubba early in the summer, about how he ran around and did it with girls in Louisiana, did things with them that he wouldn't do with Mae Maude — morally committed, as he was, to marrying a virgin. His own grandparents were big deals in Knoxtown, county seat of the next county over from ours; they were the only people in either county who had a recognizable name statewide. They ran their town's bank and owned mills all around. Their son had gone off to Louisiana to manage investments they had down there, but everybody knew that Bubba would come back to play ball for the university, just like his dad. Bubba's senior year in high school, his football games in Louisiana made the sports page in our newspaper. They even ran his picture, smiling in the end zone after catching a touchdown pass and holding the ball up over his head in one hand and his helmet in the other. It was paired with an old picture of his father at the university in pretty much the same pose. They looked just alike.

Some people have a stereotype of Bubbas as the guys who hang around filling stations and fix old cars, but the name was only transferred to them as a joke. This Bubba of Mae Maude's was more the certified classic type: first-born son of a prominent family, given title to that diminutive, endearing, and childish mispronunciation of Brother, with all the rights and privileges appertaining thereunto. The right of primogeniture, long-since abandoned in the law, lived on in the South in the granting of "Bubba" as an honor-able title of birthright and in the natural behavior of those upon whom the title was conferred. I had known several such Bubbas, and I knew what this one would be like. He would have the confidence and authority that comes from having everybody know that the future belongs to him. He would be in charge. But I should have realized that this one would be warped by the fact that he was an only child and had no one to be Bubba over.

"He's gonna be here for a week," Mae Maude said. "Then he's going to New York before football starts."

"New York!" I'd never been north of the next state — actually, never north of the southern part of the next state.

"His daddy's got business people up there. They're gonna show him around."

I pulled up in front of the schoolhouse. We couldn't be alone together inside, but it was okay to sit in the truck.

"I've got some Cokes inside," I said. "You want me to get you one?"

"Okay."

When I got back in the truck, she snuggled up against me again and said, "I don't want to talk about Bubba. He makes me mad, kinda." I didn't want to talk about him, either. So we were quiet for a while.

Mae Maude's hand got icy cold from holding the Coke, and when she put the bottle down on the floorboard and turned and slipped her hand under my tee shirt and up onto my chest, it was enough to give me a gen-uine out-of-body experience. I squeezed her shoulders really hard, and with my eyes closed I could see us both from my spiritual position outside the truck. Mae Maude turned all the way around on the seat, put her knee between my legs with her arms around my neck, and kissed me right on the mouth. My lips were smashed against my teeth, but I pushed back at hers, and I felt like I could hear horns blowing all over the place, loud enough to wake the dead — loud enough, in fact, to yank my soul back into my body as I opened my eyes and knew it was our horn blowing because her rear end was on the horn button on the steering wheel. She just kept pushing at me and sitting on the horn like she didn't even hear it.

"Don't," I said. "Get off the horn!"

"Oh, who cares?"

"I care. You want to get us in trouble?"

I pushed her off to the other side of the seat, looked out the back window, half expecting the sheriff or the executive committee of the Women of the Church to come screeching into the driveway, and then, seeing nobody anywhere, tried to pull myself toward Mae Maude for another hug. She was laughing and pushed my hands away.

"You better get yourself back to your mama's before dark, Bo Fisher," she said, "so you won't get in trouble." I hated her smile. "Take me home," she said. So I did, shifting gears by myself.

That's pretty much how the week went, with Mae Maude getting closer and closer, and me trying to keep it going, but something always happening to stop everything. Still, with nearly eight weeks to go before school started, the summer had real possibilities.

———— • ————

Then Bubba arrived. Bubba with his red Corvette convertible roaring back and forth on the road to town. Bubba with his blond crewcut and square-jawed big smile. Bubba with his tee-shirt sleeves rolled up tight above his biceps. Bubba with his left hand tapping the horn and his right arm pointing to the sky like a victory wave to anybody who might be on the porch of the store when he went past. He looked just like his picture, like somebody had made arrangements for him to spend his whole life crossing the goal line. Mr. Samuel Do-Boy did a little wolf whistle every time the red Corvette went by.

I never waved back at Bubba, not once, and didn't pay him much attention. He came before lunch every day, drove off with Mae Maude back toward town or down toward the river, brought her back after suppertime and left again each night, I guess, after I had gone home.

Late in the week, the camp truck broke down. I had to leave it in the shop in town, but I caught a ride out to the camp with some of the workmen on Saturday, thinking I'd just stay out there overnight for a few days and, for once, avoid the rule about spending Sundays in town for church and Sunday dinner. My mother thought otherwise. Bubba stopped at the store late that same day and said she had called his grandmother to see if I could get a ride back into town with him when he came through that night. I could have shot her. But I told Bubba I'd be waiting at the schoolhouse when he was ready to go back.

Behind the wheel of his car, Bubba Wilson was willing to forego the evolutionary advantage of opposable thumbs with the ability to grip. He drove with his wrist. It looked a lot cooler. His right hand hung down limp over the top of the steering wheel, his left hand outside the car over the edge of the door and floating up and down on the air blowing past us. His blond crewcut was too short to blow around; it just sort of quivered in the wind. Bubba hunched his body toward me so he could talk above the noise of the wind. If I had been Mae Maude, I would've thought he was going to kiss me.

"It's always hard leaving Mae Maude," he said. "Know what I mean?"

"I guess," I said. If I'd said no, he would think I was stupid. If I'd said yes, he might think I was messing with Mae Maude. So I just said, "I guess."

"We oughtta just keep going to Louisiana," he said. "I could show you some girls down there like you've never seen around here. And they'll put out like you wouldn't believe." His voice was low and moved at a playful and lumpish kind of pace, his blue eyes blinking slowly — too slow for a guy. More like a girl. I wondered if Mae Maude and those girls in Louisiana liked that. "You'd know what to do with them, now, wouldn't you, bud?" He asked it like he actually wanted to know the answer. He had shifted his left arm to the wheel and hit me on the leg with the back of his right hand.

"I think the girls around here are just as pretty as anywhere else," I said, unwilling to give him the answer to his question.

"Yeah, but I'm talking about real women. Know what I mean?" He squeezed my leg so hard it hurt. His opposable thumb worked fine.

"How about holding on to the steering wheel?" I said. "The curves around here are tricky. They're not banked right."

"That's a colored church, isn't it?" he said as we passed the entrance to the settlement.

"Yeah," I said. I wanted to tell him what I had heard about it, about how the men from the settlement who had worked at the quarry had picked up stonecutting and construction skills from observing the white workmen, how they had salvaged granite blocks after the quarry closed and dragged them up to the road and built that beautiful blue granite church in the middle of this poor countryside. But I was pretty sure Bubba wasn't interested.

He proved I was right beyond all doubt. He stood up in the car, holding the wheel with one hand, and yelled at the top of his lungs, "I smell a gar." I was surprised he knew that joke from all the way down in Louisiana, but it was really dumb of him to say it out here where we knew people, and where they knew us. My mother would have killed me if she thought I had yelled it out right here in our own county. Of course, Bubba thought all those colored people were total strangers, or worse, just because he didn't know them, but I can guarantee they all knew who he was. He yelled it again, "I smell a gar!" and looked at me for the straight line, "A ci-gar?" which I refused to deliver from the floorboard where I had squinched down out of fear. And disgust. And maybe a little guilt. So Bubba just turned and shouted, "I smell a nig-gar." It was the wrong place for it, and it was the wrong people to yell it at. I thought of the people who had built that church and about Mr. Samuel Do-Boy and others who were now sleeping in the settlement back in the woods behind it, and I wondered if Pollo was there, too, and could hear all this yelling. I hated Bubba Wilson.

"That's not funny, Bubba," I said, sitting back up in the seat.

"Aw, it is, too," he said. "It's a joke. You're just a candy-ass little sissy." He had sat back down and leaned toward me again. "You need to grow up, bud. You might not be such a bad kid if you'd just relax and have a little fun." He pushed my shoulder with his, but I leaned away and didn't say anything to him or even look at him. "Anyway," he said, "niggers don't care. I've never seen one smart enough to pick his nose and poot at the same time." If I had said anything back to him, I would have told him I bet such intellectual feats were routinely practiced in his family, but neither one of us said anything else until we reached my house and I thanked him for the ride.

"I'm sorry I cut you down," Bubba said. "Don't let it bother you."

"Doesn't bother me, one way or the other," I said, getting out of the car.

"Well, it takes a real man to apologize, to admit he did something wrong," he said. "And I'm apologizing. You ought to accept it." He stuck out his hand to me.

"It's okay," I said and shook his hand. His grip was so tight, I wondered if he just wanted to prove he could hurt me. I squeezed hard, mainly to keep my hand from crumpling.

"You're not a bad guy," Bubba said. "Maybe we'll get together sometime," he said, which I doubted, but I wasn't about to argue with him.

———

It was never clear whether the Sunday-at-home rule was more important for the dose of morality at church or the dose of vegetables at home. In my mother's mind, morality and vegetables were closely connected, anyway. She could, for example, tell the state of teenagers' moral fiber by watching the level of their enthusiasm for more collard greens. As far as she was concerned, if a Presbyterian had some unlikely need to get right with God, going back to the buffet for seconds on vegetables was a far more acceptable way of dealing with it than going forward in an altar call at church. It was less showy and considerably more convincing. And more productive, too.

After my father's sermon that Sunday morning, I needed to do something of just that sort. When he took his text from the Westminster Catechism instead of the other Holy Scripture, I should have known I was in trouble. But his choice of the Seventh Commandment, "Thou shalt not commit adultery," was just not something that concerned me personally. Truth is, I would have given my left leg just for a chance to violate that one. But when Dad ran through the rest of the Catechism questions about it, I squirmed.

QUESTION: *What is required in the Seventh Commandment?*

ANSWER: *The Seventh Commandment requireth the preservation of our own and our neighbor's chastity, in heart, speech, and behavior.*

It always struck me as unfair how the Westminster Assembly of Divines, "that Presbyterian Parliament" as Dad called it, had managed to broaden the commandments, handing down to future Presbyterians tougher rules than God gave Moses. Why did they think God only said "commit" if He had really meant to rule out even thinking about committing? Besides, He only made it the Seventh Commandment, not the First. So why make a federal case out of it? In any event, I was clean enough on "speech"; "behavior" was basically okay — I coveted Bubba's opportunities, but that was a different commandment; and "heart"? Well, "heart" might be a problem.

QUESTION: (Dad read on from the pulpit, glancing down at me) *What is forbidden in the Seventh Commandment?*

ANSWER: *The Seventh Commandment forbiddeth all unchaste thoughts, words, and actions.*

Trouble creek. The more I thought about whether my behavior amounted to unchaste actions, the more I remembered Mae Maude in the truck with her hand up my shirt, and the more I had certifiably unchaste thoughts. Right there in church. The sermon had me in a circle of sin that was dragging me under. I wondered if somebody had actually come up the driveway at the schoolhouse and seen Mae Maude and me in the truck and had reported it to my mother, who had told my father, who was now practically announcing it to the whole congregation. He could have at least looked at somebody else. As it was, he might as well have just said it right out loud: "Bo Fisher, you stay away from that girl out in the country."

Typical of my father, the sermon was a mix of vigilance and forgiveness, but the members of the congregation, those that I could see without turning my head, didn't look very forgiving. I thought about Sister Holy Ghost's dead-eye stare. These people were just as good at it without even looking at me. I could tell by the way they held their heads absolutely still that they knew every unchaste thought I had ever had. And the ones I was having right there. I wondered if my mother noticed.

At dinner, I had seconds on collards, grits with red-eye gravy, black-eyed peas, corn, and even on squash. And thirds on collards, for good measure.

"Boy, these sure are good, aren't they?" I said.

"Why, Bo," Mama said, "I don't think I've ever seen you eat so many vegetables." She must have been very encouraged.

———

The days went back to normal, the way they usually do when Sunday is over. The camp truck was fixed by the very next day, and I went back to my regular schedule, which mostly meant getting to the store in time to see Bubba's car go by and hear Mr. Samuel Do-Boy's wolf whistle. I was there so much that Douglas the bookkeeper finally gave up on avoiding me and just stayed at his post, bent over his books behind the counter, when I came in. He did not look like somebody who expected to have much of a conversation with me, but I took his presence as a compliment that maybe he thought I was not as bad as most white people.

Some days Pollo was there, too. We talked some about the old bicycles he kept fixing up for people in the settlement. Nobody out there had a car, so bicycles were the way people got around. Or else by walking. A church up North somewhere collected old bikes when people didn't want them anymore and delivered them to the settlement. Nobody owned any particular bike; people in the settlement who needed to go somewhere would just take any available one. A couple of the really old bikes had been made into wagons that could be pulled behind other bicycles, and people used those to haul vegetables and berries and other stuff, like straw baskets that they made, up to the store to sell to the delivery men who would then carry it all off to sell to their own customers in towns all around.

Pollo's job of bicycle repair was not so much a job as an assignment for the community. It was what he did in exchange for food and a place to live and the rights to "buy" a certain amount of Cokes and things at the store, which is what Mr. Samuel Do-Boy and Douglas kept track of in the book under the counter. Pollo was good at what he did. He knew every tool and exactly how to use it. The bicycles were all shiny and ran smooth and quiet. They just looked either funny and fat or stripped down and primitive because they were such old models.

The tools Pollo used were once Mr. Snoddy's, and Miz Snoddy Senior had left them at the store. In fact, the whole store went right on like Mr. Snoddy was still there, except for everybody was better off without his peculiar personal habits. Miz Snoddy let Mr. Samuel Do-Boy and Douglas the book-keeper run the store for her. She signed order forms and credit slips whenever they needed somebody's signature, but the way Pollo told it, she sounded like the Queen of England signing whatever Parliament told her to. Now, with her gone, too, it looked like the store would just keep going on as if nothing had happened. Miss Templeton could sign things.

The store had become an extension of the little church at the Rocks, with the elders and deacons in charge of economics as well as theology. Pollo was confused about a lot of it, but somehow there had been a complicated set-up with Miz Snoddy and the store and the settlement and the little church at the Rocks and some white church in the North, and somehow it worked. The church was the settlement's connection to an unseen but approving world vaguely to the North, while the store was its connection to the very different world that surrounded it at the Rocks.

Once, Bubba stopped at the store and came up on the porch.

"Hey, bud," he said to me. "How're you doing?"

"Okay," I said. I knew he knew my name, but nobody's individual name made much difference to Bubba.

Pollo was sitting on the ground, working on a bicycle right beside the porch. He put his tools down and looked up at Bubba, but Bubba didn't see him, so Pollo went back to working.

"I was just thinking about that time when we rode into town," Bubba said to me, like it was something that had happened a long time ago. "I was thinking you might want me to bring you a girl out from town sometime," he said. "I could show you some stuff to do with her." He winked. He was acting like Pollo was deaf, or maybe invisible.

"I can't usually stay out as long as you do," I said, immediately hating that I had said that, because he might think I actually knew about when he came and went, or that my mother kept track of when I did. He didn't seem to notice it.

"Well," he said, "you could drop me off at Mae Maude's whenever you had to leave and you could just take my car and take your girl home." He stopped and leaned against the porch railing. The plan was making him think harder than usual. "Then you'd have to come get me, and I could take you home," he said.

Too bad his idea was so dumb. I could see myself driving into town in that red Corvette, my left hand riding the wind, my right wrist draped over the steering wheel, and me hunched over toward some girl next to me. But I could also see the houses in town, and the lights coming on, and the faces in the windows, and a dozen people going to their telephones to call my mother.

"I don't think it'll work," I said. "But I'll let you know."

"Well, I'm going down to Mae Maude's," he said, like maybe I wondered exactly where he might be going. Pollo kept messing with the bicycle and didn't even look up.

"See you," I said and watched him fall into the Corvette and drive off down Brickstore Road.

"Trouble on wheels," Douglas the bookkeeper said, inside the store.

"Uhm-m-hmm," somebody answered.

The people at the settlement had lived together so long — all their lives, actually — that they could deliver whole paragraphs of conversation in a single grunt or nod of the head, and I had become familiar enough to understand much of it. An uncompleted three-syllable "uhm-m-hmm" was an affirmation of whatever had just been said and an encouragement to the speaker to continue along that line. The two-syllable "umh-hm," accented on either syllable, was an affirmation of the point made but also recognized the authority of the person making the point; it would not have been used to encourage speculation from just anybody. A curt "hmh," a kind of snort or vocal sneeze, meant something along the lines that everybody in the world already knew whatever had just been said, or that it was wrong, and that in either case nobody wanted to hear any more about it. So when Douglas looked up from his books and said "Trouble on wheels," there was a predictable response.

"Umh-m-hmm."

"Already got two girls pregnant."

"Umh-m-hmm." This time, it was a whole chorus of voices.

"Down in Lu-zan."

"Umh-hm!"

The colored world was a mystery. It existed right alongside the white world as a separate world of its own. It absorbed everything that went on in the white world but remained almost totally invisible to that world. I knew white people who would talk freely and openly about their most delicate family secrets as if their cook, who was in the room with them at the time, would never have any reason or opportunity to tell anybody else. They seemed to think their colored help simply vanished at the end of the day, only to materialize again the next morning in the kitchen without having any other life experience in the meantime — or more rationally, if pressed on the matter, that the help went home at night to sleep and returned the next day without having told Miss Sarah Mitchell's cook or Dr. Beddingfield's driver or the Johnsons' colored man every single thing they had seen and heard on the previous day.

Actually, most people did not have a full-time colored man; there was a sort of time-share arrangement with them. People had one on Mondays or Tuesdays or some other day. So they were a little more discreet around one of them, realizing that on Wednesdays he might be at the Duncans' house up the street, and there was no way of telling what he might say there. Otherwise, colored people were free to gather information and observations about white people, free to discuss it among themselves, free to store it in their communal memory, free to do anything except acknowledge any of it during their working hours in the real world. I felt a little proud that Douglas had accepted me well enough to let me hear what he knew.

Most white people took no particular interest in the world of colored people, their understanding of it consisting mostly of funny stories about what colored people did or said or were reported to have done or said. It wasn't important whether anyone actually did or said whatever was report-ed; the integrity of the story — and the humor of it — required only that the colored person in question, or some other colored person, might con-ceivably have done it or said it. These stories, white people were free to share with each other at any time, even with colored help in the room with them ("Isn't that right, boy?") who would smile weakly or sometimes broadly and say "Yes'm, it is" or "Yes, sir," no matter what they were actually thinking.

But I thought about all of that much later. That afternoon at the store, as I watched Bubba drive off toward Mae Maude's house, I thought only of Mae Maude, sitting in that Corvette right where I had sat, with Bubba's wrist lying across the steering wheel and the other one probably lying across Mae

Maude's leg, and his hair quivering in the wind, and his voice bumping along like the bass part of some piece of beach music, and his blue eyes blinking real slow. I didn't want to think about it at all, but I thought about it all night.

———

Then one morning Mae Maude came walking up to the store alone. "Hi," she said as she came up the steps.

"Hi."

"Bubba's gone to New York."

"Good," I said. "I mean good he's going to New York. Good he gets to. I hope he has a good time." I could feel my face getting red, a little.

"You want to get a Coke?" she asked.

"I've got some stuff I have to do at the camp." I started toward the truck.

"Can I go?"

"I don't care."

We rode in silence while I figured out what I might have to do at the camp besides just checking on the workmen. We turned in at the schoolhouse and drove around the long loop to the cabin sites. The work crew was finishing up the second cabin, and I told Mae Maude I had to clean up Cabin One before they could move in the bunks and mattresses. She said she'd help.

I never saw anybody swing a broom that hard. From behind the cloud of dust she stirred up, Mae Maude started in about Bubba. It didn't matter to her, I guess, whether I wanted to hear it or not.

According to her, the week had not been all that much fun. Bubba had talked about all the girls he'd been seeing in Louisiana, mostly low-life types that let him do whatever he wanted to. He described everything about them in lurid detail, and she repeated most of it to me, getting madder and madder as she talked: how they all looked, what they said, which ones would put out and which ones wouldn't, how they did it, what they liked to do and didn't like to do, what different ones sounded like, even what each one said afterward, which he thought was really funny. I couldn't tell what Mae Maude really thought about Bubba, but I thought all the stories were pretty good stuff. And I thought if I could move to Louisiana, I'd have an incredible head start with the girls in that town. But it was weird hearing it all in Mae Maude's angry voice, the rhythm of it keeping time to the sweeps of her broom, the source of it hidden by dust that was getting so thick we almost couldn't see each other.

"If you wouldn't push so hard, there wouldn't be so much dust," I said when she started coughing so much she had to stop talking. She threw the broom against the wall.

"I'm gonna jump in the lake," she said. "I need to clean up. And cool off." She had dust all in her hair and eyebrows and a lot of it stuck to the sweat on her skin.

I watched her walk off through the woods toward the little pond that was to be the camp lake. We had swept up most of the big stuff in the cabin, and I decided to hose down the windows from the outside while the dust settled inside. When the work crew at Cabin Two went off to the store for their lunch break, I went down to the pond to see if Mae Maude might want to go get some sandwiches.

She was sitting in the sun on the brand new dock, her legs pulled up in front of her and her arms wrapped around her knees. Her shirt and Bermuda shorts were soaking wet.

"The guys have gone to lunch," I said.

"Good. I was afraid they were watching."

"Nope. There's nobody here."

She stretched out her legs and lay back on the dock in the bright sun and closed her eyes. She put her hands behind her head, her wet hair curling around her wrists as she moved her head slowly back and forth. I could see everything about her through a flimsy cotton blouse that stuck to her wet skin like glue. I hadn't really paid all that much attention to Mae Maude's looks when we first got to know each other; she was just a girl. But I looked at her there on the dock with her nipples showing plain as day through that wet shirt, and I thought she was the most beautiful thing in the world. I had an unchaste thought: I wished she was one of those other girls from Louisiana. And I hated Bubba Wilson.

Mae Maude opened one eye and smiled. "Aren't you gonna get wet?" she said.

I jumped in, tennis shoes and blue jeans and shirt and all. I didn't care if everything got wet and stayed wet. When I looked back, Mae Maude was up on one arm, laughing and watching me. I swam out to the floating dock and back, doing my best to copy Tarzan's slow, smooth strokes. Then I pushed up on the dock beside Mae Maude and sat with my feet in the water. When I leaned back on my arms with my hands pressed down on the dock behind me, little muscles stood out on the backs of my arms. I figured Mae Maude would see that.

"Better put your shoes in the sun," she said. So I did. And I took off my shirt, wrung it out, and stretched it out flat on the dock to dry. She grabbed the waist of my blue jeans.

"Is that all?" she laughed. "What about these?"

"Are you crazy?" I said. "This is not the quarry. There are rules around here. And eyes."

"Bo Fisher!" she said. "You and your rules. I don't think you'll ever do anything against the rules." She was play-pouting and turned over on her stomach.

"Anyway," I said, "What about big bad Bubba?"

"Bubba's not everything," she said. "I don't even care anything about him." She turned over and sat up, pulling her drying shirt away from where it was still sticking to her skin. Her nipples disappeared. My unchaste thoughts did not. "We didn't do anything," she said. "He talks big. And he acts big. Up to a point. Then he quits and just talks about those girls at home. I hate it." I stared at the lake and kept quiet. I didn't know exactly what she meant, for one thing, and the general direction, for another, seemed to be in my favor. "He thinks he can do anything he wants to, and I'm not supposed to do anything at all. He's stupid." I knew the right points and all the rules to bring to this argument, but they were in Bubba's favor, so it would have been pure-tee dumb for me to get into it. "I don't want to talk about Bubba," she said. I waited for more, but she didn't say anything.

"Mama says I might can stay out here in the new cabin if I get it cleaned up," I said, leaning back on my arms again. "That is, now that there's more people around and stuff going on," I added in deference to my mother's sense of the rules of propriety. "I have to find somebody to come out with me. But only if I want to stay all the time."

"Who are you gonna get?" Mae Maude asked. It couldn't make any difference to her, since she didn't know anybody in town anyway.

"I don't know. It has to be the right person." It had to suit me and Mama both, but I didn't say that.

"I'm hungry," she said. "Can you take me home?" I took her and then went back to camp and worked my fanny off cleaning Cabin One. I told the guys working on the next cabin that they could bring out the bunks for the first cabin any time they wanted to.

———

It took several days for my mother to round up sheets and towels and lamps and curtains and supplies for the cabin. The bunks still didn't show up, but I took all the other stuff out there. One of the old ladies in our church donated a radio and, incredibly, a television set. My mother was tempted to keep the television at our house in town. The world of technological change was clearly overtaking our family. Here was a "used" television set being discarded for a newer model, and our family was nowhere near getting its first one. Still, the old lady intended it for the camp, not just for the preacher's house, so out it went. My parents thought maybe it would be a good thing, anyway, that maybe I would pay more attention to the news of the day. The Democratic National Convention was about to be televised for the first time ever, and that was a big deal.

And that's how it happened that I learned to French kiss while Adlai Stevenson was accepting the nomination of his party for President of the United States.

Since there weren't any beds in the cabin yet, I figured there weren't any rules about not being in there alone with Mae Maude. Officially, my bedroom was still at the schoolhouse. And her mother thought it was a good idea for her to know more about current events, too, and that it would be perfectly all right to be watching the Democratic National Convention on television.

Her mother would probably be entertaining the leading local Democrat at home again that night, anyway. After her encounter with Sister Holy

Ghost, Cora had become the socialite of the season. Without the nightmare of the screaming fits, the Young Senator had become a frequent and apparently satisfied nighttime visitor. Only we knew, as he did not, that Cora's days were occupied with a whole group of "delivery men," which we thought was a perfect category for them, whether they really drove delivery trucks or arrived in their police cars or were salesmen who had heard about Cora from somebody and came by to check things out. Cora was making up for lost time, and the Young Senator seemed more than willing to do his part. We figured he told his wife he was going to another one of the frequent and interminable political meetings out in the county, but we doubted that his interest in politics would take him away from Cora, even to watch the Democratic National Convention on TV at the camp. I was pretty sure Mae Maude and I would be alone.

I was actually interested in the convention. I had liked Adlai Stevenson since 1952, when I was the only person in my class at school to admit being for him against General Eisenhower, except for the kids from the mill village who would have voted for any Democrat. But that night in Cabin One, Adlai Stevenson outdid himself. He kept setting me up to say serious, smart, important things about national policy in between kisses, while Mae Maude taught me to kiss the way she said Bubba said French people did it. It was not clear whether he meant French French or Cajun French, but Louisiana had plenty of both. I figured that must be one really hot place.

I could tell Mae Maude was impressed with my political opinions, because she kept wanting to kiss again every time I said something really good. Bubba, I can guarantee, did not talk about stuff like that.

Ever since that night, I have had a soft spot in my heart for Adlai Stevenson. But there were plenty of people around who thought that Adlai Stevenson was generally bad news. They talked about him all the time. Even Mae Maude had heard some of it.

"They say he's a nigger-lover," she said once when I came up for air.

"What? Who?"

"Adlai Stevenson. They say he's a nigger-lover," she said. Probably what Bubba had said.

"You shouldn't say that word," I said. Mae Maude sat up and looked at me like I had dropped some kind of a bomb.

"Are you for integration?" she asked.

"I think so."

"Bubba's dead set against it."

"Well, surprise," I said. "Bubba doesn't exactly strike me as a big liberal. Anyhow, since when do we care about Bubba?"

"What's a liberal again?" she asked. "I never can keep it straight."

"A liberal is somebody that likes to kiss like this," I said and returned to the previous matter on our agenda. Adlai Stevenson carried on in his thin impassioned voice, looking earnestly through the magic of television into living rooms around the country and into Cabin One. I imagined people all over America, French kissing on their couches. It was a great speech.

Of course, Adlai Stevenson was not really a liberal like Averill Harriman and Carmine DeSapio of New York, and it was important to people all across the South that the Democrats not let the New York-Tammany Hall-Big Labor-Red Communist liberals take over the party. Adlai Stevenson was a moderate. That was as far as he could go and still get any votes from Southern convention delegates. Without those votes, he didn't have a chance. And without a moderate nominee, Southern Democrats, who were arch-conservatives and segregationists, risked losing control of their home states and counties to the Republicans. So an arrangement was made that worked out for everybody.

I tried to explain to Mae Maude the difference between conservatives and liberals and moderates on race. That was the only issue that made any difference to anybody, anyway, and it was getting to be important to know who was who in those categories. In some places, it was important for social standing; in others, it could be a matter of life and death.

Conservatives, like the governor and every local elected Democrat we had ever heard of, were totally opposed to any mixing of the races. They were in favor of any force necessary to stop it, to keep it from even coming up in discussion, if they could help it. Bubba Wilson's family was in that camp, and they had already decided to bolt to the Republicans unless a third party was formed. But the problem with the Republicans was that nobody could be sure what they would do. Local Republicans could be way more moderate than local Democrats. Still, they would never be as bad as the national Democrats like Averill Harriman and Carmine DeSapio. While some people like the Wilsons went ahead and pulled the switch, most die-hard conservatives held on with the Democrats and hoped for the best.

Liberals like Harriman would flat-out send federal troops into the South and force the mixing of the races. We didn't personally know anybody in that camp. I thought I was probably about the closest one to it in our town, but I always wondered if maybe there were a few others. Nobody who was a liberal would ever want to say so; anybody who did might just as well move out and go on up north.

Moderates were more socially acceptable. They came in two shades. Supreme Court moderates accepted the court's 1954 ruling against segregated schools and thought integration was mostly a good idea, but they wouldn't actually send in troops to force it on people. That's what I said I was. Anticourt moderates thought the court and the federal government should stay out of it altogether and leave the issue to the states to decide, but they thought people should be nice to Negroes and give them better schools and jobs and houses and all. My father was in that camp, along with a lot of other people, but most conservatives couldn't see any difference between that and the hated liberals, and there were endless efforts to flush out the moderates or at least edge them back toward a conservative view.

Moderates would have been better off if well-mannered people, many of whom were conservatives themselves, had been more influential. Nice people like Bubba's grandmother, Mrs. J. Arthur Wilson as she called herself, thought it would be better just not to talk so much about race at all. She had found that the subject caused people to raise their voices, even if they agreed with each other, and she was generally not in favor of anything that had to be discussed much above a whisper. "We do not speak of integration in my home," she explained quietly. "But if we did, we'd be opposed to it." To which my mother responded later, when she heard the remark reported, "Well, we could hope she'll learn to keep her own mouth shut." Tiring of a subject that was beginning to dominate every conversation, and disliking any argument that could not be won quickly, Mama added, "It wouldn't be all bad if silence became contagious around here."

My mother thought it was "common" to be in any political category at all. She just reacted to each event as it came up, based on whatever seemed to be right at the time. It was a comfortable position for her, but it was confusing to the general public. There was huge pressure to declare total and clear allegiance to one group or another.

"Billy Graham is a moderate," I explained to Mae Maude.

"Billy Graham! He's a Baptist."

"And a Christian," I said. "I think that's his point." Mae Maude looked like she didn't get it. "He's asking preachers to teach people about integration and get everybody ready for it. He's not for any violence or big-time resistance."

"Bubba would say that's just like surrendering to the liberals," she said. Bubba would have been right. Moderates were just different from liberals on the "how" and the "when" of integration, not on "whether," but they had the advantage of sounding fuzzy about it, and it stirred up less trouble, without people getting really ugly. Just the same, I didn't want to explain anything to Mae Maude that she might repeat to Bubba. Ugly could be terrifying.

"Billy Graham is not the surrendering type," I said, hiding behind the preacher's robes as progressive Southerners were learning to do. When Billy Graham disclosed himself as a moderate, it created a place of refuge for other people in that category who needed a strong hand to hold onto. General Eisenhower and Adlai Stevenson were among them, along with a lot of ordinary people and even some newspaper editors and academics who might not otherwise have been so thick with the evangelist. Or so attentive to him. And conservatives, who had thought the preacher was a regional hero, were baffled.

Billy Graham's refusal to segregate his crusade revivals was like massive distant thunder rolling across the South, sounding to some like the promise of sweet rain and to others like the approach of a bad storm. There were people, of course, who misjudged the sound and stepped out into the open too soon, only to be struck down by savage streaks of swift and deadly lightning. The summer of 1956 was a tricky time.

"Did you hear that?" I said when Adlai Stevenson called for a "New America," where "freedom is made real for all without regard to race."

"No," she said.

"Listen."

"The civil rights plank of the Democratic platform substitutes realism and persuasion for the extremes of force and nullification," Adlai Stevenson said.

"What?" Mae Maude said.

One of the reasons Adlai Stevenson had lost the election in 1952 was that every time he said something, somebody else would have to explain it. Or maybe that was the only way he managed to get any Southern votes at all. Sometimes it's better not to be crystal clear. I explained what he meant this time for Mae Maude and added, "That's what a moderate is."

"What do you think Pollo is?" she asked. I was stumped. It was the first time it ever occurred to me that the categories were only for white people. Colored people couldn't be moderates or liberals; they were either sensible or uppity or agitators.

"He's probably sensible," I said. "He can't do anything about it, anyway, so he'll wait and see what happens." I hoped I was right about Pollo, because sensible was the only way to survive as a Negro. The Klan and its more socially acceptable ally, the White Citizens Councils, wouldn't tolerate uppity colored people, let alone agitators.

When Adlai Stevenson moved on to foreign policy, I decided French kissing was all I needed to know about that subject, so I attacked it again with all the cool vigor I could manage. In that area, I was not going to be a moderate. I remembered a warning from my eleventh-grade health teacher about the point in the process of making out "when psychology leaves off and biology takes over." I know exactly what made me think of it. "Hands above the waist" was the antidote for it, and I was alert to the situation. Maybe I was more of a moderate than a liberal after all.

"You know what?" Mae Maude said. "You kiss as good as Bubba."

"I don't see how you can kiss him," I said. "Do you like that tobacco smell?"

"Tobacco? Bubba doesn't smoke."

"Yeah, but he chews. I've seen that little can he carries in his back pocket."

Mae Maude laughed. "Those are rubbers," she said.

I was flabbergasted. I had never heard a girl say that word — didn't even know they knew it. And I was embarrassed that I hadn't known what it was in Bubba's back pocket.

"Bubba always carries some," she said, "but he never uses them. He does with other girls, but not with me. I'm supposed to be pure," she pouted, tracing a circle around my ear with her finger.

I don't know why Bubba didn't do it with Mae Maude, but I thought I would if I ever had a chance. I had no idea how to get to that point, but figuring out how to get equipped seemed like the first order of business.

———

I had never even thought about needing a rubber, but I spent the whole next day concentrating on that problem and on nothing else. What if I didn't have one when the time came? What if I didn't know how to put it on? I figured I'd better get two, so I could practice with one. I wasn't sure it could be saved to use again.

I had seen rubber machines in the men's rooms in filling stations when we went on trips, but I couldn't risk trying one of those in our town. I was sure the machines would make noise when the quarter dropped or when the handle was pulled, and I could just hear the old guys around the station snickering. Anyway, they would know that I could go to the bathroom at home, and there would only be one reason for going to the bathroom at the filling station in town.

So I had to find a station out in the country where nobody would know me. I went to about twenty of them. Nothing. Not a single machine. Each place, I would go into the bathroom, find the walls bare of machines, flush and leave. If they had called a convention of filling station guys from around the county, they would have compared notes and wondered why the white boy in the camp truck had to go to the bathroom so many times in one day. Worse, maybe they all knew exactly what I was doing and would decide to tell my mother.

Then it hit me. In the country, the machines were probably in the colored restrooms. I needed Pollo.

I went into town for the night and told my mother that I thought Pollo wanted to stay with me at the cabin, and I asked her if he could be a sort of grown-up version of the colored playmates we all had when we were little, to keep us out of trouble. To my surprise, she did not resist at all. She said she had seen Pollo several times when she had gone out to the camp and stopped off at the brick store. She had even talked to him. She liked the way he carried himself, she said, and the way he said, "Yes, ma'am." In Mama's book, a person could go a long way on posture and manners, white or colored.

"Miss Templeton has taught Pollo a lot of things you wouldn't normally expect," she said. "Including good manners. You could probably take lessons." She smiled and mussed my hair, even though she knew I hated that. I didn't say anything about it. I didn't want to start an argument, and I didn't want her to start guessing at my plan for checking colored restrooms. She said she thought it might be nice for Pollo to have a good comfortable bed to sleep in, and she said she would go out and set up everything the next day.

The workmen had brought out some single bunks and some double ones. Mama made up a single one in the counselor's room for me and decided that Pollo would like an upper bunk in the main room. The TV, she decided, could go back to town "for safekeeping," she said, "now that you'll have Pollo to keep you company. Besides," she said, "the convention is over." It was dirty pool, but I let it go. I wanted the TV, but it was a minor thing compared to my real target, still sitting in a machine somewhere in a colored restroom yet to be located. We moved the TV to her car. She instructed me the whole time we were working.

"You be careful," she said. "There's no reason to tell everybody in the world about Pollo being here. You just mind your own business, and you'll be all right. Why don't you keep fixing your meals over at the schoolhouse? Then you and Pollo can come over here after supper. You ought to be outside in the mornings before the workmen get here. You can both work on fixing up the vesper dell that Dad wants. That'll explain why Pollo's around so much. You'll be fine. Just mind your own business."

My business was something she hadn't thought about. After she left, I went in search of Pollo. He should have been surprised at my invitation to move into the cabin, but he didn't show it. He just said, "Okay." He was pretty much free to go wherever he wanted to around the Rocks. He didn't even have to tell anybody.

After supper of chili and Cokes at the schoolhouse, we went to the cabin. There was nobody around. I took all the stuff off my bed in the counselor's room and moved it to the upper bunk next to Pollo's and beside an open window where I could get some breeze.

"You'll break your head if you fall off of there," Pollo said. He lay down on the bare mattress of the lower bunk.

"Here," I said, "I'll help you move your sheets down, if you want to." I wanted him to be comfortable and happy. While we made his bed, I told him what we were going to look for in colored restrooms. He was mystified.

"What's a rubber?" he asked. It had not occurred to me that I would have to describe one, but I did the best I could. He looked at me like I was crazy when I told him what to put it on.

"Why?" he wanted to know.

"So you won't have babies," I said. "Don't you use them?" I just wanted to sound like I knew what I was talking about, but I was also actually interested in the answer. I knew that colored people did it all the time, and I wondered what Pollo did about it. I had heard about the rhythm method and thought maybe that was the answer, but I didn't have any idea how somebody would actually do the rhythm method when it came right down to it. I figured that knowing exactly the right rhythm, which I did not yet know, was probably the key to it for people who didn't use rubbers.

"Use them?" he said. "For what?"

"For messing with girls," I said.

"I don't do that." He was serious. "If you even touch a girl at the settlement, people would whip your tail."

"Then you don't need a rubber," I said.

"Yes, I do. I want to see one." Then he asked the direct question I didn't want. "You ever use one?" he said, looking me right in the eye. I hesitated.

"No," I said. "Not really." He was still looking at me. "Actually," I said, "I've never even seen a real one. Just pictures." Pollo smiled.

"Good," he said.

The next morning, we drove clear across to the other side of the county. I didn't think it would look too unusual for a white boy and a colored boy to be riding together, as long as it was in a work truck. Pollo sat on the edge of the seat, bouncing along with the truck and looking out in every direction at every thing we passed by. He looked like he was really excited about riding in the front — or maybe about the rubbers we were looking for. The farther we rode from the Rocks, the more curious he became about everything along the road: "What's that? Where does that road go? What do they do in there? Why are they burning those woods?" I didn't know half the answers.

"Who's that?" Pollo asked when we passed a couple of colored men who were walking beside the highway.

"I don't know," I said. "Why?" It didn't make any difference who they were, really. As long as they didn't know me, there was no threat that they could tell my mother. And Pollo certainly didn't have to worry about anybody telling his.

Pollo watched the two old men out the rear window, but he didn't say anything. After that, he was quiet and just faced forward, with his eyes on the road. I figured he was getting serious about the job he'd have to do if we found a machine.

We hit the jackpot at the first stop. While Pollo took two of my quarters into the restroom for colored men, I went in the filling station and fished around in the Coke box for two bottles, making as much noise with the icy water as I could, so the guy behind the counter wouldn't hear anything from the restroom.

It didn't help. Pollo's first quarter rattled and clanged like a pinball machine. It couldn't have been any worse if it had set off blinking lights. I picked up a Coke and swished it around; my hand was already frozen bluish pink. Pollo was apparently having trouble with the handle, like it would crank part way down and then flap back up. It sounded like he was trying to start a motorcycle in there. One of the mechanics came in, and I saw him and the guy behind the counter smile at each other. Then Pollo must have hit the coin return. We heard the quarter fall out — the whole world could have heard it — and the process started all over again. I wished I had a glove for my frozen hand as I kept swishing the icy water around and around.

When the noise finally stopped, I took the Cokes to the counter to pay, trying not to look at the guy. Then the second quarter went down. My whole body froze. Pollo was slamming the handle like he was going to rip the machine out of the wall. The guy at the cash register kept looking over my shoulder at the wall where the noise was coming from. I tried to look like I didn't know anything and didn't hear anything. But my face was as hot as my hands were cold. I could see the headline in the next week's newspaper: "Bo Fisher and Local Negro Arrested for Destruction of Rubber Machine." I'd be in trouble with the sheriff, the Women of the Church, the Ku Klux Klan, and my mother, all at the same time.

I paid for the Cokes and then went and sat in the truck, wondering if Pollo could get himself home if I just drove away. I had already started the motor when he came out of the restroom. He was smiling. And waving the packets of rubbers in the air.

"Wipe the smile off your face," I said. "And put those things in your pocket. You want everybody in the whole world to know what we're doing?" He put them in his pocket. But he kept smiling. His mission had been accomplished.

When we got back to the cabin, he handed me a packet. "One for you," he said, "and one for me." I stared at the package in disbelief.

"Tahiti Blue!"

"The red ones wouldn't come out," he explained.

"Didn't they have any that were just regular? Like skin color?" I said.

Pollo looked at me and grinned. "You mean black?" he said. "Nope. They didn't have any."

The package said Tahiti colors would "enhance your enjoyment." It didn't explain how.

"Let's try them on," Pollo said back at camp. It was a big mistake, but much better that it happened with Pollo than with Mae Maude. Pollo looked at mine and laughed out loud.

On him, Tahiti Blue looked dark and metallic, like some mysterious magnetic shroud. On my white skin, it looked like a bright blue neon tube. Or one of those light sticks they sell at the circus, the kind that glows when you rub it. I was sure Bubba would never put on Tahiti Blue, no matter how much enjoyment it promised to enhance. I rolled it back off, threw it at Pollo who was still laughing his head off, and went to the shower. We had wasted half the day for nothing.

———

"How many colored people are there?" Pollo asked that night from his bunk into the darkness of the cabin. I was almost asleep.

"What?" I said. "Where?"

"All over."

"I don't have any idea. A lot." The cabin was so dark I could not see from my bunk to Pollo's. We sounded like a radio show.

"Like how many?" he said.

"Pollo! I don't know how many colored people there are. What difference does it make?"

"I saw some by the road today and at the filling station. I didn't know them."

"Big deal. I didn't know them, either. You don't know all the colored people in the world."

"I made a list of all the ones at the settlement for Miss Templeton. She wanted me to put them in order by the alphabet. I thought all the colored people were here. I thought everybody else was white."

"Not by a long shot," I said. I couldn't figure out how anybody could be as smart as Pollo and still be so stupid about some things. But I guess he had never been very far from the settlement. And everybody who came out from town or somewhere was white. Like the guys who drove the Coca-Cola trucks and the other delivery men who supplied the store. Or the sheriff and his deputies. Even the workmen at the camp; nobody would have brought colored men from town to do that work. If they had wanted colored people, there were plenty of them already at the settlement, right next to the camp. So I guess Pollo had no reason to know. But anybody could have figured it out. "I think it's about half and half, white and colored, if you think about the whole world. There's a lot of colored people."

"Does anybody know their names?"

"Well, a lot of them are named Roosevelt," I said. Pollo didn't seem to think that was funny. The cabin was quiet. "In the Tarzan books, they have names like Mbonga," I said. "If you went to Africa, you'd find a bunch of them." Silence. "Do you know where Africa is?"

"Of course I do," he said. "I've seen it on Miss Templeton's globe. I know all the continents." After a while, he added, "I've never been to Africa." He said it quietly, like a confession, like I might not have known. "I didn't know there were colored people there," he said. Dumb, I thought.

"The Tarzan books call the Africans 'blacks,' but it's the same as colored," I said. "Who did you think all those people were that are always with Tarzan?" He could have thought it was just apes, of course. But his answer surprised me.

"I don't know anything about Tarzan," he said, "except you talk about him all the time."

I couldn't believe there was anybody in the whole world who didn't know Tarzan. We had a bookshelf full of Tarzan books at our house and a drawer full of comic books. During the summer, the picture show in town ran old Tarzan movies for the three-day mid-week slot nearly every week. And I had seen just about every Tarzan movie they had ever made. Pollo didn't say anything else. He must have fallen asleep.

"Sweet dreams," I thought. "Tomorrow, you're going to Africa."

Chapter Three

THE VAULT OF THE TREASURES OF OPAR

The forest god found a ready welcome in Pollo's world alongside the sun god. I went into town and returned with several Tarzan books, which Pollo grabbed like they were bars of actual gold from the Temple of Opar. I told him that *Tarzan of the Apes* was the one to start with, and he took that one into the cabin and stayed in for a day and a half until he finished it.

I worked at the vesper dell by myself. We had already cleared an area at the bottom of a hilly path that ran from the cabins over to the schoolhouse, in a natural dell surrounded by tall pines and thick underbrush. I cut down some smaller pines in the woods, stripped their long skinny trunks of branches and bark, and tied them to trees around the edge of the clearing, creating a kind of fence to define the worship area. I left an opening beside the path — and another behind the altar, since I knew that people who were moved during vespers to "dedicate their lives to Christ" or just "to indicate a willingness to consider full-time Christian ministry" would sometimes be asked to meet back there for prayer as the candlelight procession of other campers would wind its way back up the path to the cabins for sleep. I wondered if maybe they would call that one the "Prayer Gate."

I figured Pollo probably didn't know anything about all that, but he would have to be impressed with all the work I had managed to get done. As it turned out, he didn't even ask about it. He was holed up in the cabin with his book like some convict in a cell. He hardly spoke when I brought him his food, just kept reading. When he didn't show up at the schoolhouse for supper the second night, I took some food back to the cabin again. Ham and tomato sandwiches and milk. It looked like a pretty good supper to me.

"I like Kulonga," was all Pollo said, tapping the book with his hand. Apparently, he had finished it. I didn't even remember Kulonga from when I read it. He was obviously not a big deal in the story. Pollo had dog-eared the page where he appeared and opened the book to show me. I read while Pollo ate. Kulonga was a majestic warrior, son of Mbonga, the king of the first tribe of black people that Tarzan ever saw. In the part that Pollo liked, Kulonga was stalking Horta, the wild boar. Tarzan watched in awe from the trees as Kulonga moved silently and swiftly through the jungle, a "sleek thing of ebony, pulsing with life," naked except for an oval shield on his back, bands of metal around his ankles and arms, a huge ring in his nose, and tufts of bright feathers in his hair. Kulonga had three parallel lines of color tattooed on his forehead and three concentric circles on each breast. When he raised his arm to throw his long, slender spear with the poisoned tip, "muscles rolled, lightning-like, beneath his sleek hide," the book said. Horta the boar never even saw him or heard him coming. Kulonga was magnificent, and Tarzan learned many things from watching him, like how to shoot arrows and how to make fire. But Kulonga also killed Kala, the ape-mother of Tarzan. So, after a few pages, Tarzan killed Kulonga.

"Is Kulonga in some other books?" Pollo said.

"Nope," I said, adding what I thought was obvious: "He's dead."

"I thought he might come back."

"He's not a god. He's just a guy," I said. Pollo opened the book again to the dog-eared page and read the part about Kulonga to himself, again.

Before we went to bed, Pollo moved his stuff to an upper bunk. He didn't say anything about why. After we turned out the light, he said, "You want to hear about Kulonga?"

"I don't care," I said. He probably just wanted to tell it. I already knew everything I needed to know about Kulonga, but I was curious about whether Pollo would get it right.

In the darkness, he recited the story of Kulonga, word for word. I bet he didn't miss a one. Whenever there was a pause, I would say, "Uhm-m-hmm." I could almost see the majestic Kulonga on the ground below our bunks, "a sleek thing of ebony, pulsing with life." Pollo stopped before he got to the part about Kulonga killing Kala, the ape-mother of Tarzan. So, as far as his story went, Kulonga lived on.

"What's 'sleek?'" Pollo wanted to know.

"Shiny," I said. "Smooth. But not soft or weak. More like strong and hard, but kind of graceful. Do you know what 'lithe' is?"

"Like Hermes?" he said.

"Who's that?"

"Hermes. Mercury. The Greeks called him Hermes. Miss Templeton's book said Hermes had a 'lithe form.' He was a wrestler and a runner. Maybe he was sleek."

"Probably," I said. "You know Daphne? The one you told us about? Apollo's wood nymph that was such a good runner? She could have been sleek."

"But not Bacchus. Or the Cyclops." He was quiet for a minute, apparently thinking through an alphabetical list. "Or Eros."

I started at the top and found a good one. "Adonis," I said. "Adonis was sleek."

"Nanh," Pollo said after a minute. "A wild pig caught him and killed him. He might have looked sleek, but he wasn't really." Then he added, "Sleek is good. I like it."

"Hmh," I said. I didn't really mean it, but I was tired.

Actually, I loved talking about the gods with Pollo. When it came to myths, Pollo had to be the smartest colored boy in the county. And maybe not just colored. He had read everything Miss Templeton had about gods, and he knew them inside out. And alphabetical. And which ones were Greek and which ones were Roman, which was not something I could ever get straight. We had a course in mythology in the seventh grade, but none of my friends in town thought it was very interesting, so we never talked about it. I couldn't get over it; I thought it was the most interesting stuff I had ever heard. Or seen. There was a picture of Perseus on the cover of the book, completely naked, holding his bloody sword in one hand and Medusa's decapitated head in the other. It was totally different from anything in our town. Perseus was sleek.

"Icarus!" Pollo said suddenly into the darkness. "Icarus was sleek like Kulonga. Icarus' father taught him the stuff that got him killed, same way Kulonga learned from Mbonga. Being sleek is dangerous."

"Hmh," I grunted again, and I meant it this time, because I was just about asleep. Then Pollo said something that lit up the dark cabin.

"I bet Icarus and his father were black like Africans," he said. "Like Kulonga. If they hadn't been," he said, "the sun would have burned them. Like it does you." My eyes were wide open. The thought of Bubba Wilson listening to this conversation crossed my mind. "And Apollo had to be black," he added. "The sun god couldn't have been white." Crazy. I knew Apollo was white, but I wasn't sure I could prove it, so I didn't say anything.

I don't know how much longer Pollo stayed awake, but I was awake for a long time, thinking about whether any of the gods were black. I didn't think it could be, but I didn't really know. Nobody ever mentioned their color. The picture of Perseus on the front of my book was actually a statue, so there wasn't any color in that. All the other pictures I had seen just showed white gods, but then I wasn't sure the painters would really have known. I fell asleep thinking about sleek black gods. I would have bet two bits that Pollo did, too.

———

The next morning, I handed Pollo *Tarzan and the Jewels of Opar*. "Here's a good one," I said. "You'll like Mugambi. He's in some other books, too." Mugambi, an "ebony Hercules," was the faithful companion of Tarzan for a lot of adventures. He was swift of mind and swift of foot, and he rescued Tarzan — and Jane, too — from all kinds of troubles. He was sleek.

Pollo took the book and disappeared. He was gone for three days. I worked on the vesper dell by myself again, using some logs we had already notched and setting them up on stones to create woodsy pews. The place was really looking good. I couldn't decide whether to put up a cross at the front. I was pretty sure there was a rule against religious symbols in Presbyterian churches, but I didn't know if anybody had thought about making rules for Presbyterian vesper dells. It would have been easy to make one with two small tree trunks. I could even have made it out of dogwood, like the original.

In the afternoon of the first day that Pollo was gone, Sister Holy Ghost walked up behind me in the vesper dell and scared the bejeezus out of me. "Yoo, hoo," she said in a shrill soprano that shattered the quiet woods and made me think I needed to Get Right with God right away. I do not know how she got there without making any noise on the path. She looked kind of dumb, standing there in the middle of the woods in her high heels and veiled hat and white gloves. She had heard from our family's cook in town that Pollo and I were staying together at the camp. She thought that was good, she said. And she hoped we were being good. I said "Yes, ma'am," thinking probably everybody would agree that Sister Holy Ghost deserved a "ma'am."

Sister also knew that her new ally, the Young Senator, was going to a political meeting out on Brickstore Road, she said, and so she had caught a ride to the schoolhouse with him. She had just put some fried chicken in the ice box for our supper, she said.

It is hard to believe, but I lied to Sister Holy Ghost. I said that Pollo was working, too, but on the other side of the camp, but I would see him at suppertime and I knew for a fact that he would love the fried chicken. She smiled. I hoped it was because she believed me. I didn't want her telling our cook or my mother that Pollo was missing and that I was alone.

Sister had not been much of a mother to Pollo, even though that was all the family she had. Her own mother had died in childbirth when she was born, an only child. Her father had been banished from the settlement when it became known that he had delivered Sister to Mr. Snoddy to pay his debts. She herself had gone off to town after Pollo's birth and had grown up there and became a fixture at the House of Prayer as Sister Holy Ghost. I wished that everybody there had known that Sister Holy Ghost was born a

Presbyterian, but I don't think they had any idea where she came from. She had not returned to the Rocks until the Young Senator engaged her to help with Cora and brought her out to the Snoddy place on the Fourth of July. So far as I knew, the fried chicken delivery was just the second appearance of Sister Holy Ghost out there. Anyway, she said she was going back up to the main road to wait for the Young Senator. He had said he was just going to have a quick political meeting that afternoon. I smiled and said, "uhm-m-hmm," but Sister Holy Ghost was already walking back up the path to the schoolhouse.

I didn't actually worry much about Pollo until the second full day he was gone. I checked at the Snoddys, then Mae Maude and I went to Miss Templeton's and to the settlement and to the quarry. He was nowhere. The men at the brick store had seen him once, when they said he came by there and picked up some bicycle parts and some tools. Even Douglas said so. Mr. Samuel Do-Boy acted like that was not odd at all, but Pollo's bicycle was still at the cabin, and it worked fine.

I figured Pollo could take care of himself, wherever he was, but I was going to have trouble with my mother if she found out that I was living at the cabin alone. Still, until she found out, it was all opportunity if I could find a way to get around the Seventh Commandment's prohibition of adultery in thoughts, words, or — I should be so lucky — deeds. Even Bubba would have thought I was growing up.

———

Cora had no idea that my mother had raided the cabin, taking the television set back to town. We didn't lie to Cora; we just didn't mention it. And she was preoccupied with her own hectic schedule. So she thought nothing of it when Mae Maude told her she was going back to the camp with me. We were free and alone. Just the same, we followed some rules. Instead of going into the cabin, now just a TV-less bedroom, we took a couple of Cokes and went down to the new swimming dock.

The night air was hot and damp. We sat on the edge of the dock with our feet in the water. The lake was creek-fed and warm, not at all like the cool clear spring water at the quarry. That night at the lake, the air and water were so close to the same temperature, we couldn't feel anything but the sheer surface of the water around our ankles as we made slow patterns with our swinging feet, rippling the reflection of the moon into slow-dancing lights.

"Don't you wish the whole world could be like this?" Mae Maude said.

"It is," I said. "This is the way the whole world is." I lay back and looked up at the stars. "Look, there's the universe in total peace right in front of us." Mae Maude scooted over and lay back with her head on my stomach. I tried not to think about the Seventh Commandment.

"It's not this peaceful everywhere," she said. And it's not adultery, I told myself as I touched her hair, if we're really in love.

"I'd feel peaceful anywhere I could be with you," I said, hoping it sounded like true love. And I meant it. "It's not the place that's not peaceful. It's the people in it." I touched her face with my hand, and she kissed the tips of my fingers. But she was not thinking about love.

"Bubba says there's gonna be real trouble if Negroes try to go to school with us," she said after a while.

"Nobody's talking about that around here," I said. "There's nothing to worry about."

"He says they might try it in Tennessee. There's a bunch of men in that new Citizens Council that might go up there. Bubba says they're worried about outside agitators showing up."

"They're the outside agitators themselves," I said. "They're just going to make trouble, sticking their noses in other people's business."

"Bubba says it's better to fight it out there than to wait 'til it gets here. That way, nobody that we know would get hurt."

"That doesn't make any sense. What difference would it make, who gets hurt? People are people, whether we know them or not."

"Bubba says he might go, if some of the football team goes. He says he would be protecting me," she said, turning over so that her face was right in front of mine. She dragged her hair back and forth over my chest and face and added in a more teasing way, "Bubba would protect me from anything."

"Too bad he's not here to protect you from me!" I grabbed her head with both hands and pulled her to me. We kissed hard. It was as good as we had ever done it. I was really glad Bubba was in New York.

Mae Maude lay back on the dock beside me. "Do you know all the stars?" she said.

"No. Some. Pollo knows them all. There's Scorpio," I said, pointing. "See those bright stars in a big arc, right there? With the curving tail hanging down like a scorpion's stinger?" I had leaned over on my elbow so that my other arm was pointing right up above her face. When I brought it down, I just let it fall across her shoulders. Sleek-like. "That's Scorpio," I said and leaned over to kiss her again. I wondered if I should try to tell the myth of Scorpio, except I couldn't think of it. All I could think of was how Scorpio's stinger had scared the horses that were pulling the sun god's golden chariot when Phaëthon was driving, even though he'd been told he shouldn't. I moved my arm down across Mae Maude's chest, and she didn't say anything. She just kept kissing. So I put my hand under her shirt, and she still didn't say anything. Phaëthon completely lost control of his horses, and they raced through the heavens, banging Phaëthon and the bright sun chariot from one star to the next, setting fire to everything they touched. The air was so hot and muggy, it was hard to breathe. But my hand kept moving, sort of slowly across damp sticky skin. There wasn't anything under her shirt but skin. Then the horses of Phaëthon plunged downward and practically set the whole earth on fire. They scorched the mountaintops, turned wooded fields into deserts, turned the Ethiopians black, turned the seas into sand pits, turned... I hoped Mae Maude hadn't noticed that I forgot to keep the kiss going while I was testing how far she'd let my hand go. I hadn't realized how hard it is to move your hand and your mouth like that at the same time, and breathe, too. And I had no idea what happened to Phaëthon. I think he died. When I stopped everything to get my breath and think for a minute, trying not to breathe too hard, I just left my hand where it was.

"Do you think it's good for Pollo to be so smart?" Mae Maude said. I was not thinking about Pollo. And I couldn't answer the question with my hand under her shirt. It's even harder to think and feel than it is to kiss and feel. So I took my hand out.

"He's okay," I said. "He's the smartest colored boy I ever met."

"Do you think he wants to go to school with us?"

"I don't think it's crossed his mind," I said. "But I'd go to school with him. Wouldn't you? You don't need any protection from Pollo."

"Bubba sure doesn't think we should be in school with him or any other colored boys. At least, not me. He's seen you and Pollo together at the store. He wanted to know if you were making friends." I hadn't thought of Pollo and me as friends, but it didn't bother me. "Bubba thinks that's un-American," Mae Maude said.

"I think it's un-American to be as dumb as Bubba," I said. "Do we have to talk about him?"

"No," she said. I snuffed the conversation with another kiss. This time, I was kissing and thinking and feeling all at the same time. I unbuttoned her shirt and rubbed my hand around, but I couldn't figure out how to see, so I had to stop kissing. Mae Maude kept her eyes closed and starting humming that same tune from "Out of the Ivory Palaces" that I had heard so often from Cora. I couldn't decide if that was a good sign or a bad one. Mae Maude's voice was soft and low and full. I kept rubbing and listening. And looking.

Mae Maude was sleek, no doubt about it. She looked like the girls in *Esquire* magazine. Just as smooth and firm and shiny in the moonlight. Except her nipples were darker. The girls in *Esquire* had nipples that mainly made a pointy shape but were about the same color as the rest of their skin. I had thought maybe that was a difference between boys and girls, but Mae Maude's were darker, just like the guys I had seen, so there might have been some photographic technique in *Esquire*. Actually, one of Mae Maude's was darker than the other one. Or maybe it was just the moonlight. But one looked darker, and it looked like it was closer to center than the other one, too.

I suppose the total number of paired breasts that any guy ever sees in the flesh, without the effect of photographic technique, is relatively small in comparison with the whole population of women in the world, so it can be risky to generalize. In my case, the number I had seen was exactly one. One pair. And that one was also Mae Maude's — at the quarry when we went skinny dipping — and I had been too self-conscious about my own body parts there to focus much on hers. The *Esquire* girls didn't really count because of the camera effect, and the naked pygmy ladies in *National Geographic*, exciting enough when there was nothing else to look at, didn't count at all because they were so saggy and brown. As far as I knew, the concept of asymmetric nipples could be a generally accepted thing and perfectly normal for real American girls. But it was a surprise to me, just the same. I didn't have anything to measure with, but judging by my hands, I could swear one of her nipples was almost half a knuckle closer to center than the other one. I glanced at my own; they looked alike. I didn't want to check them out right there, because Mae Maude would have wondered what on earth I was doing, but when I checked later in the cabin, I found that mine were exactly equidistant from the center line, as expected, and also from my belly button, which I had not expected. A perfect equilateral triangle.

Mae Maude was technically a scalene triangle. Three unequal sides. I did not know then, of course, whether that was a permanent condition or just transitory; it seemed reasonable that nipples might develop at different rates or even that they might migrate, the way a flounder's eye moves around to his other side because of the way he lies flat on the bottom of the river — I mean I knew nipples wouldn't go that far, all the way around to the back, but I thought they might move sort of imperceptibly, like over a long period of time. And a very short distance. Half of a knuckle, for example, didn't seem impossibly far. I could not think of anybody I could ask. Miss Templeton would very likely know, but it was hard to imagine asking her the question. So I could not really account for the difference between Mae Maude and me.

I also could not then have accounted for the effect on me of Mae Maude's open shirt. I couldn't decide if it was psychology or biology, but I was aware that I was dangerously close to some transition point. Her skin was so tight it was shiny, but it showed no understructure of bones or muscles; it was all soft, smooth sloping lines. I marveled at mounds and curves that looked so firm and taut and felt so soft and supple. As I moved my head from viewing position to kissing position and back, my mind moved from geometric measurements to a world of Tahiti Blue. Sleek Tahiti Blue. Sleek Tahiti Blue diesel-engine passenger trains, racing through the woods and out onto the swimming dock. In the dark of my mind, Tahiti Blue didn't look so dumb, after all.

The trains had incredibly loud horns. Irritatingly loud horns. And distracting. And it wasn't a train; it was a car horn up on the hill behind me somewhere, and it sounded like it was stuck. The same thing had happened once before, and I hadn't handled it well, so this time I tried to screen it out.

"Who's that?" Mae Maude said.

"It's still me," I said.

"No, dummy. The horn."

"I don't know. I don't care." But she was trying to push herself up, looking up the hill toward the cabin. The only vehicle in the camp was the truck Mae Maude and I had driven over. When I looked to see if some other car was visible through the trees, Mae Maude started buttoning her shirt.

"I guess we better go check," I said, surrendering.

The horn stopped when we were about halfway up the hill. There was no other car or truck anywhere around that we could see. Just the camp truck. We didn't see anybody.

"I don't know how my mother does that," I said. Mae Maude didn't get it.

"Your mother's not here," she said.

"Well, not really," I agreed, conditionally.

"I better go home," Mae Maude said, taking my hand and leading me to the truck. She shifted gears all the way to her house.

When I got back to camp and went into the cabin, there was a note stuck on Pollo's bed. I recognized part of the text from the note Tarzan had left on his father's cabin in Africa after he learned to write:

> *This is the Place of Pollo. Do not Harm*
> *The Things that are Pollo's. Pollo Watches.*
> *Pollo has Found the Jewels of Opar.*

I couldn't be sure what things Pollo was trying to protect. Or what he had been watching. Tarzan had posted his notice after he saw white people messing with his cabin on the African beach; he had books and furniture and things in there that were left over from his parents. In our cabin, everything there was mine, so Pollo was probably just playing some game. If so, it wouldn't be hard to figure out where he and the jewels of Opar would be.

———————

I pulled up in Mae Maude's yard the next morning and honked for her, and she came out still dressed in her pajamas. If a girl in town had done that, she would have been risking her reputation and her neck just to show the boy she really liked him. I wasn't sure what it meant out on Brickstore Road, if anything, but I liked it. When I told her that we were going to the quarry, she went back inside and then came out looking like a dream come walking, with a pair of cut-off blue jeans hanging loose and low around her hips, the legs rolled up into tight cuffs high on her thighs. And she had on a sleeveless cut-off tee-shirt that hung down just over the tips of her breasts, leaving a lot of skin in clear view down to below her navel. I hated that we were going to look for Pollo. And I hoped we would never find him.

The ledge at the quarry was not the most likely place to catch him, but it was the right place to start. Mae Maude saw the first evidence even before we stepped out on the ledge: a long rope of woven vines, hanging from one of the pine trees that leaned out over the pool.

When she reached out to grab the vine, bracing herself against the trunk of the tree, I could actually see the round undersides of her breasts, hanging there like Golden Delicious apples in the Garden of Eden. No wonder Adam got in trouble. And no wonder he needed a fig leaf.

"You could swing out over the water with it," Mae Maude said, stretching. She was talking about the vine.

"Except you can't reach it," I said. The only way to get to the vine would have been to climb up into the tree, and then the vine would have been useless for swinging because it would have been hanging directly below. "Maybe there's something you use to pull it back to the ledge."

We spent a little while looking for a hook of some kind, but there was nothing. While we were staring at the vine again, back on the ledge, we saw smoke coming up through the rocks on the far side of the quarry. It seemed to be seeping up through a dozen different crevices and around boulders that had fallen into a haphazard pile, probably with the very last dynamiting ever done at the quarry. A good many of the boulders were covered in moss, and in some places the smoke seemed to be coming right up through mossy ground. I wondered if that's what the exit path looked like to Adam after he was banished from the garden for tasting Eve's apples.

"What's that?" Mae Maude said.

"I don't know. It's got something to do with the Temple of Opar. You can count on that," I said. "I hope he doesn't set the woods on fire."

"Let's check it."

We ran down the narrow path to the lower ledge and went straight into the water without stripping off anything except shoes and socks. I thought about suggesting more, but it was kind of creepy to think Pollo might be watching us. Tarzan was always alert when he knew the jungle had eyes. We swam to the other side, toward the smoke. "Be careful," I said. "The rocks could be hot."

The rocks were cool as could be. We climbed up to the top on that side, walked around in the wispy smoke, even pulled up some of the moss to see where it could be coming from. There was no source apparent to sight or touch. Or sound. There was no sound of any fire. Or anything else, for that matter. The cracks in the boulders led nowhere, and the spaces between the boulders just led to the next boulder below. The smoke seemed to be coming straight out of the middle of the rocks.

There was total silence in the jungle, same as when the animals have scattered from Numa the lion. Numa might have been jungle-smart, but I guarantee Numa would have been stumped by this smoke with no fire. I suppose Numa might have sat quietly until somebody came back to tend the fire, but we were not that patient. Besides, Numa didn't mind creepy situations. I did.

"Pollo!" I called. "Pollo! We give." Not a sound. "Pollo—o—o! Come on out." Nothing. "Else we're going home," I shouted. Still nothing. Mae Maude and I climbed back down to the water and started to swim across.

As soon as we were in the water, there was a blood-curdling yell from somewhere above us. "Ah-i-a-a-ah-i-ah-i-ah!" Like the smoke, it also seemed to have no source, ricocheting off the quarry walls in a way that made it impossible to get any sense of its direction. Then we saw him, standing on the upper ledge beyond the one where we always sat. He was beating his fists on his chest, looking up at the sun so that we could only see the bottom of his chin. And he was wearing nearly nothing. Although my mother had sent many a box of clothing to African missions, she would have been quite surprised to find one of her towels here in the quarry jungle as a loincloth on Pollo. There were also some silvery things around his wrists and upper arms and on his ankles, and there were chalky circles on his chest. "Ah-i-a-a-ah-i-ah-i-ah!" I was dumbfounded. Mae Maude was smiling.

Pollo looked down, picked up the end of a rope vine that was tied to the branch of an oak tree growing halfway between where he was and the ledge with the pines, jumped off into the air from a height none of us had ever even thought of attempting, swung on that vine down into the space beneath the pines, and grabbed the top part of the vine we had been unable to reach. As he swung back toward the quarry wall on the first vine, he let the second one slide through his hand until he was holding the end of it. Then, just before the backswing hit the wall, he dropped the first vine and swung out over the water on the second. It carried him down toward the water and then back up again. As it lifted him to the far end of its arc, he turned loose and did a swan dive into the water. Johnny Weissmuller never did it any better. When Pollo came back up to the surface, Mae Maude and I were looking at the most teeth I think I have ever seen. His smile was triumphant.

"Pollo!" I said, "You could have killed yourself."

"I nearly did, learning how," he said. "I hit that wall over there about a dozen times until I figured out the right places for the vines."

"It was beautiful," Mae Maude said to the same big smile. "Can we do it?"

"I don't think we should," I said. "What if the vine breaks?"

"It won't," said Pollo. "I've done it about a hundred times. It's a little scary at first, but it's really fun."

"What's all this?" I said, tapping the woven silver band that he had put around his arms, just above his biceps. He had the same thing on his wrists and ankles. Big smile again.

"The jewels of Opar," he said to me. Then he looked at Mae Maude. "You want to do the vine?"

The two of them swam to the other side of the pool, climbed up on the lower ledge, and then walked up to the high spot where we had first seen Pollo. I stayed in the water, to pick up the pieces. I think I was more nervous than both of them put together. On the way up, Pollo reached out and fairly easily grabbed the end of the first vine as he went up the path, taking it with him the last thirty steps or so. He had to stop once and wring out his loin-cloth; terry cloth is not even close to the same thing as a lion skin.

Pollo showed Mae Maude where to stand on the edge of the cliff and talked her through the steps of the swing. As Pollo held her with one arm and maneuvered the vine with the other, it looked for a minute as if he might swing off into the jungle with her under his arm, looking for all the world like Tarzan and Jane. Or Mugambi and Jane, I guess. Actually, Mae Maude's browned skin was close to some of the lightest color in Pollo's, except she would have had tan lines, and I knew he didn't. He was really a kind of light bronze all over, but there were highlights of deep yellowish gold or brass that showed through in places, like a bronze statue when it's polished. It was easy to picture them as brother and sister — or as the twins they nearly were, which Mae Maude knew nothing about.

The vine lengths and placement must have been perfect. Mae Maude had no trouble at all, negotiating it perfectly on the very first try and jumping feet first into the water when she completed the swing. I had no choice but to try it, too. Pollo talked me through it. He sounded confident that I could do it. When I jumped, I forgot to let go of the first vine when I picked up the second one and ended up dangling above the water, holding onto both vines. Mae Maude was laughing out loud. I joined her. "Look at this," I said. "Now what?"

"Just turn loose," Pollo said. "With your right hand," he added. Otherwise, I would have gone the wrong direction and hit the rock wall.

We must have swung on the vines for an hour, practicing different dives and falls from the end of the second vine. After the first few swings, it wasn't scary at all, and it was the most fun imaginable. I thought about telling Pollo to put on some pants, but I decided nobody was going to see us, and all they could see, anyway, would have been the hollows on the sides of his fanny. Everything else was covered by his towel loincloth. Besides, if anybody found us swimming together, what we were wearing would have been the least of our problems. I thought about it deliberately, and I decided I really didn't care.

"You want to know a secret?" Pollo said.

"What secret?" I said just at the same time as Mae Maude said, "Sure."

"The hidden treasure of Opar," he said. "It's near here."

"Where?" I said.

"Take a deep breath and follow me." With that, he was underwater. Mae Maude and I both followed, but we couldn't find him. Both of us came back up for air, but there was no sign of Pollo.

"Where is he?" she said, too quick to sound cool.

"I don't know," I said and went back under, swimming back and forth until my chest hurt. I came up gasping, close to panic, and shouted to Mae Maude, "I don't see —" I was cut off by another shout.

"Ah–i–a–a–ah–i–ah–i–ah!" It was coming from inside the quarry wall. Mae Maude looked at me.

"I have no idea," I said, rolling my eyes. I had never known anybody like Pollo. At a time when my friends were intent on growing up and becoming cool, Pollo was really just a man-sized boy. He was reveling in boyhood, but with a strength of mind and muscle usually attained only after boyhood has been forsaken. It was weird. I didn't know anyone else who would have spent the time, or had the skill, to weave those heavy ropes from old grape and kudzu vines. Or anyone else our age who would swim away and hide and then do a Tarzan yell from inside a rock wall. One of the reasons that summer was so much fun is that Pollo so freely did so many things that white boys our age thought they had been obliged to outgrow. That and the fact that Mae Maude was almost as freely doing other things that white boys our age only dreamed about.

Pollo came back up between us. "Go down about five feet," he said. "It's hard to see, but there's a hole in the wall. It's really just a space under a boulder that's wedged into another one. Go through there and you'll come up behind the boulders in kind of a cave. It's okay. I've been back there a lot."

Inside the cave was a ledge big enough for us to sit on. Bigger. We could have stretched out. It was dark, with the only light coming through a vertical dynamite hole in one of the boulders and through a couple of cracks near the water line. Pollo had put some stuff on the ledge, bicycle parts and tools and rocks and things piled up in a little mound.

"The jewels of Opar," he announced, smiling, "right here in their sunken treasure vault. Just like the real thing." There was a fire smoldering on the far end of the ledge.

"The smoke!" I said. I had forgotten all about it. "That's where it came from."

"You can put sticks down that dynamite hole for the fire," Pollo explained. "If you build it over there, the smoke will go up into those cracks and work its way over to some other cracks before getting to the top. By then, it's twenty feet, and more, away from the point that would be above the vault.

There's no way anybody could find the vault, even if they saw the smoke. If you brought food in here, you could stay a long time. There's not even any way bugs or animals could follow the smoke to the fire."

It was fun to be in there, but it was cold and a little creepy. We went back out, swam across the pool, and went up to the ledge to dry off. Pollo and I went behind a tree and wrung out our pants — wrung out my pants and his towel — and put them back on. We stretched out in the sun on the ledge. Mae Maude had picked some clover from the edges of the path; she sat down beside me and started slicing the stems with her fingernail and threading them into a clover chain.

"How'd you make those?" I said to Pollo, pointing to the rings of silver around his arm. The ones on his upper arms and ankles were snug-fitting and intricately woven straps of heavy silver wire. Around his wrists were loose rings that jangled when he moved them.

"They're bicycle spokes," he said.

"Did you make them right on your arms?" I asked. "What if you want to take them off?" Pollo reached up and flicked a couple of the spoke ends on the band around his upper left arm. The strap opened on hinge-like pivots on the back side and came off in his hand. He gave it to me, and I couldn't resist trying it on. It was easy; when I snapped it closed, it looked like it had been woven right on my arm.

"Let's all wear them," said Mae Maude.

"I made some extras," Pollo said. "They're in the vault."

"Not me," I said, unsnapping the one from my arm. "I can't walk around with that kind of stuff." The truth is, I was sorry. I thought Pollo looked cool, and the one I tried on made my biceps look a little bigger. But it was also true that I couldn't go around looking like that. Pollo put it back on his arm.

"Here," Mae Maude said to me as she lifted a clover chain toward my neck. "You can wear this."

"Me Tarzan," I said, pushing the clover away. "Him Kulonga. Him wear jewelry." It was a strategic mistake. Mae Maude stepped over me to where Pollo was sitting, leaning back on his arms with his legs stretched out in front of him. She sat down between his legs, facing him, and straddled his body with her legs. Pollo sat quiet and still while Mae Maude fixed the clover chain around his neck and arranged it on his chest.

Pollo was not even close to equilateral. His nipples were sort of close together, with long lines from there down to the protruding knot of his navel. Isosceles is what he was. I wondered if Mae Maude could see the difference. I wondered if the difference might be racial. I wondered, what if race were not a matter of biology, after all, but just a matter of simple chest geometry, would people then be divided up by nipple arrangement instead of skin color? And I wondered if they would stay separated by that arrangement for very long. I knew at least one equilateral who could get really excited about a scalene. If I hadn't been such a moderate, I would have thought there ought to be a rule to keep a scalene away from an isosceles.

"Tell a myth," she said to him. She was not apparently thinking about triangles; she was working with crescents, threading a second chain of clover stems and flowers onto the one she had fixed around his neck.

"You know Daedalus?" he asked. I did, but I didn't say anything. He didn't look like he was talking to me.

"Nope," Mae Maude said.

"He was a builder. One of the best. And an artist. And he invented all kinds of things. He taught his son, Icarus, everything he knew how to do. They built beautiful buildings. Palaces and temples and stuff."

"I thought they were gods," I said. Mae Maude had started a third clover chain, attached to the second, so that it began to look like an entire breast-plate of chain mail in clover.

"Daedalus and Icarus were mortals. They worked for King Minos. Only Daedalus did a favor for the queen that made King Minos really mad." He had his head down, watching Mae Maude's hands working across his chest. "The thing is, she fell in love with this bull, a real one, but they couldn't possibly be together because they were totally different, so Daedalus made up a disguise, a wooden cow that she could get inside of, and the bull thought it was a real cow. And nobody stopped them, because they didn't know it was really the queen in that disguise." Pollo either had a better book than I did or a better imagination. Miss Templeton could not possibly be the source of such a story. And anyway, I doubted the whole thing. It sounded like maybe Pollo had borrowed the Trojan horse for another erotic adventure in story-telling.

"Did it work?" Mae Maude asked, drawn somehow to the logistics of the event more than to the likelihood of it.

"Yep," he said. "That's how the minotaur came to be. He was half human and half bull, the child of Miz Minos and her stud." I had never heard a guy use that word with a girl, but Mae Maude didn't say anything, just glanced up at his face and back down to the clover chains. I had not ever seen anything about where the minotaur came from, but Pollo's explanation had the ring of truth to it, and it made me think maybe there was a lot of stuff missing from my book.

Mae Maude was either satisfied or distracted. She kept putting her hands under the clover chain breastplate, palms down and fingers spread, raising the clover chains up and letting them settle back onto Pollo's chest. If she had thought of it, she could easily have measured his nipple placement. "Anyway," Pollo said, "the king was really mad, and he put Daedalus and Icarus into the prison that he had made Daedalus build for the minotaur."

"Why was the minotaur in prison?" Mae Maude asked, starting another chain on Pollo's chest.

"He was dangerous," Pollo said. "He ate people. And he was also really embarrassing to the king. The king couldn't have something like that just running around the palace, reminding people what the queen had done. So he made Daedalus build a prison that the minotaur could never find his way out of. Then later he put Daedalus and Icarus in that same prison. Daedalus knew the only way out was to fly, so he figured out how to do that. He asked the queen to bring him some wax and feathers, and he invented a way to make these big wings that attached to his arms and back. He practiced with them until he could actually fly. Then, when he was sure he knew what he was doing, he taught Icarus. They escaped by flying over the walls of the prison and out over the sea." By the time Mae Maude finished adding the fourth strand of clover, the breastplate covered so much of Pollo's chest that nobody could have known whether he was isosceles or not. "The thing was, they had to not fly too close to the sun, because it would melt the wax on their wings and the feathers would fall off. Daedalus told Icarus about that before they flew out. But Icarus got so excited about flying that he soared up over the mountains and far out to sea." Pollo had his arms out like the wings of a bird turning and gliding through the air. "He got higher and higher. He could see forever, all the way to the end of the earth, but he couldn't see what was happening to himself. He got closer and closer to the sun." He had definitely gotten Mae Maude's attention; they were looking right into each other's eyes. Pollo brought his hands down to her face and tucked her hair behind her ears. "When he had gone too far," he said, "too far to stop himself, the feathers started coming out of the melting wax in his wings, and he fell straight down into the sea and drowned."

"Don't myths ever have a happy ending?" Mae Maude asked, pouting a little.

"Well, they named an island for him," he said to her. "And the sea around it." Then he said to me, "I've been thinking about Kulonga and Icarus."

"That's two totally different stories," I said.

"Not really. Both of them got killed."

"Who's Kulonga?" Mae Maude asked.

Pollo recited the story for her with the description of Kulonga that he loved so much. This time he told the story all the way through to the death of Kala, the ape-mother of Tarzan, and to the death of Kulonga. When he reached the point of Kulonga's death, Pollo pulled his legs out from under Mae Maude's and stood up. He walked over to the rim of the ledge and looked down into the pool. Speaking so softly that I had to strain to hear him, he finished the story, telling how Tarzan dumped the body of Kulonga from the high trees into the middle of Mbonga's village, how Mbonga the king confronted the body of his dead son, how the people of the village believed that Kulonga must have offended the god of the jungle, the "Munango Keewati."

"See?" Pollo said, turning to face us. "Icarus did what his father told him not to do. He flew too close to the sun. On purpose. Or because he couldn't help himself. Doesn't matter; he did what his father told him not to. But Kulonga did exactly what his father taught him. He was what he was supposed to be. An archer. A hunter. A warrior. He was so good at it, he just attracted too much attention. If he hadn't, he would have lived." Pollo did not look like a boy, standing there on the ledge and looking down at us. Or sound like one. He looked grown up, even in his towel loincloth and bicycle-spoke rings and clover chains.

"He killed Tarzan's mother," I said.

"No, he didn't," Pollo corrected me. "He killed an ape. Tarzan just thought it was his mother. Tarzan was wrong. Kulonga was right. And Kulonga was killed." We were all three quiet for a minute. "Kulonga did what was right. And then somebody else decided it was wrong."

"It's just a story," I said. "Probably, Edgar Rice Burroughs didn't mean anything by it."

"They forgot all about Kulonga, like he was nobody. They didn't name anything for him or write any more stories about him. He was a warrior and a prince, and his name never even came up again. That's why I made these silver bands. To remember Kulonga."

———

That night, Pollo came back to the cabin. I didn't want him to feel too bad about Kulonga, which I thought was a ridiculous thing anyway, so I told him how much fun the vines were at the quarry pool. "You're as good as Johnny Weissmuller," I said. There was an old Weissmuller movie playing that week in town; I had seen it twice when I was younger.

"Who's that? I'd rather be Tarzan."

"You can't be Tarzan," I said. "You have to be Mugambi or somebody." I didn't really understand why he would want to be Tarzan anyway, since Tarzan was the one who killed Kulonga. Pollo didn't always make good sense. "Weissmuller plays Tarzan in the movies." There was only one possible reason for somebody not to know that. "You've never been to a picture show, have you?"

"I guess not," he said. He didn't even know what one was. I completely failed at explaining a picture show, so I told him I would take him to see Weissmuller. Pollo didn't seem to be very impressed.

"Why can't I be Tarzan," he asked, having held the question all that time. We had finished undressing and were standing there with our towels wrapped around us, ready for showers.

"Tarzan was English," I said. "White." Then maybe I pushed it too far. "Like me," I said. As I stepped around Pollo on the way to get the first shower, he ripped my towel off.

"Tarzan didn't have a white butt," he said, smiling. "The book said he was bronze from the sun, and he didn't wear any pants until he was a lot older than we are." He was probably right about the color, but that was not the point. Then he dropped his own towel as he turned and went ahead of me to the shower. "He looked more like this."

"Except he didn't have kinky hair," I said. I do not know why I said it. It was another one of those things nobody was supposed to mention around colored people. And I knew it. So I was not surprised at the reaction, except for Pollo's big smile. He wheeled around, lunged at me, knocking me onto a bottom bunk, then dragged me onto the floor and straddled my stomach, with his knees pinning my arms to my side and his hands holding my wrists flat down against the floor beside my shoulders. It hurt.

"Give?" he said. "Can I be Tarzan?"

"I give," I said.

"Say 'uncle,'" he said. Say "uncle"? Ridiculous. Colored people all over the whole world were complaining about being called "uncle" by white people, and I had been doing my best to avoid offending anybody with it. Now, here was Pollo demanding it. So I just said it kind of under my breath. "Out loud," he said, pressing down harder with his knees. It hurt, and I was tired of the game, and I was tired of having to worry about what I said to colored people or Negroes or whatever they decided they wanted to be called instead of "uncle" and "auntie," so I yelled it out at the top of my lungs, and it felt good.

"Uncle!" I shouted at him. And Pollo never really knew why I said it, because he thought he had made me do it.

Chapter Four

—■—

At the Temple of the Virgin

I t was not easy for a white boy and a colored one to go to a picture show together, but it could happen. There were all kinds of rules against it, but they could be gotten around and nobody would care that much, depending on how it was done.

There was only one theater in town, and we parked the truck about a block away from it. I sent Pollo straight to the colored ticket line, and I went around the block to come up from the other side. He had no money for a ticket but thought they could just write it down, as if Mr. Samuel Do-Boy and his sidekick Douglas were going to show up in the ticket booth of the Bijou Theatre with their little credit book. I didn't bother to explain it; I just gave him thirty-five cents and told him how to buy a ticket.

There were separate lines for colored and white, even though they went right up to the same little hole in the window at the ticket booth. Pollo was already in line when I got there, but since they always served anybody in the white line first, that line moved a lot faster, and I was inside the lobby when he came in. There were no ushers or anybody to tell people where to go; everybody just knew that whites sat downstairs and colored sat up in the balcony — "up in Heaven," white people said as a joke.

Most of my friends were jealous of the colored assignment upstairs and thought it was really boring to sit on the ground floor. We promised we were going to change the rules when we grew up. In the meantime, although we knew older boys who had been up there, nobody in our group had ever tried it, and I was nervous, trying to look cool while we waited to be sure there was no one watching before slipping up the steps to Heaven. They could arrest white people for that if they saw it happen, or at least stop them, but nobody would actually go up to the balcony to check. They did check downstairs, and they would fry a colored person if they found one sitting with a white person down there. But upstairs was easier.

My mother said there were also rats and roaches in the balcony, because colored people didn't keep it clean, but I figured she just said that to keep me out of the balcony without having to use a racial rule. Still, I was nervous about that, too.

"Hey, Bo," somebody said right into my ear. It was Victor, a colored boy who had been my paid playmate when we were little. We didn't see each other much anymore, but we had been buddies before we started school. Even after they separated us for school, we had fun for a few summers, but we had drifted away to different sets of friends. I was glad to see him at the Bijou. Victor was the kind of guy who would know how to do anything.

"Hey," I said. "This is Pollo." It was strange to be introducing two colored boys, but they didn't know each other — Pollo didn't know anybody — so it seemed like the thing to do. "He's from out in the country. Pollo, this is Victor." It was easy, but I was glad none of my friends were listening. I would have never heard the end of it.

"We want to watch the movie from the balcony," I said to Victor.

"You can't go up there with a colored boy nobody knows," Victor said. "They'll think you're going to Heaven." So he knew the joke, too, but I didn't get the point. "You better both go with me," he said. He glanced quickly around the little hallway that separated the lobby and the restrooms from the theater and went up the steps with a nod to us to follow.

"Heaven" was no joke. There were some ratty old sofas on the landing at the top of the stairs, and some colored people were sitting on them like they were waiting for a bus or something instead of going to a picture show. I heard their voices while we were going up the steps, but they stopped talking when we walked by. From that area with the sofas, there were two doors into the balcony seating — not doors, really, but just openings covered with dark curtains.

Every time the curtain opened to let somebody in, it would spill light into the balcony for a second, and as we went in, I saw a section in the back corner where a couple of rows of chairs had been taken out, leaving a big open area in front of the chairs against the back wall. I started for it, thinking it would be great to have room to stretch out. There was nothing like it downstairs. Victor grabbed my arm.

"Not there," he said. "That's Heaven." He pulled me across the aisle into the center section, and we sat on the back row right under the projector, with me sitting between Victor and Pollo. We could hear the projector running the whole time the movie was on. I didn't like the sound, but it was interesting to see the shafts of light through the cigarette smoke rising up from the downstairs area; it created a kind of cloud cover for the movie, making it feel like we were right there in the jungle with Tarzan.

Not ten minutes into the movie, a flash of light from the curtains on our right announced the arrival of somebody, and I looked just in time to see two shadowy people go into the open area Victor had kept me out of. Must have been girls; there were two distinct giggles. Two seconds later, a colored guy got up in front of us and went back to that dark corner, and while I was watching him, I saw a white guy come through the curtain and go to the same place. The light didn't shine all the way back into the corner, so I still didn't see the girls, but I recognized the guy. I didn't know his name, but he worked at the filling station on the edge of town out toward the camp. It was one of the places I had looked for rubbers, and I was a lot more worried about him seeing me in the balcony than he was about me seeing him. Groans and grunts joined the giggles.

Pollo didn't see any of that. From the first jungle drum to the last elephant trumpet, he sat up on the edge of his seat with his face toward the screen. A couple of times, he glanced back at the projection booth like maybe he thought that might be Africa back there, but he didn't miss a thing about the movie. I was a lot more interested in Heaven.

Once, the curtains let in light without anyone coming in. When it happened a second time, I saw two white girls who were about to collapse from stifling their laughs and who apparently couldn't quite get up the courage to come all the way through the curtain. The third time, they made it. I had seen both of them in town, but they were older than me and I wasn't sure of their names. They had both graduated, and I thought maybe one of them was the older sister of a girl in my class. Right behind them came a big colored boy with shiny hair that was plastered against his head in rows of wavy curls and a white guy with a duck-tail hair-do and a pastel pink shirt that matched the thin pink belt in his baggy charcoal gray trousers. I wouldn't have noticed all that, probably, except that I knew a couple of other guys who had the exact same outfit. They followed the girls into the dark corner, and I wondered if the girls could tell which guy was which in the dark. Maybe by touching their hair. And maybe not; they would get greasy hands from touching either one.

People came and went through the whole movie — not all that many, I guess, but enough that I lost track of the number and racial composition of Heaven's happy population. But the number and composition were both surprisingly complex. Whatever the actual number, it was much bigger than the number of known liberals in the whole county. The governor and all those politicians trying to fight off integration would have been alarmed to know where they were losing the battle. Over there in Heaven, biology ran rampant, trampling psychology all over the place — and politics and economics and, I happily supposed, morality.

Whatever it was that motivated the people who made the rules about who had to sit where, Heaven seemed to be exempt. I wondered how the people over there would feel about the rules when they came back down to earth — and how they would vote. I figured people had to be way more than just moderates to go to that dark corner.

Weissmuller did his thing on the big screen. He swam, he swang, he swatted evil Arabs, and he sat around in his skimpy loincloth, with a lot less coverage than he would have gotten from my mother's terry cloth towel, and with Maureen O'Sullivan's hand on his leg. I didn't think they could have changed the movie since it came out originally, but I did not remember noticing all the times Jane would put her hand to her head in a near faint over some surprising sound or sight and then, with a deep sigh, let it fall to rest on the inside of Tarzan's leg. I didn't think that happened when I was younger and saw that same movie. Twice. Maybe I was just more alert to it since riding around with Mae Maude. Maureen O'Sullivan looked like she was getting ready to shift gears. Tarzan did a lot of "sitting there, waiting," just like me in the truck.

Toward the end of the movie, Heaven's gates opened up and everybody left. At least, a lot of people left. It was too dark to see if anybody was still over there.

"You better go," Victor whispered to me, "before there's people in the lobby." I told Pollo, but he wanted to stay to the end, so I told him I'd wait for him in the truck. I couldn't believe all the people slipping out of the balcony and crowding the downstairs hallway. I figured it would only get worse if I waited, so I went down with my head toward the wall and scratching my hair like I had fleas so that I could hide behind my arm. Somebody said "hey," but I didn't even look up, on the theory that if I answered, it would be a lot harder to make the case later, if necessary, that it had been someone else coming out of the balcony with a case of fleas.

"I'm going to Africa," Pollo said, when he got in the truck.

"I'm getting out of town," I said and turned into a side street to use the back road out to the camp and stay off Main Street.

"They have really big trees," he said. I figured he meant in Africa.

"And really big snakes," I said. "And crocodiles."

"We could learn how to kill them, just like Tarzan."

"What do you mean, 'we,' paleface?" That was Tonto's line in the joke where the Lone Ranger wonders what "we" are going to do when he and Tonto are surrounded by other Indians, and Pollo probably didn't get it. It didn't really fit as a comment to a colored boy, anyway. "I'm not going to Africa," I explained.

"Why not?"

Given a choice at that moment between Africa and the balcony Heaven, I'd be in Heaven faster than the speed of light. Given a choice between Africa and anywhere else, Africa would still be no higher than second. But I didn't think I needed to tell that to Pollo. I just said, "This is the first time you've ever even been to town. Don't you think you better digest that before you start planning an African safari?" He was quiet for a minute.

"Tarzan got himself all the way to Wisconsin," he said in a kind of snotty tone.

"Right," I said without arguing the point, but what I meant by it was that there was exactly the same likelihood that Pollo would get to Africa as there was that Tarzan actually went to Wisconsin, even though I knew that story. Pollo sat up on the edge of the seat and grabbed the steering wheel.

"You could teach me to drive," he said. I slapped his hand away as the truck hit the shoulder and pulled back up on the pavement.

"Well, don't try it until I tell you to," I snapped. He was still on the edge of the seat. "Besides, that would only get you as far as Charleston. It's a long way from there to Africa." He sat back in the seat and sulked a little bit.

"I can't get to Africa if I can't get to Charleston," he said after a while and then didn't say anything else all the way to the cabin.

———

Mae Maude was surprised the next afternoon when she came out of the house and saw Pollo behind the wheel of the truck. As he looked out at her, I could only see the back of his head from my seat beside him, but I knew she was looking back at a whopping big set of teeth from her side. I had been trying to teach those teeth to drive for most of the morning on the camp roads. And I couldn't help smiling myself.

"Pollo!" she yelled and smiled back at him. I would have been surprised if he could have formed any words at all through that monster grin, and in fact he said nothing, just kept holding the steering wheel with both hands, right on 10 and 2, as instructed. He was actually a pretty good student.

"You want a ride?" I asked her. I got out and let her into the front seat between Pollo and me. It was the first time we had sat that way, but there was no other way to do it. I couldn't let her ride in the back by herself, and I couldn't get back there and leave her alone in the cab with Pollo, so we just squeezed in together. Besides, I was tired of all the protocol and really didn't care what anyone might think. But I hoped Bubba wouldn't see us. Pollo let the clutch out too fast, and the truck lurched and died. The smile went away.

"That's all right," Mae Maude said, patting his leg. "It's happened to me, too."

He started the motor again and eased out into the driveway and up Brickstore Road. He drove so slow that he never had to get out of first gear. We were moving along in slow motion, and I thought the three of us were in absolute heaven, sitting there together on the front seat of the truck — except that I had learned in the balcony of the picture show that Heaven was a lot better even than that. But if I could have had just one picture of that summer for the memory book my mother was keeping up for me, it would have been that one. Not skinny-dipping at the quarry pool, even if I didn't have to worry about my mother seeing it, not Cora and Sister Holy Ghost, not even Cora and the Young Senator, certainly not me in Bubba's Corvette, not Mae Maude's scalene torso — well, maybe that one, but I would definitely have to worry about my mother seeing it — and not even the swinging vines. The real picture, the only one I really needed, would have been the picture of just the three of us, sitting together in the cab of the camp truck, Pollo driving, all three of us smiling, riding down lonely Brickstore Road, moving so slow that measured against the earth's rotation we were probably not moving at all. It felt like we could be in there together forever.

"Does old Do-Boy know you're doing this?" Mae Maude asked before we reached the store.

"Yes, he does," I said, "but I wish you wouldn't call him that."

"That's what I call him," Pollo said. "Same as everybody. That's his name."

"Well, they shouldn't," I insisted. "That can't be his name. Anyway, I know it's not his whole name. I call him Mr. Samuel Do-Boy."

"And he thinks you're stupid," Pollo said.

"I bet he thinks I'm nice. I'm the only one who calls him something besides 'Do-Boy.'"

"Anyway," Pollo said, "he knows I'm learning how to drive. He just said to be careful. When we get to the main road, I have to let one of you drive."

"It's too dangerous with other cars," I explained, but we all knew perfectly well that there was hardly ever any traffic out there — maybe a car now and then or a delivery truck, but singular, almost never plural. I felt sure Mr.

Samuel Do-Boy wasn't afraid of the traffic but more the reaction of some white driver who might see Pollo driving the camp truck.

At the store, we bought some Cokes. Nobody had said a thing, but all the old men in the store were looking at us and smiling big. Except for Douglas. I never saw him smile.

"Well?" said Mr. Samuel Do-Boy.

"He's doing great," I said. I really meant it.

"Uhm-hm," came the chorus. I was honored.

"Wouldn't that be something?" said Mr. Samuel Do-Boy.

"Uhm-m-hmm."

"A boy from the settlement."

"Uhm-m-hmm."

"Driving."

"Uhm-hm." A couple of men slapped their knees, and others bent over in their rockers, unable to contain grins that turned their whole bodies into crescent smiles. They probably thought Pollo would some day be driving a big delivery truck. I wondered if they would have been smiling so big if they knew that he was planning to take the camp truck to Africa.

I took the truck down the main road to the turn-off into the settlement with Mae Maude shifting gears and then stopped to let Pollo back behind the wheel. As he drove through the settlement, we created a sensation. People came running out to wave to us like we were conquering heroes, and little children ran along beside the truck chanting, "Pollo! Pollo!" There was plenty of time for them to call everybody out of the little shacks to see us. We were going so slow, they could have published a newspaper about it before we got to the other side of the settlement. Pollo, already the darling of the community for his success with Miss Templeton's tutelage, looked that day like the Hope of the Future. I wondered what they would think if they could see him in the quarry swinging through the trees in his towel loincloth. I guessed they would think that he was wonderful at the quarry pool, too. And that's where we went, but without the cheering throngs. Just the three of us.

We took turns on the rope vines until we were exhausted. We were all three really good at it. Mae Maude and Pollo even learned to swing together. I was not about to try that, but I was jealous as all get out. They looked for all the world just like the movie. I felt like Boy. Or Cheeta the chimp. While they were going back up to the high ledge, I went underwater to find the opening to the hidden vault, thinking I could surprise them some way from inside the quarry wall. I went under about ten times, but I could never find the way in. It was supposed to be about five feet down, I remembered, and under a big boulder that was wedged into another one. Still, I could not find it and just gave up.

When everybody was tired of swinging, we went up to our ledge, popped off the tops of our Coke bottles on the edges of the rocks, and settled back to enjoy the day's several triumphs.

"How far do you think Charleston is?" Pollo said. I knew why he was asking, and I knew it had not been far from his mind all morning. Mae Maude laughed.

"I don't think the camp truck would make it, if that's what you're thinking," she said, with no clue as to how far Pollo really was thinking of going. He was staring at his Coke and running his finger around the lip of the bottle.

"There are other trucks," I said. I knew he was being serious. "People go there all the time. It's not that hard." He took a big swig of his Coke.

"Would you go to Africa?" he asked Mae Maude.

"Africa! I don't want to go to Africa. I don't even know exactly where Africa is."

"I can find it," Pollo said. "You'd like it."

"I don't have any intention of going to Africa," she said. She turned and leaned back against his shoulder. "I plan to stay right here. In fact, I'm not going to move from this spot until you tell a story." There was a long silence. I didn't know if it was because he really wanted to talk about Africa or because he hoped she would never move.

"You want to hear about La, the High Priestess of Opar?" Pollo said.

"I don't care," Mae Maude said. I think that's exactly what she meant.

Pollo cared. La, High Priestess of the Sun-Worshipers of Opar, was not a random choice. He told us quickly of Tarzan's search for the sunken treasure vault of Opar, of how he set out with the Waziri, Mugambi's tribe who were Tarzan's most trusted black warriors, of how the search party was trailed by the traitor Albert Werper. Then Pollo stood up and walked around the ledge, looking for the passage into Opar and mumbling about stacks of gold ingots and mountains of jewels that had belonged to the rulers of Atlantis.

He had Mae Maude's rapt attention. As he slowly and carefully climbed onto the sheer rock wall behind the ledge, describing the ascent up the great rock face of the ramparts of Opar, he could easily have been Tarzan himself.

Then Pollo jumped down and spotted the witch-doctor crouching behind the pine that leaned out over the water of the quarry pool, repeating that wise man's warning in a weird scratchy voice as he was apparently hearing it: "Turn back. Turn back before it is too late. I see bad days ahead, and danger lurks behind." The little witch-doctor gasped his last and crumpled in Pollo's hands; he dropped him ceremoniously into the quarry pool and watched him sink beneath the water.

Pollo turned and reported the capture of Tarzan by the grotesquely deformed and hairy creatures who were the priests of Opar. Forcing his wrists together behind clenched fists, he dragged himself to the feet of Mae Maude, and laid himself out on the ledge to be prepared for the sacrifice. With his eyes half open, he saw the high priestess herself, La — incredibly beautiful and, of course, naked from that intercontinental and timeless scarcity of clothing that afflicted all Pollo's heroes. As for La, he said, she gazed on the most perfect man she had ever seen, so unlike the warped and repulsive men of her own kind, he said. She sent the priests away, saying that she would torture this man herself and prepare his body for the sacrifice. Pollo took Mae Maude's hand and held it above his chest as if she held a dagger, poised to drive it into his heart. I was clearly reduced to audience in this act but lucky, I guess, not to be one of the disgusting Oparian priests. It was possible that I was expected to play the part of Werper, but I was not about to. I just watched. Pollo dropped his own hand and waited with dignity for the end, just as Tarzan had.

But passion for the form of the man before her transformed La into a "pulsing, throbbing volcano of desire," he quoted — as least, as far as I could tell, he quoted; I didn't think he could have made that up — as "she ran her hands in mute caress over his naked flesh." Edgar Rice Burroughs could not have imagined the drama that Pollo was giving this recitation. Even Mae Maude was getting into the act, her hands tracing the skin of the glistening body bound at her feet. Whatever the throbbing volcano might have in mind for the body laid out before her, Mae Maude's hands were drawn to the silver bands around its arms, perhaps as a more practical object of desire. As for La, she had gone so far already that it inflamed the priests, and they rushed in to take her away to become a sacrificial offering herself. Messing around at the wrong time in the wrong place, she had put herself and Tarzan both in imminent danger.

Pollo jumped up and turned his back to Mae Maude, protecting her from the onslaught. The vile and hairy priests of Opar never had a chance, as Pollo kicked several into the quarry pool and knocked one or two up into the trees. He grabbed one from behind, put his knee into the hairy back and snapped its nasty neck. A couple of others were stabbed with the ceremonial knife he took from La. Finally, with a foot up on one of the dead bodies littering the ledge, Pollo beat his chest and let out that primitive cry of victory: "Ah-i-a-a-ah-i-ah-i-ah!" But he wasn't smiling. His face had turned hard, and he kept on fighting his imaginary monsters, fighting so fiercely that I thought I might have to get up to calm him down. He looked like maybe some kind of strange biology was taking over.

"Why do they have to fight so much?" Mae Maude said. Pollo stopped but said nothing. He walked slowly around the ledge, clearing it of debris and dead bodies with his feet.

"That's what life is," he said, finally. "I've got it written down on a piece of paper in the vault: 'In the clash of arms, in the battle for survival, amid hunger and danger, in the face of God as manifested in the display of Nature's most terrific forces, is born all that is finest and best in the human heart and mind.'" I recognized it from the book as Tarzan's defense of African civilization against the fat, opulent pretense of European society. "'In the face of God,'" Pollo repeated, "'as manifested in the display of Nature's most terrific forces, is born all that is finest and best.' That's what happens in Africa. That's what made Kulonga what he was. And Tarzan. And Mugambi. That's what I want to happen to me, even if I have to go to Africa by myself. That's what I want to think about all the time when I'm wearing these silver African bands."

"I think that's beautiful," Mae Maude said. "I think we should all wear one to show that we believe it." She was going to have one of those bands, come hell or high water. Or throbbing volcanoes. But it was just for the jewelry. I knew perfectly well she didn't really care about the clash of arms. Or the face of God. Or about Kulonga. Or Mugambi. Or probably Pollo, for that matter. Or maybe even me. But I cared about Pollo, and I hated for him to think he would be alone. Even if we weren't going to Africa with him — which didn't exactly matter since he wasn't really going, either — we could at least remember the summer together. I wanted Pollo to know that I cared. And I wanted Mae Maude to care about me.

"You remember what Tarzan said to Jane and Mugambi?" I asked Pollo.

"About what?"

"When their plantation was destroyed by the Arabs and the Opar treasure had all been stolen. Tarzan said to Jane and Mugambi, 'When everything is gone, we still have love and loyalty and friendship.' The three of us have all that, too. We still will, even after this summer is over."

"Well, then, we could wear anklets like Pollo's, just to show that we mean it," Mae Maude said. "That we're friends forever." She was not going to give up. "You could put your sock over yours, if you have to," she said to me. "Then all three of us would have the same thing. We'd be the only ones to know what it means." Pollo looked at me.

"If that's what you want," I said to him, "I'll wear one, too." Pollo smiled. "But it's not an anklet," I said. "It's called a leg band."

"I'll be right back," he said. "They're in the vault of Opar."

"How do you find the opening?" I asked. "There must be a landmark." He told me without hesitating.

"When you take the vines," he said, "you have to drop off the second one just before it starts to swing back. That's exactly where the opening is." With that, he was gone, off to the upper ledge, gone to retrieve matching leg bands from the sunken vault of Opar to mark his friends forever. We watched in awe as he looped down from the first vine to the second and then disappeared into the water.

"Bubba's back from New York," Mae Maude said when Pollo was out of sight.

"Oh, wonderful," I said. "Why does he always have to mess everything up."

"He doesn't mean to. He doesn't even know he's doing it."

"Well, I'll agree he doesn't know he's doing it," I said. "But he means to."

"He's been back since Wednesday. I've told him every day that I didn't feel good."

"Well, tell him again."

"I can't. He's coming tomorrow, no matter what. It's the last day before he has to start football practice. It's not such a big deal. We could all be together. We could show him how to swing on the vines. I bet he'll like it. I bet he'll be really good at it."

"I won't bring Bubba to the quarry," I said. "He'll do something to mess it up. The last time I went to town with him, he did that 'gar' thing when we went past the settlement. I'm not ever going even close to there with him."

"What 'gar' thing?"

"If you don't know it, I'm not telling you," I said. It was hard to believe she had never heard it. "He just yelled 'nigger' as loud as he could, just sort of stood up behind the wheel of his car, with the top down, and held his nose and yelled it out. He thought it was really funny."

"He doesn't talk that bad around me," Mae Maude said. "It must be something about you that made him do it."

"Come on, Mae Maude. I couldn't make Bubba do anything. I don't even want to be around him. I don't think we ought to even talk to him, let alone be nice."

"Well, we're gonna be nice tomorrow. It's his last day before he starts football practice. Then he's gonna be gone. And he's gonna be a real big deal at the University. You might like knowing him." She looked at me and smiled. "Anyway, you don't want me to be alone with him on his last day, do you?"

Pollo came back up the path with his hands full of curled bicycle spokes, and we stopped talking about Bubba. But I would have bet that Pollo would have agreed with me. We put on the leg bands, and Pollo adjusted them so they didn't clank when we walked.

"You know Bubba?" I said to him. "The guy in the red car?"

"Yeah. I know all about him. Why?"

"I just wondered. He's coming out tomorrow. Mae Maude thought maybe he would like to come swing on the vines. You think he'd like that?"

"I don't know," he said. "How would I know?" The attempt at nonchalance was too obvious.

"Well, I don't think he would. But I guess we have to entertain him before he goes off to be a big star at the University."

When we were back on the main road in the camp truck, Pollo said, "Let me out at the cabin. I want to check something on my bicycle." So we did. Then I took Mae Maude home.

"Do you think Bubba will like Pollo?" she said.

"Not a chance."

"You can't be so certain. They don't even know each other yet."

"Yes, they do," I said. "I'm certain. There's not a chance. I don't think we ought to even take Pollo with us." I was not sure how to accomplish the separation without also separating myself from Mae Maude and leaving her alone with Bubba, but it turned out not to be a problem.

When I got back to the cabin, I found myself alone. Pollo's bicycle was gone, and he never came in that night. I would have bet he was sleeping in his Oparian vault. And I hoped he would stay there until Bubba left.

———

The next morning, Bubba roared past the store on his way down to Mae Maude's, signaled an ordinary routine everyday-type touchdown as he went by, then came back up with her just before lunch time. He was dressed in tennis whites and was probably mad when he heard the plans for the day. Mae Maude explained again in my presence, as if I had never heard of it, that we were going to make sandwiches together at the camp pond, and we bought some stuff to add to what she had brought from home. She was not wearing Pollo's leg band, and I thought that was a good thing. Mine was covered up by my socks.

We left the camp truck at the store, and the three of us piled into Bubba's car. Mae Maude told me to get in on the passenger side and then stepped over me and sat in my lap with her arm around my neck. I didn't even look at Bubba the whole way over, hoping he'd think I was just furniture. We turned in at the schoolhouse and drove around the long loop to the cabins, parked up on the hill, and took our bag of lunch stuff down to the dock.

Of course, the first thing Bubba did was take off his shoes and socks and his shirt. I took a look and decided to keep my shirt on. He had a rich boy's tennis tan, with his face and forearms and legs much darker than his feet and shoulders and chest. He would probably think I looked like country. But that wasn't what got me. I always thought I did pretty well compared to Pollo; he was tall and strong but kind of thin. But Bubba was all muscle, covered with bulges and ripples. And hair. Even with his jock look of shaved ankles and feet where they would be taping him up for football, he still had more hair on his legs than Pollo and I had on our whole bodies, both put together. It looked like Bubba lemon-juiced all of his, head and arms and legs, to make it blond in the sun. I would have bet two bits that he did. But I wouldn't have mentioned it for a hundred dollars.

At least, he was equilateral like me. Sort of. With him, there were so many muscular mounds and ridges between the points of the triangle, the measurements would have to be made "as the crow flies." Everything he had was bigger, and the lines were longer. But he was clearly equilateral. I thought maybe it might be a racial thing after all. And male.

I kept my mouth shut and my shirt on, ate my sandwich, and thought up different reasons why I would not be able to go swimming with Bubba. I took off my shoes and, in a stroke of genius, reached into my sock and unhooked the silver leg band so it came off inside my sock, and Bubba never saw it. I was pretty sure he would not like the whole idea of anklets on a guy.

When Bubba finished talking about New York, he started talking about football. He was sitting on the end of the dock with his feet in the water, and Mae Maude was beside him. I had my legs pulled up in front of me, leaning back on one elbow and wishing I could be somewhere else. While Bubba was still talking about New York, Mae Maude leaned away from him and back against my legs. That's about when he switched to football, talking about working out and banging people around, and she pulled her feet up on the dock and when I put my legs down flat to keep her from leaning against me, she just sat there and started playing with my feet. Bubba said he could do fifty push-ups easy and a hundred sit-ups, then put his hands and big arms behind his head and demonstrated sit-ups right there on the dock. I'd never seen a guy do that without hooking his feet under something, but I'd never seen a guy with a stomach he could actually flex, either. Mae Maude started pulling my toes.

"This little piggy went to market," she said. "This little piggy…"

"Mae Maude!" I said. Here was this rich bully of a football goon flexing his muscles at us and talking about banging people around, and she was playing with my feet. "Stop it," I said. "Bubba's talking."

But Bubba had stopped talking. He stood up like some menacing monument, looking down at the two of us. We looked dumb, even to me. Bubba's eyes were blinking a lot faster than usual. I figured I was either going to get beat up or we were going swimming. Bad news, either way.

At that very moment, Pollo came out of the woods and walked onto the dock. I was relieved that he was dressed normal and didn't look like Kulonga. The idea of African warriors around our lake would have been as hard to explain to Bubba as jewelry on boys. Mae Maude stood up. I knew she was nervous.

"Bubba," she said, "this is Pollo."

Nobody said anything.

Pollo looked straight at Bubba, waited, looked at our bare ankles and then out at the lake, pulled off his shirt, waited, stepped out of his shoes, waited again without looking back at us, dropped his pants on the dock, stood there for a long minute, waiting in his undershorts and the woven straps of bicycle spokes on his ankles and upper arms, jangled the loose bands around his wrists, and then dived into the water and swam out toward the floating dock, sleek as all get out. I was transfixed by the grace of it all. Bubba was not.

"I'm not swimming with a nigger," he said. I wanted to tell him he'd be smart not to go after Pollo in the water, but I stayed on my rear end and my elbows, trying to be small.

"He's not a nigger," Mae Maude said. "He's a friend. And don't say that word again."

"Nigger, nigger, nigger," Bubba said. There was a hard edge to his words that I had not heard before. "That's what he is, that's what he was, and that's all he ever will be. You can't make him something else, Mae Maude."

Pollo pulled up on the floating dock and stood up facing us, his legs spread apart and his hands on his hips. He looked like a warrior prince, with the sun glinting off the silver around his ankles and arms. I looked at Mae Maude. She was crying.

"What's wrong with you, Mae Maude?" Bubba said. "You turned into some kind of a liberal?"

"You don't have to be a liberal," she said. "You just have to be nice."

"Not to niggers, you don't," Bubba said. "You got to keep them in their place. Or else they get in trouble." He looked at Pollo out on the floating dock, held his nose dramatically, and yelled: "I smell a nig-gar!" Pollo jackknifed into the water and started back toward us. "Swimming with you sure as hell ain't their place," Bubba said to Mae Maude.

"Stop it," Mae Maude said.

"Wait 'til the sheriff's people hear about what you're doing, swimming with a colored boy out here," Bubba said. "You know what they're gonna do? Probably shut down the camp." He was right. They had already closed the swimming pool in town just because somebody had asked a question about integrating it.

"Bubba," Mae Maude said. She didn't finish whatever she was thinking.

"Bubba nothing," he answered. It made no sense, but it sounded forceful. "I'm leaving. And I'm not coming back. Ever." He picked up his shoes and shirt and walked off the dock and into the woods, sort of skipping as he pulled on each shoe, then heading up the hill to his car.

"Bubba!" I called to him. "Wait up." He kept walking.

Pollo came up from underwater and rested his arms on the dock.

"I'm sorry," Mae Maude said to him. She was still crying.

"Bring Mae Maude over to the schoolhouse," I told Pollo. "I've got to stop Bubba." I ran as fast as I could, but he was already in his car and backing away from the cabin when I got to the top of the hill.

"Bubba! Wait up," I yelled. "We don't have a car." I have no idea why he stopped. Not because I told him to. Not to be nice. Not because he cared whether we had to walk back to the store. Maybe it was manly. Anyway, he stopped.

"Get in," he ordered and then scratched off toward the road before I could get the door closed.

"Bubba," I said, "there isn't any reason to tell anybody anything."

"The hell there ain't," he said. "I don't know what kind of camp you got going on out here, but it ain't American. I'm gonna see to it that it's shut down."

"It's Presbyterian," I said, "and nobody's gonna shut it down, because there's nothing 'going on.' What are you gonna say, anyway?" He drove past the schoolhouse and off toward the store. "What's anybody gonna be mad about?"

"That you all are out here swimming with niggers. That's enough."

"And that you left Mae Maude down there alone with one of them?" I said. He took his foot off the accelerator, and the car slowed down. Bubba gripped the steering wheel hard with both hands. "She didn't go down there by herself," I said. "You took her. Then you ran away when one nigger showed up." I cringed at my own words, but I had to find the right button to push. "Doesn't sound All-American to me," I added. I saw the back of his arm flex and knew it was coming.

"Sonofabitch," he said and hit me backhanded across the mouth. I hated him, but I knew I had him.

"Big man," I said. "But if you tell on Pollo, I'll have to explain how it happened." He pulled in at the store and stopped beside the truck.

"Get out," he said. He was back on the road toward town and out of sight before I could start the truck. I didn't spit the blood out of my mouth or check my teeth until he was gone. Everything was okay; it was just the inside of my lip that was split and bleeding.

———

I drove back to the schoolhouse to wait for Pollo and Mae Maude, figuring they would walk over on the path down through the vesper dell in the woods. It was a hilly path, but it was shorter that way than along the road that looped around from the cabins.

The sound of a car on the loop road surprised me. It seemed to stop at the far end by the cabins. I hoped to high heaven it was not Bubba. I thought about driving the truck around there but didn't really want to confront him again and couldn't figure out what I would do if he was really there. Besides, Mae Maude and Pollo had plenty of time to get away from the lake and cabins and ought to be arriving at the schoolhouse any minute. So I waited there.

There was no sound of anybody anywhere. After a while, I left the keys in the truck and walked down the path to the vesper dell, moving quietly so that Bubba would not hear me if that was really him at the other end. I reached the entrance to the clearing where vespers would be held during camps and saw Bubba himself standing behind a tree, just watching something.

"Shhh," he said with his finger across his lips. In that split second, before Bubba even finished his "shhh," I saw them. There was Pollo with his pants off again. There was Mae Maude pushed against the little altar of tree trunks, with her clothes on the ground. There was a scream, a shriek. Pollo turned towards us, all in that same split second, and Mae Maude screamed again, a piercing scream that didn't quite sound like words. Pollo turned and took off through the woods.

Bubba and I bumped into each other trying to get through the little gate.

"See about Mae Maude," I yelled so he could hear me over the wailing. "I'll catch Pollo. I know where he's going." I was afraid Bubba might actually catch him if he tried; I knew I could not. I ran off after him as Bubba went to Mae Maude.

I never saw Pollo. I kept running, partly because I could still hear Mae Maude screaming and I didn't want to deal with that. I ended up at the schoolhouse and waited for the screams to stop. I knew Mae Maude well enough, and Pollo, too, to know what had happened in the vesper dell. No way could it have been rape, with the way she had egged him on all summer, but it wouldn't matter; it would be rape when Bubba told it, and Mae Maude would have to go along with it. And Pollo would pay hell for it.

When the screaming finally stopped, I went back down the path to the vesper dell. I didn't see anybody around, but I heard a low guttural kind of moaning. I went in and found Mae Maude alone, crawling in the dirt, still naked, whimpering low like a wounded animal, gathering her clothes. Either it was a good act or I'd have to change my mind about Pollo; it didn't look like she had exactly volunteered.

"I didn't do it," she croaked out when she saw me. "He raped me."

"He's gone," I said. "I couldn't catch him." I sat down beside her and held her shoulders. There were splotches of dirt all over her.

"He raped me," she said over and over again. Looking at her, I thought it might be true. Still, it shouldn't have been that much of a surprise to either one of us.

I had never been so disappointed with anybody in my life as I was with Pollo, even if Mae Maude did tempt him beyond "the point where psychology leaves off and biology takes over." Pollo knew all about that. I had told him. And he should have known that the psychology of race required him to keep the biology of sex in check. I hadn't said that to him in so many words but, Lord, how could he not know it?

I should have been disappointed in Bubba, too, except that it was totally in character for him just to leave Mae Maude alone there in the woods. He was such a jerk. I hoped he wasn't out looking for Pollo.

I managed to get Mae Maude's shorts on her, wrapped her shirt around her, and carried her to the truck. She was pitiful. She lay curled up on the seat while I drove to the cabin. I took her inside and turned on the shower. She cried the whole time and kept saying, "He raped me," like I didn't know that or wouldn't remember it. The truth is, I just didn't know what to say back.

"What happened to Bubba?" I called in to her.

"He went away," she said between sobs. "He said I was a nigger-lover. He said he couldn't have a girl like me. A girl that messed with colored boys. He said he'd never see me again."

She came out of the shower wrapped in one of my mother's towels and stood sniffling at the far end of the room from where I sat on the bunk.

"Come here," I said. She didn't move.

"He raped me," she said.

"I know. I know." I went and picked her up, put her on the lower bunk and covered her with a sheet. Then I lay down beside her, just hugging her and saying nothing until finally she was quiet and still.

"Better get dressed," I said after a while as I gave her a squeeze. "I have to take you home."

"Where's Pollo?" she asked.

"I don't know," I answered. It was the honest truth.

———

When I took Mae Maude home that night, it was the last I saw of her or Pollo or Bubba. I went back down to the Snoddy place every morning for several days, but Cora said Mae Maude didn't feel well and didn't want to see anybody. I didn't say anything to anybody about the whole thing, and nobody seemed to be making any big to-do about it.

Summer was over. After a couple of days, I closed up the cabin and went back to town. I waited for action from Bubba or his family, but nothing much happened. I guessed he was afraid I'd tell that he had run away when Pollo showed up at the lake or, worse, that I had seen him hiding behind a tree at the vesper dell, just watching, not going in to protect Mae Maude. Anyway, nothing serious came up. Once, my mother asked if Pollo had been swimming with us. She said Bubba's grandmother thought Bubba might have seen us and just thought somebody should know.

"No, ma'am," I said. "That's not true. Pollo was swimming when Bubba was out there, but he was swimming by himself." Nobody mentioned it again.

School and football games and weekend movies began to fill my time and my mind, and my thoughts about the Rocks were gradually less frequent and less painful. A couple of Saturdays, I saw Victor uptown and wondered whether he knew where Pollo was. Having introduced Pollo to the larger colored world, I wouldn't have been surprised if they all knew exactly where he was and how he was doing, but I didn't ask. I was supposed to know, and I didn't want to let him know that I didn't. So I said hello to Victor and we talked about simple stuff ("How's school?" "Fine." "Good.") and neither one of us mentioned Pollo. After that, I could go for days in a row without a single thought about the summer at the Rocks.

Nothing unusual ever happened in our town, but there were two events that fall that turned heads. One, a girl from a farm near town — a wonderful girl that everybody knew and admired — had entered a beauty pageant sort of as a lark. To everyone's surprise, including hers, she won a trip to the finals in California, representing the whole U.S.A., and was selected Miss Universe of 1956. It was on television. People around town agreed, with a smile and a wink, that she was "one of the prettier girls in the county." I wondered what Bubba thought about it; Miss Louisiana had not even come close.

When Miss Universe came back to earth from California, there was a parade in her honor on Main Street. They had a float for her to ride on. The governor was there. The whole town turned out, not just the colored people who normally packed Main Street on Saturdays, and everybody had a good time.

The very next weekend, on a Sunday afternoon in mid-October, there was another parade. This one was the Ku Klux Klan; they had not marched in our town since the late 1940s. There were not many colored people on the street on Sunday. My mother thought we should all stay home, too, but I wondered how the Klan could be scary, dressed in sheets, so I went to watch.

They were scary. There were about forty of them, in white robes with red and gold borders and decorations. A mixture of American flags and Confederate battle flags flapped fiercely in the wind, crackling like the flames of a big bonfire. The snapping flags and dull footsteps of the marchers were the only sounds. One of the Klansmen turned his head and looked at me as they went past. It was creepy. Like the others, he wore a tall mask so that there were just eye-slits where his face should have been. Cowardly, but evil looking. At least, to me.

Two little colored children sat on the curb, smiling gleefully as if they were watching a company of clowns from the summer carnival. They looked disappointed when the parade went on by and none of the clowns did any tricks. Sister Holy Ghost was standing behind the children, staring back at the white sheets as they went by. And not smiling.

When I went home, my mother said she had heard that the chief of police was among the marchers; she was furious about it. And one of her friends had heard that some of the football players from the University were also in the group. "I hope Bubba Wilson wouldn't get involved in anything like that," she said.

At Thanksgiving, I went out to the Rocks again. The sting had worn off from the last days of summer out there, and I missed everybody. Except Bubba.

I might as well have stayed home. The Snoddy place was boarded up. The schoolhouse and cabins were locked up tight. Nobody at the store had seen Pollo, they said, since before I left camp at the end of the summer. Cora, they said, had gone off with the guy who drove the Coca-Cola truck, and Mae Maude was at Miss Templeton's. They said they thought maybe she was going to have a baby, smiling at me when they said it. It wasn't happy news to me — or funny, either.

"Did you see the cross down by the lake?" Mr. Samuel Do-Boy asked me. He was looking at me sideways, not smiling, waiting for an answer.

"Who put a cross down there?" I said. "I don't think that was in the plans. How long has it been there?"

"Oh, 'bout five or six weeks. Since the middle of October."

"I'll have to go check it out," I said. "I hope it fits in."

It did not. At the end of the long swimming dock, where I had sat with Mae Maude so many times, and also with Mae Maude and Bubba, and right where Pollo had dived into the water with his woven bands of bicycle spokes, there was an ugly and primitive cross of two-by-fours. Charred. A brilliant blue sky with puffy clouds highlighted the reds and yellows of the trees around the lake, and all those shapes and colors swirled and dissolved into the blackened hulk of that cross as I connected "the middle of October" with the Klan rally in town and understood what had happened.

"No!" I shouted, not really meaning to. "No—o—o—o—o!" it came back to me as a scream from the far side of the lake and again from the hillside behind me: "No—o—o—o—o!" A white heron started up from the edge of the lake, and a flock of crows flew out of the trees with a chorus of calls in perfect harmony with the echoes of my own cry. I ran toward the end of the dock, joining with nature in revolt against the cross that stood there mocking the very God of all creation. I grabbed it out of the cement block that held it upright, raised it up over my head and threw it with all my strength into the lake.

It floated. It came back up to the surface and turned lazily in the sun, mocking me. Without any thought for the cold air, I stripped down, dived into the water and dragged the God-damned cross back to the dock. I threaded it through the cement block, right up to the cross bar, and pulled it back into the lake and as far away from the dock as I could get it before it began to pull me under. I let it go, then went underwater to watch it sink to the bottom, its cross bar waggling back and forth as if it still had some life in it, struggling to get back to the air and light. A puff of dirty silt welcomed it to its final resting place.

As I pulled up on the dock and gathered up my clothes, I felt the cold for the first time, and I thought of Mae Maude and Pollo and me swimming together in the cool water of the quarry pool. Bubba Wilson was right about one thing: I had made friends with Pollo. Friends. Not like a moderate being nice to a Negro boy. He had become my friend. That ugly cross made me want to tell Pollo, made me want to call him my friend. Out loud. I wanted to sing out, "I went to the rock to hide my face," and hear Pollo shouting back, "The rock cried out, NO HIDING PLACE!" but my thoughts were overtaken by a jumble of memories and images.

What came through the jumble, of all things, was the Fifth Commandment, crowding everything else out of my mind. Not the commandment itself, not the "Honor thy father and mother" text, but the explanatory answer that goes with it in the Westminster Shorter Catechism, the part about the honor "which belongeth to everyone." The reason my father required memorization of the Catechism, he said, was not so that we might know the answers when questioned at church but so that we might know the way when challenged in life. Standing there on that cold dock, my mind focused involuntarily on an answer that burned away the pretense of that ugly cross and burned away my own pretense, as well.

QUESTION: *What is forbidden in the Fifth Commandment?*

ANSWER: *The Fifth Commandment forbiddeth the neglecting of, or doing anything against, the honor and duty which belongeth to everyone in their several places and relations.*

I stood there in that place that had seemed so beautiful to us, stood there naked as the day I became a part of God's creation, stood there hating the Klan for dishonoring my friends, stood there looking up at the sun crossing the sky in its golden chariot, stood there guilty as sin. And I cried. I cried for Pollo and for Mae Maude. And I cried for myself, stung by my own failure against the claim of the commandment, angry at the overt violation represented by that burning cross, and unable to stop the march of my memory through the Catechism.

QUESTION: *Which is the Sixth Commandment?*

ANSWER: *The Sixth Commandment is, "Thou shalt not kill."*

QUESTION: *What is forbidden in the Sixth Commandment?*

ANSWER: *The Sixth Commandment forbiddeth the taking away of our own life, or the life of our neighbor unjustly, or whatsoever tendeth thereunto.*

If I had neglected the honor of my friends since the end of the summer, I had done far worse by walking along with them in the weeks before that, leading them — or following, it didn't matter which — right into the path of ignorant violence. "Whatsoever tendeth thereunto" was broad enough to cover me and Bubba and the Klan all at the same time. Mae Maude and Pollo were not exactly faultless, either, but there are special requirements for those who have been instructed.

As I dressed, I thought again of that afternoon at the quarry pool, and the images of Pollo and Mae Maude fought for space in my mind:

The Fifth Commandment forbiddeth the neglecting of the honor which belongeth to everyone,

I went to the rock to hide my face,

The Sixth Commandment forbiddeth the taking away of life,

The rock cried out—

Or whatsoever tendeth thereunto,

No Hiding Place!

The Fifth Commandment forbiddeth...the Sixth Commandment requireth... And then I remembered the Seventh Commandment, the one that forbiddeth adultery and requireth the preservation of chastity in heart and speech. And I wondered if I would violate the Commandment, sort of secondhandedly, just by remembering previous unchaste thoughts. And then I remembered some of those thoughts. And then I smiled.

———

Miss Templeton was on the top step of her porch before I reached the bottom step. She did not look inviting, even with her teeth already in.

"Afternoon, Miss Templeton. Is Mae Maude here?"

"Mae Maude is not receiving visitors." It was the same icy line I had heard from Cora after I took Mae Maude home at the end of the summer, one of those female things that guys are supposed to pretend they understand. Mae Maude had plenty of time to be feeling better, but maybe she was embarrassed, even though I already knew everything. I wasn't sure how to ask.

"Is she, you know, okay?" I said.

"You'd best leave Mae Maude for me to worry about. She'll be fine."

"Yes, ma'am," I said. "Have you seen Pollo?"

"You leave Pollo for God to take care of, young man," she said more sternly still. "There is certainly nothing more that you can do for him."

"Yes'm, but I sure would like to know where he is, just so I could talk to him."

"There's been too much talk already. If you want to help, don't you bring up his name ever again. Not to anybody. He is not here. He is in God's hands. He is not your concern." Concerned or not, I was obviously not going to find him through her.

"Do you know about the cross at the lake?" I asked Miss Templeton.

"Of course," she said. Of course. She knew everything.

"Does...?" I do not know why the question was so hard to ask. "Does Pollo...does he know?"

"He does," she said. There was silence as I looked up toward the roof of her house and around at the kudzu to keep her from seeing the tears welling in my eyes.

"Miss Templeton?" I said. I looked right at her. "I didn't have anything to do with it."

"We all had something to do with it," she said. "But I know that you are not to blame." She must have seen something in my face, because she slumped a little and said, "Don't worry, son. Everything's going to be all right." She stiffened again and added, "Don't ever speak of this again."

Delphine Templeton stood there in her loose dress that looked a little like a dirty choir robe, with wisps of gray hair sticking out all around her pale white face, then stepped back into the shadow of the kudzu-draped entry to her sanctuary. The house looked like nobody had lived there for years.

Summer was more than just over. With Miss Templeton's dismissal, the summer of 1956 was gone forever, as if it had never been at all. I had no idea then how hard it would be for any of us ever to get the good of it back, how hard it would be to recover something that was never there.

Chapter Five

———

"COME ON OUT, WHEREVER YOU ARE"

Odd. The summer I spent in the country dropped from my mind as if it had been the trunk of some fallen tree, floating waterlogged for a time below the surface of the lake, then sliding away to the bottom without any warning and without any immediate reason. With a teenager's attention to the surface of life, I saw no ripple, heard no splash, took no notice of the loss. I did not feel it begin to go. I don't even remember forgetting it.

That it came back to me with such force after ten years was a total surprise. I had graduated from high school, gone to college, joined a fraternity, bought a tuxedo, and worked at summer jobs farther and farther from home, pushing the geography and general dimensions of my life far beyond the small town of my parents and their friends — and of my own friends there. When I went back, I went back only to the house, not really to the town, and certainly not to the life of that place. I became less than a tourist, just a player touching base by habit, wrapped up in my game and not paying much attention to the base itself.

Unsatisfied after college by several years of teaching school and unsure of what I wanted to do, I went to graduate school. There, I walked into a maelstrom of conflicting opinion and challenge to nearly every shred of order and tradition I had known.

The Duke University graduate school grabbed my mental and moral shoulders and shook me hard. I had expected something more contemplative, even musty. But Duke rocked. In medical research and in literary criticism and in the study of primates and even in the current rage of "student unrest" — and certainly in basketball — there was a drive to beat the established universities at their own games and to beat them so convincingly as to make Duke itself the standard for future competition. Matchbooks in the university dining halls carried an etching of the Duke Chapel's soaring Gothic tower and a quotation from the president of the university: "We will not rest until we are a national force in every field that legitimately concerns us." Fraternity parties and basketball victory celebrations operated on the same principle. Life beat so strongly at Duke, in mind and body, that the dust expected to give character to the carved-stone capitals and cornices never even had a chance to settle.

My field was history, and the strength of the graduate history program then was its emphasis on telling the story. No historian strayed very far, or wanted to be caught straying at all, from the rigorous pursuit of the facts. Facts were essential, and disciplined research was required for their recovery. But at Duke we were taught a historian's job was to find the truth — and that facts alone are never truthful. They have no meaning without the suppositious story, ephemeral or eternal, in which they occur. Without some such story, history has no reality. So, at Duke, they taught us to tell stories.

I'd just started a class assignment to "create a fictional account of an actual historical event" when my mother called. She wanted me to come home for the weekend.

"Your father has a funeral to do on Saturday out in the country," she said.

"Anybody we know?" I asked.

"The Church at the Rocks has had some trouble. It's been in the papers here."

"Like what?" I said.

"Their preacher's been put in jail, and they asked Dad to help with a funeral out there this weekend. People are saying the Klan is involved somehow, but that hasn't been in the paper. Come on home, Bo. I think you should."

I didn't think, for one second, she was scared. More likely, she sensed a "teaching opportunity" in getting me involved in this experience. Or she might have been looking for a more active ally than my father. Either way, I sensed a crusade in the making.

My mother subscribed to what was known in her youth as "muscular Christianity." Over the years, the Christianity portion of the concept had gained some flexibility in her view, but the muscular part was rock-hard solid and unyielding. I have known other preacher's wives who took more of a "sweet Jesus" approach; they ruffled no feathers, made no waves, just stood around gently smiling. In Sunday school, kids ran over them. Kids did not run over my mother. She was not into "suffering the little children" to do whatever they wanted, or adults either; she was more excited by the example of cleansing temples and driving out money changers. She never exactly gave the impression that she could walk on water, but most people in town came to believe that if she smote the waters, the waters would flat-by-God divide in two as if Moses himself had struck. In a time when muscular Christianity had gone soft, Mother became the model of a muscular Presbyterian.

Not that she wasn't fun. Church Family Game Night, in fact, was her thing. Other people were there to foster congregational relationships; Mother was there to win. For her, it was the same thing — just a case of defining the relationships. Whether the contest was a relay race or horseshoes or comedy skits, her teams always won, and they always had more fun than anybody else. She poured that same competitive energy into everything she did, whether she was organizing support for world missions or arranging table decorations for church suppers.

Raised in an era when segregation was a given fact of life, Mother did not challenge the system. But she had an irresistible impulse to attack when people in her circle said dumb things about what she regarded as poor and defenseless colored people. Like some other preachers, my father received his share of hate mail for his straightforward openness to integration. But the hate mail that came to our house was always anonymous. People don't mess with somebody who can bring plagues.

So when she called, I went home.

When I pulled in our driveway on Stonewall Street, my father was sitting with a tomato sandwich on the front porch steps, admiring his fresh-cut lawn. He shook my hand and said it was good to see me. Mother came with a glass of iced tea for him, kissed me on the cheek and said she'd get some tea for me. She returned with a pitcher on a tray and a plate of cookies — before I even saw them, I recognized the aroma as my grandmother's teacake recipe. This was a serious visit.

Mother and I pulled up rockers on the porch behind where Dad sat on the steps. I asked nobody in particular who'd died out at the Rocks.

"Joe Douglas," Dad said without turning around. Mother nodded firmly, as if to let me know he was telling the truth. Dad must have had eyes in the back of his head. "Don't say anything, Julia." She didn't say anything. But she nodded at me again to let me know he hadn't told the whole truth.

"I remember Douglas," I said. "He was an old man when I knew him. Did he die of old age?" In our town, that was the most frequently cited cause of death.

"He was run over," Dad said. He looked like he was explaining it to his tomato sandwich, which he kept turning over for examination before taking a bite.

Mother couldn't hold back any longer. "Right in front of the store," she said. Then she added with a nod, "The Klan."

"We don't know that, Julia. This must be your homemade mayonnaise." My father was serious about tomato sandwiches: white bread, tomato straight from the garden, mayonnaise, salt and pepper, nothing else — served slightly soggy and at room temperature. I never actually saw him turn one down for violating his principles, but sitting there on the steps, he apparently had hold of a good one.

"I spent the whole summer just trying to get Douglas to look at me," I said. "Meekest man in the whole world. What could the Klan have against him?"

"That's exactly what I'd like to know," Mother said, totally and probably intentionally missing my point.

"Did you know him?" I asked the back of Dad's head.

"Don't you remember?" he said between bites. "You knew Joe Douglas in town when you were little. Great tomato sandwich," he finished with a flourish. I knew Mother knew he was wiping his mouth with his hand and then licking his fingers, and we both knew that's why he didn't turn around.

"I don't remember," I said.

"That's not possible, Bo. Joe lived right up here on Stonewall Street, up behind the town clock at the Douglas place. You went up there with me one time. Remember when Tack Sullivan died?"

I did, and I remembered Joe, just didn't think I knew he had a last name. It seemed a long time ago. "Yes, sir," I said, trying to sound like I was only answering the question he had asked.

"Joe's been out at the Rocks since then," Dad said. "He kept the books for the old Snoddy store. That's where they found him."

I was glad he wasn't looking at me, so I didn't have to worry about what might be showing in my face, whether surprise or embarrassment. Or guilt at never connecting Douglas at the brick store to the "colored man" I had known only by his first name when I was a boy. In truth, I had never expected to see that Joe again after Tack Sullivan died, and so I wasn't looking for him, not at the Rocks, not by any name.

———

Tack Sullivan died the summer I was nine. It wasn't that big a deal. If more people had known about it, I could have easily forgotten the whole thing. He'd lived alone at the volunteer fire department across Stonewall Street from our house — a sort of resident social director for the firemen, those civic heroes who volunteered mainly to play gin rummy every night at tables behind the fire truck. He had come up from Charleston longer ago than anyone could remember, but he didn't seem to have any connections either in town or down there. His absence from the fire department during the summer of 1949 caused very little comment. ("Tack here?" "Nope." "Deal.") It wasn't the first time he had disappeared for a while.

That summer was hot and dry. By August, we had to come in before lunch and stay in until after supper. If we went out in the afternoon, we could get polio, everybody's mother said.

The police shot a mad dog one afternoon, right in the middle of Stonewall Street, in front of the church next door to our house. He was a big dog, and from our front hall I saw him jump straight up in the air when the bullet hit him. For several days after that, we couldn't go out at all, but I didn't know for a while that the problem went way beyond mad dogs and polio.

The day the mad dog got shot, in the playground beside the fire department, just over the stone wall that bordered the sidewalk, they found a grocery bag with fingers in it. Bloody human fingers, cut from somebody's hand.

No one said anything about it to us children at first, but they had to tell us eventually so we'd stay inside. And we stayed. Nobody wanted to run into Finger Man and come back with stumps for hands.

Marcie Pratt was our cook then. After the bag of fingers turned up, she didn't have much time to clean the house, since she began leaving right after lunch and lingered most of the morning at the front windows upstairs. Her father would come for her, just in time to get leftovers from lunch, then walk her the three or four blocks into the dusty winding streets where most of the colored people then lived — and still do. But Marcie continued to bring her nephew Victor with her in the mornings, so I would have someone to play with and so he could still collect the small allowance my mother paid him for that duty.

Victor was my guide to better living. He taught me how to shoot marbles and kept me from stepping on cracks in the sidewalk. He told me things my parents would not have mentioned: "Put a pin in the ground on a rainy day when the sun is shining, and you can hear the devil beating his wife," and "In Baltimore, they got 'rest-u-rahnts' where colored people can sit down at the table and eat right next to white people," and "Episcopal babies don't have foreskins." Victor knew some incredible stuff.

On the other side of the church next door to us was an alleyway leading to the rear of the stores along Main Street. There were usually discarded boxes and crates we could use for building things. With the Finger Man around, Victor and I were confined to the yard, where we could be seen from the porch, but we persuaded my mother to watch as we went to get a big refrigerator box from behind the furniture store.

At the beginning of the brick wall that separated the alley from the churchyard was "Jelly Roll," an old black man who sat there every day. I'd thought the discovery of the bag of fingers had changed everything, and I was surprised to see Jelly Roll at his post. When we were close to him, the old man took his hands out of his pockets, rubbed them together, and said the only thing he ever said: "Je-l-ly Ro-o-ll."

"Well, at least they're not his fingers," I said.

"The fingers were white," Victor said.

I looked at Jelly Roll again. White fingers made a big difference. What if they were white kid fingers? Jelly Roll could even have done it to somebody who came through the alley. I said nothing. I wanted to get the box and get back to the house.

That's when we saw Miss Mattie Douglas crossing Main Street and starting down Stonewall past the courthouse. Alone. Victor and I were crawling side by side in our box, moving it forward like the track of a tank and bringing it back up the hill in the side yard. He was still relaying bits of what he had somehow learned about the fingers ("there was only nine of 'em") when the window flap we had cut out rolled to the front, giving me a view of the street. I stopped crawling and poked Victor's arm with my elbow. We stayed there on our hands and knees, heads touching, staring at Miss Mattie as though she were some mysterious apparition in the viewfinder of our periscope.

"What's she doing?" This, just barely whispered.

"I don't know."

"Where's she going?"

"I don't know."

"She oughtta not be out there by herself."

"What you gonna do about it?"

"I don't know."

We watched Miss Mattie walk down past the fire department, nod and glance in as she always did, turn at the playground and go up Lafayette Street past the library and out of sight.

"They gonna find Miss Mattie in a grocery bag next," Victor said. "My mama says white ladies' be-hinds look like two heads of cauliflowers, anyway," he added.

The route Miss Mattie took was the one she always took. Her daily activity — her only activity, so far as we knew — was to walk from her house at about 10:30 in the morning, cross Main Street beside the town clock, then go all the way around our block to Main again and into Mr. Simpson's grocery store. There she would buy whatever she needed for the day and then, although the store was just steps away from the town clock, she'd go all the way back around the block and come home along Stonewall.

In this way, she had to pass Tack Sullivan twice each day when he was around. At that hour of the morning, he would invariably be tilted back in a worn-out cane chair in front of the fire department, his still-blond hair falling forward over his forehead like a hat. If he was awake, they nodded to each other, and he'd touch his hair where the brim of a hat would be. That exchange had become so much a part of Miss Mattie's routine that she was apparently unable to stop it even when Tack was not there. She simply nodded at the wall as she went by.

Miss Mattie's house stood back by itself behind a short row of sycamore trees. She lived alone, except for her yard man, Joe, who lived behind the big house in a little one-room building left to him by Miss Mattie's father. In the afternoon after Miss Mattie's solitary walk, my father decided to visit Joe in his little house. Victor and I tried to get him to judge whether she was being brave or just crazy. He had said only, "She may not know; I'll talk to her."

Clearly, someone had to look after Miss Mattie's safety, but we thought going to Joe was as brave or as foolish as Miss Mattie's walk past the playground to the grocery store.

Joe himself was reliable and certainly well enough known and respected in the town. But he was also physically capable of killing nearly anybody, and he had developed an attitude that had not gone unnoticed. The previous year, he had been the first black person to vote in our town after a judge in Charleston said the Democratic Party couldn't keep Negroes from voting in the primary if they could read. And earlier that same summer, in 1949, he had snapped at me for my perfectly courteous greeting, "Hey, uncle."

"I'm not your uncle," he said angrily. "Never was, never will be." Then he added, "I have a name." I was afraid to call him anything at all after that.

Before Dad went up to see Joe, he asked me out of the blue if I wanted to go with him. I had no idea what good he thought I would be, except maybe I could run for help if we needed it. If he thought I could do anything else, he must have been disappointed by the way I held his hand all the way up the street and dragged along a half-step behind him — except for when we saw Jelly Roll and I stepped up the pace to get past him in a hurry.

"Hello, Jelly Roll," Dad said.

"Je-l-ly Ro-o-ll," Jelly Roll said, rubbing his hands together.

After we crossed Main Street, Dad looked down at me and said, "This will be one of those times for children to be seen and not heard. Okay?"

"Yes, sir." It would have suited me not to be seen, either, but I didn't want to miss this event. I knew Victor would die and roll over when he heard where I'd been.

At Joe's open door, I dropped my father's hand and stood with my hands on my hips. Dad stepped into the little house and said hello and shook Joe's hand just like it was a regular pastoral visit. Dad sat on the one chair in the room; Joe sat on the edge of his cot. I sat down in the doorway with one foot in the yard.

Joe was then in his middle or late fifties. He was still big and still strong. He had close-cropped gray hair that clung to his head in tight coils like wire shavings against a magnet. His skin was a creamy brown; his eyes, dark and steady. He was smart. Everybody in town knew that. Mr. Horace Douglas, Miss Mattie's father, had taught him to read and to count. Mr. Horace had raised him from the time he was a boy, in many ways treating him like the son he never had. Some said that was the reason Joe had so much trouble knowing his place when people started stirring up the order of things between the races.

"Joe," Dad said that afternoon in the little house, "Miss Mattie's got to be told what's happened. It's not safe for her to be out alone."

"I told her, Preacher," Joe said quietly. "Ain't nothing more gone happen. She'll be all right."

"You've done a fine job of looking after her, Joe. And the yard is a garden spot. I've admired your roses all summer."

"Miss Mattie's favorites," he said. "Mister Horace, he planted them for her when she was just a little girl." He chuckled. "Those roses near as old as me. I been taking care of them and taking care of Miss Mattie for almost forty years. After all that time, I know Mister Horace don't want me to give them up now."

Dad shifted his weight in the chair, brought his hand up to support his chin, and waited. The way he listened made people talk.

"We been through times, Preacher. Don't nobody know it, but we been through times, ever since I came here."

"Weren't you born on this place?" Dad asked.

"No, sir. I was living out in the country. Mister Horace, he used to visit us when I was just a boy. I remember one day my daddy had an awful argument with him, and Daddy says he was gone move his family to the city. Mister Horace says he'd help us get a place to live, and the thing was over and done with. But later, Mister Horace, he comes out and says we can't support the whole family in the city. Since I was already 16 and the biggest one, Mister Horace says I could come work for him. So he brought me up here and put me in this little house."

"He took good care of you, didn't he?"

"He did. He did. And I got to take good care of Miss Mattie. She was just a young lady when I came here. Shoulda been married, but she wasn't. I remember her just standing up there at her window whilst I was working in the yard here. I thought, What's a young lady like that doing all cooped up in a house? But she just stood there watching."

"Is she in the house now? I think I should talk to her."

"Yes, sir. You go on around to the front. She'll come to the door."

They were both standing now. Dad took Joe's hand in his and told him, "Joe, I'm your friend and Miss Mattie's friend. Let me know when I can help you." With that, he stepped into the brightness of the afternoon, down onto the bald clay spot of a stoop, and out into the green separating Joe's house from Miss Mattie's. I was already ahead of him, but not too far. As we walked through the hedge in the side yard, I heard the screen door close at the back of the big house.

There was no answer at first, so Dad turned the bell a second time. Miss Mattie pulled back the curtain at the sidelight, then opened the door. "Hello, Miss Mattie."

"Good afternoon; won't you come in?" She motioned him into the parlor on the right. I followed as quietly as I could, since neither one of them seemed to think I was there. It was bright in the parlor, with the sun shining directly into the windows through thin white cotton curtains and halfway across the floor. Miss Mattie took a straight chair by the fireplace; Dad and I sat on the sofa against the far wall.

"We've had some trying times," Dad said. "I hope you've been all right."

"My father..." she said. Her brow wrinkled, her head tilted, her hand turned in her lap as if it expected to make some point, but her voice had quit.

"Mister Horace?" Dad prompted.

"Yes. Will you have some tea?" I was hoping she would offer cookies, but Dad turned the conversation back and tried to pick up her thought again.

"No, thank you, ma'am. Mister Horace passed away many years before I came here."

"Yes. The third of November, nineteen and ten. His forebears settled this town." She paused. "He was so strong. He always knew what to do, knew everybody in town, and they respected him. He helped them — never gave anyone money, but he always knew what they should do. He would know what to do—" her hands, lying very still in her lap, opened and closed again as she added, very quietly, "now."

"Your father would want you to be careful," Dad said.

"He said, 'Be strong, Mattie; be strong.' But he was sure he knew best. I was twenty-five, afraid of being an old maid. All my friends married, and there was no one else, but he said I should wait, that I should be worthy of Mother." She smoothed her skirt. "He said he would take me to Charleston, but then he died." She looked up at my father. "I had no way of knowing he would die." I had no idea if she and Dad were talking about the same thing or not.

They talked about some other things — finally, about the roses blooming on her fence and then of the plans to repair the town clock.

"It never has agreed with itself," she said with a slight smile. "The east side facing me has held pretty steady, but the west face has counted time differently since its first hour." The town clock was then 116 years old — the oldest continuously working wooden clock in America, a status of honor that rendered the precise current time of day more or less irrelevant. "Father's people built it," said Miss Mattie.

"I always heard that Tack Sullivan came up from Charleston with the ballast brick for the clock tower," Dad said.

"No." She corrected him without the least sign of a smile. "Mister Sullivan came in nineteen-ought-nine. I was in Main Street with Father, and we saw him coming on his horse. We were right by the Confederate monument." She stopped, then added, "He tipped his hat to us, but Father put his arm around me and drove the buggy home."

The sun and its window-shape on the floor reached Miss Mattie's feet, crossed at the ankles in front of her chair. The open toe of her right shoe was torn loose from the sole, exposing a little toe curled arthritically across the one next to it.

"Did Tack stay here in town then?" Dad asked.

"Oh, yes. He even came to the house after a few days, but Father said I mustn't see him, said we knew so little about him, said he would ask about among his friends in Charleston. I never knew if he heard anything. He never mentioned Mister Sullivan again."

"Did you have family in Charleston?"

"Mother's people, only. But I never knew them. Mother died when I was born, and Father buried her here. Her family never forgave him. He would often say, 'Mattie, you carry your mother's life in you. You must be worthy of her.' I think he felt that Mother's family would take care of me, would introduce me in Charleston, but he never took me to them. I tried to tell him, but he wouldn't listen. I suppose he didn't want to impose. He was so strong and self-reliant. I even tried to hurt him, but it was foolish; he merely thought me disrespectful of Mother's memory — she was so lovely, so pure, so proper. Then he died."

"I'm sure the memory of your mother and father is very much alive in your example," Dad said. "You have reflected both his strength and her purity."

"I have wanted to," she said. Dad had said exactly the right thing.

"But I worry about you being here alone," he added, "especially just now. This is not a good time to be alone," he said, "either here or out on the streets."

"I have been through a great deal," Miss Mattie said. "I shall be strong enough to survive this. I shall be all right."

The Town Clock struck five. Dad stood and looked out the window; the east face of the clock showed five-thirty. That would make it nearly six on our side. In any case, we should be home. As we walked to the door, Miss Mattie thanked Dad for coming. Nobody mentioned me.

"I shall be all right," she repeated. "Nothing really has changed."

We left her and walked home. I didn't have much to tell Victor, except that I had been to Joe's house and returned. He pretended he was not all that impressed.

The very next morning, Miss Mattie was back out on the street again, walking down Stonewall past the town clock to Lafayette and up past the library. A little later, she came back along the same route with her bag of groceries. Then for a few days, she did not show up. I thought maybe she had taken Dad's caution to heart. It didn't take Victor long to think of other possibilities. "Maybe the Finger Man got Miss Mattie," he said.

On Sunday morning, Miss Mattie missed church, as Victor and I suspected she would. I wrote a note on the bulletin and handed it to my mother. During the second hymn, she looked back and confirmed the absence. She mentioned it to Dad immediately after the service. "I know," he said. "I'll go up to see her after dinner."

He didn't have to. Joe was standing at the door to our side porch when we got home. Dad shook his hand in full view of a few straggling church members, just like Joe was a regular member of the congregation, and invited him into our house.

As Dad took Joe into his study, I heard Joe say, "I ain't done nothing wrong, Preacher, but ain't nobody gone believe it." The remainder of the conversation stayed locked behind the study door.

Miss Mattie was dead. That much I learned right away. She had not died the way Victor and I would have guessed, of course. She had not been feeling well for several days, but she had dressed for church that morning and had sat in the parlor by the mantelpiece for a moment before leaving the house. Without any struggle, she simply slipped away. Dad and the undertaker found her there later that afternoon, propped against a pillow. She was wearing her white eyelet dress and her pinpoint-perforated laced white shoes. The open toe had been repaired. A white rose was in her lap.

Before going to Miss Mattie's house, Dad drove Joe to the bus station and bought him a ticket for Charleston. Unexplained arrivals and departures were a lot more frequent and a lot less bothersome to people then than they are now, and Joe's disappearance was the end of the story as I knew it then.

—◆—

Joe's story — leaving things mostly said and unsaid just as Dad told me there on the front steps — began with Mr. Horace, who had brought Joe to the little house beneath Miss Mattie's window in 1909. Mr. Horace had spent a great deal of time with Joe, teaching him to read, teaching him manners, teaching him simple carpentry skills with the ancient tools in his shed. Mr. Horace was good to him, treated him as much like a son as any white man could treat a black one, promised him the security of a home, a trade, and a protector.

On a night in late summer of 1910, Joe sat on his cot, watching the darkened windows of the big house. His door opened and Miss Mattie came in. He stood quickly. "Miss Mattie…"

"I thought you might like this," she said, reaching past him to place a dish of berries on the table.

"Miss Mattie, you shouldn't be here." Joe looked quickly toward the house, to see if she'd been followed, but all was dark in the house, and still and quiet in the yard.

Then Miss Mattie crowded Joe against his cot, and he pushed her with the back of his hand. She stumbled and he reached for her to prevent a fall. "Mattie! Go to your room." It was Mr. Horace, standing in the open doorway of Joe's little house.

Joe said nothing to Mr. Horace but did as he was told, stepped out into the yard, stood against the front of his little house, silently took the lashes of the buggy whip, knowing that Mattie would see this punishment from her window.

Afterward, he lay on his bed in the dark, hurting from the torn relationships even more than from the welts on his back. He scarcely moved at the surprise of a hand soothing his skin with liniment.

"It's all right, Joe," Mr. Horace said as he gently, gently spread the cooling balm. "It's all right, son."

The events of that night were never mentioned again until Joe recited them to Dad in his study on the day Miss Mattie died. There was never any suggestion that Joe should leave, not from Mr. Horace, not from Miss Mattie when her father was gone, not from Tack Sullivan when he began coming to the house in the darkness, not even more recently when Joe had insisted Sullivan could not stay there as ill as he was, and certainly not when Miss Mattie's strength had failed her and she could not get beyond Tack Sullivan's fingers.

It was Joe who preserved the yard and the house and the family name. It was Joe who steadied Miss Mattie and steadied the world around her. When Tack died in the upstairs room, it was Joe who rescued Miss Mattie from the bloody chore she could not complete when, in her distress at the idea of having Tack Sullivan's body discovered in her house, she began to carve it into little pieces for disposal in grocery bags she thought she'd drop off around town. It was Joe who took away the knives in the night, cleaned the blood from the floor, and moved the body. Miss Mattie never asked what happened but simply went on with her life. She awoke that Sunday morning just as usual, dressed for church, and sat down to rest for a quiet moment in the parlor. And so it was Joe, at the end, who found her there and mended the toe of her shoe and placed the rose in her lap.

The day after Joe left town, they buried Miss Mattie beside her parents in the church cemetery. For the large crowd in attendance, Dad's prayer noted the example of her strength and purity. A day or two after the funeral, on his way to a meeting at the school, Dad took me with him up Stonewall Street past the town clock. This time, he took my hand and stepped quickly behind Miss Mattie's hedge. Dad closed up Joe's little house, scattered some leaves to hide some freshly dug earth just under the back of Miss Mattie's house, said a prayer for Tack Sullivan there, and asked me to help him straighten the clean white latticework that always made the place look so tidy.

"Is there any thing you want to talk about?" he said to me.

"No, sir."

As we stepped back into Stonewall Street beside the white roses on the fence, Dad checked his watch against the east face of the town clock, accepted the mismatch, and said it was time for me to go home. Then he hurried off to his meeting at the school.

Time moved on into fall, and things turned gradually back to normal. We became bolder and bolder in our new after-supper game, dancing around the shrubbery with our hands in front of our faces, ready to run to home base from whoever was "it," risking the "loss" of one finger every time we were caught. By the next spring, we barely remembered the reason for the game and its song:

> *Finger Man, Finger Man, come on out,*
> *I got ten fingers* (or nine or eight...) *in front of my snout.*
> *I'm not afraid of another scar,*
> *So come on out, wherever you are.*

I felt stupid about forgetting Joe, not knowing him all those years ago when Pollo and Mae Maude and I would go down to the brick store for a Coke. He had known me, and it'd taken him weeks and weeks of Cokes to stop hiding in the back room whenever I'd come around. And where was Pollo now? Would I recognize him if I passed him on the street? The ten years that separated me from that summer at the Rocks suddenly seemed like no time at all. I could see the cabin and the vesper dell, the ledge at the quarry, the dusty road through the settlement.

And that's when I saw the newspaper article, folded open by the edge of my mother's plate of cookies. "Arrest in Incident at the Rocks," the headline said. My mother did even the most casual things with a purpose more or less in mind, and I knew this was the reason I'd come home. A preacher, Rev. Paul Templeton, had been arrested in the settlement for inciting a riot. There were names and places I recognized in the story, others I did not. But I knew enough about the Rocks to believe that I had a leg up on understanding the facts and turning them into truth for my class assignment back at Duke. I followed Mother inside and asked her how exactly I'd go about talking to a prisoner down at the jail.

The sheriff looked up from behind his desk and spoke without waiting for any greeting from me.

"Your mama says you want to talk to the prisoner," he said.

"Yes, sir." I would have added something more courteous, like "if that's all right with you," but he was already standing up and reaching for his keys and I thought there was no reason to mess with whatever force he felt from my mother. I doubted she had asked him if it would be all right.

In all the years I had lived in that town, I'd only seen the jail from the outside. It stood beside an open field where we'd flown kites as youngsters, and I'd studied the fortress of thick brick walls and the black iron bars on the windows of the second floor. It was a place that struck fear into the hearts of youngsters. As fourth graders, or maybe fifth, we tried to turn that fear in our favor, going regularly into the dense woods beyond the kite field and behind the jail to smoke rabbit tobacco rolled in dead oak leaves, knowing that decent people like our parents would never dare to spy on us in such a place. One afternoon as we struggled to keep the fire alive inside the damp rolled leaves, we heard a gunshot from the jail. We ran. It would be hard to say whether we were more afraid of the bullet itself or of the ghost of some unknown and now departed person at whom the bullet might have been aimed. The effect was the same. After that, we smoked our rabbit tobacco in the tall weeds behind the courthouse right on Main Street, significantly increasing the chances of being caught but reducing the chances of being killed. The jail was not a place we ever wanted even to visit, let alone be put. I realized how much I still felt that way as I followed the sheriff toward the back of the building.

On the first floor, behind the sheriff's office, was a large holding cell where a couple of seedy old white men slept off drunken stupors on narrow cots. The sheriff unlocked the door, and we walked through that cell to an open door in the inside wall. "Nigras," the sheriff said with a studied effort at correct pronunciation, "are upstairs. We only got the one up there right now."

"There's not a separate entrance?" I asked. As youngsters we had been puzzled that there was no entrance visible from the outside other than the front door, not even a fire escape like the one at the school. We had heard there was a passageway for colored people to be taken in — or, worse, out — without anybody knowing.

"We usually just go through here so they don't get too familiar with everything. This way, if they ever managed to get the door open upstairs, they'd just end up locked in this cell down here. Wouldn't do 'em much good. Besides, bringing 'em through here has a sobering effect on these guys. Even drunks don't like the idea of having to mix with criminal nigras."

At the top of the stairs, a locked door opened into a dim corridor. On one side, a row of solid doors; on the other, a row of cells that were totally visible, separated only by walls of bars. The cells were considerably smaller, darker, and more numerous than we had imagined as kids when we counted the windows from the kite field. In fact, only every third cell had a window at all. None had a cot. Or any plumbing. There was a short stool and a bucket, nothing else.

The lone prisoner on the second floor wore a baggy black and white striped jumpsuit. He crouched on the little stool in his cell, his elbows on his knees, the hard fist of one hand planted tightly in the palm of the other. A chain on the floor disclosed the promise of leg irons under the loose folds of his pant legs. His hair was a bushy mass, flattened on one side with what looked like dried blood. He showed no recognition that anyone had entered the cell.

"Bo Fisher's here to see you, boy," the sheriff said. "Get up."

"No, no," I said too quickly but not wanting to irritate the guy if I was going to be left alone with him. "It's okay."

The sheriff shrugged. "I'll leave the stairway door open," he said as he backed out of the cell and slammed the door behind me. "You can call when you want out."

The slamming cell door turned me into a twelve-year-old. I flinched hard, turned half toward the corridor, and wanted to call the sheriff right there from the distance of five or six feet, except that I saw the uniformed son of a bitch looking back at me, smiling, and I knew he would have enjoyed it too much. I watched him disappear through the stairway door, found that I was breathing very fast and unable to swallow, and I wondered if there might be some way to get a glass of water.

Then the prisoner, without moving his slumped shoulders, raised his head slowly and looked at me.

"Hello, Tarzan," he said.

I stared. He stared back at me. One of his eyes was swollen shut, and his whole face seemed to sag. I took a step toward him as an old memory took hold, then glanced back to be certain we were alone. I tried to lick my lips, then wiped my sweaty hand across them.

"Pollo?" I said. He dropped his head again, and I could see nothing but matted black hair, black and white stripes, a fist, and the chain between his bare feet. "Pollo?" He looked up again, and this time I saw him. "Pollo!" I dropped to my knees in front of him and touched his hands, but he leaned back against the wall and let his arms hang down loose beside the stool. But he didn't take his eyes from mine. "What are you doing in here? I was looking for Paul Templeton," I said, "the preacher who was arrested for starting a riot. Where is he?"

"Here I am."

"What?"

"That's me. I'm the preacher. I'm Paul Templeton. But there wasn't any riot."

"What happened?"

He just shook his head.

"Pollo," I said, getting back on my feet. "We've got to get you out of here."

"Hmh." I knew what that meant, but I wasn't sure whether he didn't want help or didn't think I could deliver. I delivered.

"Sheriff!" I called. "You're as good as out of here," I said to Pollo. I decided the interview could wait. Besides, I had no idea what to say to him. Having been so alike during our summer together in the country, we could not have been more different facing each other in that dark cell. I raked my car keys on the bars and shouted again.

———— ◆ ————

At home, I reported to Mother that Paul Templeton was actually our old friend Pollo from camp. She showed no surprise. And no indecision. She went to the telephone and dialed long distance, asking for a man whose name I recognized as head of the presbytery organization that included the Southern, or white, Presbyterian churches in our county. My mother's voice was so well-known in that office, it would have been redundant to identify herself.

"Howard," she said, "have you been reading what's going on out here at the Rocks?" No chit-chat. Just a short pause. "Well, the boy they've got in jail is a Presbyterian preacher. I want you to get him out." There was a long pause as she listened to Howard. She rolled her eyes at me while Howard went on with whatever he was saying. Then her left hand moved up to battle stance on her hip. "Don't you 'Miss Julia' me," she said to Howard, "I don't care if he's black, white, blue, or striped. Or guilty. That boy is a Presbyterian. It overrides everything else." Any objection could put Howard on very shaky ground. "What? It makes no difference that he's a Northern Presbyterian, Howard. What kind of Presbyterian do you expect a Negro to be? And anyway, this is a Southern Presbyterian calling you. And he's a Southern Negro. So that makes us responsible." Another pause. "Well, what's the number up there?" She wrote it down. "Thank you, Howard. Good-bye."

"Well, Dixie dew!" she said more or less to me as she looked for something in the desk drawer. "Exactly what we get for electing a weak-kneed man as executive." Then she added as an afterthought: "And a Baptist as sheriff." The war was widening. I would not have put money on the sheriff or the Baptists for anything in the world.

She didn't call the Northern number at once, but rather called our own Southern headquarters in Atlanta for an introduction to somebody up there, implicitly acknowledging the possibility that people in New York City might not recognize her voice, even if they were Presbyterians.

"It'll take a couple of days," she said to me after explaining things to the Northern Presbyterians. "We'll wait. I don't want the sheriff stirred up until I'm ready for him."

———

In the ten years since my summer in the country, life at the Rocks had changed. For one thing, the camp sponsored by my father's church struggled on for a summer or two and then was abandoned. For another thing, although the main road along the ridge line was still in place, what little traffic it had known was now drained off into the double slashes of a huge new interstate highway knifing across the nearby countryside.

Miss Templeton, for yet another and more major thing, was dead. The Klan's blackened cross down at the lake had shaken her badly, people said, finally claiming her as its victim. She had died after Pollo's homecoming as pastor in that summer of 1966 and was buried, not in the old graveyard of the abandoned white Presbyterian Church just down the main road from her house, but in the cemetery of the "Church at the Rocks," with the Rev. Paul Templeton officiating.

All that, I learned standing around after Douglas's funeral. I was surprised at how easy it was to fall back into normal conversation with people I had not seen for ten years. In fact, people had changed remarkably little. Mr. Samuel Do-Boy still had an air of unmistakable authority despite being quite a bit stooped over. And Sister Holy Ghost stepped right out of 1956, without changing so much as a hair on her head — or the hat and veil that covered it.

"Miss Templeton wrote some folks up north," Sister said.

"Philadelphia," prompted Mr. Samuel Do-Boy.

"Hmh!" said Sister, apparently not feeling the need for any prompting.

The upshot of this struggle for control of history was that Miss Templeton had written to the Philadelphia congregation that had sponsored the Church at the Rocks since after the Civil War. She reminded them of their support during the strife of Reconstruction, of the waning of their relationship through the last several decades, and of the urgent need for their attention now in the crisis of a new civil rights struggle. In response, the Philadelphia congregation funded scholarships for the sons and daughters of the settlement, re-establishing an old tie between the white Northern congregation and Charlotte's Johnson C. Smith University.

Cora Snoddy had sold all her farmland to the settlement, by way of the Northern church Miss Templeton brought to her as a purchaser, saving only the old house on Brickstore Road. Then, in return for the Young Senator's help in dealing with the estate of Mrs. Snoddy Senior, and perhaps for other services rendered as well, she gave him the house as a hunting lodge. And she ran off with the driver of a Coca-Cola truck and never came back.

"Hunting lodge," I said. "What would anybody hunt out here?" Silence.

Sister looked at Mr. Do-Boy. Mr. Do-Boy looked at his feet. Finally, Sister looked at me.

"Sugar," she said.

"Ma'am?" I thought she was calling me that.

"Hunting sugar," she said. Oh. I looked at Mr. Do-Boy. He was still studying his feet. "That man has a problem."

"Young Senator?" I asked as soberly as I could. In fact I remembered his problem very well. But Cora, they had said, was gone.

"You know his wife?" Sister said. She was talking only to me. It did not appear that Mr. Do-Boy would be solving the problem of his feet anytime soon. "Came to the House of Prayer one night, said she wanted us to know she'd been born again, said her virginity'd been miraculously restored. She said God told her to announce that to somebody, and she just knew we would understand better than her white friends. Now, if that woman's a virgin, that's the biggest miracle we will ever see." I studied Mr. Do-Boy's feet. "Anyway," she said, "anybody could understand if that man goes hunting."

Young Senator was very open about his visits to his hunting lodge, his car becoming a familiar sight on the ridge road: a big black Cadillac with a bumper strip on the back in bright red-white-and-blue: "Jesus ♥s You." Sometimes, he stopped in at the brick store to shake hands, his camouflaged hunting pants always freshly pressed, with a smooth crease in each leg. "Gonna do a little hunting," he would say, but nobody ever saw a rifle or heard any shots from the fields down at the end of Brickstore Road.

He had his own driver, a black man from town who wore a chauffeur's cap and stayed in the car when the Young Senator went into the store. His job was to see to it that the car and its owner were returned home without any public notice or embarrassing traffic accident. The guy drove like the very Devil, but the highway patrol knew to leave the car alone. There had been debates at the store about whether Young Senator's companion was in the trunk or under blankets on the floorboard of the back seat.

"Cora never came back?" I asked, adding innocently, "Or Mae Maude?"

"No reason to," said Mr. Do-Boy, liberated by the change in subject matter. "Everything they had is ours. Except for the house."

I wanted to know more about Mae Maude and the baby I guessed she'd had, but Sister and Mr. Do-Boy had lost track of her. It was just as well that

Mae Maude had stayed away. It might well be that she was perfectly happy not to see Pollo ever again. Or me, either. I was never sure how she really felt about Bubba; she could easily have blamed the two of us for losing him.

One other subject seemed deliberately unmentioned. The Klan?

"We don't know that," Mr. Do-Boy said.

"Hmh! We certainly know they were here last week," Sister said.

"Hmh! Doesn't mean they had anything to do with Douglas," the old man said, looking older.

"Did you report that they were out here?" I asked.

"Hmh!" said Mr. Do-Boy. "Who you want to report it to? Anybody you could report it to was most likely out here wearing a sheet. Irritate those people and they just keep coming back."

"Hmh!" Sister said. "They'll never turn you loose until you show them you're not afraid."

Mr. Do-Boy looked at her with a cold fixed stare and pulled himself up as tall as his bent back would let him go. He spoke very softly: "And is that what Douglas learned?" There was silence for a long uncomfortable moment. Then the two of them walked off in different directions, leaving me standing there by myself.

———————

By mid-week, Mother was ready for the sheriff. She marched into his office at the jail with a telegram and money wired from up North. I was back at school, but it was easy to imagine the scene, with Sheriff Poston and his deputies jumping up at her entrance like a covey of quail flushed up by a snarling bird dog. Quail are not confident birds; they just make a lot of noise rustling out of their bushes when threatened and then jump up in the air, flapping their wings and hoping to God they can fly. That same hope must have filled the sheriff's office when Mother showed up, the men rattling chairs and desks as they got to their feet and flapped their arms, not know-ing whether to salute or reach for their holsters, try to fly or just stand at ease.

Mother sprung Pollo from jail, took him to our house for lunch, fed him some vegetables, lectured him on the civil part of civil disobedience, reminded him what a privilege it is to be a Presbyterian, told him to get a haircut, and drove him back out to the Rocks. She called me on the telephone that night. She'd had a good day.

Chapter Six

———◆———

JESUS IN THE DRIVEWAY

For Pollo, his day of deliverance from jail had not been good at all. "Age," he said to me when I went back down to the Rocks the following week, "ain't always wisdom. The trouble with church elders is they're too old. They got no notion of what's going down." His voice and his words had taken on a hard edge consistent with the hardness in his eyes, but it seemed just a little practiced. Like his stance, with legs spread apart and arms folded across the bold patterns of a bright dashiki, it probably would have been more effective on some television news report than it was with me, standing there in the yard of the little church. But his hair was impressive; it had been teased back out into a full round Afro, a dramatic improvement over his appearance when I found him at the jailhouse.

We met in the cemetery behind the church, and he was standing by a tall marker with a building etched into the stone, a building in flames.

There was an angel rising up from it, his wings outstretched toward the heavens, his head bowed and sad. He might easily have been Icarus — black Icarus, with short tight coils of hair, a wide nose, full lips. I had never seen a Negro angel; to this day, I have not seen another. There was no halo, only the flames from the burning building licking at his feet.

I looked at the inscription: Edouard DuBois, 1898-1910.

"French?" I asked.

"Not likely. That's little DuBois," he said. Do-boy. "He was the brother of Mr. Samuel DuBois. You remember him. The one you used to call by his whole name."

Black people have a decided advantage in the fact that no one can see them blushing. I walked around to the back of the monument, hoping Pollo hadn't noticed, and I remembered my consternation as a teenager at a dignified man being called "Do-Boy," as though every address was an order and a put-down. It had been me. I'd created the insult in my own mind, every time I spoke the man's name. DuBois! I blushed again.

On the back side of the tombstone was an inscription:

> *Angel,*
>> *Rising From the Fiery Flames,*
>> *Arriving At the Seat of Mercy,*
>> *Call Again Our Names.*

"Mr. Samuel DuBois ran the store," Pollo said. "Still does. And he's the Clerk of Session at the church. Was then and still is. This Edouard was his little brother. He was killed in the fire at Centennial."

"What fire?" Centennial College was a Presbyterian school for Negroes, a leftover from the Reconstruction-era Committee on Freedmen of the Northern church, and the pride of moderate and progressive church people throughout the state. When liberals began talking about the immorality of having separate schools for whites and Negroes, moderates had sided with segregationists and with the Negroes themselves to keep Centennial open as an historic symbol of the church's support for the education of the race — and as an opportunity for Negroes to run their own institution without being smothered in the bigger and better white schools. Centennial had high visibility among church people all through the early years of civil rights battles until it finally gave up the ghost under financial pressures in 1958. I was surprised that there could have been some important fire that nobody had mentioned. "I've been on the campus," I said, "for a YMCA interracial conference. I even read the history of the school so I wouldn't seem like such an outsider. I guarantee there was nothing anywhere about any fire."

"Sometimes, being white is even worse than being old," Pollo said. "At least, my black elders have a memory. Who wrote the history you read? I guaran-damn-tee it was no Nee-gro. Look at you, Mr. Big-Time Education; you don't know shit from Shinola."

Gratitude was not a strong suit of this new Pollo — "Paul," as he asked me to call him from now on, "Pollo having died a long time ago." He was right. A lot of him did seem to have died. But I thought I could help bring him back if I could be patient and supportive and understanding. For starters, I could easily understand his anger. He had been beaten, politically and psychologically, as well as physically. Even the act of rescue had gone sour after my mother had brought him out of jail and delivered him to the Rocks. He led me to his study, and offered me a chair.

The small granite paperweight bearing his new name caught my eye. I picked it up. "I don't understand this," I said.

"It's easy," he said. "When they sent me away, I had to change it."

"I'm sorry," I said.

"A name is a name," he shrugged. "It doesn't matter." It should, I thought, if you're the sun god, but I kept quiet, and he went on to explain that the burning cross at the lake in the summer of 1956 had frightened Miss Templeton badly and changed the course of his life. "She knew," he said, "what it meant."

"Everybody knew what it meant," I said. It meant that the Klan had heard about Pollo and Mae Maude, but I kept that thought to myself.

"That's not what I'm saying, man. She could see what it'd do to me, to the Rocks, to folks at the settlement. And what she saw, she didn't like worth a damn. Me, neither, but I thought we ought to fight it. I was angry."

"I was there, you know," I said, wondering if he had somehow forgotten that I knew all about it. "You couldn't have fought it. They would have killed you. I know they would have."

"You don't know half what you think you know," he said.

I know what I remember about you, I thought. And I remembered Mae

Maude, her hand on my leg as she shifted gears in the camp truck, how we wouldn't talk for miles and miles, and how all that touching seemed so loud. I wondered where she was now and how she remembered things, me and Pollo, all that time ago. I wondered if the whole summer was spoiled for her by its last violent moments, or if she'd come to see how narrow the path had gotten that led her and Pollo into the vesper dell.

"The elders agreed with the old lady," Pollo went on. "They didn't want trouble. So they sent me away. The new name was easy. Pollo was too noticeable, and I didn't have a family name, anyway. So I took Miss Templeton's. From then on, I was only around other blacks, and nobody saw any connection with anything."

"But you came back," I said.

"Yeah. I sure did."

I took a pad and pencil from his desk. "What happened?"

———— ✦ ————

I received a B+ on the paper — from a professor who was generous with As. "Perhaps not enough distance from the event and its consequences for true history," he noted. "But good effort. Keep at it." He added as a postscript after the grade: "And probably too much story for the weight of available facts." Over the years since then, I could not leave it alone. In so many ways it was the story that brought Pollo and me back together. And it would turn out to be the story that parted us. I have revised and revised it as I gained information and insight from people who were participants. I don't know whether it is "true history" even now, but I believe the truth of it.

———— ✦ ————

QUID PRO STATUS QUO
HISTORIOGRAPHY ID-511
BO FISHER

Paul Templeton leaned back in his chair and waited for his unexpected white visitor to say perfectly predictable things.

"Gweat sermon, Pweachuh."

"Praise God," Templeton said. He intended it as a pastoral instruction, but it came out louder than he expected, covering a stifled laugh. The Deputy's high, scratchy voice was a constant surprise, forced through his pinched little mouth that turned his *r*s into *w*s. Like chicken lips on a pig's face, Templeton thought — and wondered how in heaven's name he would get through this conversation with a straight face.

Templeton graduated from the seminary just two months earlier, in June of 1966. He was brand new to the pulpit of the Church at the Rocks, but he had grown up in the community, and he knew this man's appearance at church was a sign of the season: Election Day is on the way, he thought.

When Templeton first stepped into the pulpit that morning, he had seen the Deputy toward the back of the church. The pale and round white face looked like a moth hole in the congregational tapestry of rich browns — or maybe an empty placeholder for some absent member. It irritated him. For starters, the Sheriff sending a Deputy was a put-down, most likely aimed at the new Preacher's youth and inexperience more than at the church itself. Probably thinks he put me in my place, Templeton thought. Just the same, if the Deputy wants to be seen, let him be seen. So he invited him to one of the pulpit chairs.

The Deputy squeezed his wide body out of the pew only after six other people stood up and moved. He paraded down the center aisle in his baggy white suit, mopping his face with a handkerchief, and took up residence in the pulpit as if he were some kind of dignitary they should be proud to have in attendance. All through the sermon, the Preacher felt the Deputy's eyes on him, placid eyes, not reacting to the enthusiasm building in the congregation. During the hymn after the sermon, the Deputy sang out in a high raspy tenor easily heard above the congregational harmony.

"Amazin' gwace, how sweet de sound..."

Gwace? Templeton concentrated on his hymnbook, but he couldn't resist scanning ahead for more trouble. He saw it coming:

"Dat saved a wetch like me..."

He looked up in time to see the entire bench of deacons break into broad grins.

"Let's sing all five verses," Templeton said in the pause after the first verse. He winked at the deacons and then glanced at the Deputy. Sorry S.O.B., he thought. I ought to call on him to "pway."

"...and gwace will lead me home."

At the end of the service, Templeton ushered the Deputy to the door and let him shake hands with the departing members. Those who spoke thanked him for coming. One or two had concerns about someone in jail, and the Deputy wrote down the names.

"Zeb? Yes, indeed. Zebedee."

"Zebalon," the woman corrected. Zeb's name was added to the list on the scrap of paper.

"He your boy?"

"Yes." The woman's eyes were watery, even through the veil of her crinkled straw hat. The Deputy touched his beefy hand gently to her shoulder and moved Zeb's mother along toward the door.

"Know him well. Too well. I'll tell him you asked."

The Deputy had turned back toward the line when a thought came to him. He put his arm again around Zeb's mother. "Zeb's not a bad boy, you know," he whispered. "He's no twouble to us, weally. Just can't stay away fum de joy juice. Den he wanders all over town. It scares people. He don't mean to, I don't think. But we have to take him in. We take good care of him 'til he gets wight again. Tell you what. If you'll keep him out here and keep him out of town, I'll let him out. Can you do dat?" She nodded without looking up, trusting this implausible looking white official could do whatever he wished. "I'll get him back out here dis afternoon," he said. Then he went back to the Preacher's side to greet the last few worshipers.

"What's your name?" the Deputy said to a small round boy who waited at the end of the line. The boy sidled up to Templeton, grabbed on to the full sleeve of his robe and looked up at the Deputy without raising his head.

"Folks call him Pup," Templeton said.

With difficulty, the Deputy lowered himself to the boy's level and held out his hand. "I'm glad to see you, young man," he said, smiling. But the boy turned his head into the dark folds of Templeton's robe.

"He's the best man I have," Templeton said, emphasizing man. "Straightens up the church after worship. Keeps everything in order around here." The Deputy tried to look around behind the Preacher, bracing himself with one hand on the floor. If he says "boo" like Pup's some kind of baby, Templeton thought, I'll put a knee in his face. The Preacher looked down at the two of them as if he were some giant oak, a berserk hog circling the base of his trunk to catch a squirrel. He wondered if Pup might suddenly take off and climb up his robes to his shoulders. The look on Pup's face said that he had already thought of the same thing. Templeton put his hand on the boy's head, partly to reassure him and partly to keep him on the ground. "Go put the hymnbooks back in the racks," he said, and Pup was released.

The Deputy grabbed the Preacher's arm and pulled himself back up. "Cute," he said, red-faced and huffing, either from the boy's rebuff or from the heavy effort of descending and ascending.

"He's twelve years old," Templeton said, knowing that the Deputy had misjudged Pup's age because of his size and demeanor.

"I love little kids," said the Deputy.

Templeton laughed. "Pup thinks he's a man."

"Does he talk?"

"No."

"Oh," the Deputy said with genuine sympathy. "Deaf and dumb." Templeton looked quickly at Pup making his way through the rows of pews in the empty church.

"He hears everything," he said. "And he's very smart. He reads. And writes. He knows everything that goes on in the settlement. Just doesn't talk."

"Can we talk?" the Deputy said. "I mean you and me? Somewhere besides wight here?" And so Templeton had taken him to the little study behind the choir loft, where now he waited for the man to state his business.

The Deputy hoisted one leg up on the other, grabbed the arms of his chair, and leaned more or less forward in his most intently sincere posture. "De Wocks is impawtant to Shewiff Poston," he said, "if you know what I mean."

Templeton knew what the Deputy meant. "De Wocks" translated as "the Rocks," a self-contained rural settlement of black people isolated in the country by the abandonment of a big working quarry forty years before. The people were poor, but they had a strong sense of community. They voted. For nearly twenty years, since the first Democratic primary open to Blacks in 1948, the Rocks had returned unanimous votes, with nearly a hundred percent voter turnout. As a precinct, it had unusual weight. Paul Templeton, probably alone, thought the community had not been adequately compensated for its loyalty.

The Sheriff and his Deputy were clearly among those who thought otherwise. The Sheriff's job was to coordinate payments for those candidates endorsed by the party's county committee. In the early days, a small donation to the proper hands could carry the Rocks, but successive preachers had escalated the price, and the 1964 election cost a small fortune. In the Sheriff's view, enthusiastically shared by the Deputy, it had been a mistake from day one to substitute cash for other kinds of persuasion. It had tempted the preachers into greedy grasping. The system was a lot less corrupt, they agreed, before these people could vote, and a lot more democratic before the prices got so high. There was something distasteful about relying on rich people for money that then went into the pockets of people like those at the Rocks, but the county party's dwindling margins of victory made it impossible to adjust the payments downward.

"That's what the goddam Republicans did," Sheriff Poston had explained to his Deputy. "Goddam two-party system just puts money in the pockets of colored preachers and makes it more and more expensive to run the government."

Preachers who used the money for urgent needs in the community — basic things like food, heating oil, medical care, funeral expenses — saw the system as a reasonable way to redistribute wealth. For Paul Templeton, younger and more idealistic, the system was a cheap pay-off. By opening the Democratic primary to black voters, the federal court had altered the fundamental relationship between the people and their rulers, and the rise of the Republicans had created actual value in black voting power. But with the trading of cash for votes, the system absorbed that power comfortably and managed to avoid any real change.

What Templeton wanted was not little bits of cash but a serious investment in public facilities: paved roads, water and sewer service, electricity, a health clinic, a new school, a simple thing like a telephone — the things that would make it possible to recruit private investments, jobs. That, he knew, was the only solution to chronic poverty at the Rocks, poverty so grinding on a daily basis that it prevented attention to long-term solutions. As far as he was concerned, his own church leaders had become part of the problem, settling for a role in distributing the funds provided in election years.

"Forget the fancy stuff," one of his deacons had warned. "When the bag man comes, think of that money as bags of groceries." "Don't get too big for your britches," another one said. "All that fancy college education you got won't do people no good if they can't eat. You cross the Sheriff, and he'll fix it so we get less than nothin'." He looked sideways at the young Preacher's collegiate haircut and added, "Don't let that big Afro go to your head, son. It ain't extra brains."

Now, Templeton looked across his desk and felt embarrassed. The Sheriff had set him back by sending this Deputy instead of coming himself. Still, he had no choice but to try.

"The children here need a better school," Templeton said.

"I wemembuh when dey wud'n any school," said the Deputy pleasantly. "Shewiff Poston helped a lady set up de old schoolhouse. Fact, de Democwatic Party collected books in town and sent 'em out."

"Exactly," Templeton said. "Those were old books then. They're just about useless now. Why should these children have inferior books?"

The Deputy stared at Templeton. He was pleased with himself for remembering the book drive. What more to say about it, though, was out of his range. He was glad to get the assignment to cover this precinct, but the Sheriff simply told him to deliver the money and use his judgment, same as he had before in smaller, less important precincts. His judgment before, however, always had to do with how much money to deliver, never anything about schools and books. He reached for the money in his pocket. That must be what he's fishing for, the Deputy thought. Maybe he's embarrassed to ask. Maybe he don't know how it works.

"It's impawtant to de Shewiff," he said. And then he had a brilliant idea as he spread the bills on the Preacher's desk, in front of a framed photo of schoolchildren. "You could buy a lot of books."

Or groceries, Templeton thought. He looked at the money and said, more aloud than he meant to, "Yessir, yessir, three bags full." The Deputy's eyes narrowed in deep thought.

Pup walked in through the open door, went to a small cabinet behind the Preacher, and laid down the chalk and eraser used in the church for the blackboard that listed the hymn numbers. He turned, half hidden by Templeton's robes, looked at the Deputy and narrowed his eyes in the closest thing he could manage to a threatening frown.

"That's a good man," the Preacher said. "Run on home. I'll be there directly. Ask Aunt Stitch to save me some dinner." Watching Pup go out through the back door of the study and down toward the settlement, Templeton thought of all the mornings he had watched from this same window, Pup and the other children dragging themselves up that path from the settlement to the schoolhouse, the day's natural joy and excitement silenced by the hunger in their stomachs. He looked again at the Deputy's money on the desk and calculated: two hundred breakfasts.

"Deputy," he said, "the county can get federal money for hot lunches and breakfasts for school children. How can we get that money for the Rocks?"

The Deputy was baffled. He didn't have a clue how they had gone from books to breakfasts. But he understood the point of the question. He reached into another pocket. He figured he didn't have to say anything. Oblivious to Templeton's calculations, he put two hundred more breakfasts on the table.

It was the Preacher's turn to be baffled. He stared at the stack of bills. Maybe that's the way they do it, he thought. He and the Deputy were caught up in a system neither of them understood and both of them opposed, and the system was working in spite of them. The Deputy, more comfortable with his role than the Preacher was with his, said nothing. Templeton stood up and walked to the window.

"You see that road between us and the cemetery, Deputy? Looks like a driveway, doesn't it? It's really not a road at all, just a wide footpath. But that's the road that goes down to the settlement. You ever been to the settlement, Deputy?"

"I had to awest a couple boys," the Deputy answered, then added, "I don't like to do dat."

"No, of course not. But at least you know what the settlement looks like, don't you? Did you see any paved streets, Deputy? No, they don't have any paved streets, do they? Just dirt alleys between the houses. Did you go in any of the houses, Deputy? They're just shacks, aren't they?" He was talking faster now. And louder. "Look like backyard playhouses for some child in town, don't they? Isn't that right, Deputy?" He turned and looked at the Deputy. "It's not right, Deputy; it's not right at all for people to live like that. Why haven't those streets been paved, Deputy? Why is there not a single telephone for these people? Why do they still have only one water pump for all those houses? Why do they still have outhouses around the edge of the settlement? Why do they live like that?"

The Deputy had no answer. It was beyond him why people would live like that. Probably something in their character, he would have thought. But he wasn't thinking. He was nervously patting his pockets, waiting for the Preacher to calm down.

Templeton put his hands on his desk and leaned over it toward the Deputy. Speaking quietly and deliberately now, he said, "That's why people are marching all over the South, Deputy. Do you understand that?"

The Deputy's face made it clear: He understood nothing. But he found what he was looking for, and in the silence he set the table for two hundred more breakfasts.

Templeton wondered how many more pockets of money the Deputy might have. He was tempted to keep fishing, but he refused; he had bigger fish to fry. This man with his pockets stuffed with money and his "bwain" stuffed with cotton had stymied him. "Deputy," he said slowly, "why are you here?"

Now that's a dumb question, the Deputy thought. He reached instinctively for another pocket.

"No, Deputy," said Templeton, holding up his hand to stop him. "Why," he said, "are you here?"

"Dis," he answered, relieved to get to the point of the conversation and pulling out a sheet of paper from his pocket, "is why." He was pleased to get to this stage of the game without emptying his pockets of cash. "De ballot," he said. "It's impawtant to de Shewiff." He placed the list of candidates in front of the Preacher, careful not to get it too close to the pile of money.

Templeton read the list, then walked around the side of the desk. He thought of the children walking hungry to the old schoolhouse, and picked up the money.

"Deputy," he said, "I want you to tell the Sheriff something." He folded the list of candidates around the stack of bills and stuffed them back into the Deputy's pocket. "You tell him I'd be happy to see him in church."

Templeton stood in the doorway and watched the Deputy drive away with the money. He had no idea how he would explain this to his deacons, but he had one very clear thought: I did my job. They'll have to pay attention to the things my people really need.

———

When he reached town, the Deputy also did his job.

"New pweachuh-boy at de Wocks gonna be twouble," he reported to the Sheriff. "Talked about marchin'. Got a big Afwo," he said, using his hands to shape one around his own head. "Maybe we should bwing him in."

"Gotta be careful these days," said the Sheriff. "Is he smart?"

"Don't think so. He asked some dumb questions about schools and books and bweakfasts and stuff. Like I should pave some woads and do somethin' about pwivvies. And a telephone. Like I might have one of those in my pockets. Dumb stuff. He gave de money back to me."

"Probably thinks he's Martin Luther King or somebody," said the Sheriff. "But if he was, he wouldn't be out at the Rocks. Just keep an eye on him. He'll slip up. The ones with too much mouth always do. When he does, three or four days in jail will smart him up." The Sheriff winked at his Deputy. "It'll be good for his the-o-logical education."

"Wight," said the Deputy. "He just needs a little instwuction."

"Watch him," the Sheriff said. "But be careful. You have to be smarter than him."

"No pwoblem."

The Sheriff watched his Deputy lumber off toward his car. He couldn't be sure what they might be up against at the Rocks, but the Deputy's report worried him. He hadn't met the new Preacher out there and didn't want to. He was tired of dealing with those people. He'd let the Deputy handle it. But as he watched the Deputy's wide backside moving off toward the car, he couldn't stifle a thought: "Heaven help us," he said.

— ◆ —

Before another Sunday rolled around, the truck from the telephone company pulled up to the Church at the Rocks — part of the company's community outreach program, the driver said.

That day, in late summer of 1966, the settlement gained its first telephone, installed in the Preacher's little study behind the choir loft.

Paul Templeton was pleased. He wondered if the Sheriff himself would show up for church on Sunday morning. "That's progress," he said to several deacons who had come up from the settlement to witness the installation. Some of them smiled. Some of them did not.

None of them knew that the shiny new black telephone was connected to a silent party line with one other instrument — one without a listed number — or even a mouthpiece — one that sat with only its earpiece activated, adding to the clutter on the Deputy's desk.

— ◆ —

The telephone was a major event. After church on the first Sunday after its installation, a small multitude crowded into the little study just to have a look.

"My, my, my," someone said.

"Uhm-m-hmm." A chorus of women's voices.

"At the Rocks."

"Uhm-hm."

"Have you used it?" This, to the Preacher.

"Yes," he said.

"Uhm-m-hmm." An expectant silence.

"The first call was to Gloria at school," he obliged.

"Uhm-m-hmm?" A louder chorus. And a lot of smiles.

"Then I called some of my college friends," he said after a long silence during which the smiling chorus stared at the machine, waiting but not looking at him.

"Who's paying for those calls?" asked a deacon who had stepped into the room behind the ladies. He was not smiling.

"There's no charge," Templeton said. "The telephone company said it's part of their outreach program. They want us to use it."

In fact, it had been difficult at first to use it at all. Templeton was prepared to pay personally for the call to Gloria, but the Operator said there was some problem with the line.

"I want to call Charlotte," he said. "To Johnson C. Smith University. Can you tell me how much it will cost?"

"That's long distance," she said, with an attitude he recognized.

"I know where it is," he said. "And I know it's long distance."

"You can't do that," she said.

"I can pay," he said, emphasizing each word.

"There's a problem with your account," she said, just as deliberately. "It says 'special.'"

"It's just new."

"No, it's something else. I'll have to call you back."

He thought she would call back immediately, and he sat at the desk arranging what he wanted to say to Gloria. He could easily envision her at the other end of the line. He knew the dorm at Smith, knew the hall, knew the phone, and he knew she would be proud of what he had done. Not so long ago, she had been one of those children trudging up to the schoolhouse with an empty belly, but she would understand the importance of standing up to the Sheriff. She believed in change.

But the Operator did not call back that afternoon. Or the next day. Or the next. He set the telephone on the floor beside his desk, a useless toy, and he resolved never to use the thing at all. Or even think about it. When it finally rang for the first time while he was preparing his sermon, he jumped out of his chair. Only on the third ring did he lean over and look down at the telephone on the floor. It rang twice more before he picked up the receiver.

The Operator's news was exciting. "Of course," Templeton said. "It was supposed to be good for us!" She explained that some arrangements had to be made, but there would be no charges for the use of the telephone, not even for long distance calls, and the telephone company wanted him to use the phone as much as he liked. He could call anywhere. He told her he would remember the company's generosity and asked her to reach Gloria DuBois at school in Charlotte.

"He's just another pig," Gloria said when he mentioned the Deputy.

"Have you seen him?"

"Don't have to. He's a cop. They're all pigs."

"Of course." Templeton smiled. A college education is a wonderful thing, he thought. But Gloria took off again before he could comment.

"Maybe he needs a visit from Stokely. Give the pigs a dose of Black Power."

"Oh, come on, Gloria, you're not buying that stuff, are you?"

"Stokely says Black Power is the only way to get anything from white people, anything worth having."

"Stokely says. Stokely says. We sure do seem to be taken with what Stokely says."

"Well, he's man enough to say what needs to be said. The question is, are you man enough to have him come say it at the Rocks?"

"Look," he said, "in the first place, Stokely Carmichael would not come to the Rocks. Not enough TV cameras on our situation out here. And in the second place, there's nobody at the Rocks who would buy all that Black Power stuff. Get this picture in your head: Stokely Carmichael, all of age 24 or whatever he is, tall and fierce, face to face with Mr. Samuel DuBois, age 70, bent over and all soft and cuddly — one panther ranting about seizing power for blacks and one old cat purring about how 'the Lo-o-rd provides for colored people.' Mr. DuBois can't even say 'Negro' yet, Gloria." He paused, but she said nothing. "I have to work with what's here," he said. "And we're making progress."

"Hmh," she said. "Not very fast, you're not."

"We got this telephone," he said with some pride in his voice.

"Look, Paul. The student council is bringing Stokely to Smith in a couple of weeks. I bet he'd drive me down to the settlement on his way back to Atlanta."

"I don't think that's a good idea."

"I do. Besides, I'd like to get to know him."

I don't think that's a good idea, either, Templeton thought, but what he said was, "When is he coming?"

"The 9th. Friday. We'd come down there that night."

———

"Stokely Carmichael, you dumb ass," the Deputy said into the dead end of the telephone he was holding at his desk in the Sheriff's office. "Best not be marchin' in dis town."

"Who?" asked one of the checkers players at the other desk in the room.

"Stokely."

"Who's that?"

"Stokely Carmichael! You as dumb as he is. Don't you watch TV?"

"Yeah. A lot. So who is he?"

"Didn't you see de march down in Mississippi dis summer? Almost got some people killed."

"He the one I saw rolling on the ground with the buckshot in his back-side?"

"Dat was James Meredith. You don't know enough to deserve being pwotected fum niggers."

"They all look alike, anyway. Everybody knows that."

"Well, dey don't all act alike. It was obvious which one was Stokely, standin' up tall as he could, wight in de fwont of de march, just askin' to git hisself shot. I don't know what held 'em back." The Deputy shook his head in mock befuddlement. Or possibly not mock at all. "Talkin 'bout black power," he added.

"I know him," the second checkers player chimed in. "He's the one says he's a panther or something."

"He's a pussy, is what he is. When he totes his black ass into dis county, he's gonna get it filled with more than buckshot." They laughed. "Let's go see ol' Lester."

Lester Driggers held court at The Fork, the truck stop he owned and operated on the outskirts of town, where the by-pass cut off from the main road. The regular customers were the only customers; their clothes, their color, their sidelong looks, their dangling cigarettes, their demeanor as they sat backwards or forwards in their chairs, leaning over the tables of greasy burgers and beer bottles and dirty ash trays, all made it clear that anyone with any difference would be unwelcome and in trouble. Very fat and very skinny seemed the only acceptable options.

The Deputy was perfectly at home at The Fork, and he liked the way his uniform set him apart from the rabble. He never took a place at a table, but always pulled his chair out into the open space as if to oblige everyone in the room with an unobstructed view of his eminence. He pulled one fat leg up on the other and settled his hat on his knee, turning it so that the badge faced forward.

"What you boys think about havin a bunch of Black Panthers in town?" He nodded at Lester as if the two of them knew what the answer would be.

"They not anywhere near here," a short and skinny young man said. He turned his chair around and leaned back against the wall. "They not that dumb."

The Deputy laughed. "I wouldn't say dat," he said. "You don't know how dumb dey can be." A couple more men turned their chairs around. "Dey sure as hell plannin' to come." More chairs turned. The Deputy lifted himself out of his chair and began to pace. He looked like he was addressing the jury. "De 9th. Next Friday. Stokely Carmichael hisself. I don't know how many he's bringin' wid him. Maybe we ought to organize a little welcomin' party."

"Naw," said the skinny little man. "Why don't we have us a coon hunt?" The room erupted in laughter and the scraping sound of chairs turning back to their tables. The Deputy nodded to Lester Driggers and made his way to the door.

———◆———

On Tuesday, the 6th of September 1966, in mid-day, Stokely Carmichael's schedule changed. A white Atlanta policeman attempted to arrest Harold

Prather, a Negro, on suspicion of car theft. When Prather ran, the policeman shot him. Within the hour, Carmichael's Student Non-Violent Coordinating Committee had a sound truck covered with "Black Power" slogans roaming the neighborhoods around the shooting, calling for a rally at 4:00. They boomed up and down the streets: "Handcuffed him and then shot him in cold blood."

Neighbors reported hearing Carmichael's voice: "We're gonna tear this place up, 'cause we're tired of these racist police killing our people."

"Atlanta's just a cracker version of Watts," somebody said, talking about the Los Angeles ghetto recently burned out in racial rage. "Atlanta needs to learn a lesson."

At 4:00, hundreds showed up for the rally, including the police and Atlanta Mayor Ivan Allen. As Allen attempted to quiet the crowd from atop a patrol car, the rally turned to riot. The crowd overturned a radio reporter's car and beat the man inside. Fifteen others were injured. The police arrested ten people at the scene and arraigned two SNCC members for operating a sound truck without a permit. Stokely Carmichael was missing. A warrant was issued for his arrest: inciting a riot and disorderly conduct. The news of the riot was carried on national television that night and in most east coast newspapers on the morning of the 7th.

Lester Driggers was watching at The Fork. "You see that crazy nigger in Atlanta?" he asked a table of card players. "That's the one coming up here. Calling po-lice 'white devils.' He ain't seen white devils yet." He turned and frowned at several men sitting at the bar. "Making all that trouble and scaring people to death," he mumbled, setting off a whole chorus of nods from the bar.

"You think he's got guns, Lester?"

Lester Driggers laughed. "How many niggers you know got guns? Only thing Stokely Carmichael's got is a mouth. You hear what he said down there? Talking about killing white po-lice. It's plain criminal, is what it is."

"Nobody around here is gonna listen to any of that stuff. Not even our 'Ne-gro' niggers."

"No. You're right. But I tell you one thing that boy Stokely can do. He can flat draw a damn crowd."

"We can do better'n that," one of the card players laughed.

"Yessir, I do believe we can."

Lester Driggers made the plan. Friday night, they'd get a crowd together out the old ridge road, past the little church to the old brick store, down a dirt drive at an abandoned house. "No big talk in town, now," Lester Driggers said. The bar was nodding again and leaning back in their chairs. "No sir. We'll save our talk for when it damn well counts for something."

———

Friday broke crisp and cool after an overnight temperature of near 50, a record low for early fall. But the first rays of sunshine brought full notice of the heat to come. Summer was not done; thermometers would reach the mid-80s by afternoon. There was no sign of any rain, the weather turning a monotonous hot and dry wheel across the South. People were happy just to have the nighttime respite.

By lunch, The Fork was steamy. The Deputy found Lester Driggers there with a dirty apron around his waist, serving the unusually big and unusually noisy crowd. The regulars were there in force, clumped together, talking and glancing sideways at newcomers whose tasseled loafers and sweaters looped around their shoulders gave away their city origins. The Deputy smiled at the air of excitement all around him. He took a place at the end of the bar.

"You see Cwonkite last night?" he said quietly to Driggers, who was making change at the cash register next to the Deputy.

"Yeah. Didn't mean to, but I couldn't remember when that new Tarzan series was supposed to start, so I turned the TV on too early." Driggers handed some change to the customer without looking at him and turned toward the Deputy. "It was pretty good."

"Good! You thought the news was 'good?'" the Deputy whispered heavily, leaning toward Driggers so that he had to brace himself on the cash register.

"Not the news. I thought Tarzan was good," Driggers said, smiling from the side of his mouth and apparently oblivious to the drift of the Deputy's conversation. "Or pretty good, anyway. The new guy looks a little fruity. Smiles like a queer. But he was pretty good. Not as good as Weismuller.

There won't ever be anybody that good. Anyway, it was good to get Billy Graham off the screen. I don't know why they think we're interested in the London Crusade. I doubt I'm going to London to be saved."

"I don't give a goddam about Billy Gwaham," the Deputy said. "Or Tarzan, neither. Did you see what Cwonkite said about Stokely? Or did you forget Stokely?"

Driggers' face turned stone cold. "Shut up, fool," he whispered. He stood up, surveyed the crowd, and nodded to the Deputy to follow him to a back room, closing the door behind him. "If you can't use your brain, use your eyes. Look around out there. I don't know who they all are, and neither do you. You ever hear of F.B.I. informants?"

"What do we do about informants?" the Deputy asked a little sheepishly.

"We don't do nothing about informants. That's Bobby and Cecil's job, not yours. Maybe you don't remember your job. Your job is to do what you're told. Do you remember who got you your job? That's who can take it away from you, too."

"I am doin' my job, Lester," the Deputy said. "What do you want?"

"I want you to go out to the Rocks and arrest that Stokely guy and that preacher boy who invited him up here. But not until I give the signal."

"Dat's what I was doin' my best to tell you about," said the Deputy. "Stokely's not there. If you watched the news, you'd know dat. The po-lice are looking for him in Atlanta. He's a fugitive from justice. Dey gonna awest him down there." The Deputy was pleased with himself.

"You're a total fool," Driggers said. "Why do you think they didn't already arrest him in Atlanta? Because they couldn't find him in Atlanta. Because he ain't in Atlanta, dummy." He waited for a dramatic moment. Then he leaned toward the Deputy and said slowly, "But we know where he is, don't we?"

"You think Stokely's — ?"

"Can you think of a better place to hide out?"

"Well, that means we got us a — "

"A panther and a preacher." Driggers smiled and then laughed out loud. "Two pussies for the price of one." He hustled the Deputy towards the door. "Now you go on. You don't need to know nothing about what's happening here. You wait for a sign out by the road. You'll see us drive by, going back to town, then you get yourself out there and arrest them once we're gone." He ushered the Deputy across the crowded room. "Better bring some help," he added.

───────

Sunset came at 6:40, just after the evening news began. From a television left on at The Fork, Walter Cronkite addressed the darkening room with the news of the day: Stokely Carmichael had been arrested in Atlanta. But The Fork was empty. The crowd that had gathered all afternoon was already gone in a stampede of cars, heading off toward destiny and the rare opportunity to combine their racist view of the world with the capture of a genuine wanted criminal.

───────

The first car down Brickstore Road was a black Cadillac with a "Jesus ♥s You" bumper sticker. The owner undoubtedly knew nothing about Lester Driggers' plan. Nor did the three boys from the settlement who had been designated nighttime security guards at the store up on the main road. But the boys saw the familiar fins of the big car slide by in the dark with the headlights off.

They knew where the car was going. The old Snoddy place down at the end of Brickstore Road had become a hunting lodge for the owner of the Cadillac, but he only came at night, and there was intemperate speculation as to the nature of the hunt. The boys had trailed the big Cadillac down to the house before and found it hard to spy, as the windows were still boarded up. They had gone back when the house was empty, but all they ever found was a lot of empty liquor bottles.

Here was their chance to catch the man's "hunting" partner. They could already sense the drama of their report to the community at the settlement; they would be heroes.

They had no idea how heroic they would have to be before they could ever get back to the settlement — or how their story, told over and over, would become a vivid part of the history of the place.

The boys had been engrossed in old Tarzan comic books they had found under a ledge at the quarry pool near the settlement. Concluding without much discussion that Mr. Samuel DuBois, the church elder, would not look with favor on pictures of near-naked people, they had squirreled the books away in the back room at the store, hiding them under an old pair of dark suit pants in a cabinet there. Security duty was not demanding, and the boys had memorized every word and every image of the comics.

A squabble over which of them could claim to be the bronzed and heroic Tarzan had resulted in a compromise: All three took the names of African warriors — Mbonga, Mugambi, and Bazuli. They were in agreement that nobody would have to be Achmet or Abdul, the evil Arabs. But they argued incessantly, especially after dark when there was nothing else to do, over the proper identity of each one's namesake among the strong but generic brown men in the pictures. They were on their pallets and in the midst of just such an argument when the approaching Cadillac silenced them. The three watched the car turn down Brickstore Road, and without a single word, mounted their bicycles and took up the hunt in the dark of a moonless night.

By the time the boys reached the clearing around the house, the car was dead to the world in the grass beyond the gravel drive, leaving reptilian tracks across the yard. The boys propped their bikes against trees by the road and started toward the breaks of light in the boarded windows of the house.

"They're already inside. Come on." A step into the clearing.

"Wait!" Whispered. "What about the driver?" Retreat to the trees. "You think he's still out here?"

"Maybe in the car."

The threesome stared at the car as if it might suddenly spring to life, whip around and fix them in its headlights.

More whispers: "I don't see anybody."

"He could be lying down in the seat."

"Go get up closer."

"Who?"

"You. We'll keep an eye on you. You can be the scout."

"Big deal. What am I supposed to do?"

"Get where you can see into the car. See if anybody sits up when we make a noise."

"Well, wait 'til I get set."

The youngest of the three boys stepped slowly into the clearing and then raced across the front yard, ducking behind the trunk of a one-sided tree. There was no movement in the car. The older boys waved the scout off toward the crape myrtles at the far end of the side yard; when he reached the safety of those trees, he disappeared from their view. The woods were extraordinarily silent, as if mice and birds and everything else that might move were as transfixed as the boys. Occasional early-browned leaves from the tall tulip poplars made soft pats on the ground behind them.

"What do you think?"

"Nothing."

"Think he's all right?"

"I don't know. I want to get out of here. It's creepy."

"We can't leave him."

"I can." There was no sound anywhere.

"Think we better go get him?"

"Not me. You go get him."

"Chicken."

"You're a bigger one."

"What's that? You hear something?"

"What? Sh-h-h. It could be them."

"Who?"

"Them, dummy. Or the driver. Shut up."

"I hear a car."

"It's just somebody up on the main road."

"What if it's robbers going to the store?"

"Shut up, will you? Look! There he is." The scout ran out from the woods near the back of the house, having circled all the way around to an old storage shed just in front of the Cadillac. Only his movement was visible in the deep darkness; when he stopped still, he disappeared. "Get me a rock. If I can hit the car, the driver will jump up if he's in there."

"Wait a minute. That car's getting closer. Sounds like more than one." The boys turned toward the sound and saw a line of headlights curving through the trees along Brickstore Road. The scout must have seen them, too. He had vanished.

Cars spilled into the yard around the Snoddy house. Headlights went dark but interior dome lights lit up as doors opened, illuminating the white-robed passengers emerging like ghosts from a fleet of coffins. The sound of doors slamming sounded like gunshots. The lights went off in the house.

Among the gathering group, the boys saw fancy robes mixed with crude wrap-around white sheets. Headdresses varied from imposing tall pointed spires to simple hoods made out of pillow cases, but each one masked the man within with equal and evil effect.

One of the tall spikes nodded toward the Cadillac, "I told you he was with us." Their surprise at the hunter's presence for their rally was undoubtedly equalled by the hunter's surprise at the arrival of company.

Several of the sheets unloaded stacks of wood from the back of a pickup truck. In the center of the front yard, they made a rough teepee of logs. Someone splashed gasoline onto the logs, the boys reported, and then poured more over a piece of cloth wrapped around a pole, lit a match to that and stuck the torch into the pile of logs. The whole teepee flared into a tall flame racing toward the sky, and sheets floated like moths toward the light of the fire. The front of the Snoddy house was spotlighted.

The two older boys from the settlement sank back into the shadow of the tall poplars, wide white eyes in their dark faces making them the negative image of the Klansmen on the far side of the bonfire. Their scout was nowhere to be seen.

They watched the side door to the house creak open, and two sheet-enshrouded figures emerged.

"Hey!" called one of the shiny satin hoods from the front yard. The two from the house stepped toward the big black Cadillac, and one of them opened the passenger door for the other one. "Glad to see you," yelled the satin hood and started towards the car.

The dome light from the Cadillac cast itself over the shrubbery near the house, and the two boys under the poplar trees saw their little scout crouched beside a tall, leggy nandina bush, right in the path of the approaching Klansmen. But then the car door slammed shut, and the scout disappeared again in the dark shrubbery. A crowd of Klansmen gathered around the figures from the house, grunting their greetings and slapping the newcomers on the back.

One of the figures from the house stepped out unsteadily and began shaking hands with the circle of Klansmen, his shiny hunting boots and the cuffs of his creased camouflaged pants showing beneath his sheet. He kept looking back at his companion, who stood rooted to the ground beside the car, hands tucked firmly into the folds of the sheet. It would have been hard for the boys under the poplar trees to guess who was most uncomfortable: the wobbly figure in the creased pants, the mystery companion, or the scout behind the scraggly nandina.

"We got to do something," the oldest boy whispered.

It wasn't long before the rattle of bicycle wheels on gravel caused the whole group to turn toward the Brickstore Road. The bicycle raced into the light of the bonfire and off across the yard toward the one-sided tree. "Kree-gah!" the cyclist yelled at the top of his lungs, "Mugambi bundolo!"

"Hey, we got us a coon right here," shouted one of the Klansmen. He took off running toward the bike, followed by flowing sheets and robes taking up the chase, the creased cuffs lagging behind.

Only the mystery companion stayed in place. As soon as the Klansmen cleared the side of the house, that frozen figure melted toward the nandina bush and stuck out a dark hand to the little scout hiding in its shadow. The sheet opened and engulfed the boy in its folds, then moved off beyond the far end of the car and into the woods at the edge of the side yard. The sheet released its guest into the darkness of the woods, returned to the driver's side of the car, got in and started the motor, turning the car around to face Brickstore Road. The creased hunting pants fell into the car on the passenger's side, but late-arrivals had blocked the way out, and the big black Cadillac fell silent again. The Klansmen were in full pursuit of the screaming bicycle and saw none of this.

The boy on the bicycle had disappeared beyond the one-sided tree and into the dense woods behind the crape myrtles. Some of the Klansmen pulled up into a huddle, but others charged into the woods, snagging their sheets on the blackberry brambles that grew helter skelter along the edge of the woods. The whole scene quieted as tall white figures bent over to disentangle their robes from the thorns.

"Kree-gah!" This time, the sound came from behind the Klansmen, where Brickstore Road entered the Snoddy yard. The bicycle raced out of the dark across the gravel, right into the glaring headlights of the Cadillac and off toward the house. "Bazuli bundolo!"

"There he is!" White sheets rushed back from the one-sided tree and the blackberry thicket, coming together like a ground fog and flowing around the edge of the house. The bicycle vanished behind the storage shed at the end of the drive. Several of the Klansmen pulled up at the side of the Cadillac.

"Think it's time to go?" one of the satin robes asked, huffing the words into the window on the driver's side. A nod in response. "Right," said the Klansman as if the driver had spoken with authority. "There's bigger fish than this little pickaninny." He put two fingers into the sides of his mouth and let out a shrill whistle. The running Klansmen stopped dead in their tracks and looked back at him. "Come on," he said. "We got better things to do."

"What's better than teaching this little jungle bunny a lesson?" asked a muslin sheet.

"Have you forgotten about Stokely Carmichael?" The tall satin hat turned back to the Cadillac. "Stokely's a lot more important than this kid, ain't he?" he said to the driver. Another nod. "Right," said the Klansman. "That's what I thought, too."

During the general argument that followed as to the relative importance of their original plan as compared with the importance of teaching a lesson to this one boy who was making monkeys of them, and long before the group of sheets could agree to begin organizing their motorcade, the three boys regrouped and rode their bicycles off through the woods toward the main road.

———

When the boys arrived breathless at the settlement, they fell onto the front steps of Mr. Samuel DuBois's house and blurted out the news of what they had seen. It was almost midnight, and still no sign of the moon.

"Call Sister Holy Ghost," the old man said.

"In town?" the boys asked.

"She's at Aunt Stitch's place," he said. "Go on. She'll be waiting."

How he could have known that was beyond understanding. Aunt Stitch went to bed at 9:30. She expected her house to settle into respectful quiet by then, and she was rarely disappointed, by anything or anybody. And Sister Holy Ghost lived in town, ministering to the wider world through the House of Prayer for All People.

Nevertheless, Sister Holy Ghost stood at Aunt Stitch's door as if she had in fact been waiting. The boys started stammering out the news they had been told to bring, but she held up her hand for silence. She tugged at the veil over her face, then stepped between the boys and off to the home of Mr. Samuel DuBois. The boys followed at her heels.

"You were right about the cars," she said. Mr. DuBois said nothing. It was Joe Douglas, the deacon who assisted him at the store, who spoke.

"Where's the preacher?" Douglas asked.

"Not at the house," she said. "In his study at the church, most likely."

"Well, then, he's in trouble. And we're in trouble."

Douglas led her into the house, and told the boys to gather everyone as quietly as possible at the head of the lane leading to the church. "Tell them all to wait for me," he said.

The people from the settlement reached the churchyard just in time to see a stream of cars come up the main road from the store and pull off onto the lawn. White-robed Klansmen burst into the night. Mr. Joe Douglas, Sister Holy Ghost, and three young African warriors in the lead of the procession heard the car doors opening and slamming shut. And they saw the last car in the motorcade slide on by, like the Levite skirting the man who fell among thieves, passing by on the other side. It was a big black Cadillac with "Jesus ♥s You" on the bumper and two flat-hooded Klansmen inside. It did not stop, but raced off down the road toward town.

The Deputy sat for a long time in the squad car, hidden from the main road by a row of scruffy cedars. "Goddam Lester Dwiggers," he said out loud, rubbing his hands together and blowing on them. "How long does he expect us to sit out here in the cold?"

"Yeah," said one of the two men in the back seat. "Of course, he got a fire to stand around. He don't even know it's cold." He cackled. "Probably."

At ten minutes before midnight, as the moon rose at last over the dark horizon into a starlit sky, the Deputy leaned forward over the steering wheel and squinted into the headlights of an oncoming car. He hit his floodlight. The car swerved across the center line, then steadied and returned to the right lane, blinding the Deputy with its highbeams. It sped by, a big black Cadillac with a bumper strip that said "Jesus ♥s You." In the driver's seat was a hooded Klansman, a second figure slumped against the door on the passenger side.

"Dat's it," the Deputy said. "It's over." He turned the key in the ignition and pulled into the road. A half-mile or so from the settlement, he picked up speed, turning on the flashing red light and siren. As he made the curve just before the Church at the Rocks, his headlights caught a crowd of Klansmen still milling about in the yard. Every white hood snapped his way.

"Somethin's wong," the Deputy said. "Dey supposed to be gone." He made a split-second decision without ever slowing down. Lights flashing, siren blaring, he blasted right past the church, his siren fading to a whine in his race to nowhere.

For a moment, the tableau was frozen in place, ghosts at the steps of God's house. Then one of the Klansmen with a two-by-four on his shoulder started an eerie, taunting chant:

"Sto-o-oke-ly-y! Sto-o-oke-ly-y!" The drawn-out vowels slithered into the night like long wisps of vapor. "Sto-o-oke-ly-y! Sto-o-oke-ly-y!"

Hidden in the underbrush, the people from the settlement huddled against the chill in the air and the chilling sight on the grounds of their church. Sister Holy Ghost was at their center, sniffing the air for clues and ready to lead her charges off in any direction. Only her eyes moved. She squinted at the window of the pastor's study, straining to discern any movement inside.

"Sto-o-oke-ly-y! Sto-o-oke-ly-y!"

"Down," Sister whispered. Children dropped to the ground all around her, and most of the adults too. Only Sister and Douglas remained standing, watching, not moving, waiting for some expected spirit to point them in one direction or another. Douglas looked at the window of the pastor's study and frowned at Sister.

"Sto-o-oke-ly-y! Sto-o-oke-ly-y!" One Klansman nailed the two-by-fours together in the shape of a cross; another dug a hole. They sunk the base of the cross, packed it with dirt so that it stood upright. Others brought short logs and kindling from the trucks, others made torches, dipped in buckets of kerosene. But most of the Klansmen only milled about in the yard around the church, calling "Sto-o-oke-ly-y! Sto-o-oke-ly-y!"

Then a harmony joined the chant across the lawn. The sound seemed to come from the dense trees themselves, as if their echo had picked up the wrong cue. But it grew louder, and the chanting grew weaker as the Klansmen turned this way and that, unable to determine the source of the disembodied song:

> *On a hill far away,*
> *Stood an old rugged cross,*
> *The emblem of suff'ring and shame....*

Then the bodies appeared; rustling through the underbrush, dozens of black people — men, women, and children — led by Sister Holy Ghost, who fixed her gaze on the shiniest of the satin robes standing by the planted cross, directly in line with the steps of the church.

"I smell a gar!" yelled one of the Klansmen to nervous laughter from his comrades. "A ci-gar?" came the set-up line in the same voice.

"Shut up," commanded the shiny satin sheet in a harsh whisper. "It's Sister Holy Ghost. What's she doing out here?"

There was no sound until the hymn began again in a low and melodious mezzo-soprano, and the group from the settlement started forward.

> *And I love that old cross,*
> *Where the dearest and best*
> *For a world of lost sinners was slain....*

The man in the satin robe turned toward the advancing group and crossed his arms over his chest.

"Excuse me, sir," said Sister as she stopped in front of him, "but we're just going into the church."

"You ain't going nowhere," said the Klansman.

"It's time for our usual 'Midnight Watch,'" she explained. But no explanation was really necessary. The group following her had kept moving when she stopped, flowing around her and around the wide stance of the Klansman as if they were just two boulders in the stream.

"Wait a minute!" the Klansman shouted at the group, turning to stop their progress toward the door of the church. As he turned, Sister took a small sidestep and passed him by, placing her arm around one of the children straggling along near the end of the procession.

"Thank you, sir," she said to the Klansman. She rejoined the group and took up their song:

> So I'll cherish the old rugged cross,
> 'Til my trophies at last I lay down;
> I will cling to the old rugged cross,
> And exchange it someday for a crown.

"The hell with them," the Klansman said. "Light it up."

Inside the church, the soft and steady moonlight gave way to the wildly dancing red reflections of the burning cross in the yard. The people took their seats in the pews and bowed their heads in silent prayer. It was only a matter of time.

Sister was ready in the aisle when the door burst open and slammed against the wall. The satin-robed Klansman waved a torch, the fire come inside now. "Where is he?" he demanded.

"The people are praying," Sister whispered. Her hands were clasped at her waist.

The Klansman stopped and looked at the bowed heads all around him. "Where is Stokely?" he whispered back.

"There's no one here by that name."

"We know damn well there is," he said. Another figure stepped into the aisle behind him, a fat man in a robe that looked borrowed from a thinner model or perhaps bought in a much earlier time. The buttons around his middle strained against his girth, and those at his open neck fell back in relief.

His hood flopped to one side, and he had to adjust the eye slits constantly in order to see.

"I assure you there is no one here by that name," said Sister.

"Well, where's the preacher?"

"He is not here." Her eyes looked steadily into the blank slits of the satin hood and did not shift left or right.

"I don't believe that," the Klansman said and pushed her aside. He and the fat man moved down the aisle, their torch sending black sooty smoke toward the ceiling and filling the room with the thick sweet smell of burning kerosene. Sister glanced at Douglas who stood up at the front of the church, blocking the aisle.

"Will the children come forward for prayer," Douglas said aloud. "Don't mind our visitors," he added with sudden volume, as if to announce their presence. The two Klansmen were now surrounded by children of all sizes pouring out of the pews and kneeling down in the center aisle around Douglas. "Let us pray," he said.

"I'll check the study," the fat Klansman said in a high raspy voice. He braced himself on the ends of the pews as he stepped over the children and made his way toward the door beside the choir loft.

"Ouch," said one of the children and hit the fat Klansman on the leg. "You on my foot."

"Sowwy," said the Klansman.

"We'll start the sentence prayers with you, Daniel," said Douglas, "and continue around the circle."

"Dear Lord, watch over us tonight and every night," said the strong voice of a teenaged African warrior. "And deliver us from our enemies," he added just a little louder. Then, after a moment, more quietly: "Thank you, Lord, for Douglas and Sister Holy Ghost."

"Thank you, Lord, for this place," said the next.

"Thank you, Lord, for our houses."

"Thank you, Lord, for food." Somebody giggled. The prayers moved on around the group, connected by a predictable stream of consciousness.

The Klansman in the satin sheet was swamped in kneeling children. He shuffled one way, and then the other, his robes cumbersome in the tight quarters. Finally, he snapped at the fat man ahead of him, "For God's sake, help me out of here," and the fat man nudged a few more children aside.

They ducked into the study with the torch, leaving the sanctuary again to the light of the cross still burning in the yard. The sentence prayers continued.

"Thank you, Lord, for trees."

"Thank you, Lord, for woods." Another giggle.

"That's the same thing," someone whispered. The pressure to come up with blessings not already mentioned is the principal reason people pay attention in sentence prayers.

"Okay: thank you, Lord, for grass." More giggles. "Well, there's nothing else left," the struggling voice whispered in defense.

The prayers stopped with the sound of breaking glass and falling furniture from the study. Little eyes opened wide, but neither Douglas nor Sister Holy Ghost flinched.

"Lord, the moon was so late tonight," Sister Holy Ghost said, picking up the prayer. "It seemed so dark. But now it's out. Thank you for the moon, Lord. It reminds us of the sunshine coming in the morning, when all the fears of the night will be burned away, when all the lights of these men will be put out, when all us will see clearly by the light of your love. We are not afraid, Lord. Morning will come. Your morning. The morning of your kingdom. And all us will be there with You."

The two Klansmen brought their torch back into the sanctuary, but they had not found the preacher.

"Thank you, Lord, for your everlasting arms," said Sister. The satin robe pushed Douglas aside and started back through the crowd of children, up the aisle and out of the church, with the fat man in tow.

"And so we pray," said Douglas, "as our Lord taught us to pray:"

"Our Father," the children picked it up in unison as the two Klansmen moved through them with their torch, "who art in Heaven, hallowed be thy name..." The door slammed at the back of the church, and the sanctuary fell dependent again on the light of the burning cross outside. "Thy kingdom come..."

The yard was in an uproar. Before the two Klansmen could announce their search had come up empty, a small boy from the church ran headlong into the backside of the satin robe, his fists pummeling the slack folds. Two other Klansmen grabbed the boy and pulled him away.

"Well, he's little, but it's all we got," one of them said. It was impossible to tell which of them was talking. "Let's have some fun."

"Better clap your hand over his mouth so he won't yell," said the other.

"He won't say nothing," the fat Klansman said. "He can't talk." The boy stared directly back into their masks. "Turn him aloose," said the fat one. The two who were holding the boy turned their masks to face the preposterous suggestion. "Turn him aloose," he said again.

The fat Klansman pulled a pistol from under his robe and aimed it at the boy's legs. "Better git, boy," he said. The boy strained against his two captors and stamped at the ground, kicking them in the shins. "Let him go," the fat Klansman insisted. He held the pistol against the side of the boy's head and leaned over toward him. "Better wun your legs off, son. Wun fast as you can."

The boy stared at the floppy hood hanging blank on the Klansman's face. The eyeholes were dark and lifeless. "Wun, Pup," the hood said, more softly. "Wun," it whispered. The boy broke loose from the men holding his arms and took off across the yard, not toward the settlement but toward the ridge road.

"Bobby! Cecil!" said the fat Klansmen. "Follow him." Hoods snapped back and forth as the men surveyed each other. They all looked more or less alike. "Which one's Bobby and Cecil?" the fat one asked.

"Right here," said one of the muslin sheets. Another hand shot up.

"Hurry!" said the fat Klansman. "Don't lose him." They were off and running. "But don't get too close! If he stops, you stop. Wait for us."

The fat Klansman pulled off the sheet that covered his uniform and walked over to the squad car. "You boys go on home," he called to the group in his high raspy voice. "I got me an awest to make." When nobody moved, the Deputy walked back into the crowd and said with as low a voice as he could manage, "Git your asses out of here. Shewiff don't want y'all out here at all. If you still awound when I make an awest, I'll have to awest you, too." This time, the rest of them moved off toward the fleet of cars and pickups pulled up into the yard.

The Deputy Sheriff drove toward the brick store, slowly, without any siren and without any lights. He was not surprised at the direction Pup had taken. And he was certain that the frightened boy would lead him to his target.

Bobby and Cecil were standing by the side of the road just before an abandoned house where a white woman named Delphine Templeton once lived. The Deputy pulled the squad car off to the side, grabbing the bullhorn from the dashboard and closing the door behind him just enough to shut off the dome light without making a sound.

"He went in the house," one of the Klansmen whispered when he crossed the road.

"Get them sheets off," the Deputy said. Cecil yanked off his hood and unbuttoned his robe, dropping them both to the ground. He and the Deputy stood together, staring at Bobby struggling to pull his robe off over his head. His feet and legs came free, but the rest of his body churned in the sheet, an occasional arm flailing out and then disappearing again as he worked himself into tighter and tighter coils.

"Help," Bobby said. Cecil looked at the Deputy.

"We ought to just leave him," the Deputy mumbled. "But go on. Git him out."

The three of them stopped at the edge of some overgrown wild roses in the front yard of the dark house. The kudzu was so thick across the porch that there was just a dark slit in the foliage where somebody might go up the steps and to the door. "Go to de back, both of you," the Deputy said. "I betcha a dollar dey'll wun out dat way. Got your guns?" Both of them pulled pistols from their holsters. "I'll count to a hunnerd, den start. Now git." Although the chirping and shrill grinding of crickets and tree frogs was so loud that it would have taken a sizable noise to be overheard, he added a warning, "Don't make no noise."

The Deputy waited until the two men were out of sight, then started counting slowly to himself. He looked up at the moon, as big and full as a dinner plate. He studied the spray of the stars across the sky. He didn't know any of their names, but he had been taught them, he thought, as a child. His breath fogged on the air around him, and then it was time to go.

"...Ninety-seven, ninety-eight, ninety-nine," he said out loud and clicked on the bullhorn. It came to life with a burst of static. The woods went instantly silent and alert. "Okay," the Deputy shouted toward the porch, surprising himself with the volume he got. "Templeton! We know you in de house. You come on out. We not gonna hurt you. We know you got Stokely in de house wid you. Dat's who we want." There was silence from the house and from the woods. "You know he's a wanted cwiminal, Templeton? Stokely

Carmichael is wanted by the po-lice in Atlanta. And de F.B.I. in Washington, D.C. You gonna be in a heap of twouble if you hidin' him." Nothing but silence. "Come on out de fwont, Templeton. We not gonna hurt you. You got my pwomise on dat. If you can't git Stokely to come out, we'll come git him if we have to tear de house down." Still silence. "Okay, boys," the Deputy Sheriff said to nobody, but still talking through the bullhorn, "go back to de back. Dey might wun out dat way." There was a brief silence and then a gunshot from the back of the house.

"Stop!" The shout rang out while the sound of the shot was still echoing through the woods. Then silence again. The Deputy dropped the bullhorn and pulled his pistol. He had not actually expected to have to use it. There were muffled voices and the sound of commotion from the back of the house.

"Hey, Deputy," a voice bellowed. "Come on back. We got him!"

The Deputy drew his flashlight with his free hand. When he turned the corner of the house and shined the light into the back yard, he found Bobby and Cecil standing over a dark figure crumpled at their feet, face down, his body twisted to one side and his knees pulled up to protect his stomach.

"Did you shoot him?" the Deputy asked. There was blood on the back of the man's head and on his shoulder. His shirt and pants were torn. There was no movement.

"Naw, just roughed him up a little bit. He tried to get away. He's lucky it was us and not the Atlanta po-lice."

Cecil kicked the man in his rib cage. "You not going anywhere now, are you, boy?" There was no protest or response.

"Bad ass panther," Bobby laughed. "Ain't nothing but a pussy now." He added a kick to the man's butt.

"Stop it," the Deputy said. "Turn him over." The two men stuck their feet under the inert form and rolled him over onto his back. The man coughed and turned his head to one side. The Deputy Sheriff shined his flashlight into the swollen face. The crickets and tree frogs had started up again, and the yard became noisy and crowded.

"Dat's not Stokely Carmichael," the Deputy said.

"'Course it is," said Cecil. "Who else would be running away?"

"We caught him," Bobby added. "It's gotta be Stokely."

"It's Templeton," the Deputy said under his breath.

"Who?"

"Templeton. De pweacher. How you gonna explain you shot a pweacher?"

"We ain't shot nobody," said Bobby. "Just beat him up a little."

"It's de pweacher," the Deputy repeated. "How you gonna explain you beat up a pweacher?"

"Wadn't just us," Cecil said firmly. "You told us to get him. You in it, too." After the Deputy said nothing, Cecil added, "Besides, he was resisting arrest."

The Deputy shined the flashlight into Cecil's face. "For what?" he asked.

"I don't know," Cecil said, shielding his eyes. "Ain't 'resisting arrest' enough?"

"You gotta be being awested for something," the Deputy said, exasperated.

"How about if he was incitin' a riot?" Bobby offered. "I heard of that."

"Maybe," the Deputy said, turning the flashlight back to the man at his feet. "Dat is what he had Stokely here for."

"Fact, he was harboring a criminal," Bobby said. "Ain't that enough to arrest him?" The beam of the flashlight jolted up toward the trees.

"But we ain't got Stokely," the Deputy said. "We got no pwoof he was here." He shoved the flashlight into Cecil's stomach at point blank range. "Take dis and go in de house," he said. "If we find Stokely, den Templeton was harbowing a cwiminal." Cecil stood still, pointing the flashlight toward the back porch of the house. "Go wid him," the Deputy said to Bobby. "I'll guard de pwisoner."

"Big deal," Bobby said.

"Go on," ordered the Deputy. "You better find somebody in dat house. Use your guns, if you have to."

As the two men went off into the dark house, the Deputy squatted beside the form of Paul Templeton and gently turned him over onto his stomach, keeping his head turned to one side. "You gonna be okay," he said. He straightened Templeton's legs. With some effort, he pulled his arms out from under his body and brought them together behind his back, snapping them into handcuffs.

When the Deputy stood up, he could see the flashlight moving from window to window in the house. There was no sound anywhere. He pulled his pistol again and pointed it toward the back door, holding it there until the flashlight appeared and started down the steps into the yard.

"Find him?" the Deputy said, staring into the darkness behind the beam of light.

"Nope," Cecil said.

"We looked everywhere," Bobby added.

The three men spent a long minute staring at each other and at the body on the ground. "Well," said the Deputy, "dey ain't nothin' to do but git dis one outta here. Watch him while I git de car. It'll just have to be incitin' a riot."

For that offense, compounded by his resisting arrest, the Rev. Paul Templeton spent ten nights in the jailhouse in town. His parishioners went quietly on with their lives, intending to draw no further attention to themselves and assured by the Deputy, who visited them twice in the first few days after the arrest, that their preacher was in good hands and was simply being detained by the F.B.I. because of the suspicion that he was connected to the criminal element that had threatened to burn down half of Atlanta. The Deputy explained that the criminal element was a danger to the settlement as well, seeing that people who followed the likes of Stokely Carmichael had repeatedly burned down their own homes and neighborhoods in other places in the country. If that weren't enough to convince good people to keep their heads down, he reminded them of the threat from the other side, as the Klan pursued its own pledge to bring the bad element to justice. "Dey'll burn down anything, you know," he said, then corrected himself. "Well," he said, "dey don't burn down dey own stuff, but dey'll burn down everybody else's in a minute."

On the tenth day after his arrest, Paul Templeton was released without public notice or explanation. The charges were dropped without comment.

———

There was a fragment of the story I did not include in my graduate school paper because it would have left the story open-ended. The facts were simple. Two days after Pollo's arrest, Joe Douglas, a gentle man who stood up to the Klan, was found dead in the road in front of the brick store.

Chapter Seven

———

RAILWAY TO THE SUN

The tower of Duke Chapel is always described as soaring, and it is that. Solid and majestic, at the end of a long drive, it anchors the Gothic campus that spreads out from its base — anchors, really, that entire part of the world. But it's inside that the chapel sheds its heavy granite skin and lifts itself, truly soaring, toward the sky.

Just beyond heavy carved doors, in a cool sunken vestibule, a short flight of stairs leads you into the chapel. There, thin beams of color ride through the airy loft to strike the north wall. Rising stone columns stretch to support ribbed vaults in the ceiling, where all the shimmering architectural activity comes finally to rest on flowered stepping stones that mark off the lengths of the nave high overhead. The experience of the chapel interior is sudden and momentary, because as soon as you recognize the shape of the space, the idea of Church takes hold, and quiet awe overtakes the dramatics of Gothic architecture.

It's the great joke of the Goths on the Church of Rome that its grandest cathedrals are sanctuaries to pagan sprites stolen from the uncultured north. It is ironic, maybe even outrageous, that the joke should then be played on these unsuspecting Methodists, but the joke has actually gained strength in the translation. The gargoyles and fairies of the Duke Chapel nearly dance from their high perches. As a defense, a thousand patriarchs and apostles in stained glass and stone keep watch. Except for Lazarus, they do not sleep, or even blink, their bug-eyed faces alert to any giggle, any scraping sound, any moving feather, as the sprites settle down under the cover of shadows in the loft.

The angels keeping the apostles company at Duke are white. Not white stone. White race. I'd never noticed them as anything other than generic angels until I saw the tombstone in the cemetery beside the Church at the Rocks. That one black angel, distinct and powerful and haunting, rising from the flames of a burning building, had made all these other angels perched about Duke Chapel seem trivial and meaningless. And very white. A few have Greek lips or curly hair like the Greek gods, but the weight of all their other features makes it clear that angels are white. It's possible, of course, that the saints with whom the pale sarcophagal effigies of the Dukes keep company in the Chapel were all actually white, as were the Dukes themselves and the heroes of their faith: John Wycliff and John Wesley, Thomas Jefferson and Robert E. Lee, and the others who stand in stone at the chapel doors. They are accurately and honestly white. But all the angels too?

On Sunday, the 9th of October 1966, I sat in the crowded chapel listening to the Right Reverend James A. Pike. He was the former Bishop of the Episcopal Diocese of California, twice charged with heresy and only once acquitted, and his invitation to the pulpit at Duke had created some controversy.

He satisfied his critics and his supporters both, arguing for a return to basic beliefs. "The Muslims," said Bishop Pike, "go into Africa offering one God and three wives; we Christians go in and offer three Gods and one wife. We don't stand a chance." Nervous laughter from the congregation. "We'd better decide," he said, "just what is important and what is not." All around the chapel, good Christians squirmed, whether they were wives or not, knowing perfectly well what's important.

It's unlikely that Bishop Pike intended to remind me of Mae Maude

Snoddy, but that's what he did. I'm not even sure why. I hadn't thought about her much in the ten years since our summer in the country. Now, as Bishop Pike talked on about his new form of fundamentalism, my mind wandered. I looked at the granite ledge over the reredos in the apse of the chapel and thought about Mae Maude and Pollo and me on the ledge above the pool at the quarry. The stone in the chapel alone probably equaled the entire output of the quarry at the Rocks. I studied the figures in the stained glass and wondered if the heretical Bishop Pike had ever pondered the possibility that Mary Magdalene, fixing him with a frozen stare from the clerestory window in the transept to his right, might have been either isosceles or scalene, one of her hands covering some critical proof. I wondered if there might be a special name in geometry for the flattened isosceles triangle formed by the pendulous breasts of Mary Salome. I noted with some satisfaction that Duke's Adam is an equilateral; Eve, a scalene. And I decided I would find Mae Maude.

———•———

I thought she might have gone back to Louisiana, since that was the only other place she knew anything about. Mrs. J. Arthur Wilson, Bubba Wilson's grandmother, might have the key I needed. I called her from Duke to ask if she knew the name of the town where Bubba — and Mae Maude, although I did not mention that to Mrs. Wilson — had gone to high school. "This is Bo Fisher, Mrs. Wilson; Morrison and Julia Fisher's son? I'm looking for a friend who might have some connections where Bubba went to high school."

"Bo!" Mrs. Wilson said, "Bo Fisher! I don't know when I've heard from you." Never was the correct answer to that, but I decided to just let her go on not knowing.

"Bubba went to high school in Louisiana," I said. "I thought I might be able to locate somebody through that high school, but I don't know where it was."

"Well, I am so thrilled to hear from you, Bo. I think about you so often."

I could guarantee that Mrs. J. Arthur Wilson had not given me two thoughts in ten years, but "I think about you so often" is exactly what she said. There is a certain quality of lie that is entirely within the bounds of propriety in the world of Mrs. Wilson. "Are you taking good care of yourself, Bo?"

"Oh, yes, ma'am. I'm doing just fine. I'm looking —"

"Where are you now, Bo? Aren't you at some school up North? We've all been so worried about you."

"Yes, ma'am — I mean, no, ma'am, there's nothing to worry about, and it's not up North, exactly. I'm at Duke. And I met someone who had some connections in that town where Bubba went to high school, but I can't remember the name of the town."

"Minor," she said, "Minor, Louisiana." Finally. Like finding a small gold nugget after panning all day in a shallow stream. "But I don't think Bubba or his parents would have anybody left there." She paused, and I waited, wondering what I would say if she mentioned Mae Maude. "It's a poor little town, you know," she said. "Hardly any white people at all, and none of those that would really be in our set. Bubba played ball with those people," she said. She would have been surprised to know what else he had played. "His daddy always said that was good for his development as a ball player, but I was more concerned about his development as a gentleman." Maybe she did know. "I don't think he had actual friends there, though. Did he ever mention any friends to you, Bo?"

"Well, yes'm," I said, being totally honest, "he did. One or two." I wondered if Bubba's memory of those girls in Minor, Louisiana was as vivid as mine. I wanted to ask Mrs. J. Arthur Wilson if knowing exactly what girls liked to do, and how they did it, and even what they said afterward qualified them as friends.

"You ought to call Bubba," she said. "I know he'd love to talk to you."

"Yes'm, I thought about that," I said, and I had thought about it, but what I thought about it was that there was no way in hell that I would ever call Bubba Wilson.

"Bubba's finished law school, you know," Mrs. Wilson said. "Practices right here in Knoxtown. But he's out of town quite a lot. Up at the capital, mostly. I think he represents some companies that have an interest in the Legislature."

"Well!" I said, with more surprise in my voice than I intended. "I'm glad to know he's doing so well." I could see Bubba Wilson slapping backs and squeezing legs and blinking his eyes real slow around the Legislature. I guessed he'd be pretty good at it. "Well, Mrs. Wilson," I said, "I enjoyed talking to you. I just needed to know the name of that town."

"Minor," she said. "Minor, Louisiana. But I don't think Bubba has any connections there."

"No, ma'am, I suppose not. I just needed the name of the town."

"Minor," she said. "Minor, Louisiana. Are you taking good care of yourself, Bo?"

"Yes'm, I am," I said. "Well, I have to go now, Mrs. Wilson."

"Well, now, you take care, Bo. How are your parents doing?"

"They're doing great," I said. "Mother's expecting me to call any minute now," I outright lied to Mrs. J. Arthur Wilson, "so I guess I'd better go. Bye, Mrs. Wilson."

"Bye, bye," she said in the distance as her phone was already on the way to its cradle. After holding me on the phone for twice as long as I intended to be there, she had hung up before I did.

———◆———

Pollo's mind was on something else — himself. When I told him I wanted to try to find Mae Maude, he just shrugged his shoulders and then said, "I don't think they want me to stay here."

"Who?" I said. "If you mean the Klan, I'd say that's fairly obvious. But you can't let that stop you."

"I can't stand up to them if I have to watch my backside all the time. I have to have the support of my people. Else I can't make it." Pollo was more depressed than I had seen him since that day in the jail. "It's my own elders I'm talking about," he said. "My own elders."

"Come on. We've been through all that," I said. "They'll come around. What else can they do? They don't have a lot of options."

"The status quo is more than just an option for people without power. Look at Mr. DuBois," he said. "He's made it a long time just riding along with the way things are. He's not willing to risk anything in the hopes of things getting better."

"Because he doesn't really believe things will get any better," I said. "But you know damn well they can. And you know the system will only respond to demands. It's sure as hell not going to get better on its own."

"Yeah, but it can get a whole lot worse on its own. Mr. DuBois thinks I've cost the settlement a whole lot of progress by shutting down the payments from the sheriff."

Pollo's reception back to the settlement after his jail time had been cool, and remained that way. Mr. DuBois had met him at my mother's car and said, "Well, fancy pants. You made your point with the sheriff. Now he made his. Now what?"

"Now we take them to court," Pollo had said.

"Whose court you planning to take them to," Mr. DuBois asked, moving right up under his face and looking into his eyes, "somewhere in New York, maybe? Who you think runs the courts in this county right here? Same people that run the highway, boy. Same people that can shut down this high-way out here and shut off the trucks that carry our baskets and food to the people who are paying us for them. Same people that send the county nurse out here. Same people that can stop sending her out here, if they take a mind to. Same people that used to give us money at election time for things peo-ple really need. Do you understand what I'm telling you, boy? We get along by going along. Been doing that for a long time. It is not your job to upset all that."

"We have a right to all those things," Pollo said, "a right. My people don't have to depend on gifts."

"And while you're making that point, the gifts will stop. And your people will starve because you want to make a point. Maybe the first thing you ought to learn is that we're not your people. We were God's people before you got here, and we'll be God's people after you leave." He turned and began to sidle away. "In the meantime, you stick to preaching. That is," he shot a look back over his shoulder, "what God's people need from you."

So Pollo went back to preaching. And Mr. Samuel DuBois went back to managing the church and the store. And Sister Holy Ghost went back to tending the relationship between the sheriff and the settlement.

According to Pollo, Sister had come to his defense with the elders. But they were less interested in that than in the possibility someone might find a way to restore the sheriff's payments for the election. Because Pollo was opposed to the whole thing, he was excluded from the discussions about that matter.

"It's a corrupt system," I said to him. "There's no obligation to be honest about it. Why don't you just take the money and then let people vote however they want to vote? It's a secret ballot, you know. The sheriff will never know how any one person voted."

"Not exactly," he said. "Not out here. What they do is give us ballots that are already marked. We distribute those to people when they go to vote. They pick up their blank ballots at the polling place, put the pre-marked ballot in the box, and bring the blank one back to us as proof that they didn't cast some secret vote of their own. Then we turn those in to collect the money."

"But you could expose that with a good newspaper reporter."

"Right. And lose the money. And lose my church. Mr. DuBois has already said he's not going to 'explain things' to me again." Pollo was quiet for a minute, looking down at the ground. When he spoke again, it was without looking up. "They don't even trust us to mark the ballots ourselves," he said to the ground. "Probably don't think we're dishonest, just dumb."

On election night, I watched county officials tally the paper ballots at tables behind the truck at the Volunteer Fire Department in town. Results were posted by overhead projector on a big screen set up in the back of a pickup truck. When the unanimous votes went up from the precinct at the Rocks, I knew the elders had made their deal. There would be an emergency fund for the settlement. And Pollo would not administer it.

I tried to point out some positive things in Pollo's situation. There weren't many. But there was Gloria. Well, not Gloria exactly, but Gloria as illustrative of the young people Miss Templeton had taught and sent off to college, and those who had hopes of going off to college and were likely to find the status quo unacceptable. Gloria herself, ever since Pollo's beating and jailing, had treated him the way some people treat a woman who's been raped, like spoiled meat, as if he had let himself get beat up and done nothing about it. Stokely Carmichael, as she pointed out, had eluded the police until there were plenty of reporters around to publicize his arrest, and had remained conspicuously in jail, and expected to inflict more damage on his captors than they could ever inflict on him. In her mind, Pollo was a pathetic substitute.

But there were other young people in the settlement who saw in Pollo the first glimmer of possibility. I could see the adulation whenever they were around him. I thought he should concentrate on those kids. "Mr. Samuel DuBois is history," I argued.

"Well, his history is very much in charge of the present," Pollo said. "And he's got hold of my future."

"Only temporarily," I said. "These kids are the real future. Miss Templeton saw that." What I really thought was that their hero-worship would revive Pollo's crushed spirit, and that was at least a start.

For whatever reason, Pollo took my advice. He started an after-school Bible class for teenagers in his study at the church, and they gravitated to it as a sort of social center away from teachers and parents and elders. "Soldiers of Christ" was approved by Mr. DuBois as a perfectly acceptable name for the group — with a nod to his preacher's growing maturity in the role to which he had been called. "Onward Christian Soldiers" became the closing hymn at each meeting, a fine if unlikely theme song for the budding liberation theology testing the waters at the Rocks.

At Thanksgiving, the teenagers were joined by older students home from college, and the group outgrew the little study. With the approval of Mr. DuBois, Pollo opened Miss Templeton's abandoned house, and the group spent the holiday washing and dusting and sweeping and sawing and hammering — with an occasional rousing chorus of "Onward Christian Soldiers."

I heard the racket when I pulled up at the brick store on Saturday of Thanksgiving weekend, looking for Pollo.

"What's going on at Miss Templeton's?" I asked Mr. Samuel DuBois.

"Big doing's," he said.

"Uhm-m-hmm," from the men sitting around the stove.

"Young people working for Jesus," Mr. DuBois said.

"Uhm-hm," came the chorus. I thought it was unlikely, and the look on my face gave me away.

"Yes, they are," Mr. DuBois said. "Pollo has them. They've been studying the Bible every day. Now they're fixing up a place that can be a regular little seminary like we used to have, long time ago. Pollo wants a place where he can teach, and the children can study. And sing. And have Bible games and such. Place they can go after school and Saturdays."

"Uhm-m-hmm."

"When the chores are done, of course."

"Uhm-hm."

"Well, I think I'll go over," I said. "I was looking for Pollo."

"He'll be glad to see you."

The kudzu at Miss Templeton's house had been cut back to outline the front porch without engulfing it, and the steps had been sanded clean. Inside, people swung brooms and mops over what looked like freshly sanded hardwood floors. A group of youngsters crowded around an out-of-tune upright piano where somebody was pounding out a revival-style rendition of "What a Friend We Have in Jesus," complete with heavy bouncing bass and riffs wherever there was the slightest opportunity. I wondered if anybody else in the whole world had ever put one right after the very first word: "What" [a backhanded riff across the entire keyboard from left to right] "a friend we have in Je-" [ba-ba-ba-ba in the bass] "-sus!" The kid was surprisingly good, and the crowd obviously loved it, slapping themselves on the back and fake-swooning with every riff across the keyboard. A smaller squadron of teenagers was busy carrying bricks and boards, measuring against available wall space, apparently for a bookcase.

Pollo called to me from the back hall. He seemed genuinely glad to see me. "Bo Fisher! Come on back!" It was the most animation I'd heard in his voice since we were teenagers. He turned toward a crew installing screen wire on the back porch. "What do you think?" he said to me.

"What in the world is going on?" is what I said. But what I actually thought was that the plan to rebuild Pollo's spirits was working just fine.

"It's going to be a community center for young people," he said. "Like a rec hall or something. Or a combination of that and a library. Guess what we call it."

"The Ramblin' Wreck Hall?" I said. It was the best I could do in a hurry.

"Nope," he said. "The Oracle." He beamed, teeth from ear to ear.

"The Oracle? I don't get it."

"Come on. Think. Didn't I teach you anything about mythology?" He smiled even more broadly, but I didn't think it was funny. His spirits were so high he was on the edge of having the big-head. But in a way, that's how Pollo always was. "It's a place where the kids will come for the truth about the world and the meaning of it. That's what always happened in this house, anyway. And it's not something I can do at the church. And it's not something the kids will get at school, either. Everybody will leave me alone here." Just as they did with Miss Templeton, I thought.

"Where'd the screen wire come from?" I doubted the elders had authorized any of the election money for this project.

"Town," he said. "Sister Holy Ghost rounded up stuff from people. Your dad helped. Didn't you know that?" I didn't.

"Well, yeah," I said. "But I didn't know he could get screen wire. Who's playing the piano?"

"Zeb. Zebalon. He's the only one who can play like that."

"I don't remember anybody named Zeb," I said.

"He's younger than we are. Music was the only thing Miss Templeton could teach him. He dropped out of school and went into town. Became the town drunk. It's too bad there wasn't a night club or a bar or something where he could play." It was an odd thing for a preacher to regret.

"Hymn tunes go over great in a bar," I said.

"The way he plays them, they might have. But he can play anything. Anyway, he's been back out here since late summer, and we're trying to keep him away from town. And hooch. Now that we've got this place open, and with the piano and all, I think he might stay put."

"You should feel good about this place," I said.

"We've still got a lot of work to do," Pollo said. "Hard stuff. And we don't have what we need to get it done."

"Like what?"

"The roof, for one thing. It leaks all over the place. But we don't have shingles and roofing nails. Otherwise, we could probably fix it ourselves. The underpinnings are another thing. A lot of the wood pilings that the house sits on are rotten. That's why the floor sags in some places. It would take some heavy equipment to jack the floor up and replace the piers. We just don't have any money for that kind of stuff."

"Yeah," I said. But I was thinking this was surely a problem we could handle in town.

"It's okay," he said. "It'll hold for a while."

———————

Mother thought I was barking up the wrong tree, expecting our congregation to come up with money for a house that nobody was even going to live in. "If people were burned out," she said, "or thrown out, we could get some help. But a place for teenage foolishness? No, sir." But Dad saw what I was getting at. He was the one, after all, who had championed the camp, years before, and always pushed for budget money for young people's programs. Just the same, he acknowledged it would be a hard sell in our congregation. About a week after I returned to school, I got a letter from him.

"Dear Bo," it said. "I talked yesterday with Dr. Miles MacDonald (reminded me of old Miles Bigger out at the Crossroads!) in the Northern Presbyterians' foundation offices in Philadelphia. He was very interested in the community house at the Rocks and said there was some endowment that might be able to help. He wanted to know if Pollo could come up to meet with the board. I told him Pollo had no funds, and he said they could pay for the trip. They'll send enough for you to go with him. (I told him you were a good friend and could help to be sure nothing goes wrong with the trip.) Can you make it? They have an annual Christmas meeting coming up next week. The two of you would have to take the overnight train. He's wiring the money. I was pretty sure you could work it out to go along."

Nothing could have kept me from it.

And nothing could have been worse than that train ride. For one thing, the crowd on the train wasn't exactly friendly. Most of them were black, but there were a few whites who sat by themselves toward the front of the car. Nobody sat near us. They looked at us like we were freaks. Or Freedom Riders. Every time the train stopped for passengers, I worried that some Klansman might board and start a fight. But I couldn't see moving to a seat by myself, either. It was 1966, after all, not 1956. And we were headed north. I know Pollo thought about it, too. He even asked me whether I thought it was a good idea for one of us to be awake all the time, "just to watch our suitcases," he said. "Your mother will jerk a knot in our heads," he said, using the words of her explicit threat, "if we lose those things."

Turned out, neither of us could sleep much, anyway. The train didn't roll along toward Philadelphia. It jerked. And it stopped at every cowpath we came to, either to let somebody off or somebody on. Mother had packed some ham sandwiches and Oreo cookies to munch on through the night, but she used butter instead of mayonnaise on the sandwiches because she was afraid the mayonnaise would go bad before we could eat it, so by morning my mouth was a nasty mixture of ham, butter and Oreo chocolate. Pollo's, too. I had to tell him once to sit up straight because his head was falling over on my shoulder and his breath smelled bad.

I had been in the North a number of times, but it was a surprise, anyway, to see so many blacks and whites in the train station. A lot of them seemed to be talking to each other and maybe going to some place together. There was a saying at home that in the North, whites said to black people: "Rise as high as you want to, but don't come any closer," while people in the South said: "Come as close as you want to, but don't rise any higher." Dad always said that the bad part of the Southern attitude would be easier to correct than the bad part of the Northern attitude, and that we'd be more likely to get it right eventually. Just the same, they seemed to be getting pretty close to each other in the Philadelphia train station. Some of the blacks had on suits and ties, and some of the whites wore shabby coats and broken down shoes and looked like they hadn't shaved in a while.

I was about as liberal as anybody could be on the subject of integration, but I found myself surprised all the time by unexpected circumstances. When I went to brush my teeth in the train station, it was the first time in my life that I had been in a rest room with black people who were strangers. I was surprised that I noticed. And disappointed in myself. But when I had to choose to stand behind either a black person or a white one waiting for a sink and then follow one of them, using the same sink to brush my teeth, I flinched. I probably blushed. I was really embarrassed at my reaction, even if it was only superficially racist. So I walked around for a minute or two until there were a couple of sinks open and then went to the one where a white guy had been, as if I hadn't noticed who had been there. I actually wouldn't have hesitated a minute to follow Pollo, but with strangers, it seemed different. Anyway, with our teeth brushed and my hair combed and Pollo's puffed and our clothes totally wrinkled, we went out and took a taxi to Dr. Mac-Donald's office.

———

The foundation and the archives of the UPCUSA — United Presbyterian Church in the United States of America, the awkward name of the Northern Presbyterians — were housed in a mansion that had been turned into offices. There was a man at the front desk, rather than a woman, as if to prove immediately that this really was a different country. He looked like a squirrel in a green visor, nervously gathering papers from the top of his desk and stacking them in neat little piles. He looked at us and said to me, "Well, you must be Bofisherr. 'Sthisyerr friend?" He spoke so fast, I almost didn't get his question. And, like a lot of Yankees, he was strong on consonants and not so good with vowels. He was looking at Pollo with his lips pursed and his head cocked to one side.

"Yes," I said rather suddenly. And proudly. "Yes, it is my friend." Pollo's stern look at me prompted the right name just in time. "This is Paul Templeton," I said.

"Reverend Paul Templeton, isn't it?" the Squirrel said.

"Yes," Pollo said, sticking out his hand. "How do you do?"

"Oh, I'm fine," said the Squirrel, smiling, "very fine. And I hope you are, too." He took Pollo's outstretched hand in both of his, turning it back and forth as if he were considering the best way to crack it open. "We've been so looking forward to your visit." ("Farrd t'yerr visit" is what that sounded like.) "Did you have a good trip up from the South?" the Squirrel said to Pollo, speaking slowly now and more loudly, as if maybe I had just introduced him to an exchange student who spoke Swahili as his native tongue. Pollo just looked at him. I think the accent was maybe more of a problem for him than for me.

"Not such a great trip," I said. "We look pretty scruffy. Is there a place where we could change clothes?"

The Squirrel, who evidently saw no reason to give us his name, directed us to a small apartment that was generally reserved for missionaries home on furlough and would be home for Pollo and me while we were in Philadelphia. It was just a bedroom with a sitting area and a bathroom, like a very nice hotel room. We took turns showering and shaving and then dressed for our meeting with Dr. MacDonald. Mother had given us both a little lecture about the appropriate clothes to wear to a meeting in Philadelphia. She had embarrassed me by asking Pollo if he had a suit.

It occurred to me that the apartment was just like being in the cabin again back at camp, which was the last time I had been that intimate with a black person, but I didn't mention it because I didn't want Pollo to think I thought there was anything unusual about it. I couldn't help noticing that he had changed considerably — no longer the tall, skinny kid I remembered, but now filled out into a very impressive, slender but solid-muscled man. His coloring, even in December when my summer tan was almost gone, made him look like the picture of vigor and health. "Sleek," I thought as he stepped out of the shower, and I smiled as soon as I thought it.

Pollo put on his dress shirt with gold-looking cuff links and a gold collar tab that made his tie stand out from his neck. He even had a bright hand-kerchief for the coat pocket of his pin-striped double-breasted suit. He made me look a little tired in my blazer and Bass Weejuns, but I thought I was probably more correct for Philadelphia. Mother, of course, would have sided with him. Pollo spent a long time in front of the mirror, adjusting his tie and puffing up his hair so that it was perfectly round. He never asked me how I thought he looked. When we were both presentable, we went back to the front desk.

"Well," the Squirrel said, "you look very nice. I'll call Dr. MacDonald."

Dr. MacDonald was shabby. And bent over. He looked like an Elder Squirrel who was perhaps training the younger one at the front desk. Without straightening up, Dr. MacDonald looked at Pollo with obvious admiration. Too obvious, I thought. "Ah," he said, turning to me, "you must be Bofisherr." It was hard to know whether he thought I "must be Bo Fisher" or "must be Bo, for sure." It always interested me that Southern accents are reproduced phonetically in books and newspapers as dialect, as if we were speaking something other than the written language, while New Yorkers and Philadelphians and Chicagoans, even though their speech patterns are just as distinctive, are rendered in print as perfect standard English. It would have been just as reasonable, I always thought, to render Southern accents with correct standard spelling and put the various Northern accents in dialect. But it never happens.

Dr. MacDonald, in any event, was only the second person we had met in Philadelphia, but he was also the second one in a row to guess that I "must be Bofisherr." It seemed to me just as obvious that Pollo "must be" Paul Templeton, but I suppose they thought it inappropriate in Philadelphia to make that assumption based on a guy being black. They probably guessed — and maybe correctly — that I would be less offended by a greeting based on being white.

"Yes, I am Bo Fisher," I said. "And this is my friend, Paul Templeton." The Younger Squirrel shook his head knowingly. Dr. MacDonald took Pollo's outstretched hand, smiling up at him broadly, and bent over even more, as if he were greeting the new king of the forest. Pollo stood ramrod straight, even leaning back a little. It looked like he thought he deserved the homage or maybe that he was just wary of what the old man might do next. But the Elder Squirrel just nodded some secret message to the younger one, then stepped back and motioned Pollo and me into his office.

Dr. MacDonald's office was an orderly clutter of books and papers. There were so many neat stacks of things on his desk, on the floor, on cabinets, and on chairs that I wondered how there could possibly be that many different categories to put things into. The number of stacks suggested that maybe they were just randomly placed and then compulsively neatened.

"Here," Dr. MacDonald said as he took a pile of yellowed pages from one of the chairs in front of his desk and started toward a long table in the corner of the room, "I'll put Dr. Van Deusen over here in the nineteenth century where he belongs." Nothing random about it, apparently. "Please sit down."

Dr. MacDonald sat on the other side of his desk from us in a cane-bottomed swivel chair that lifted his feet off the floor and made him look like he had found a good place to perch. He leaned over with his elbows on the desk, resting his chin on his tented fingertips. I wondered if maybe he was about to pray. But he just gazed at Pollo and smiled.

"We're so very happy to have you here," he said. "You remind us of a young man from the Rocks who came up here many years ago." He paused, still smiling at Pollo as if he might be waiting for a response. Pollo glanced quickly at me, but I had no clue to offer as to where this line of conversation was going. "Perhaps you know him," Dr. MacDonald said. "Sam, his name was. How is he?"

"Sam?" Pollo said.

"DuBose, I think," said Dr. MacDonald. "Sam DuBose. He came up here after the great fire at Centennial Academy." The phrase came out as "'fterrthfie-errr," but the reference was clear.

"DuBois, you mean," Pollo said. "Mr. DuBois. He's fine. Still fit as a fiddle. Still runs our church; he's the Clerk of Session. And he still runs the store we operate for the community. He's very much in favor of our project." It was a nice effort at turning the conversation to our subject, but it didn't work.

"He didn't run anything, of course, when he came up," Dr. MacDonald said. "He was really just a young man. We brought him up, ostensibly to report on the fire but really to protect him, and he stayed for a year or two. Lived with a family..." he said, leaning back in his chair with his eyes closed and pursing his lips, apparently rummaging through stacks of stuff in his mind. "Harrisons, I think, or Hendersons," he said. "They were members of Third Church. Great friends of the Kirkpatricks who, as you know, have always," he said, opening his eyes again and smiling at Pollo, "had such an interest in Centennial. You attended Centennial, did you not?"

"Yes, sir," Pollo said, ignoring the impossibility of answering a question turned in on itself with an inverted negative. "Until they closed it," he added. "Great shame," Dr. MacDonald said. "Great shame."

"When exactly was the fire?" I said. "I don't know anything about it."

"Oh, it was a very long time ago," Dr. MacDonald said. "Do you know Sam?"

"Samuel," I said. "Yes. Mr. Samuel DuBois. But what did he have to do with the fire?"

"You would have to ask him that question," Dr. MacDonald said. "I was just an assistant at that time. I didn't actually attend the meetings of the trustees then. So I'm not entirely familiar with the report. But I picked up Sam — Mr. DuBois as you call him, although I'm certain DuBose was his name — I picked him up at the train station and brought him here. And then took him to the Hendersons, or Harrisons or whoever they were, and sometimes took him messages from home. Since we were nearly the same age, I was responsible for rounding up a set of clothes for him from my friends. He was a very nice young man. Very smart. After he left, we lost touch until the trustees sent the nurse down there to look after people in the smallpox epidemic. She stayed on at the Rocks, and I kept up with Sam for a while through her."

"The nurse?" I said. "Miss Templeton?" I looked at Pollo in surprise and found him gazing back at me with the look of someone who has done his homework and is waiting impatiently for another kid to solve the problem to which he already knows the answer. "Did you know that?" I said.

"Of course," Pollo said. "That's why Dr. MacDonald is interested in the Delphine Templeton Community Center." Although I knew the reason for our trip, the Templeton Center was news to me as a name, and I decided to butt out of the conversation. I'd thought I was the one who set up this meeting — or at least my father had — and that I was there as Pollo's guide, but he and the Squirrels obviously shared some connection that excluded me. I simply looked back at Dr. MacDonald.

"The trustees," he said. "It's the trustees who have an interest in the center. They have always been very proud of the work Miss Templeton did." He turned to Pollo. "You know we're having dinner with them tonight."

"Yes, sir," Pollo said.

"Do you have dinner clothes?"

"Just these."

"Well, we can fix that. Dickinson has already called down to the tailor's. They have tuxedos for rental now. It's a new day, you know. Not everyone has his own. No stigma to renting one." I wanted to tell him that I actually had my own tuxedo at home, but I didn't want to embarrass Pollo. I also wasn't sure I could still wear mine after five or six years, but I wasn't sure that made any difference in this situation of just wanting the Philadelphia Squirrels to know that I was not some country bumpkin who did not have his own tuxedo. I really wanted to ask if he expected people to travel with their tuxedos in 1966 if nobody told them they were going to a formal dinner. As it was, I couldn't think of a good way to say any of that before Dr. MacDonald added, "We'll take care of the expense, of course. You'll just have to go along with Dickinson to get measured." So the Younger Squirrel's name was Dickinson. Too bad. I would have bet money on Nutley.

Instead of leading us to the tailor's place, Nutley took us back to the missionaries' apartment and measured us himself. Had his own tape measure, for some reason. It was a little weird having somebody like that get intimate with the inseam, but it was more convenient than going to the tailor. Nutley called in the measurements by telephone, and the proper outfits were delivered to us in less than an hour.

———

"Philadelphia is wonderful," Pollo said as we were dressing, but I wasn't sure he was really thinking about Philadelphia. He couldn't pull himself away from the mirror, and the truth is he looked great in his tuxedo. In fact, he looked taller and bigger in general. The tux changed the whole impact of his Afro, making it look almost like some kind of top hat — or ermine crown. Elegant is probably the right word for his appearance. It was at least that, and maybe close to regal. I thought he would knock these Philadelphians out. There was no way, I thought, they could possibly deny him the money he had come for. We waited in the apartment until 7:00 as instructed, then went to the front door of the Historical Society building to meet Nutley. He was standing beside a long black Cadillac limousine, talking across the top of the car to a uniformed driver on the other side. "It's the Kirkpatricks' car," he said to us. "They sent it for you."

Pollo and I sat quietly in the back seat, facing Dickinson and trying to look like we did this just as often as he did. We did not look at each other, but I'd love to have known what was going through Pollo's mind as we pulled through an ornate gate into a long drive, circled a fountain, and stopped in front of a modest door. The house was huge. Had they built it with the same porch-to-dwelling ratio we use in the South, it would've had two dozen columns across the front. It briefly crossed my mind that we had been brought to the servants' entrance, but then a servant stepped up to the car to open Pollo's door. I wasn't surprised he wore a tuxedo, but I was surprised he was white. That would have been regarded at home as the height of pretentiousness, a total misfit for a house with no columns. Pollo got out but stood stone cold still beside the car, looking up at the house. I had to push him aside to get out.

"Looks like a dormitory," he said under his breath. Then he took a deep breath and stuck out his hand to the man who had opened the car door. "Mr. Kirkpatrick?" he said.

"He's on his way," the man said with the slightest smile.

Another white man, a man about my father's age and also wearing a tuxedo like the man who had opened the car door for us, came out through the door of the house and extended his hand to Pollo. Neither of us made any move toward him.

"Reverend Templeton," the second man said, approaching in full stride.

"Mr. Kirkpatrick," the first man said, still holding the car door.

"Mr. Kirkpatrick," Pollo said, a little too loudly to the advancing man as he took his hand. "Mr. Kirkpatrick," Pollo said to me, smiling. "This is Mr. Kirkpatrick," he said again as if I might be having trouble understanding that this "must be" Mr. Kirkpatrick.

Before I could report that conclusion, Mr. Kirkpatrick turned to me and said the inevitable, "And you must be Bofisherr." The doorman looked at me, smiling, and nodded in agreement, as if I had just been granted a title of nobility by the local lord.

I was getting used to all the consonants, like picking up a foreign language when it's necessary. I was a little proud. "I am Bo Fisher," I said, accenting it properly in hopes they might all begin to get it right.

It was a mystery to me why anybody would want to take a perfectly rich and melodious language and give it such monotonously hard edges. A simple phrase like "Good morning" from the lips of a woman in, say, the Lowcountry of South Carolina will take on the shape of a palm frond slowly rolling on the upward drafts of a gentle breeze, showing first its firm thrust and then turning up to reveal its soft and silvery curving underside. Like any other work of art, it permits a wide range of interpretations; it invites an unforeseen response to provide a meaningful aesthetic and personal context. The same phrase from a New Yorker or Philadelphian, if offered at all, will take the shape and character of an old clock's inner gearing, quick-grinding a grudging single second of squandered time. It does not invite a response.

"Nice to see you, Dickinson," Mr. Kirkpatrick said to Nutley, who had climbed out of the car and stood behind Pollo and me. The Squirrel could have helped with introductions, but he just stood there smiling and rubbing his little hands together.

Mr. Kirkpatrick took Pollo by the shoulder and started back into the house. I looked at the doorman, and he nodded again and held out his hand to indicate that I should follow Mr. Kirkpatrick. Then he and Dickinson went off toward the far end of the house. Another doorman waited for our coats. I noticed his tuxedo had brass buttons, or gold, unlike the black buttons on ours and Mr. Kirkpatrick's — a lot more subtle distinction than we would make in the South in a similar situation. In Philadelphia, the buttons on the tuxedo were the only way anybody could tell that the doorman was not actually a member of the family. Or that Pollo was not the doorman. Pollo had apparently caught on to the system and did not speak to the man, but I said "Hey" to him as I went past, just to watch him smile in surprise.

"Good evening," he said pleasantly.

"We've been looking forward to your visit," Mr. Kirkpatrick was saying to Pollo. "There are some people in the study that I want you to meet before we go in to dinner with the trustees. It's a bit of a show in there; you'll feel more comfortable if you've met the family first. We want you to feel quite at home."

There was very little chance that either of us would feel at home here. I wondered if Pollo remembered Edgar Rice Burrough's description of Tarzan's ancestral home in England. This could have been its duplicate. The study was a dream: walnut paneling, leather easy chairs, bookcases reaching up so high there was a ladder on rollers to access the top shelves, a fireplace with a roaring fire, and two beautiful girls that turned out to be Kirkpatrick's daughters.

"Margaret," he said to one who looked about our age, "this is Reverend Templeton."

"Please," said Pollo, extending his hand to her. "I'm Paul. And I'm very happy to meet you." Margaret took his hand but said nothing.

"And this is Emily," Mr. Kirkpatrick said, motioning to a younger woman who wore a simple shift dress with black boots in contrast to her sister's gown.

"Hello, Paul," said Emily. She stuck out her hand a little stiffly but very deliberately, the way a woman might think a man would do it, and smiled up at Pollo.

"And this," said Mr. Kirkpatrick, "is Bo Fisher. He came up with Reverend Templeton on the train." I can't remember now whether he had actually adjusted his pronunciation or whether my ears had just begun to accommodate it. But I do remember the first touch of Emily.

"It's an awful ride, isn't it?" she said, extending her hand to me in the same stiff way she'd greeted Pollo. Her grip was firm and confident, but her hand felt smooth, as if she were wearing invisible silky gloves. "Welcome to Philadelphia."

"Thanks," I said. "It's nice to be here. And to come to such a wonderful house."

"Hello," said Margaret. She could speak, after all. "It's nice to have you both here," she said to me.

"Glass of sherry, Reverend Templeton?" asked Mr. Kirkpatrick. Pollo nodded in assent, and Emily poured one for him as Mr. Kirkpatrick retrieved his own highball scotch, judging by the open bottle beside the wine decanter. It looked to me as if the sherry must have been a ministerial deference, rather than the sign of a limited bar list, and so I answered with "bourbon and water, please," when asked. I needed something stronger than sherry.

"Bourbon," Mr. Kirkpatrick said with some surprise in his voice and then smiled. "Of course." He went to a tall cabinet and unlocked the door. "Bourbon," he said again as he ran his hand across the labels of a couple dozen bottles. "Good." he said, "we have it right here," as if it should be a surprise to find bourbon in a liquor cabinet. At home, it would have been a surprise to find anything else. Well, not at my home, where there was no liquor cabinet at all, but at any home that had one.

Margaret took her place beside Pollo, not saying anything but looking up at him as she sipped her sherry, so I turned to Emily, who was looking from her father to me and hiding a smile behind her fingertips.

"You mentioned the train ride," I said to her. "Have you ridden that train up from the South?"

"Too many times," she said. "I go to Duke." She said it the way the British do, "Diuke." And she said it with just the slightest lilt.

"Really," I said. "What are you studying?" I was hoping for history.

"Greek," her father said. "Or Greeks. As in Sigma Chi and Beta Theta Pi." He laughed and gulped down the last swallow of his drink.

"Daddy," Emily protested. "Well," she said, her head tilted and a little pout on her face, "I do have a good time." She smiled, and I smiled back at her. "I love it down there. But fraternities and sororities are just part of it. There's a lot going on at Duke. I'm only a sophomore, so I'm still learning about a lot of it." She sipped from her glass of sherry, looking at me with big eyes over the top of the glass. I had seen that look a hundred times from girls at home but had not expected to encounter it in Philadelphia. I bet Emily fit in well back home — a kind of Southern Belle with consonants. I wanted to keep her talking, more to look at her than to listen.

"Margaret graduated from Mount Holyoke," Mr. Kirkpatrick said before I could tell Emily I went to Duke, too. He turned to Pollo. "I believe your school is Johnson C. Smith," he said. "We've had a connection with the university for years through the foundation and our church." They talked for a while about the state of the university and its seminary. Pollo explained that he had started out at Centennial, which Mr. Kirkpatrick seemed to know, and that he had transferred to Smith because Centennial had been closed, which Mr. Kirkpatrick thought was "a great shame, a great shame." He said, "We supported Centennial for a long time, but there came a point at which the program just could not be sustained." Nobody asked me where I went to school.

Margaret had sat down in one of the leather chairs while Pollo and her father were talking; Emily sat side-saddle on the arm of the sofa. They both stood up again when Mr. Kirkpatrick announced, "Here comes Mother." Mrs. Kirkpatrick glided into the room, the flashing silver points of her shoes under her long skirt providing the only evidence of mechanical effort in her movement.

"Brad," she said to Mr. Kirkpatrick, "everything is ready. They're waiting for us in the dining room." Mr. Kirkpatrick made the necessary introductions, and Mrs. Kirkpatrick made the necessary arrangements. "Margaret, you take Mr. Fisher; I'll go in with Reverend Templeton." She stepped toward Pollo, and he put out his arm for her as if he had done this a hundred times. "Emily can come with Father," she added.

We formed a little processional: Mr. Kirkpatrick and Emily in the lead, Margaret and I following. Mrs. Kirkpatrick was talking so softly to Pollo that

I could not hear what she was saying, and they did not move when we started across the foyer. When we stopped at the door of the dining room, I looked back and saw them still standing in the study. They made a striking couple, she looking up at Pollo, her face flooded by the light of the chandelier, and Pollo basking comfortably in the brilliance of the Kirkpatrick sun.

The front end of our little parade entered the dining room without any notice from the trustees and their wives, gathered in their tuxedos and evening gowns around the longest dining room table I had ever seen — or have yet seen. But heads turned and conversation stopped as Mrs. Kirkpatrick and Pollo appeared in the doorway. Mr. Kirkpatrick clapped his hands twice and announced, "Ladies and gentlemen, may I present our special guest, Reverend Paul Templeton, about whom you have already heard and from whom you will hear directly a little later in the evening." The trustees applauded. Pollo bowed slightly, as if this were the most normal thing in the world, escorted Mrs. Kirkpatrick to her place at the head of the table, and stood behind the chair she indicated to her right. It was hard not to be proud of him.

"And this," Mr. Kirkpatrick said with a gesture in my direction, "is Bo Fisher. Some of you will remember his father from our site visit to Centennial College some years ago." Several trustees said "Hello" as Mr. Kirkpatrick was saying "Please be seated." It wasn't much of a welcome, but at least I had some connection to this affair other than through Pollo, even though I had no idea what connection my father had to their Centennial site visit.

Huge arrangements of Christmas-red gladiolas divided the long table into sub-cultures, so that I spent the evening with those people seated directly around me and in between two of the massive flower arrangements. We were six: Margaret and Emily; a Miss Mills, who was introduced to me as the longtime secretary of the Kirkpatrick Foundation; Dr. MacDonald and Dickinson, and myself.

Miss Mills nodded to me from across the table. She was a slight woman, a little wrinkled, with gray hair that fell in uneven wisps from the top of her head in a short modern chop that might have looked wonderful on a young blonde. Miss Mills kept her lips pursed — so pursed that her whole body appeared pursed. I suspected that her legs, at least, were pursed primly beneath the table; she gave the impression that she was engaged in some serious, albeit pleasant, effort to keep lips and legs properly and politely together. Still, there was the tiniest furtive smile playing at her mouth, alerting a careful observer to the possibility that it might overtake her best intentions at some unexpected moment, forcing her into a broad and disastrous smile, leading her legs to relax and part in the midst of dinner. I thought it unlikely that she could manage much conversation without risking the loss of critical leg control.

Our little group appeared to be staff and onlookers for the banquet, lucky not to have been seated at a separate table. I could not see Pollo at all, and Mrs. Kirkpatrick only when she sat up straight or leaned to her left. When she leaned toward Pollo, I lost her behind the gladiolas.

But the flowers holding our small group captive gave me an opportunity to concentrate on the Sisters Kirkpatrick. I had difficulty getting any response other than a smile out of Miss Mount Holyoke, who was seated between Dickinson and me, but Emily seemed interested across the table when I mentioned to Dr. MacDonald (with a glance to be sure she was listening) that I was a student in the graduate school at Duke. Emily had not met any graduate students, she said. She did not know where graduate students lived. She did not, in fact, know much geography around Durham other than the East Campus, which housed the Duke University Woman's College. And she knew, of course, the Gothic West Campus for men several miles away, which housed the indoor stadium where she cheered for the Blue Devil basketball team — and which also housed the Greek fraternities where she partied, after games or just in general.

Emily was disappointed in one aspect of her experience at Duke which she hadn't been able to overcome with Yankee ingenuity: she had met few Southerners. "I know they're there," she said, "but they're not Betas or Nu's." Most of her friends were from Philadelphia or New York, although she had run into students from New Jersey everywhere she went on campus. She guessed that the Southerners on campus grouped together and distanced themselves from others because, she said, "they hate Yankees, you know." She delivered all that information after I said that I was a student in the graduate school at Duke and before I could say another word. At the description of herself as a hated Yankee, she rolled her eyes and paused in her peroration.

"We don't hate all Yankees," I said. I'm sure I flinched at saying the word. Like "nigger," "Yankee" was a word my mother taught us not to say, on the principle that it was offensive. As a kid, I became a fan of the Brooklyn Dodgers in order to avoid that word. I knew better now, knew that people in the North even called themselves Yankees, knew that "Yankee ingenuity" was not just another slur — or at least it wasn't taken that way. I just couldn't stop the trained flinch.

"At least," I joked, "we don't all hate all Yankees." Nobody smiled, except for Miss Mills, who couldn't seem to help it. "And it's hard to find enough Southerners at Duke (I said "Dook" deliberately) to group with. I think I know every one of them. So I could easily introduce you to some." No smiles anywhere in the group, other than the one still sneaking up on Miss Mills' pursed lips. I had no idea what was wrong with this line of conversation, unless maybe they didn't like being called Yankees by a Southerner. I took a desperation shot. "I know they'd like you," I said to Emily. She smiled. I studied the plate that a tuxedoed waiter had set before me and withdrew from the conversation. Dr. MacDonald picked it up with a question to Margaret about the girls' prep school where she was teaching, and the talk went off down that track.

The waiter was black. All the waiters were black. And all the doormen we had seen were white — apparently some color-coding of the household staff for clarity of command. I wondered if Pollo noticed. Although I could not see him or Mrs. Kirkpatrick on the other side of the flower arrangement, I could hear their voices.

"I've been in the South many times," Mrs. Kirkpatrick was saying. "We often winter in Florida."

"I don't think many Southerners go there," Pollo said. Good for him. I hoped she got the point that Florida is not the South. And he could have added that "winter" is a verb only for birds.

"It's wonderful," she said. "Always nice and warm. Are the winters warm where you live?" They went on talking about the weather, and I tuned out. "Is that not so, Mr. Fisher?" Dr. MacDonald asked. I had no idea what the subject was, but I was tired of inverted questions that assumed concurrence with whatever point had just been made.

"No," I said perversely, "that is so." I smiled. Miss Mills' face lit up in a twinkling grin, perhaps from having contended with those inverted questions throughout her long career with Dr. MacDonald, and I could have sworn that the tablecloth rustled provocatively above her lap. Everybody else in our little group stared at me blankly. They — or maybe the long trip or the tension of being out of my natural habitat — had hooked a very snotty aspect of my personality. I realized I wasn't going to get through the evening unless I could shape up. "I'm sorry," I said. "It was just a little joke. Very little." Emily smiled; the others did not, but at least they looked away, at each other or at their food. "I'm afraid my mind wandered," I said to Dr. MacDonald. "What is it that you were asking me?"

"About Centennial," he said. "Is it not true that most of the students there transferred to Johnson C. Smith when the college closed?"

"I don't really know," I said. "To tell the truth, I didn't even know it had closed. I went to a conference there once when I was a freshman in college. It seemed like a pretty lively place."

"It revived wonderfully after the fire," Dr. MacDonald said. The phrase came out as " 'fterrthfie-errr" again.

"I didn't know anything about the fire, either," I said, taking pains to pronounce it correctly. "I'd love to hear more about it."

"It isn't appropriate dinner conversation," Dr. MacDonald said.

Emily spoke up before I could say anything else. And just as well, because I had no idea what to say to that. "You went to a conference at Centennial?" she asked.

"Yes," I said.

"I'd love to go to a conference at a black college," Emily said just as Margaret spoke up: "Is that where you met Reverend Templeton?"

"Poll — Paul?" I said. "No. I suppose he might have been there at the time, but I didn't know it." It had not even occurred to me as a possibility until that very moment. "I knew him a long time ago, when we were young, but we hadn't seen each other for years until just recently."

"I think it's wonderful that you take an interest in him," Emily said. She glanced at Pollo, who was on her side of the table about three seats away, then leaned toward me and continued softly, "In fact, I don't know a single black person. I would love to, but no black people live in this part of Philadelphia. And I haven't met even one at Duke."

"Well, I know a few of them on campus," I said. "I could introduce you to them." I wanted to ask her who cleaned her room or did her laundry or served her plate in the cafeteria. Those people were certain to have been black, like those who were serving at dinner in her own home, but I presumed that she was not used to thinking of them as black people. Or maybe not as people at all. Still, I knew that she really was talking about students. I could not imagine what they would make of her, but I could certainly introduce her.

"Would you?" she said. "I think that would be wonderful."

There was a pause, because the obligatory "Oh, it's nothing," seemed inappropriate.

"Do you think," she said, leaning toward me and lowering her voice, "that he would come speak to my sorority?" She glanced again at Pollo.

"Why?" I said.

"We're very interested in black people," she said, and I thought she blushed just a little. "I mean," she added, "in civil rights. We even thought about asking a black girl to become a sister. There's one that we heard might run for Homecoming Queen, and we thought she would probably be good to ask, but nobody knows her. Anyway, we want to be more involved. Maybe he would talk to us about what we might do to help."

"He might," I said. "I don't think he's ever been to Duke."

"We really have a great group of girls. Last month, we canceled our Christmas dance at the country club because they don't allow any black members. The student council is thinking about a rule against places like that, too. He might be surprised at how supportive the campus is."

"Well, yes, I bet he would be. I'll ask him." I caught myself thinking how hard it would be to recruit these Yankee ingenues for a Freedom Ride. Just the same, Emily herself seemed genuine in her interest.

"Perhaps you could take Emily down to see the project at the Rocks," said Dr. MacDonald. "We ought to have someone from here take a look."

"I'd be glad to," I said. "I'm sure my mother would be happy to invite her to stay at our home." I was at least sure of that. Emily just smiled.

The conversation drifted off to things Philadelphian, and I concentrated on the plates being delivered by the tuxedoed crew. I noticed that no one else said "Thank you" for what was put before them or for the dirty dishes removed by white-gloved hands, so I began saying it louder and louder. The waiters smiled, but it was hard to tell whether they were happy about my courtesy or laughing at it. Other than a few glances, maybe to see what I was being served that made me so grateful, no one else reacted in any way.

Emily's idea of bringing Pollo to Duke was a good one. I could see myself giving him a tour of the campus, surrounded by granite walls and towers, and it would be like we were looking for the right ledge in a huge quarry. I could see Pollo swinging on a vine from one of the turrets. I could see Mae Maude with us. I looked at Emily; she had definite possibilities as a substitute for Mae Maude, although it was interesting that I hadn't thought of it until I thought of Mae Maude. Emily might even be better than Mae Maude. I had no idea, for one thing, what Mae Maude might look like after so many years. Frankly, I was afraid to find out. I had the name of the town in which to start looking for her, and for weeks now, I'd let it slip from my mind. I thought of Bubba's grandmother saying how Bubba didn't have any connections there anymore. Maybe I didn't either. Mae Maude sure hadn't come looking for me.

But I knew Mrs. J. Arthur Wilson, arbiter of taste in Knoxtown and its contiguous counties, would be proud to see me sitting in a tuxedo at the great table in the Kirkpatricks' mansion. It was exactly the kind of place she would imagine Bubba frequenting in the capital city. And the Kirkpatricks were, I thought, exactly her kind of people, just with an opposing point of view.

From the other side of the gladiolas, I heard the word "redneck" and perked up my ears. Mrs. Kirkpatrick was leaning toward Pollo, so that I could not see her face behind the flower barrier, and she was "appalled" by the "ignorant rednecks" she'd seen on her trips to the South. She didn't explain how she came to conclude they were ignorant — most likely a geographic guess on her part. "I would be ashamed if there were people like that in Philadelphia," she said. I wondered if she had been to the train station. "It leads one to think ill of all white people in the South."

"They are ignorant," Pollo answered, not clarifying that he didn't mean all of us. "They're trapped by their own history and ignorance. The South is a violent, ignorant place." I felt my face begin to flush. I thought if I heard "ignorant" one more time, I would stick my arm through the gladiolas and grab the Reverend Mr. Templeton by the throat. "We have to deal with the rednecks all the time," he continued. Then the doorman announced that dessert and champagne would be served in the music room, and Pollo's next words were lost in the rustle of feet and pleasant chatter toward the door.

I felt a tug at my sleeve. Miss Mills took my arm as if it had been offered. I smiled at her.

"I like you," she said. "You're feisty." That attribute is not always positive, but her squeeze on my arm was reassuring, and I was glad to find any affection at all in the room. It occurred to me that the vote on me now stood at one "for" and some unknown but large number "against." I fervently hoped that Emily could be recorded as an abstention, at worst.

Thanks seemed inappropriate, so I patted Miss Mills's hand on my arm and said, "It's nice to get to know you, Miss Mills. I'd love to know more about your work at the foundation."

"Drop by to see me tomorrow," she said. "I'll tell you about the fire." She deliberately said the word the way I had pronounced it and smiled at me again. Then, with another gentle squeeze on my arm, she slipped away.

Chapter Eight

———◆———

PLAYING WITH FIRE

We settled into the chairs before the fireplace in the music room. Dessert was served, and a waiter made rounds with glasses of champagne on a silver tray. Then Mr. Kirkpatrick stood and introduced Pollo again, describing him as a sort of "Moses for his people," intent on bringing them out of the wilderness of poverty and ignorance and into the light of education and achievement. Mr. Kirkpatrick concurred with the opinion he ascribed to Pollo, that "those people" could be as smart as anybody, and he was glad to find somebody — especially "one of their own" — willing to take up the task of deliverance. He noted, too, the risk inherent in the role of such leadership, "Southerners being so notoriously violent in their resistance to even the most basic of civil liberties that we take for granted in Philadelphia but that are denied to Negroes all across the South."

Not all Southerners, I wanted to say, and I wondered why my very presence in that room did not make an adequate statement of that fact. Had Mr. Kirkpatrick looked at me, he would have seen the grimace on my face, but he was busy making eye contact with the trustees. I briefly considered throwing my champagne at him to make my point. "They are apparently unwilling," he continued, "to honestly face the guilt they bear in this matter." Guilt! "And ignorance," he concluded, ignoring the fact that he had just split a goddam infinitive, "can be intimidating."

"But it's not always intimidating," Mr. Kirkpatrick said with a smile. "I heard just this morning of a white Southerner — no offense, Bo — who was stopped for speeding on the turnpike. When the patrolman said to him, 'Do you have any I.D.?' the Southerner looked at him quizzically and said, 'About what?'" My self-consciousness turned to embarrassment and then to humiliation in the applause and laughter that followed. "Get it?" he asked, as if they might not have known why they were laughing. "I.D.," he said. "That's the way they pronounce 'idea.'"

No one even glanced in my direction — for which I was grateful, because I was blushing again. But then I was irritated. They seemed not to care whether I thought it was funny, or even that I was there at all. "Well," said Mr. Kirkpatrick, raising his glass of champagne to Pollo, "I give you a far better representative of that poor region, the Reverend Paul Templeton."

Pollo did not look at me either. Instead, he looked directly at Mr. Kirkpatrick. It crossed my mind that he might do the honorable thing and wring the neck of our elegant host, but he only stuck out his hand and said, "Thank you." The group around me applauded, as patron and parson posed hand in hand, the picture of thralldom, although it was risky to guess this early in the relationship which of them was liege and which of them, thrall. I felt certain that every one of the trustees would've bet on the wrong man. As the applause subsided, Pollo turned to the group, in his most serious demeanor, almost glowering, and said, "You have no I.D.," then flashed that gorgeous smile that I had seen a hundred times, ten years before, and not at all recently, "No I.D. at all, how glad I am to be here." Laughter and applause erupted.

Pollo held out his hands for quiet, and perfectly respectable trustees looked up at him with the wonderment I'd seen on Mae Maude's face at the quarry ledge. Pollo must have recognized it, too. He stretched himself an additional inch or two and threw out his chest as if he expected someone — Margaret Kirkpatrick, perhaps, or maybe the venerable and pursed-legged Miss Mills to begin splicing clover chains around his neck.

"It is a remarkable thing," he said with precise enunciation, "to be here in this beautiful room with all of you. Just three months ago, I lay on the dirty floor of our county jail, my body beaten, my spirit broken." He was speaking now in a near-whisper. Trustees leaned forward so attentively, they appeared to be trying to read his lips. "I was put there on that floor," he said, "by the Ku Klux Klan. And by the police. There is no real difference." Trustees nodded solemnly to each other, as if they knew what he said was true.

"And they are very good at what they do," Pollo said. "It was not my first encounter with the Klan. Ten years ago, they tried to track me down. They left a burning cross in the midst of our settlement as a sign for anyone who might challenge them, or offend them." Pollo's voice began to rise. I felt certain he would not tell them what the offense was. "My offense ten years ago? Being black. That was my offense." He was practically shouting at the trustees. "Being black. Nothing more. Being black. It is an offense they cannot forgive. Ten years later, they found me. I was right where they had looked." He smiled. "These are not rocket scientists." Light laughter from his audience.

"As I lay on that floor in the jail, lay there in my own blood, lay there broken and dejected, lay there wanting to die, I was redeemed from despair by a single image: the face of Delphine Templeton. Delphine Templeton, who came to our community with the support of her fellow Philadelphians so many years ago. It was Delphine Templeton who taught me that my humanity was greater than my blackness. It was Delphine Templeton who hid me away from the Klan when I first attracted their attention. It was Delphine Templeton who sent me, with your help, to Centennial Academy and to the college and to Johnson C. Smith and to the seminary. It was Delphine Templeton who sent me away from danger and then called me back to service."

He did not say that it was Bo Fisher who got his butt out of jail.

"There are other young people in our settlement who will never know the tutoring of Miss Templeton. But they need the same lessons. They share my offense. They are black. And they live in a world that will not forgive them for that offense. And yet, they must be equipped for service in that very world. A world that takes offense because they are black." Pollo walked a half-circle in front of the fireplace, looking directly at each of the trustees.

"Miss Templeton's house still stands in our community," he said. "It is there in that house that I want to establish a center for the encouragement of black children to reach their full potential. The Delphine Templeton Community Center can be a place where they learn that it is no offense to be black."

Pollo turned toward the fire, turning his back on his listeners, letting the room fall silent. Just as the trustees began to squirm and glance at each other, he wheeled around. "I need your help," he said. "Without funds for repairs, the house will collapse, and the dream of Delphine Templeton will collapse with it. I hope you will not let that happen."

The art of approximate truth had been a specialty of Pollo's since I had first known him. He could always tell a story to make his point — especially to impress a girl, although these men in Philadelphia seemed just as taken by him. I knew exactly what he was doing, weaving another myth there in the music room of the Kirkpatrick mansion, a myth in which truth was not to be found in the details. For Pollo, truth was a matter more related to impression than to any particular facts. In this case, the trustees were impressed.

I was not. I was offended, not because Pollo was black, but because I was a white Southerner and had been made a pariah for that reason alone. Also, I had become suddenly invisible, and I wasn't sure which was worse.

Pollo stepped off to the side of the fireplace, and there was total silence in the room. Mr. Kirkpatrick was obviously not sure whether this "Moses to his people" was finished, or whether he might yet turn again and smite something. Finally, the host stood and, watching Pollo's back, thanked him for bringing such a powerful message. He noted that the trustees would be meeting officially the next morning and invited Pollo to the meeting. He said nothing at all to me.

As the group broke up, I left by a side door. I wanted to explain to all of them that the South portrayed tonight was a sort of fiction, not untrue but not exactly true, either, but the evening was Pollo's. I did not want to undo what he had achieved for himself. I found myself in a back hall, and one of the waiters let me out through the kitchen door. I walked all the way around the house and waited in the car for Pollo and Dickinson.

The silence as we left the Kirkpatrick estate reminded me of riding in the truck ten years earlier, out in the country, riding along with Mae Maude, with Pollo in the back, and with me mad as a hornet trying to explain that Pollo was playing with fire. Riding home from the Kirkpatricks' dinner party, I wanted to tell him he was playing with fire again, that I had been exactly right the first time, and that he was doing it again. I had the strange feeling we'd returned to a moment we'd already experienced. It would have suited me if the Kirkpatricks' driver had stopped the big Cadillac and asked Pollo to ride in back, on the long flat trunk of the car. And it would have suited me even better if Mae Maude could have been sitting beside me, mad or not, instead of Pollo.

Dickinson must have sensed the tension, because he said nothing, let us into the foundation headquarters with his key and a good night. Neither one of us answered him — Pollo, probably because the little Squirrel was now beneath his notice; me, because I was steaming.

In the missionaries' apartment, we undressed in silence. Pollo dropped his tux in a heap on the floor and headed for the shower while I was still arranging mine in the tuxedo bag, cufflinks and studs put away in the little sack hanging from the neck of the hanger, tie clipped to the cummerbund. I waited my turn for the bathroom and traded places with Pollo as he finished.

When I came back to the bedroom with my towel wrapped around me, I found Pollo stretched out on the bed, with all the covers thrown off on the floor. He was lying there with his eyes closed and his arms relaxed behind his head, as if transformed by his triumph at the Kirkpatrick mansion into a freshly molded and still-warm bronze sculpture, strong and powerful and sleek, the Sun God Recumbent. I had brought flannel pajamas for the Northern cold but decided they would look stupid, so I slipped on some regular undershorts and a tee shirt.

"You ready for me to turn out the lights?" I asked.

"Uhm-hm," he said without opening his mouth. Flexed biceps were the only sign of actual life in the figure stretched out on the bed as he answered. Maybe they were a response to the tone of my voice. Or maybe they were a warning that I had interfered with the quiet repose of His New-Sprung Majesty. In any event, they did not relax before the room went dark.

I lay in bed, unable to sleep and still burning from the dinner party. I could hear Pollo's slow, steady breathing. Finally, I spoke quietly into the darkness, just to make the point, if not actually to wake him up.

"Not all Southerners are rednecks," I said. The slow and steady breathing continued. "Not all of us," I added. There was an audible gesture of inhaled and exhaled breath from the darkness.

"No," came the answer, also low and quiet, "some of us are niggers." His voice carried the tone of flexed biceps.

"That's not what I meant." I sat up on one elbow and leaned into the darkness. "Don't turn this around on me, Pollo. Anyway, didn't you notice? Up here, I'm the nigger."

There was silence and darkness. I got up, and left the room.

———

Minor, Louisiana, according to the Atlas of the Americas in the apartment sitting room, had 2,432 people. Precisely. Unhappily for Mrs. J. Arthur Wilson, the atlas most likely counted people who were not white, as well as those who were, and counted everybody as one person rather than dis-counting or footnoting the people who would not have been in her set. Still, it seemed to me that if Mae Maude was one of the 2,432 — or if she had become the 2,433rd — she should be easy to find.

I called the information operator in Minor, who told me in a foreign-sounding voice that she had no listing for a Mae Maude Snoddy. Or any Snoddy.

"Is there anybody there who has lived in Minor for a long time that I could talk to?" I asked.

"I've been here for twenty-six years," she said, "so far. All my life. Is that long enough?"

"Well, I was just thinking that in a small town like that, somebody might remember Mae Maude Snoddy and know something about where she is."

"I know nearly everybody, and I don't remember her in particular."

"Did you go to high school there?"

"You have to be a high school gradu-ate to get this job."

"Yes, of course. Did you know Bubba Wilson?" It didn't take much arith-metic to figure she could have known Bubba really well. She could have been one of those girls he told Mae Maude about. The catalog of his descriptions ran through my mind as vividly as when I first heard about them, and I wondered which one she was.

"I remember a Wilson family," she said. "No one in particular." If the Wilsons were 3 of the 2,432 people in Minor, with Bubba as big a deal as he was in that high school, there's no way she could not have known him "in particular."

"Is there anyone else in town that I could talk to?"

"There are a lot of people. It's the biggest town in the parish. But you have to ask for somebody in particular." I thought about taking a stab at a name but decided to let it go.

I called back the next morning, but the same voice was on the job again. Apparently, she was the only information operator in Minor. Maybe the only high school graduate. I was convinced that she was lying about Mae Maude. I had no idea why.

I left an envelope with five dollars by the phone with Nutley's name on it. No way would I let them think Southerners were cheapskates, too.

Afterward, I packed my things and brought them to the lobby of the building while Pollo went for his morning session with the trustees.

Miss Mills spotted me and raised a cup of coffee. "Cream?" she said.

"Yes, ma'am, and sugar. Two spoons." She looked at me and almost smiled.

"You were interested in the fire," she said through her almost smile, pronouncing the word "fi-ah," as she had heard me say it.

"Well, it just keeps coming up," I said, "and I can't really find out anything about it. There's no mention of it in the history of Centennial."

"Can you do arithmetic?"

"Ma'am?"

"Arithmetic. All the histories you've read say that Centennial was founded in 1912. Simple arithmetic is the clue to what you're looking for. Of course, you have to know some history." And so she took me on a mathematical tour of the history of Centennial, from its founding date backward.

1912 didn't add up to a hundred years from anything, other than the War of 1812. But the centennial observance of the founding of the Presbyterian Church in America had occurred in 1888, and with it, the renaming of a little school for freed slaves. So Centennial was in existence by 1888 and had a history in another town before moving to the campus Pollo knew so well. It grew into a thriving college with several hundred resident students long before its re-establishment in the capital city in 1912. The fire had burned away its official history, but it was all written down in the discolored and brittle pages bearing the minutes of the Committee on Freedmen.

———

The train ride home was almost not long enough. Pollo was full of himself after his official meeting of the trustees, reporting a grant from the Kirkpatrick Foundation that would more than cover the expenses of renovating The Oracle — or, rather, the Delphine Templeton Community Center. "And there's more where that came from," he said twenty different times.

But the real news was in my report on Centennial and the fire. Pollo had not known that the name of Mr. Samuel DuBois was then, in fact, Sam DuBose — a much more likely name in our part of the state, the same as several very prominent white families. I could guarantee it against Pollo's skepticism. I saw it spelled that way in the minutes of the Kirkpatrick Foundation in Miss Mills's office, and I saw his signature on some appended receipts.

As a young man in Philadelphia — just a boy, really — Sam DuBose had become enthralled with W. E. B. DuBois and his book *The Souls of Black Folk*, and had decided that he must also have some French and African heritage himself. To reflect his discovery, he changed the spelling of his own name, gaining an instant and distant past — and hoping to lose the more immediate past that was now remembered only by Miss Mills and, presumably, Dr. MacDonald. Later and for the same reasons, Samuel DuBois changed his brother's name on the tombstone at the Rocks. He pronounced it with no *s*, as it is pronounced in the oldest parts of the South, in places settled by the French — not the wild trappers and traders who came later to the Gulf Coast, but by the solemn Huguenots who had fled from persecution in the seventeenth century.

Sam DuBose had been spirited away to Philadelphia by the Committee on Freedmen for a report to the Kirkpatrick Foundation on the disastrous fire at Centennial. He was kept there as a precaution for his own safety. He himself thought he was being followed, according to the minutes, and the trustees believed they were saving him from a certain lynching.

The boy reported he'd been in the dormitory the night of the fire, that he heard a slight noise in the yard and went to the window. He saw the first flames come through the roof of the porch almost simultaneously at both ends of the veranda that ran the length of the building. He yelled "Fire!" at the top of his lungs to rouse his friends, saw his roommate sit up, yelled again and jumped to the porch roof below his room. Boys emerged from the burning building like wasps from a threatened nest, some jumping from windows or running out through doors, others just appearing suddenly in the air of the yard from some unaccounted opening. In the panic of the moment, Sam DuBose ran through the crowded yard, clutching at people from behind, pulling apart little groups huddled together, calling to his little brother. From the far end of the building where Eddie's room had been, he heard a cry, "Sammy! Sammy!" calling through the flames. "Here!" he had answered, "Here I am, Eddie!" But all he heard back was his own voice, calling "Here! Eddie! Here," the crackling of the flames, the frightened babble of the boys in the yard, and the roar of the fire trucks arriving to wet down the smoldering ash.

The dormitory had housed forty-six students, according to the official record in the minutes. All but three of the students escaped the fire, thanks to Sam DuBose's alarms. Among those who did not was Eddie DuBose, age 12.

The cause of the fire was never determined. The white people of the town said that local colored people, envious of the advantages enjoyed by the students able to attend the college, had burned the building in anger. People associated with the college said the Klan, fearful of an educated class of Negroes and angry at some unspecified "disturbance" in the town, had torched the place. There was no evidence, either way.

Although Pollo knew Centennial College had some history before its "founding date" of 1912, he didn't know this. It was as much a surprise to him as it was to me to learn the town where the fire actually occurred was in the next county over from ours, in Knoxtown, Mrs. J. Arthur Wilson's town.

———

Knoxtown was separated from the town where I grew up by an interstate highway and a couple hundred years. Nearer to the river than our town, it was much older than any place in that part of the state, and its comparatively long history was one source of great pride. Pride, in fact, had become such a prominent characteristic of Knoxtown that it had long since outgrown its sources. No one could even name all the sources, or cared to, for it was pride itself that Knoxtown was most proud of.

That view was not likely to change. The Wilsons and their set, who had dominated Knoxtown for at least the last hundred years, did not teach evolution, did not believe in it, and did not practice it. Most towns struggle to find some balance between the business of creating a future and the art of preserving the past, that being the tension that brings life and meaning to the present. Knoxtown knew no such tension, and they regarded changes elsewhere as examples of a natural depravity that was not unexpected in humankind, but not known in Knoxtown.

Even in 1966, the town square of Knoxtown was a tour of yesteryear: an elegant courthouse designed by Robert Mills (the architect of the Washington Monument, according to the historic marker), an opera house in which Jenny Lind, the Swedish Nightingale herself, had sung (according to another marker), and the house in which Jefferson Davis and the Confederate Cabinet "were to have met" (a source of incalculable pride, even though the meeting was never held, it having been scheduled for a day or two after the cabinet had officially disbanded in defeat, and after Jeff Davis had passed through Knoxtown alone in his retreat). There were historic markers everywhere. In deference to Knoxtown, one could become relatively well-read just by walking around the Square. There was even a bronze tablet in the sidewalk, noting for posterity that "The news of the murder of Abraham Lincoln was announced on this spot by Mayor William Tipple, a cousin of President Davis." There was no marker anywhere with reference to Centennial College.

Knoxtown must have looked very much the same in 1910 as in 1966. All the buildings were the same. Many of the citizens were also the same, just later generations of identical names with Roman numerals at the end — III, IV, and even an occasional V, like personal historic markers. The newspaper, named the *Journal* despite its being published only once a week throughout its existence, was still printed in the same building on the Square. They kept back copies as a source of pride for the town, and those copies were open to review without supervision or censorship as an example of the fact that pride knows no bounds in Knoxtown.

The Wilsons were not hard to find in the newsprint Knoxtown of 1910. Bubba's great-grandfather was president of the bank, having inherited that role from his father as the eldest son. A younger brother was president of the mill. A third was devoted to the newspaper as owner, editor, and principal reporter. Photos of the editor's brothers, always posed portraits, appeared in the paper on several occasions as civic leaders of note.

At first, I was appalled by the attention the paper gave to lynchings. "Lynching in Mississippi," said one typical front-page headline, the most prominent headline in the paper, even though the incident took place hundreds of miles from there. A sub-head added, "Large and Enthusiastic Crowd Gathers," as if it were just another gala civic event. The *Journal* reported lynchings from all over the South, no matter how distant, generally with scant notice of the alleged offense but with vivid chronicling of the abuses directed at the victim by the crowd, and always with a reference to whether or not the body was "mutilated." Mutilation seemed to be an obsession of the editor's, with many references to its practice as an appropriate deterrent to uncivil behavior, and an appropriate visual aid for colored people who might not know any better. When I checked other newspapers around the state for stories on the fire at Centennial, I found the *Journal* was not far off the standard in reporting lynchings, except for the editor's mutilation fixation.

The *Journal* was sketchy on the fire at Centennial. The event itself was reported on the front page, below the fold. The more interesting article occurred in the editorial column, just after a lead-off note about the great value of 4-H Clubs and the good quality of young people involved in the program. "Burned to the Ground" was the next sub-head. After lamenting the loss of major buildings and, incidentally, three unnamed students who burned to death in the blaze, the editor noted speculation in town that the fire had been set by local "coloreds" who were jealous of the educated class of Negroes at the college. A large reward, according to the editor, had been posted by a Northern family interested in the college, and local leaders had formed a civil committee of inquiry to bring the perpetrators to justice.

Other newspapers in the state were less certain. At the university library, I found articles critical of the climate of hatred and intolerance in Knoxtown, and specifically critical of the role of the *Journal* in propagating enmity between the races. One newspaper called attention to the short distance from the firehouse to the campus and wondered explicitly why there was delay in the arrival of fire trucks at the scene. In another paper, there was a letter from an anonymous Knoxtonian suggesting that the alleged malice of local blacks was a cover-up for a conspiracy, not specified, and referring to an earlier confrontation between Centennial students and the local establishment.

In a second trip to Knoxtown, I found the earlier incident reported in an issue of the *Journal* six months prior to the fire. "Negroes Disrupt Event" said the headline, followed by a sub-head "Local Citizens Outraged At Unruly Behavior." The event was a Klan rally, right on Main Street, where Centennial students marched down the sidewalks along the edge of the rally, singing hymns "so loudly that participants in the rally could not hear the speaker." The speaker was the president of the mill, Mr. William Trent Wilson. The sheriff, according to the article, was unable to explain the lapse in civil order represented by the ill-mannered behavior of the students, and an editorial suggested that the law enforcement official might be called to account in the next election.

In an unrelated article in that same issue, there was a report of a fire at the opera house, noting that the volunteer firemen had arrived so promptly that "next to no damage" was done. Citizens were quoted in praise of the record of the firemen in responding rapidly and effectively to fires in the town. I went out immediately and drove the distance from the fire station to the opera house and from the fire station to the large pasture which had been the site of the campus. The difference was inconsequential, but in favor of the campus.

Back at Duke, I discussed with my advisor the possibility of researching the Centennial fire as my master's thesis. "Possible," he said. "It sounds like there may be a reasonable conspiracy theory, but a theory only, and otherwise, just one sort of speculation against another, you see. It has the possibility of a great story, of course. But the sort of thing one might write for the loose standards of the popular press. Or a novel. Unless there is some direct evidence of occurrences surrounding the event, Mr. Fisher, you will undoubtedly be disappointed in your effort. It is very difficult to make history of something that has no primary sources." I decided to push it just a little further. I went back to Miss Mills.

"Yes," she said by telephone from her office in Philadelphia, "The Kirkpatrick Foundation posted the reward. The trustees were vitally interested." As to what came of it, she said the search process had been managed by local people, "people of good will and reputable character," she added with a flourish that would have been a source of pride in Knoxtown. There had been some speculation that young Sam DuBose could provide information to the trustees that had not been available to the local Knoxtown committee, but nothing had come of it, despite his lengthy stay in Philadelphia. There were no other records than the minutes of the foundation that I had already read. I was at a dead end, except for the possibility that Mr. Samuel DuBois of the Rocks, a.k.a. Sam DuBose of Philadelphia, might talk.

———— • ————

None of this appeared to be news to Pollo. He listened without any expression to what I had learned, sitting back in the desk chair of the church study with his arms behind his head. The only glimmer of interest I saw was when I said the newspaper accounts were written by the editor, Ruffin Wilson. I would have identified him, but I stopped short when Pollo leaned forward and rubbed his chin. His eyes moved from me to the wall behind me to the papers on his desk and over to the bookcase along the wall, as if he were looking for something.

"Bubba Wilson," he said. I guess he had found it.

"Yeah," I said. "The guy who ran the paper was Bubba's great-uncle, his grandfather's brother." Pollo stood up and walked to the window, clasping his hands behind his back and looking out toward the cemetery. I talked for a long time to Pollo's back. I told him every single detail of what I had learned, even inconsequential ones like the near-historic role of Knoxtown as the intended site of what might have been the last meeting of the Cabinet of the Confederacy, except for the fact that it never happened. I told him there was no evidence of Centennial College, and I told him as if I were making some kind of confession: Knoxtown had managed to remember something that never happened, while forgetting something that had.

Pollo never turned around, but I talked on. I'd started out trying to get Pollo's help in gaining Mr. Samuel DuBois's confidence, but I could have done that with a simple summary, without the effort of remembering every detail. There was more to this telling, some cleansing, maybe. As I reached the end of what I knew about the Centennial fire, I also reached the conclusion I would never know enough about it for my advisor at Duke. Mr. DuBois would be just another opinion, even if he agreed to talk about it. And there was no need to drag Mr. DuBois back to that awful time in his life, because I was coming not to care about it anymore. The telling of the story ended any involvement I wanted to have with it. I was done.

Pollo turned from the window and looked at me. "We need to tell DuBois," he said. I let the "we" slip by without a comment, without the old joke about the Lone Ranger and Tonto. "We'll tell him," he said. "He needs to know."

I said the obvious: "He was there."

"He's still there," Pollo said.

"Come on, Pollo," I said.

"Don't you see?" he said. "DuBois never left that burning building. He's still scared. If we can get him out, maybe then he'll understand what we're up against in the here and now." He walked around the desk and stood in front of my chair.

"It's history," I said, looking up at him. "It's done. Just leave it alone." Pollo stuck out his hand as if he wanted to shake hands. It seemed odd, but I took it. Instead of shaking, he reached past and grabbed my thumb and wrist in what had become a sort of black greeting to the "brothers," forming one fist with two hands. In this case, it was so that Pollo could pull me up out of the chair, but we stood face to face with our hands locked in a tight fist, and I felt awkward and proud. I had seen black brothers on campus greet each other that way, but there was usually something more to it, a series of grips, and I had no idea how to start. So I just said again, "It's history."

"History," Pollo said slowly, holding my hand still in that one fist, "history is a rotting corpse. You should know that."

I only knew one rotting corpse, and my mind raced through a series of images that surrounded it: an old one-sided tree with a group of people under it, like they were posed in a faded photograph; men with shovels, digging; Sister Holy Ghost on the wicker settee, her arms around Cora Snoddy, the two of them embracing something they hadn't been able to remember and couldn't forget; Mae Maude standing close to me, so close I could feel the warmth of her body. And then there was the fresh corpse of Mrs. Snoddy Senior in the field beyond the house, and the camp truck on the road through the settlement; an empty ledge at the quarry where I had thought I would find Pollo. An empty ledge. Pollo. The image that old corpse led me to so rapidly was not the corpse itself at all, but Pollo. Pollo sitting under the kudzu on Miss Templeton's porch, stunned by an unfounded fear, by just the mere possibility that I might have called the sheriff. And I felt the pain again, the pain of a distance that I could not cross on Miss Templeton's porch. And I worried that my eyes might water as I looked at Pollo across the joined fist of our hands, ten years later. And I did not want to let go. I cannot know, of course, what Pollo was thinking, but I heard what he said.

"We have to dig it up."

And so we went to see Mr. Samuel DuBois.

"Hmh," is what Mr. Samuel DuBois had to say about it. He hit a key that opened the drawer of the cash register and began arranging coins in the round-bottomed sections of the drawer. He looked up when I said that Dr. MacDonald sent his regards. "He still there?" Mr. DuBois said. Then he looked down again into the drawer and formed the nickels into a roll along the bottom of their hollow.

I told him how Dr. MacDonald welcomed us and arranged for special clothes and a fancy dinner.

"Tuxedos," Pollo said.

"He told us about your visit up there," I said. "He wasn't sure whether you stayed with the Hendersons or the Harrisons." Mr. DuBois reversed the whole order of the coins in the drawer, swapping the two half-dollars from the far right with a wad of pennies on the far left and then arranging the nickels, dimes, and quarters into descending order between them. He picked up the dimes, but they went back into the same slot where they had been.

"I read *The Souls of Black Folk* on the way home on the train," I said, fishing for any kind of a response.

Mr. DuBois closed the cash drawer and walked from behind the counter to a chair beside the stove.

"Did you?" he said, folding himself slowly forward from the waist and down from the knees, then falling suddenly backward the last few inches into the chair.

Pollo began to recite from *The Souls of Black Folk*, proving to me that he had in fact read it: "It is the strife of honorable men to see that in the competition of races, the survival of the fittest shall mean the triumph of the good, the beautiful, and the true. To bring this hope to fruition," and Mr. DuBois began to mouth the words with him, "we must study the South — and we must ask: What are the actual relations of whites and blacks in the South?"

"And we must be answered," Mr. Samuel DuBois concluded the quotation firmly, "not by apology or fault-finding, but by a plain, unvarnished tale."

Pollo smiled his million-dollar smile.

"But it's not true," Mr. DuBois said softly. "I knew better even then. The plain unvarnished tale is that strife does not bring the triumph of the good, the beautiful, and the true. It doesn't happen."

"Then what's more glorious than making the effort?" Pollo said.

Mr. DuBois was silent for a minute. Then he said, "Staying alive."

"You can do a lot without being killed." Pollo said.

"Now, maybe," the old man said, "and only maybe, even now." Mr. DuBois sighed. "The news makes heroes now out of people killed for civil rights. But when it was just plain human rights..." His voice trailed off. He leaned forward and picked up a piece of crumpled paper off the floor and threw it in the stove. "There's no glory in a lynching," he said.

Pollo didn't say anything, so I asked, "There weren't ever any lynchings around here, were there?"

"Hmh," he said. "What do you think the fire at Centennial was? Just a different kind of lynching." He looked at me sideways. "Did your re-search turn up the names of those boys who died in the fire?"

"No, sir," I said, avoiding the fact that I did know one of them, his brother. "Their names weren't in any of the newspaper accounts."

"Not much glory in it, was there?"

"No, sir," I said.

"Would you like to know their names?" he said.

"Yes, sir. I would."

Mr. Samuel DuBois sank down in his chair. "Samuel Jenkins, from over in Carlisle," he whispered. "Carl Duckett from Charlotte." The names seemed to come to him slowly, or maybe only painfully. When he spoke again, we could barely hear him. "Edward DuBose." Neither of us said anything for awhile. Finally, Pollo spoke up.

"You gave Edward a beautiful tombstone," he said.

"I heard him calling my name," Mr. DuBois said. "He was my little brother, and I couldn't help him."

"I read a report in Philadelphia," I said. "The fire was too hot. You couldn't get to him. He couldn't hear you calling him back."

"I lied," Mr. DuBois said.

He met my eyes, and his stare was tired and dark with what he'd lived with for fifty years. I felt foolish and naive, and I was the one who looked away.

"I lied to the trustees," he said. "I lied to my family. To our family, mine and Eddie's."

He got up and went back behind the counter.

Pollo stood in the middle of the store with his arms folded, watching. I squatted on the floor in front of the stove. We must have stayed like that for a long stretch of time before I thought of what to say next.

"There was nothing you could have done," I said. "The building went up so quick. I read that in the newspaper. You couldn't have gone back in. And there was no way he could have heard you with the noise of the fire and the ruckus in the yard." Mr. DuBois braced his arms on the counter, and his head sank between his shoulders.

"I never called him," he said.

"Sir?"

"I was afraid. I ran out of the building and hid in the woods. I was afraid they saw me."

"Who would have seen you?"

Mr. DuBois stood up straight, as straight as his stoop would allow. "I saw something that I never told," he said. "When I woke up that night, I went to the window. There was a bunch in white hoods running across the yard. The Klan. I saw them throwing torches at the building. I was afraid to yell for fear they would kill me. Not with the fire. With ropes from a tree, like they had said. And knives. I would rather have burned."

"Who said?" I said.

"Some white men in town. A couple weeks before the fire, Eddie and I were walking. Two white men picked us up and gave us a ride on their wagon. We didn't think anything about it. But when we got to the store, they grabbed us off the wagon and pushed us through the store into a back room. There was a bunch of white men back there, laughing. I didn't know any of them, didn't know why they took us there. Eddie and I were both scared. They made us stand at a table that just had a bag on it, and some of them kept yelling, *Go ahead, go ahead on.* Finally, one of the men took the bag and poured out what was in it on the table, some dark and leathery looking things. *Know what they is?* the man said. We didn't say anything. *Want me to tell you what they is?* And the others yelled for him to go on. *Nigger toes,* he said. *Nigger toes is what they is.* We didn't know what he meant. There's some kind of a big nut that white people call nigger toes, but it didn't look exactly like that. *Nigger toes,* other ones of them kept calling out. *They came from a nigger was lynched over in...* I forget the name of the place. He picked one of them up, and we could see the toenails. *They came from a nigger was lynched,* the man said. They were real toes. Eddie and I were scared. I wanted to get out of there. It was so hot I thought I could have fainted, but I had to be brave because of Eddie. I wanted to get him out of there, and I thought maybe they would start with the biggest one of us if they were going to lynch us. We didn't say anything. Just stared at those toes." Mr. DuBois was silent, staring at the air in front of him.

I thought the store was so hot I might faint. Pollo was just standing there with his arms crossed and with his eyes fixed on Mr. DuBois. I wanted to run out into the fresh air, but I didn't want him to think I couldn't take this rotting corpse as it came up from the dark, dank deep where it had been buried.

"Then one of those white men, a fat man with glasses and a suit on — most of them just had on overalls like the two that picked us up, but one had a suit and eyeglasses and beady little eyes — he took the bag again and reached down into it. He pulled out something bigger and waved it at us. *See this?* he said, sticking it in front of our faces and smiling at the men who were laughing at him — or at us, I don't know, but laughing. *See this?*"

Mr. DuBois held his hand up in front of his face as if he were holding the neck of a chicken for inspection by a customer. "*See this?* he kept saying. *Know what it is, boy?* he said." Mr. DuBois had tears in his eyes and he was talking louder. "The man said, *This is what was hanging between that nigger's legs, boy.* And everybody laughed. Somebody was holding my shoulders so I couldn't run. I don't know if I would have if I could. I thought I was going to faint. It was so hot and so loud in there."

It felt hot and loud in the brick store, too. I wanted him to stop talking, for my sake, for his own sake.

But Mr. DuBois kept waving his closed hand right in front of his own face. "Don't it smell?" he said. "Don't it smell? Don't it smell like the cock of a nigger, boy?" Mr. DuBois's voice broke. "Don't it smell like...Don't it smell..."

Sweat popped on my lip and forehead. I thought I might throw up. I wanted to stop Mr. DuBois, wanted to make Pollo stop him, wanted to run out into the yard, wanted to yell at the top of my lungs, wanted to find Miss Templeton over at her house next door, wanted it to be 1956 again, wanted to jump in the camp truck with Pollo and Mae Maude, wanted to hear Mr. DuBois whistle when Bubba drove by.

I left. And I did throw up, in the bushes outside the store. I was sweating and had cold goose bumps and I felt dizzy. Throwing up did not help, so I went and sat in the car, waiting for Pollo. He was in the store a long time.

"You happy?" I said to him when he finally came out. "You think you helped Mr. DuBois get from one place to another?"

"What do you mean, 'you,' paleface? It's your research project. And besides, we don't have the corpse yet," he said.

"What corpse?"

"Somebody, one of those Klansmen, saw Mr. DuBois in the window. He took his hood off and waved that big black cock up at him from the yard of the dormitory. Mr. DuBois ducked down and didn't come up until the whole place was on fire. He thinks he could have saved those boys if he had yelled earlier, but he was afraid the Klan would come back for him and string him up and castrate him. He's still afraid of that. Old as he is, he is still afraid the Klan will castrate him. He hid in the bushes while the dormitory burned down, and he's been hiding at the Rocks ever since. That's why he doesn't want any attention drawn out here. He's still afraid that Klansman will recognize him, after all these years. "

"I'm sorry," I said. "But I'm also sorry we made him talk about it."

"No. Black people who know better have covered up for the Klan all these years and let whites say what they wanted about that fire. And Mr. DuBois thinks he's the only one who knows the truth, and that he's not safe as long as he's the only one."

"What can we do about it?"

"We can find out," Pollo said. He looked at me and smiled. "We can dig up the body."

"How?"

"I don't know. But the first thing we're going to do is, we're going to Knoxtown."

———— ◆ ————

Pollo had never been to Knoxtown. "People from the settlement don't go there," he said. "Nobody in Knoxtown wants us there." Still, Pollo wanted to see the place. "I can go anywhere I want to," he said. "This is not 1910." At the time, 1966 seemed modern.

History does not go away, however, just because somebody decides to ignore it. I had been to Knoxtown by myself and found it welcoming enough to a Presbyterian. But then my religion was not as obvious as Pollo's skin. So when we made our triumphal entry into the city, it was not lost on me that he was sitting in the front seat with me — and in a coat and tie, since we were going to the library and the newspaper, so it was obvious that he was not somebody who might be working for me. I think we might have been okay arriving in any other town. I think. But it was not even 1966 yet in Knoxtown; we were crossing into another time as well as another place.

There were a few blacks in Knoxtown. Not millworkers; blacks weren't allowed to work there. But there were enough to fill the need for household servants and handymen. We saw several of them as we drove in. More to the point, they saw us. I suppose they all knew each other and knew that this one riding beside me in the front seat in a coat and tie was not one of them. They didn't stare, but just looked sideways at us from whatever they were doing, sweeping the walk or clipping the hedge or hanging out laundry. Pollo nodded to every one of them.

We hit paydirt, but not at the library or the newspaper. The "Knoxtown History" section at the library had nothing on Centennial College. Not a single reference. The newspaper had only what I had already seen. Nobody seemed to know what had happened to the minutes of the Committee to Restore Order, those "people of good will and reputable character" that Miss Mills had remembered so respectfully, although the newspaper had reported the establishment of the committee as a source of pride that the community intended to "deal forthrightly with the perpetrators of this dastardly deed, whoever they are."

"There's a guy out on the bypass that talks about that fire all the time," the secretary at the newspaper told us. "Crazy guy, but he's the only person I've ever heard mention it. Serves pretty good food, too," she said.

So we pulled up at Ernie's Truck Stop and Buffet at the edge of town and across from the mill. There were no trucks or cars in sight at the square little cinderblock building, but I figured people probably walked over from work or from the mill village that sprawled down the hill behind Ernie's. In any event, it looked right and smelled right for good food.

"Y'all visiting Knoxtown?" a man in a dirty apron said to us when we sat down. I answered him before Pollo could say anything smart. I was afraid the guy was going to tell us to leave, that maybe blacks still couldn't eat there, even with a white person with them.

"Yes," I said. "We are." It was obvious, anyway. "Are you Ernie?" I said as pleasantly as I could.

"E-r-n-i-c-e," he spelled. "Ernice, like Ernie with a 'c' in it. Just like on the sign outside: Ernice's Truck Stop and Buffet." He waved toward a pot-strewn counter with a dripping spoon.

"I guess I just didn't read it right," I said.

"E-r-n-i-c-e," he said again. "Ernice. Thought y'all might just be passing through," he said. "That happens sometimes." The man was so thin he could have been the shadow of the cigarette hanging out of his mouth. Most of his face sloped down at about the same angle as the cigarette, and he looked really hard and dumb, like a good candidate for the Klan. But his words were friendly — just the fact that he spoke to an interracial couple of customers was friendly, for one thing. He explained that the only lunch was the buffet, but he could bring us iced tea or water or Cokes. And he meant cokes, with a lower case 'c.' "Most folks drink Pepsis," he said, "but I got others."

We loaded up plates at the buffet: fried chicken, mashed potatoes, collards. That was the whole buffet. But it was good.

"What brings y'all to Knoxtown?" Ernice said when he brought us the tea. He looked like he might pull up a chair and join us. "We don't usually get customers this early," he said. "Nobody comes 'til the morning shift is done at the mill. Y'all on business?" I guess we looked stumped by the question, so Ernice offered some hints. "Government, maybe?" Then he looked at us and smiled around the cigarette. "Preachers?"

"He is," I said, pointing at Pollo, who actually smiled at being spotted. "Not me," I added. I decided to be direct, even though it was unlikely that E-r-n-i-c-e would care much, one way or the other. "I came over because I'm interested in Centennial College."

"Know all about it," Ernice said. He was the first person I had met in Knoxtown who had even admitted to recognizing the name without a lot of prompting. "Over on the other side of town," Ernice said. "Know right where it was."

"It burned," I said.

"Yeah. I don't think it was a real college, but they called it that."

"Did you ever see it?"

"Nope. Saw the rubble after the fire. My daddy took me over there to see it. We went a lot. I guess there's not much else to look at in Knoxtown." The Historical Society of Knoxtown would have been sorely disappointed in Ernice. "What church y'all go to?" Ernice asked. I had been asked that question by nearly every person in the South that I had ever met, but never in the company of a black person. And never in Knoxtown, where the question had a sinister kind of tone to it.

"Presbyterian," I said firmly. Ernice didn't challenge it.

"I'm a Baptist," he said. "Strict Baptist. Got born again some years ago when I was young and been living with Jesus ever since." Ashes dropped off his cigarette and onto the floor. Jesus would have overlooked it, I guessed. "Even got myself elected as a deacon," Ernice said. "And that started a whole miracle." I knew better, but I couldn't help myself. I took the bait.

"Really?"

"Yep. My wife Annie's barren. Couldn't have no kids, even though we tried." He smiled and the cigarette tilted up, "Lord knows we tried." Eyelids and mouth and cigarette all turned up everything, in fact, turned up but the sideburns. Then it all fell again. "Doctor said I didn't have the necessary stuff." He frowned. "Man like me. I don't believe that, do y'all?" It was not a rhetorical question.

"Not likely," I said.

"Annie's just barren. Then we had a baby. Ernice Junior Melton. He sure is by God a miracle. Came nine months to the day after I was elected a deacon in the Roadside Creek Baptist Church. Nine months to the very day." I wondered exactly what had been on Ernice's mind at church while he was being elected a deacon, but I kept my face straight.

"Must not have been elected on a Sunday," I said. Pollo looked at me quickly, straightening his face before turning back to Ernice. Ernice knew exactly what I meant.

"Naw, I don't hold by that," he said. "I believe you can do it whenever the time is ripe. Bible don't say nothing about not doing that on Sunday. Ain't nothing unholy about it if you do it right. And we sure as hell by God got it right that Sunday after church." Ernice actually winked at Pollo, and Pollo's face broke into a broad grin. "Don't believe I've ever seen my Annie as excited about anything as she was about me being elected a deacon in the Baptist Church." He punched Pollo on the shoulder and grinned, and the cigarette went straight up in the air again. "You know what I'm talking about, don't you, preacher?" Pollo was grinning from ear to ear.

"Y'all want to know about the fire?" Ernice said abruptly as a group came in for a late lunch. "Come back after the next shift is over."

Ernice, it turned out, had found Jesus at the expense of his father, a mean-spirited and tyrannical man by Ernice's recollection, who had spread evil in Knoxtown. The old man had been possessed by the devil and was never saved from it. He was obsessed by the fire at the Centennial campus, taking his children there over and over again, describing the fire in detail, and telling them that this was the fate of uppity niggers who forgot their place in the world. The more his father ranted about the fate of uppity colored people, the more Ernice had imagined schoolboys burning in the fire. "Made my skin crawl," Ernice told us.

At his conversion — actually, at his baptism in Roadside Creek — Ernice had begged silently for divine relief from all that he had learned from his father about those boys burning in the fire. When Annie presented him with Ernice Junior, Ernice decided that his son would never hear about or have to explain anything about the fire. Over time, it became apparent that Ernice Junior would never be able hear anything or to talk at all. Ernice took that as a sign from God that the sins of the grandfather were being visited upon this little boy of his — and that he, Ernice himself, had become "the 'com-plice" by keeping the secret of the fire. And Ernice came to believe that if he could tell the story to someone who would believe it, he could lift the terrible birthmark from his son. Until we showed up for lunch, apparently, he had not been successful. "Now it's out," Ernice said, and he told us every-thing that he knew.

"Oh, Crazy Ernice," the newspaper editor said when we confronted him with our report. "Tells that story to everybody who comes through town. Not a brain in his head. Just lies about everything. Nobody else in town has ever heard a blessed thing about that fire since it happened, unless it's some of the colored people. Some of them actually did it, you know. Nobody likes to talk about it now because it might just stir up trouble between the races, but it's the truth." His face turned cold, tight lips replacing his easy smile. "That's what the newspaper said at the time, and there's never been a shred of evidence to contradict it. Anyway," he said, his mouth relaxing again in almost a smile, "it's not likely that Ernice Melton would be the historian of Knoxtown, is it? Really. He just spins a great yarn. But he sure is a good cook, now, isn't he?"

"Does Ernice have any children?" I asked.

"Just one," the editor said. "A boy name of Ernice Junior. Born deaf and dumb, but Ernice does love that boy. Always said he wanted more, but I guess that's not what the Lord intended." Even God in Heaven couldn't have gotten Ernice elected a deacon in the Baptist Church more than once, I wanted to say, but I decided not to explain that to the editor. It stood to reason that the editor would not have any idea how stimulating such an election might be. And I decided to discount the editor and to believe Ernice, to believe him totally, from the fire to the miracle of Ernice Junior and everything in between. Ernice had had his baptism by fire, or baptism from the fire, maybe, from a fire that had burned at his insides and made his skin crawl. Being born again, he had come eventually, by way of the Baptist Church's only recorded and truly miraculous "conception by election," to father a little life that gave meaning and purpose to his own. And to preserve that life, he had been led to tell the truth.

"Don't y'all stir up trouble, now," the editor said amiably as we left, "you hear?"

———◆———

Ernice Melton had given us what we needed to free Mr. Samuel DuBois from his demon. Pollo and I waited at the brick store until everybody else had gone before bringing it up.

"We went over to Knoxtown," Pollo said.

"Why, boy?" Mr. DuBois said quickly and with just a slight menacing edge. "Why? I told you nobody needs to go over there."

"It's just another town," Pollo said quietly. "We met some nice people."

"Hmh."

"We actually met," Pollo answered, speaking slowly and stressing each word, "we met a man who knows who it was that talked to you in the store with the bag of toes. And who it was that saw you in the window of the dormitory."

Mr. DuBois literally froze behind the counter. He did not look up or move an eyelash.

"They're all dead," Pollo said. "They never knew who you were, and they never told anybody enough to be able to find you." Pollo walked around the counter and put his arm around Mr. DuBois. "The men who showed you that bag were led by Ruffin Wilson, the editor of the newspaper. He was the beady-eyed man you remember. But he was just a pawn like the others. He was doing what he was told to by his brother, a man named Arthur Wilson, who owned the bank and kept the Klan leaders in debt to him one way or another. The man who led the attack on the dormitory and saw you up in the window was the father of a man we met in Knoxtown today, a man named Ernice Melton. Mr. Melton says his father lived out the last years of his life, after civil rights began to spread, in fear that you would turn up somewhere and identify him as the one who set the fire."

Mr. DuBois did not even look up.

"About ten years ago, some young guys in Knoxtown reorganized the Klan," Pollo went on. "They tried to find you on the basis of what the old-timers remembered, but they couldn't make heads or tails of it. They think you just vanished, went up north and never came back. Right after the fire, though, they had really tried hard to figure out where you were, because they were afraid you would make the connection between the incident at the store and the fire at the school." Mr. DuBois was still looking down at the counter, but he nodded his head at this comment. "They thought you might have recognized Ernice's father as being at both places." Mr. DuBois kept nodding. "He was the man," Pollo said, "who picked you up in his wagon when you and Eddie were walking to town." Mr. DuBois's head was still nodding, and his body began to jerk under Pollo's protective arm. "And he was the man who took off his hood and saw you in the window." Mr. DuBois was rocking back and forth as if his whole body wanted to acknowledge what Pollo was saying. "They wanted to be sure you would never be able to tell anybody." Pollo held Mr. DuBois in his arms and said, "They're all dead now. The old men are all gone." Pollo held Mr. DuBois tight while the rocking and nodding stopped. "There's nobody left who knows anything." At last there was total, bearable stillness in the brick store.

Mr. Samuel DuBois patted Pollo's arm until he moved it, then looked up into Pollo's eyes, turned away again and walked out of the store.

Chapter Nine

———◆———

MINOR, LOUISIANA

There was one last body to unearth, one that would be a whole lot more appealing than the others we had dug up. This one would be vivacious and sexy, with a mischievous smile and asymmetric nipples. I was sure of it.

I left Pollo out. I'd been reluctant to get into that whole subject with him, since he had shown absolutely no remorse about what had happened in the vesper dell. Anyway, I figured he might not be somebody Mae Maude wanted to see.

And Pollo, as usual, had his own demons to contend with. The quarry company had resurfaced after a whole generation of silence. Out of the blue, a squad of surveyors showed up and began to mark off the company land with iron stakes and little red flags. They claimed not only the quarry proper but also most of the settlement, and nobody seemed to know what for. Pollo called the Young Senator at the capital to make some inquiries. He discovered that the quarry company wanted to sell the property to the state as a waste dump for prospective industrial development along the nearby interstate highway. The state hadn't expressed any interest at first, but Young Senator said the situation was changing, courtesy of the company's well-connected lobbyist, none other than our old nemesis Bubba Wilson. Bubba Wilson was another name I didn't need to mention to Mae Maude. I thought Pollo and Bubba could just fight out the future of the quarry by themselves.

I saw the survey crew on my last visit home just before exams.

"The stakes are high," Pollo had said.

"Hmh," I said. Low stakes would have been a surprise in anything that interested Pollo. Still, he made it sound pretty serious.

"They want to resettle us into public housing in town," he said. "Closer to jobs, they say, even though the only jobs for our people in town would be maids and yardmen. But they'd get us out of the way of development of this part of the county."

"Don't you all own the land across the road?" I asked. "All Mr. Snoddy's property?"

"Sure, and Miss Templeton's, too, but the company's proposal to the state says ownership of that whole tract is in doubt, because it was conveyed to an unincorporated entity of uncertain membership. It's a crock, but they could tie us up long enough to get us moved out of the way."

"What can you do?"

Pollo grinned. "We have a lobbyist with better connections." He waited for me to ask who it was, then flashed his million-dollar smile. "Young Senator, of course," he said. I guess I frowned. "I made a little pastoral visit on him down at his hunting lodge," he said.

"I know all about the lodge," I said. I always hated for him to act like he had to explain things to me. "You found out who the woman was?"

"As usual," he said, still grinning, "you know about half as much as you think you know. Young Senator's driver was William Allston, Bo. He's from town, only you probably don't know him; he's colored."

"Don't be such a smart-ass." The whole town knew William. He worked at the black funeral home, drove the hearse in a uniform that made him look like an admiral in a Gilbert and Sullivan operetta. Sometimes when people went to the city or somewhere and wanted to impress somebody, they would get William to drive them, in full regalia.

"You know who he is, Bo, but you don't know what he does." There was no point in explaining anything to Pollo when he was in that know-it-all mood. "William drove the car, and William took care of what Young Senator needed. It's not technically sex, according to Young Senator. I don't know whether that's because of racial composition or technique." The grin returned. "Maybe it's for medicinal purposes. Anyway, there was no woman."

Pollo apparently thought I shrugged.

"Don't shrug your shoulders like it's no big deal, Bo. You never saw it coming, because it doesn't fit your experience with Young Senator. Douglas, of all people, figured it out. He knew some people in town who knew William, and they knew all about it. 'Driving' white men is what William does for a living."

I wondered if that could be true. I thought about my friends in town who had laughed when we were kids about people who went to town with William Allston. It had never occurred to me that we were not laughing about the uniform.

Pollo went on. "When Douglas told me what was going on," he said, "I made a pastoral visit to Young Senator. I wasn't sure how he would react, but I figured I might be able to help him. I knew it would help us, no matter how he took it. And you know what? He thought he was doing exactly the right thing. Perfectly honorable. Didn't mind talking about it at all. He told me all about his wife's miraculous religious experience in recovering her virginity. He told me he'd been fooling around with Cora and other women when he was still having sex with his wife. But he said none of those flings ever had any chance of becoming a serious relationship. They were just healthy exercise and reduced his demands on his wife. He loved his wife. Still does. After she cut him off, he gave up other women for fear they might break up his marriage. Doesn't that sound honorable to you?"

"And William?" I said. "Is that honorable, too?"

"Was to Young Senator. 'A man's needs don't go away,' he told me, 'just because his wife becomes a virgin.' That rings true to me," Pollo said, grinning again.

I still did not see any reason to grin. Where are the naked wood nymphs when you need one? "Didn't he know he'd get caught?"

"Never thought about it. You know white people, Bo. They think whatever they do with black people doesn't count, like nobody will know. It's always a surprise to them that other black people know about it. It's an even bigger surprise if one of us mentions it."

It seemed to me that Pollo had developed a lot of ideas about white people, but there was no point in getting into that with him. Pollo's Principle of Approximate Truth was at work. "Young Senator has to figure you could tell somebody else," I said.

"He and I made a little arrangement," Pollo said. "He mentioned that through his visits to the lodge, he could take special notice of our needs at the settlement. I mentioned that he was doing the honorable thing as a faithful husband, under the circumstances God had given him, and that was his own business."

"Some pastoral visit," I said.

"It was helpful to everybody." The grin grew. "When I called about the quarry, he listened."

Pollo's confidence, born of pragmatism, was an unbecoming new characteristic, no matter how effective. But it didn't matter much to me. My thoughts about the quarry were on a much higher plane, remembering Mae Maude running down to the pool from our ledge, dropping her clothes along the way. I left Pollo to fight off Bubba on his own. I had to take exams, and I had to study the roadmaps to Louisiana. It was time to see just how much Mae Maude Snoddy remembered about me.

———

Minor, Louisiana, is not much of a town, not even much of a place. Brackish swamp water surrounds patches of gray-black ground, dirt like old ashes, and those patches come together to form causeways and small peninsulas and homesteads. The houses, scattered wherever there is enough ground to hold one, are cinderblock and sprawling. Commerce seems random, just corrugated tin sheds that might be auto repair shops, might be nothing at all, with rusted hulks of old cars abandoned in the yards. The entire area looks tentative, as if a fair-sized storm anywhere along the Mississippi might casually rearrange the whole thing.

I stopped at one of the tin sheds, one that turned out in fact to be an auto repair shop, and asked for directions to the middle of town. There was a snort from the two legs sticking out from under a car.

"What you looking for?" said another guy, standing at the open hood, wiping his hands on a greasy bandana. The pair of legs snorted again, like even this was a stupid question.

"Just the middle of town," I repeated. The disembodied legs sounded like they were hawking and spitting, but I didn't see how a person could do that, lying on his back under a car.

"This is about as middle as you gonna get," the complete guy said. "What do you need?" I decided to settle for a post office. "That's easy," he said.

"It's in the fedral building." He disappeared behind the hood of the car again, but when I didn't leave, he sighed heavily and tried again. "You saying you don't know where that is, either. It's down this road on your left. It's marked."

"It's the goddam fedral building," the legs said, as if that ought to be enough of a description for anybody.

The goddam fedral building was not the usual marble and stone monument, not even brick or cinderblock. It was tin. A large flat warehouse that suggested the local congressman was not high on the pork barrel distribution list. On the other hand, maybe it was the largest tin-sheathed building in the country. An American flag out front proclaimed, "This is the goddam fedral building."

There was no parking lot. The few cars in evidence were pulled up on what passed for a lawn. People who worked there apparently were dropped off, or else maybe they came in one of the two old schoolbuses pulled up at the front door. Inside was not unlike other federal buildings, without the marble floors, but still had the smell of a mausoleum. The post office was dead ahead, presided over by a postmistress who turned out to be perfectly pleasant and unhelpful.

"Nobody in this parish by that name," she said of the Snoddys. "I would know, you know," she added with a smile, "unless maybe they don't get any mail."

The postmistress indulged a single vanity. Not with her hair, which was mouse gray and more or less pulled back into what could have been a bun with more effort; instead, it bagged around her ears. And not with her eyes, which were also mouse gray and a little baggy. But her lips, oh, her lips: layers of lipstick in bright, bright red. I wondered if maybe for an extra dime, she would plant a fat red kiss on outbound envelopes.

"How about census records from the '50s?" I asked, knowing that I could follow a trail if I could find a toe-hold.

"Burned with the library when the high school integrated," she said, turning her lips into a pout.

"And I suppose the school records burned, too?"

"The whole school," she said. "They consolidated it after that." She waved her hand as if she might be pointing across the road, but there was nothing I could see. When I looked at the postmistress again, she was smiling. "Don't you want to ask about tax rolls?" she said.

"Burned, I suppose."

"Nope," she said, "there you're in luck." She leaned across the counter conspiratorially, apparently relishing her role as research assistant. The parish courthouse had moved to a bigger town in 1960, and federal judges now used that facility. It was a blow to Minor, but it had saved the parish records. "The tax rolls are there," she said quietly, "and birth certificates and marriage licenses. You might find something." She stood up straight again, and she winked.

The postmistress had given me one more thing to worry about: marriage licenses. I had not even considered the possibility that Mae Maude Snoddy might be somebody else these days. What if the postmistress actually knew something and was trying to warn me? What if I found her with a him? Could I pull off a "just looking up an old friend" explanation for my sudden appearance in Minor, Louisiana? Not likely. My best plan would be to go home and never mention to anyone that I had been anywhere.

On my way out of the building, I stopped at the directory posted on the wall, wondering what use there might be for a federal building when courts and records had moved away. And there in front of me was the answer, not just to that question but to The Question. Under U.S. Government — Programs, was an entry: Pre School/After School Care.

The director was listed as Mimi Templeton.

Room 15.

Had to be.

Goose bumps, standing hairs, rapid heartbeat, dry mouth, shallow breathing — I didn't make a list, but so far as I know, I didn't miss a single stereotypical reaction called for by the situation. Maybe tears, if that's one; I don't remember coming close to tears.

What was with my friends and their names? When I went off to college, my mother suggested I should use my full name, DeBault [DEE-bo], which was the family name of her maternal grandmother's French Huguenot ancestors, and far more professional sounding than Bo. I had not even come close to doing it. (A) Bo is who I already was, and (B) DeBault [DEE-bo] didn't sound remotely professional to anybody other than her, not to anybody outside Charleston. It might look good, but it would have to be explained constantly, and I couldn't go around signing letters,

> *"Yours truly, DeBault*
> [DEE-bo]."

Anyway, if Mae Maude thought she should change her name, why Templeton, same as Pollo? Maybe she didn't know Pollo had already taken it. It seemed reasonable that she would choose Miss Templeton's name on her own, and it seemed unlikely that she could have married somebody who just happened to have that name.

Room 15 was at the back of the building, down a long hall around to the back of the post office. There was a door with a window, and I walked by it three times before I could slow down enough to see anything. There were kids, all right, a bunch of them, all black as far as I could tell. And sitting crosslegged on the floor in the middle of them was Mae Maude. She was wearing jeans and a loose shirt, and she had her arm around one of the children who was trying to push another one out of her lap. I wondered if one of them might be hers.

She was smaller than I remembered, more delicate, more like her mother, and still very pretty. One of the children collapsed across her lap, and she let her long hair drag across his tummy to tickle him. He shrieked and rolled away, another child lying down for the same. I remembered her hair fanning across my chest on the dock at the camp pond, but there hadn't been anything funny about it then. I'd had the strange sensation on the dock that I was about to be snapped up and sent away for doing something really bad. I had the same feeling in the back hall at the federal building in Minor, Louisiana.

After a couple more discreet passes by the door, I sat down on a wooden bench in the hall. I hadn't planned to find her this soon, or like this at all. I imagined we would surprise each other, maybe crossing the street, going in opposite directions so there would be a suddenness to it and it would be immediately obvious whether we recognized each other or not. It would be unrehearsed, a moment that could easily go in any direction, depending on her reaction. Instead, I was about to ambush her in a situation that had built-in expectations. I could not possibly go on about my business down this hall if things didn't seem to click. What was I doing in this hallway anyhow? And that little kid couldn't possibly be hers. Hers would be ten years old — in fourth grade. Ten years was maybe longer than I had thought. Then, suddenly, there she was.

"Bo?" I jumped up and took her outstretched hand. She smiled, not big but the same smile I remembered. "I'm sorry I kept you waiting."

I had expected at least a hug, no matter what the circumstances. The much-ballyhooed sexual revolution of the 1960s had, as far as my personal experience was concerned, resulted only in women shaking hands like men. "I'm so glad to see you," I said, taking her hand in both of mine and hoping I wouldn't remind her of Young Senator. "How did you know I was waiting?"

"We don't get a lot of traffic past our door," she said, and there was that smile again, so easy for her. "Especially not people who pass by several times without coming in."

"I didn't want to interrupt."

"Are you kidding? It was all I could do to keep the children off the ceiling once they saw you. Every stranger is cause for twenty questions."

"Are you free now?" I asked. I was still holding her hand. I had held it too long, but there was no graceful way to drop it now, so I just held on as if I had meant to.

"It's nap time," she said. "Can you come back at six? That's when we're done here."

"Can I take you out to dinner tonight?" I asked.

"Around here? Not likely." She pulled her hand away and pushed her hair back. "We could grill hamburgers at my house."

"It's not that far into town, is it?"

"Not too far for me," she said. She smiled, but not like it was a big deal one way or the other.

———

The drive into New Orleans was awkward but important. People can have silence in a car when it would be embarrassing if they were just sitting together in a room. And there's an endless change in scenery to pretend to look at. We were pleasant, then silent for long stretches, and then pleasant again. I thought things were going well.

Then, "Bo, do you know that I have a son?" she said quietly. I tried not to change my breathing pattern.

"I knew you were going to have a baby, but nobody would tell me anything."

"Did you ask?" She was looking straight at me, and she was not smiling now.

"I went out to your mother's and to Miss Templeton's, but they wouldn't let me see you. I even went back out there at Thanksgiving."

"I didn't know that," she said. "I'm glad."

"Is the baby here in Minor?"

"He's not a baby anymore," she said, still without smiling.

"Practically a young man. Miss Templeton put him in Wilton Orphanage." She turned to look out her window, not at me. "They handled his adoption, and they won't give me any information about where — or who — he is." I knew the place, and I wasn't surprised that they played strictly by the rules.

"It's a pretty conservative home," I said. "I didn't even know they had integrated."

"Have they?" she asked, and there was a long silence now, not so comfortable.

Why in the world would she say that? She knew what I meant. I wished

I had taken up pipe smoking. It would have been a great time to puff and tamp and reload. Maybe Miss Templeton had passed the baby off as white. Maybe technically, the baby was white. I didn't know the rules about such things, but I did know he would've had three white grandparents and only one black. And Mr. Snoddy was both of his grandfathers and one of his great grandfathers. I bet the rules for calculating racial fractions didn't take all that into account, so maybe Miss Templeton just winged it. I bet it was easier to say the baby was white. No telling what he looked like anyway.

Mae Maude was still looking out her window, the swamp dotted with billboards rushing past. When she spoke again it was so softly I could hardly hear her.

"Bo, you think Pollo is the father of my son." There were tears in her eyes when she looked at me, and I had flashes of her mother, Cora, and one of her fits on the Snoddy lawn. Maybe, like her mother before her, Mae Maude had fabricated a more acceptable history and come to believe it was the truth. I wondered if she remembered that I knew all about it.

I spoke slowly, softly. "You told me he was," I said.

"You were there, Bo. You saw what happened."

I decided to take this one head-on. "I was there, Mae Maude," I repeated. "I saw you and Pollo. Remember? You told me he raped you."

"Pull over," she said. When I didn't, she hit my arm with the back of her hand, hard, opened her door and yelled, "Pull over!"

She was out of the car and running down the side of the road before I came to a complete stop. When I caught up with her, she stopped abruptly, and turned the other way. "It's okay," I said. "Come on back to the car. Whatever happened, it's okay."

"It's not okay, Bo," she said, and she was sobbing now, but like she was angry. Her face was bright red in the passing headlights. "Pollo didn't rape me. He's my brother. He's all the family I have. We were teenagers, and we were curious." She looked up at me. "So were you," she said. "Only you had more rules."

I decided not to dispute any of that, but the fact remained: I hadn't actually done anything wrong. Why was Mae Maude acting like I had? Her hands were clenching and unclenching at her sides, and I got the idea she'd hit me again if I got close enough.

"Let's get back in the car," I said, but she was tense and stiff, and we didn't budge.

"You left me in the woods with Bubba," she said. And that was it. My mind went racing through memory. I had followed Pollo out of the vesper dell, knowing I could not catch him, but just to keep Bubba from chasing him and doing no telling what. Mae Maude had kept on screaming — for show, I thought, or hysterical like her mother — and I had not wanted to go back down there until she stopped. I had left her alone with Bubba.

"Mae Maude," I said, but she still had things to tell me.

"When you were out of sight, he hit me. He hit me and hit me. He said I had defiled my body with nigger love." Car lights caught her face again and it was still wet, but she was not crying. She was coming at me, her words nearly spat out. "He said I wasn't fit to be his girlfriend, was not even fit to be his whore."

"I didn't know, Mae Maude. I didn't think —"

"No. You didn't, did you? You just made your guesses and figured you were right, just like always. But it was Bubba Wilson who did all that to me. It was Bubba."

Her voice broke. I stepped toward her and put my arms around her, and she didn't fight me off. I don't know how long we stood there beside the highway, but I held her until I felt her body start to calm. I could have said I'm sorry — sorry I left you there in the vesper dell, sorry I didn't come back faster, sorry I misunderstood what happened, sorry I left you so terribly alone all these years — but I thought the best way to say it was just to hold on tight. Besides, I wasn't sure what my voice would sound like.

When she was still and quiet for a while, with her head against my shoulder, I took a step toward the car, and she moved easily with me.

The boy had been adopted as an infant. Mae Maude saw him only briefly when he was born, first not wanting to see him at all, then not being able to help herself. She had mixed feelings about him, even still. There were days she had to find him, had to know something about him, tell him something about herself, and then days she'd rather just forget the whole thing. It wasn't hard. She didn't even know the boy's given name.

I drove slowly, thinking it was probably best not to get anywhere for a while. Mae Maude was quiet again. I kept my arm around her shoulders and she was tight against my side in the car. I wondered if she remembered shifting gears in the camp truck. Apparently so.

"Bo," she said finally, moving her hand to my leg, "do you want to get a Coke?"

I laughed out loud. It lacked the passion I might have imagined, but it was close enough.

So we went to New Orleans for dinner and had a hamburger and fries. It was certainly more relaxed than dawdling over a linen covered table and trying to blend in with quiet elegance. We talked about everything — everything. She remembered Pollo's jungle jewelry, and we laughed about Adlai Stevenson and his French-kiss policy. Mae Maude and Pollo had spent some time together that fall she was pregnant and deliberately chose the same last name to explain their family connection. Neither of them knew I had come out to the Rocks looking for them.

We had a long, leisurely meal under the golden arches. When conversation lagged, we were perfectly comfortable just looking at each other. "I don't want to take you home," I said.

"Who said anything about going home?" she said. "Do you like jazz?"

And so we found ourselves on a low bench on the front row in a dark and dingy room in the French Quarter, listening to the Preservation Hall jazz band. When I took Mae Maude's hand in mine, she leaned against me, and we stayed that way for a long time. I didn't even clap for the songs but used my free hand to thump the bench instead.

Preservation Hall has a way of stripping life to its basics. There is no pretense in the building or in the music — no rules, no protocol — just freedom for each musician to feel his way through, exploring his own possibility, but respecting all the possibilities of the other players. My mother would have doubted the catechism could be reinforced in such a place, but I thought my father would have understood. With the music freeing my soul and Mae Maude's shoulder alerting the rest of my body, I was ready to move on to the future.

The future turned out to be Pat O'Brien's piano bar and a tall rum drink in a hurricane glass. Nobody needed encouragement to sing along, but the management had provided an irresistible force. An old man with thimbles on his fingers and absolutely no statement in his face or body stood by the piano and tapped out the rhythms on the bottom of a silver drink tray that he held in front of him. The patterns were varied and intense. I told Mae Maude there was no telling what Sammy Davis and Fred Astaire could accomplish if they knew they didn't have to use their feet. She smiled, but I don't think she heard me. She was singing at the top of her lungs. The old man went on earnestly tapping while people put money on his tray.

I lost track of how many hurricanes we had, but I do remember a kiss on the way to the car that was French French, Cajun French and bonafide French Quarter. It was way beyond anything Adlai Stevenson could possibly have dreamed.

I do not know how we got back to Minor, but I remember clearly my dilemma when we pulled up at her house. "Do you have a couch I can sleep on?" I asked as I opened the car door for her.

"No," she said. She took my hand. "But don't tell your mother."

———

The phone rang with the flat off-key sound it always has in the morning. I was vaguely aware that it was light out, but I was in a hot cocoon of sweat-damp sheets and some thick sweet aroma that I could not quite identify. Like a stupefied firefly in the boll of a magnolia blossom, I tried to move up, shuddering to the buzzing sound each time the phone rang. It took me a minute to figure out what it was and then where it was, and when I answered it, I was still considerably less than half awake.

The voice on the other end was way ahead of me.

"Bo?" Then before I had time to answer the question, "DuBois is dead."

"What?" I said, "Pollo?" Mae Maude was not there. I was certain she had been; there were her blue jeans on the floor. "She's not here," I said.

"Bo!" Pollo was insistent.

"Yeah," I said, "I'm here."

"Did you hear me?"

"Yeah." I thought he had said DuBois was dead. "Mr. DuBois?"

"Bo, there's trouble." Dead silence. "You better come home."

"Come home? There isn't anything I can do about it."

"They killed him, Bo. And the sheriff is saying somebody from the settlement did it." Dead silence again. "How long will it take you to get here?"

"I'm in Louisiana," I said.

"I know where you are, Tarzan." That had to be true, but I couldn't think of anything to say about it. "The jungle has eyes, son," he said. I was waiting for the spear, but all he said was, "How long a drive is it?"

"Sixteen or seventeen hours. Or maybe eighteen. The roads are terrible."

"Come right now?" Uncharacteristically, it was a question and not an order. A quiet, desperate question. I couldn't tell him no. I looked at my watch.

"I guess I'll see you sometime tomorrow morning," I said.

I looked for Mae Maude but couldn't find her. Not in the house, not in town. At the federal building, they said she had come in, not feeling well, and asked for the day off. She hadn't checked at the post office or at the little grocery and drug store up the road, and I didn't think I could wait much longer. I wrote her a note, telling her what Pollo had told me. I wanted to talk to her about us, about everything, but I just said, "I'll call when I get there." And I added, "I love you." I wondered if she would believe that, and I almost tore up that page. But I was pretty sure it was true, so I left it.

The road home was a blur. Traffic, slow going my direction and fast going the other way; one crossroads town after another, so indistinguishable from each other there was no way of knowing when I crossed a state line. The roadside gradually changed, from canals big enough to swallow a car, to dry drainage ditches, to red-clay cuts and barbed-wire fences. When the radio lost all signals, which happened for long stretches between big towns, I had plenty of time to think.

So DuBois was dead. Pollo had said on the phone that the old man decided to take on the surveying crew on his own. He had told them to leave the settlement. When they ignored him, he picked up some of their equipment and tried to load it in their truck. The men had gathered around him, but his yelling at them to leave had attracted a crowd from the settlement, and the men packed up and left.

Pollo made a point of the fact that the surveyors were all white. "We gave him the courage to do that, you know," he said to me. I didn't know if that should have made us feel proud or guilty. Anyway, the men said nothing but blew their horns long and loud when they left.

"They'll be back," Mr. DuBois had said. He was right.

I wondered what the old man thought of the three of us that summer, Pollo and Mae Maude and me. I didn't recall that he discouraged us at all. In fact, he was very proud of Pollo learning to drive. And I couldn't remember him showing any fear of white people who came to the store, not the delivery men or Cora's strange visitors. Not even Bubba. I couldn't actually recall Mr. DuBois ever speaking to Bubba, but that was probably Bubba's doing. He didn't speak to anyone who was black. Without knowing anything about Mr. DuBois and his own family's history, Bubba managed to get himself and Mr. DuBois in exactly the right relationship, purely based on the color of their skin.

Somewhere before Atlanta I got behind a funeral procession and had to drive fifteen miles an hour for more than twenty miles. When we got to a small town, the police stopped traffic at the one red light so that nothing, I guess, would slow us down. I turned on my headlights and went right on through with the other mourners. So did the cars behind me as far back as I could see. The cross traffic and people pulled over to the side for respect must have thought we were burying the best-known corpse in three counties.

All the windows were down, but our pace did not stir up much of a breeze. The taste of eternity we were getting was not a taste of where any of us hoped to spend it.

When the procession finally stopped beside a small roadside cemetery in the open country, there was a moment of protocol confusion. In the rearview mirror, I could see headlights turning off and then on and off again. Presumably, the same questions occurred to everybody: Should we now pull over in respect for the family we had joined? Would it be enough to drive by slowly, or would the view of our faces confirm our insult? We apparently all reached the same conclusion at the same time. We took off like bats out of hell, lights off, faces turned away.

My eyes were dry and droopy. I turned the front vent window so the air blew directly in my face. I took off my shoes and socks. I propped one foot up in the blast of air. I counted fence posts as they whizzed by. I thought about the fire at Centennial and all we had learned about it, and I had to admit that, no matter what, we had made a lot of progress during the long lifetime of Mr. Samuel DuBois. When I couldn't stand it anymore, I pulled over on the side of the highway and slept until dawn.

Chapter Ten

———

LOOKING WHITE

I reached the Rocks a little after noon. There were cars and trucks pulled up on the grass in front of the church, with a half dozen highway patrol cruisers and a couple of television vans. There were children from the settlement standing on top of the cars closest to the building, trying to look in through the open windows. Several uniformed state troopers stood together on the lawn, just talking to each other. Some were smoking cigarettes. Two held rifles down by their sides, pointed at the ground. All of them looked toward me when I pulled up on the lawn. By the time I stepped out of the car, one of the troopers — one with a rifle — was standing directly in front of me.

"You Bo Fisher?" he said. I nodded. "I thought you might be," he said pleasantly. "Preacher wants you to come around back, through the office."

"Study," I said. The trooper turned, apparently planning to escort me. "I know the way," I said. "I'll just go alone." He peeled off toward the other troopers.

Through the open windows, I could hear someone praying, and it sounded like my father. It did not have the energy or the insistence of Pollo.

There were two more armed troopers on the steps to the study. They leaned apart so I could step between them, and I waited in the study for the prayer to end.

Funny how distinctive the sound of prayer is, as compared with a sermon. It's all just public speaking, but with prayer, there's a different volume, a different cadence, a different lift to the end of a sentence, a different way of holding on to the last syllable of each phrase. And a lot more pausing and breathing, as if maybe God might need a little time for translating into Hebrew. With sermons, a preacher speaks to be heard. In prayer, he speaks to be overheard.

At a Presbyterian funeral, the prayer is the main event, and it generally goes on forever, worse than the pastoral prayer at church. Once, when I was a boy, a woman stood up during one of my father's beautiful but interminable prayers, screamed bloody murder, then keeled over into the laps of the startled people seated next to her. It's a wonder some of them didn't die of a heart attack. Dad stopped praying and sat down, and the organist played "Sweet Hour of Prayer" about thirty times while two elders, a doctor and a funeral director, quietly vied for the bodies in that traumatized pew.

Dad said later that the woman had an epileptic fit. I didn't say anything, but I thought it might have just been her way of saying, "Will you puh-leeze hurry up and get this prayer over with?"

At length, the prayer at Mr. DuBois's funeral was finished. When I heard the chorus of amens, I opened the door and stepped into the jam-packed sanctuary, facing the congregation and blinded by the bright glare of television lights. The piano ripped into the recessional hymn, with its predictable breathing pattern covered by dramatic riffs: "What! — a Friend We Have in Je! — sus." Had to be Zebalon, the reformed town drunk, at the keyboard.

A hand clamped down on my shoulder and pulled me backward. It was Pollo, pulling me into the procession with him as he came down out of the pulpit. "Look white," he said to me with a frown. I did my best. In front of the casket, we met the line coming from the other side of the pulpit, and I was paired with my father. The two of us looked very white. One of the TV cameras at the back of the church followed us out the door.

Before I could say anything to Dad, Pollo led me to a spot beside the freshly dug grave. I found myself standing by Sister Holy Ghost, solemnly watching as the Flower Ladies handed baskets of flowers and a lot of greenery through the church windows to a line of men, passing the baskets from hand to hand, from the church to the grave. Sister's eyes were uncharacteristically soft and watery, and I was not sure she would want me to notice. I looked away but took her hand in mine. She squeezed tight. No words were necessary.

Pollo presided at graveside, with Dad standing beside him, both of them in simple black Geneva gowns despite the heat. Pollo seemed despondent, more than just professionally funereal. I shouldn't have been surprised. It was never clear whether Mr. DuBois was his parishioner or his bishop. He had played a huge role in Pollo's life, even when Pollo was just a kid on a bicycle. Now, as he buried his mentor not far from where he had buried Miss Templeton, the Reverend Paul Templeton stuck strictly to the words prescribed in the Book of Worship, exactly as Mr. DuBois would have expected.

In the cemetery, it became clear there were distinct clusters of people, not so obvious when they were scrambled in the pews. Easiest to spot were the white people, a dozen or so, all of whom I recognized from our church in town — which accounted for the cars on the lawn. There were people from the settlement. They stood bunched together like visitors, glancing around to get their bearings. Then there was a group of young people who looked very much at home, but whom I didn't recognize at all. Several of the girls wore wrap-around African style clothes and matching turbans. All the boys sported gigantic Afros the size of turbans. They milled about, rather than clustering, but they seemed to be touching base with Gloria — and with wherever the TV cameras were pointed.

The men from the settlement had built an arbor, a wood frame covered with tree branches, to protect the food laid out for lunch. My mother was there, under the arbor with some women from the settlement. I knew she had come to be "help," but I also knew she could not possibly get into that role. I could see her chatting with the other women, all the while pointing to where the food should be put, assigning Iced Tea Ladies to the ladles hanging on a huge big bucket, positioning someone to hand out paper plates and plastic forks. I knew the rule: Guests in a buffet line, even at a picnic in the country, should never have to pick up their own plates. I was certain she explained the rule as she was putting the Plate Lady in place. She could not fathom wasting an opportunity to help people improve themselves.

People loaded up plates of food and sat around on tree stumps and tomb-stones. Even the TV crews put their cameras down and got in line, most of the troopers exchanged their rifles for drumsticks, and there was a strange spirit of homecoming. All these people who didn't even know Mr. DuBois, waiting around for something dramatic or illegal to happen, still they couldn't help but grab a plate of country cooking.

I joined a group sitting on the steps to Pollo's study, away from the main crowd, in the shadow of a huge oak tree old enough to have shaded the burial of little Eddie DuBose in 1910. Dad was there, along with Pollo. Also Sister Holy Ghost and Zebalon.

"I didn't realize you'd be here," I said to Dad as I stepped over him to get to the top step.

"For DuBois?" he said. "Of course."

"I called him before I called you," Pollo said. We were all facing forward, and no one turned around. They looked like they were talking to their food. I knew from the way Pollo emphasized "you" that he was talking to me.

"Troopers," Zeb whispered. They had picked up their rifles and were moving off toward their cruisers. There was a sound of a car coming down the ridge road, and the loose feeling of community, of plenty of time for the future, seemed to break wide open. Pollo took off at a run, and I followed to see what might happen. A crowd formed, their paper plates set aside, cameras back on the reporters' shoulders.

The car pulled up on the lawn. I don't know who it was that the troopers expected, but it certainly couldn't have been Mae Maude, which is who got out. She was wearing white flats and a yellow and white sundress with a full skirt that twirled when she turned to close the door. Not exactly right for a funeral but perfect for a picnic in the country. And perfectly Mae Maude.

Pollo and I reached her at the same time. She kissed him on the lips, which I guarantee the troopers did not expect, and said, "I made good time. Thanks for the call." Then she kissed me on the cheek and said, "Thanks for the note." She took my arm as if I had been designated her escort, and we started back towards the church.

I introduced her to my father and to Mother, who was standing at the study steps with a plate of food for her.

"This is Mae Maude, Mother. She used to live out here. I was just visiting her in Louisiana." With my mother, confession was infinitely better than discovery. But I tried to make it sound like the most interesting coincidence in the world.

"So I heard," she said, just to let me know she could still discover faster than I could confess. "From Pollo," she added with a wink. It was a friendly gesture; ordinarily she would never disclose her sources. She smiled at Mae Maude and handed her the plate. "You'll need to eat, dear." I hoped Mae Maude would be able to finish all the vegetables.

I led Mae Maude to the top step where I had been sitting. Everybody else took their same places, but they turned sideways so they could see Mae Maude, who looked just as much at home as ever. She waved her fork at the cruisers on the lawn.

"Why the troopers?" she asked.

"They think we need protection," Pollo said.

"Uhm-m-hmm," said Sister.

"From the quarry company?" I asked.

"Hmh!" Sister said.

"They won't be back for a while," said Pollo. "Young Senator tied them up in legislative hearings about the damage their trucks are doing to the roads around the new quarry, over in Rutledge." He smiled. "They've reached an understanding about certain affiliations of a certain lobbyist's family. Young Senator agreed there are questions he won't ask — unless he has to."

"Uhm-m-hmm."

"The Klan?" I asked.

"Hmh!" Sister couldn't hold back. "They're already here." She waved at the troopers. "They're just wearing different uniforms today. It's just like it's always been. DuBois and Douglas both lived their whole lives believing that those white people would eventually find them. And eventually they did."

"Don't say that to Gloria," Pollo said. "Her friends are already blaming DuBois's death on a conspiracy between the Klan and the quarry company.

I guarantee that's what they're telling the TV cameras. That rumor's been going around," Pollo said, "and it's got the company worried."

Given the company's connection with Bubba Wilson, I thought it might well be more truth than rumor. I wasn't alone.

"Uhm-m-hmm," said Sister. "That's exactly why they're afraid of Young Senator's questions."

"Gloria's a lot closer to the truth than the newspapers are," Pollo said.

The papers were being fed by the sheriff, backed up by the Knoxtown *Journal*, reporting dissension in the settlement over the move to public housing. They speculated that somebody who wanted the relocation money had killed Mr. DuBois, because of his open opposition to the plan. According to Pollo, that was the real reason for the troopers' presence, sent by the sheriff to draw media attention to the possibility of violence in the settlement.

"They want people to think they're here to protect us from us," Pollo said.

"Uhm-hmh," said Zebalon. It was the only time I'd ever heard him have an opinion.

Several people from our church in town came over to say goodbye. Dad and Pollo both thanked them for coming. For some reason, Dad told them he might stick around until after dark. Nobody had asked that question. The TV cameras seemed to take an interest, filming the whole scene and following the town folk off to their cars.

The afternoon grew warm, and then late. The TV crews filmed the inside of the church and Pollo's study, the graveyard and down the ridge road toward the settlement. They filmed a few of Gloria's friends with angry, pinched looks on their faces. Finally they had to leave to make the evening news.

"Well," Dad said, standing to face us, "the television people are packing up. I think I'll go on home." He grinned at Pollo. "I'm tired of looking white," he added. "See you tomorrow, Bo?"

"I guess," I said. "Or tonight." He nodded and walked off toward the arbor.

"What did that mean, 'looking white?'" I asked.

"Protective coloration," Pollo said. "We thought we should let people see on television that there are some white people around, that we're not out here alone. That's why your father brought people out from town. That's why I need you to stay tonight."

"You think there'll be trouble?"

"Not as long as they think you're here, Tarzan." He smiled, but it faded in a hurry as Gloria came toward the study steps, flanked by two tall women just as imposing as she. They looked like they were escorting the Queen of the Nile. Pollo stood and took a step toward her, but she held up an imperial hand that stopped him in his tracks.

"Does that phone in there still work?" she asked, indicating the study door with a nod of her head. Pollo shrugged. "Well, don't use it," she said.

She told him she and her friends would spend the night at The Oracle — the Delphine Templeton Community Center — and that they would have a lookout posted on the road. The first sign of cars after nightfall and they'd be coming, not to worry. "Lawrence knows people in town who can get here in a hurry, just as soon as somebody sees what's going down." Her eyes flicked over me without any sign that she saw me. She led her parade of warriors down the ridge road toward Miss Templeton's house.

"They think they can change the world." Pollo said, under his breath. Then he added, "They may, but not tonight and not here." His eyes looked dark and cold as he watched Gloria's grand march. "Not 'til we're ready," he said. He looked at me and smiled. "Let's hope you're a big TV star tonight, Bo Fisher," he said.

"We have made so much progress in Mr. DuBois's lifetime," I said, "to have it come down to all this fear and suspicion."

Pollo looked at Sister with a little smile and said, "Do you think progress is something white people actually experience, or is it just an illusion unique to them?"

"Meaning what?" I said.

"Meaning that I'm pretty certain we don't see progress," he said. "Or look for it. Not the way white people talk about anyway."

"That's so," said Sister. "White folks are always talking about things getting better, even when they're not running for election to something."

"They think history is the movement from one thing to another," Pollo said. "For black people, history is permanent. Not even cyclical. Just permanent. Like a rock. Just sits there. Didn't really matter to DuBois whether it was 1910 or 1950 or last week."

"But he stood up to the quarry company," I said. "He never would have done that in 1910. That's the glory in strife that W.E.B. DuBois was talking about."

"You're getting *The Souls of Black Folk* mixed up with Edgar Rice Burroughs, Tarzan. What W.E.B. DuBois said is that we need a plain unvarnished tale. And do you remember what Mr. Samuel DuBois said about that? He said it's not true. He said the plain unvarnished tale is that strife does not bring the triumph of the good, the beautiful, and the true. It doesn't happen."

"Uhm-m-hmm." Sister said.

"That's what he told us, and that's what he showed us."

"Uhm-hmh!" Sister said.

"Progress," Pollo said. I wished I had never mentioned it.

Sister stood and stretched and told Zebalon he could escort her down the road to The Oracle. "That's where I'll be tonight," she said with a sigh, "keeping those people of Gloria's from burning the house down."

"Thanks," Pollo said. "G'night."

And then we were alone in the shadow of the big oak, Pollo and Mae Maude and I, sitting quietly on the study steps and looking into the cemetery. Mae Maude was holding my hand, and she was leaning against my shoulder, and I would have given anything for a dramatic recitation of one of Pollo's myths. What we needed was a naked wood nymph in full flight, but Pollo seemed done with all that. Maybe we were all done with all that. The ledge at the quarry pool was so far away, I wondered whether we would ever know anything like it again. We had been put out of Eden, and maybe it was best to hunker down and hold on tight.

The truth is, even in my memory of that summer we had first met, there was always a sadness at its core that would not go away. It was as if our friendship, Pollo's and mine, had been infected by some strange thing in the environment, something we didn't want and didn't want to talk about, something incurable, stunting, even killing.

And so I could not think of what to say now, on this night it seemed to have all come down to; the three of us on the church steps, waiting. The tombstones were so white in the gathering gloom of dusk, and we could see the red earth from Mr. DuBois's fresh-turned grave. And out there beyond what we could see, there was the old camp, the vesper dell, some rusting hulk of a truck gone to scrap. This was the place we grew up. In a way, we sat there on those church steps facing down our own history, the ghosts of

Bubba Wilson, of burning crosses, of doubts and of too much time gone by. What was there to say about all that?

"Hey!" Mae Maude bumped me sideways with her shoulder and stuck her foot in Pollo's rib. "You want to get a Coke?"

"What are the chances that Mr. DuBois kept something stronger in the back room?" I asked.

"Zero," Pollo laughed. "But we can look." He stood up and reached into his pocket. "I have the keys now."

———

I do not know whether history moves forward as the story of human progress or just sits there as testament to the immutability of human nature. It does sometimes seem to me to be a heavy weight dragging us back into the darkness, so that those who fail to learn the lessons of history are not the only ones who are doomed to repeat it.

I do know there is a great deal of darkness. But I also know that in the darkness there are moments of unmistakable light. Even if we know the moments are transitory, even if we feel the pull of the darkness, still I believe God calls us to those moments and promises that the light will not go out entirely.

IN MEMORIAM

———

Edward DuBose
Lamar, SC
Died in the fire at Harbison College
March 17, 1910
Age 12

Carl Duckett
Charlotte, NC
Died in the fire at Harbison College
March 17, 1910

Samuel Jenkins
Carlisle, SC
Died in the fire at Harbison College
March 17, 1910

ACKNOWLEDGMENTS

———

When I was diagnosed with ALS shortly after writing the first chapter of *Fire in the Rock*, my wife, Joan, and our children inspired me with their unfaltering love and their confidence that we could live with whatever the disease might bring. When it brought paralysis that left only my eyes functioning effectively, we found technological advances ready for us—in our case, with the Eyegaze System from LC Technologies. Neil Cottrell and Rusty McDonald and their team take care of me and keep my computers running, my body healthy, and my life full and good. Sally McMillan, my agent, gave me confidence and motivation.

The Novello Festival Press is a part of our public library, formed to encourage local writers. The hardcover edition of *Fire in the Rock* was their first novel, and I am grateful to them. Ashley Warlick, a successful writer and teacher, turned editor for me with persistence and diplomacy and skill and remarkable sensitivity and hard work.

I am indebted to Maureen O'Neal and her associates at Ballantine Reader's Circle for this paperback edition. I don't know what more a novelist could ask than to have a publisher who takes a story seriously and encourages readers not only to read the work but to think about and discuss it.

Fire in the Rock

JOE MARTIN

A Reader's Guide

A Conversation with Joe Martin

This interview was conducted by the author's son David, a graduate of Denison University in Ohio and now a student in the Master of Fine Arts program at Queens University in the Martins' hometown of Charlotte, North Carolina.

David Martin: Okay, Dad, your children want to know: How many of the teenage exploits in *Fire in the Rock* were drawn from your personal experience?

Joe Martin: Zero, kid. Zip. None.

DM: But everyone who knows you says Bo sounds exactly like you.

JM: Well, I think Bo is a lot like me as a teenager. He reacts to experiences very much as I would have—naively, idealistically, and often wrongly. We are also both preachers' kids, but I never experienced Bo's "exploits." And I never anticipated it would be so hard to explain that the story is fiction!

DM: How about Pollo and Mae Maude? Are they based on real people or are they composites of a lot of people?

JM: You know what? I can't think of a single characteristic of either one that I drew from someone I knew, except that your mother and I once had a beautiful bicycle tour guide in France who had, shall we say, the distinctive physical geometry of Mae Maude. But Pollo is a pure creation. One summer I saw a boy my age repairing bicycles at a country store. I saw him several times, but—just like Bubba in the book—I never even spoke to him. In a way, the character of Pollo is my apology to that boy. I often thought about him as I wrote.

DM: Is that why you wrote the book?

JM: No. I have always thought that I grew up in a remarkable little town, Winnsboro, South Carolina. Even though we moved from there in 1953 when I was twelve, I still think of it as home. It was a wonderful place to grow up—a very gentle time and town. Later I saw that there was a brutal meanness based on race that coexisted very comfortably with that genuine gentleness. And much later I began writing as a way of understanding—or at least of coming to terms with—those two very real aspects of our life.

DM: I don't think I've ever been there.

JM: Well, I've neglected your education! But it's not too late. Winnsboro doesn't change much from one century to the next. We'll go. I can show you the incredible architectural heritage we had for a neighborhood. On my short walk to school, I passed a tall town clock and marketplace built in 1833 and modeled after Independence Hall in Philadelphia, an imposing early-nineteenth-century Greek Revival courthouse designed by Robert Mills (who also designed the Washington Monument), a large granite Confederate monument erected in the middle of the street before cars were invented, and a house that the British general Lord Cornwallis used as his headquarters in the Revolutionary War. By the time I got to school I had walked through nearly two hundred years of history. Some Winnsboro landmarks such as those and some actual events (like the Klan march and the Miss Universe parade) appear in the book to give the fiction a sense of place and reality, but the stories I've told certainly didn't happen in Winnsboro and don't characterize the town as distinct from any other. In fact, Winnsboro is not unique, except for being more genteel than most places, so the story is not at all about Winnsboro but about the warped sense of race that dominated the whole South then—and did before and still does.

DM: Doesn't that compression of history have a lot to do with *Fire in the Rock*?

JM: Sure, and with Southern culture in general. On the surface, *Fire in the Rock* is literally about growing up in the segregated South of the 1950s and '60s. It's about the effect of race on perceptions and relationships. But there's a metaphysical issue at work, too, at least as I see it. It has to do with the impact of history, which is a problem that interests me. Is it a rotted corpse, as Pollo says at one time, that must be dug up and confronted so we can progress? Or is it a mute, immovable rock, as he says later, that doesn't change its meaning from one event to the next? Several stories in the book raise that question, and that's what the opening quote from *The Great Gatsby* is all about.

The question is this: Is there "fire in the rock" of history? Is there a dynamic for change, or is human nature in stasis and beyond the possibility of redemption? Or is the whole thing just beyond our ability to understand or influence?

I don't think readers have to deal with all that. The book has to work on its surface, it seems to me—on the level of the quarry ledge and Tarzan movies and Bubba Wilson's grandfather's Klan terrorism and the Philadelphia dinner and Young Senator's odd philandering and Mae Maude's geometry—or it doesn't go anywhere.

DM: That brings me back to the characters. Where did you come up with names like Sister Holy Ghost, Sweet Daddy Grace, Jelly Roll, Young Senator, and Mae Maude? It's interesting, because your children have pretty boring names: Joe B., Elizabeth, and David. I would not have minded being named Sweet Daddy Grace.

JM: And Elizabeth could have been Sister Holy Ghost?! We could have had a traveling tent revival.

DM: Did Southerners have neat names like that when you were growing up?

JM: What a question from a generation that has Sister Souljah and Eminem and Snoop Dogg! Actually, Sweet Daddy was a real person, Bishop C. M. Grace—of Philadelphia, I think—who was the flamboyant head of the United House of Prayer for All People. He traveled like the pope, complete with flowing robes and adoring throngs and a special parade vehicle. He came to Winnsboro several times while we lived there. There was a woman in town who went by the name of Sister Holy Ghost, although I knew absolutely nothing about her except for her name. At the time, I didn't know there was anything odd about it. Remember, I was twelve when we moved away. Jelly Roll was real, too. I made up Mae Maude Snoddy because I wanted her to have a name she would want to change. Then her mother changed her own name in the very first paragraph of the story, so Mae Maude was stuck with Mae Maude.

DM: And Pollo?

JM: Pollo was named for the Greek sun god, Apollo, so his name is pronounced to rhyme with Apollo. (It is *not* the Spanish word for chicken or an English game played on horseback!) There are bits of the Apollo myth throughout the book. They shouldn't get in the way of anybody's enjoyment of the story, but they explain why some things are as they are. Apollo, for example, was the interpreter of the oracle of Delphi in the Temple of Apollo—hence Delphine Templeton. And that explains the relationship of Pollo and Miss Templeton in the story.

DM: Is mythology something you studied in your graduate program at Duke?

JM: Nope, seventh grade. In Winnsboro, we had a course in Greek, Roman, and Norse mythology in the seventh grade, taught by Ida Lou Macfie, who was also the principal of the school. Miss Ida Lou scared us to death as the principal, but she was a great teacher. In almost twenty years of schooling, I never had a teacher better than Miss Ida Lou or a class better than that one.

Pronunciation of mythological characters, however, was not Miss Ida Lou's strong suit. The Valkyries, for example, came out as Wall-kirkies. Nobody wanted to correct Miss Ida Lou, so the whole class referred to Brunhild and her band of women warriors as the Wall-kirkies. That is also why Mae Maude's mother changes her name to Terpsi-core instead of Terp-SIC-kuhrie.

DM: One more character: The image of Bubba Wilson living his life like he was always crossing the goal line is powerful, yet it hints at a little jealousy. You have an older brother Bubba. Was he the inspiration for Bubba Wilson?

JM: Good gracious, no! Well, maybe in a way. Physically, they're almost a match except for hair color, but your uncle Bubba Martin was the classic

Southern Bubba paradigm: small-town firstborn of four sons, inheritor and defender of the family name, valedictorian of his class, all-state in football, soloist in the choir, president of the student body, and wanted to be a medical missionary. He could be terrifying (I had friends who were afraid to come to our neighborhood, although there was no real evidence that Bubba ever imprisoned slackers in our basement), but he was clearly what we should want to be when we grew up. And he clearly expected us to try.

Bubba Wilson is a more typical Bubba, his flaws of character masked by his family's power. Everything was given to him; nothing was expected of him. There is a hymn, "This Is My Father's World." At Davidson, it was rewritten as a spoof on people like Bubba Wilson, a good number of whom used family connections to get into the college: "This is my father's town / And all that lies around, / All that I see / Belongs to me, / This is my father's town." Arrogance without obligation, that's Bubba Wilson.

The current stereotype of a Bubba as a redneck who hangs around the filling station is a modern invention. In the '40s and '50s, those people were named Junior. There, that's a little Southern cultural history for you.

DM: Bo is not like any of those Bubbas.

JM: No, he's too naïve, too unsure of himself.

DM: Is it fair to say that Bo's dedication to doing the right thing blinds him to a portion of reality?

JM: I think that's fair. When Robert Kennedy was killed, his brother Ted said, "Some people see things as they are and ask Why? Others see things as they ought to be and ask Why not?" Well, there's another group of mostly innocent idealists who see the world as they think it ought to be and never ask any questions at all. You practically have to hit them with a sledgehammer to make them see reality. I'd say Bo undergoes quite a bit of reality therapy.

DM: What's a sledgehammer?

JM: I have no idea.

DM: But Bo is not really surprised when others act immorally. He seems to expect it. And what about the extreme guilt he feels when Pollo suspects Bo called the sheriff on him?

JM: That's a double sledgehammer. (By the way, I think a sledgehammer is like a pickax, but with two blunt ends.) Anyway, in this case Bo has no experience to help him understand: The reality is not true. The truth of that situation is a fiction. Later, as a grad student, Bo calls it the "suppositious story," the supposed context that gives a fact—the sheriff's siren, for example—meaning. It happens over and over in *Fire in the Rock*, and the tangled web of unspoken suppositious stories is a major reason we can't get beyond the racism that seems such a permanent part of our culture.

DM: Did you always feel the tension between races? Was there ever a time when you felt completely at ease, as in not worried about others' perceptions, with black friends?

JM: Yes, I always felt the tension and, no, I never felt completely at ease. There was a trickier tension between whites who were segregationists and those who were not. People had to be careful with what they said, depending on who was listening. Black people had to be constantly aware of who was who. In college, I had a summer job in the mountains. On my days off, I would hitch a ride out to the head of one trail or another, hike all day, and then hitch a ride back to town. There are not many black people in the mountains, and I was surprised one cold rainy day when an elderly black couple in an old truck stopped and picked me up. Without thinking, I climbed into the cab with the driver and his wife. We had a perfectly ordinary Southern conversation, except that I didn't know any of the people he knew in Winnsboro. When we were close to town, he asked me to get down on the floorboard. He didn't say why, and I didn't have to ask. Race was not something anyone could ever put out of mind.

DM: Would you have made Pollo sit in the back of the truck? Would you have been relieved if he chose to do so?

JM: I want to think I would have told him to sit up front with me, but I can't be sure. There was so much that we didn't question. Despite his genuinely good intentions, Bo is often caught making racially biased assumptions about Pollo. That was intentional on my part, because I have experienced it so many times in my own life.

DM: Ever been skinny-dipping in a quarry pool?

JM: Nope. My mother would have jerked a knot in my head. Besides, there were no quarry pools where we lived. I'm telling you, the novel is fiction.

DM: Okay, let's talk about the novel. Do you remember what was the "idea seed"? What was it that got the creative process going?

JM: There were three. I guess that's a hybrid. About thirty years ago, Marguerite Schumann told me of a really bizarre incident that happened in Appleton, Wisconsin. It had to do with the discovery of a bag of human fingers. I wondered at the time how in the world something like that could ever have happened in what I knew was the more genteel environment of a small town in South Carolina. So when I finally started writing twenty years later, that's where I started.

DM: What took you so long?

JM: I had to feed you. Actually, I had an absolutely wonderful but very demanding job at the bank as it grew to become NationsBank and then Bank of America, so I waited.

DM: What happened to the story?

JM: I started a short story about this very genteel lady and the bag of fingers. Its setting was a town like the one I knew. As I wrote, the tension between race and gentility quickly overwhelmed the story I had in mind, and I started all over, just to see what would happen. That became the story of Miss Mattie and Joe Douglas in *Fire in the Rock*.

DM: Is getting a girl to change gears in a truck one of your old moves?

JM: Give it up, David. The story is fiction.

DM: Survey says: That answer is a dodge. But, okay, what was the second seed?

JM: A pair of trees. One is a one-sided tree on the way to our lake house, where cattle gather for shade in the summertime. The other is a crape myrtle on my old running route through our neighborhood in town. It looks like a skyrocket when it's in full bloom, so I put it behind Cora in the opening scene and turned Cora into Miss Liberty. If its skyrocket appearance is emblematic of freedom, the crape myrtle also carries a foreboding of death, if you care about such things. Because of its wrinkly petals, that type of myrtle is named for the crinkly crape material that was used mostly for mourning clothes in the nineteenth century and maybe earlier. I love that kind of stuff.

DM: The one-sided tree is in that same scene.

JM: Yep. I gathered my characters under it like the cows I had seen on the way to the lake. A one-sided tree is unnatural, either diseased or wounded, so you know nothing good is going to happen under it. Those two trees stamp the character of the Snoddy place from the get-go just as clearly as the pristine lushness and cool clear water create the Eden character of the quarry pool. Again, nobody has to notice all of that, but that kind of scene creation is part of what I like about writing. I think it gives the developing story some integrity and structure. It certainly imposes some limits on the characters, keeps them from wandering too far afield.

What became the first chapter of *Fire in the Rock* first became another short story. It was accepted for publication in *The Crescent Review* just a month after my diagnosis with ALS. It would be my first published fiction, and that was a huge boost. The combination of the diagnosis and the acceptance of the short story focused me on the possibility of pushing the story ahead. Bo and Pollo became very important to me, and I wanted to find out what would happen to them.

DM: I want to ask you when you knew how the story would end, but you said there was a third idea seed.

JM: And an important one, as far as I am concerned. About ten years ago, I took some time off from the bank to do research on the history of the Presbyterian church in South Carolina. It was a project my dad left incomplete when he died. The result was published by the South Carolina Historical Society. Get this title: *Guide to Presbyterian Ecclesiastical Names and Places in South Carolina from 1685 to 1985.* It did not hit the bestseller lists. I bet you have never looked at it seriously.

DM: I don't think I ever heard of it.

JM: Anyway, I kept running into fragmented references to a disastrous fire at Harbison College in 1910 in Abbeville. But all I could find on Harbison was that it was founded for former slaves and had been in Columbia since around 1915. At the South Caroliniana Library in Columbia I found newspapers with predictably scant accounts of the mysterious fire. But in a box, I found a collection of unpublished papers gathered by Tom Johnson, library director and aggressive archivist. They were reminiscences written by alumni after the college closed for good in the early '60s. They knew all about the fire. Some of the accounts were written by children, now elderly, of men who had survived the fire. The story they told was sketchy but suggested a vivid, gruesome, brutal reality. The accounts were secondhand, of course, but they were consistent with what circumstantial evidence I could find: maps, contemporaneous events, and public affairs, and so on. I wanted to do a book on it, but my paralysis from ALS was gaining on me, and I realized I would never be able to complete the research. So I decided to fictionalize the story consistent with that box of hand-me-down horrors. I created a fictitious college fire in a fictitious town that has some of the wonderful landmarks of Abbeville but suggests nothing about the character of that town. The result is the story of Mr. Do-Boy.

DM: So when did you know how the book would end?

JM: Not until I wrote it. I had some ideas of where the story would go, but time after time the story wouldn't go there. I had a couple of creative control problems. Soon after I gathered the characters under that one-sided tree, they took over—and frequently surprised me. I knew that would happen. In fact, for me, that's a big part of the fun of writing: to find out what happens.

Remember we took a long winter vacation in St. Thomas? You were there part of the time. I had not finished the book as I had planned, and the publisher's deadline would pass before we came home. I was pretty close to totally paralyzed by then, so we hauled my Eyegaze computer to St. Thomas so I could work. Since ALS does not affect the eyes, there was never any doubt that I would be able to finish the book. There was some question whether three weeks would be long enough to resolve two open questions.

With three weeks left, it was clear that someone would have to die; it was not clear who. The other problem was trickier. I had not planned to bring Mae Maude back. That seems odd now even to me, given the way things turned out, but honestly when I was writing the first half of the book I just thought she was a teenage summer romance and we would never see her again.

The problem was that every woman who read the draft demanded more Mae Maude. That group included my editor, Ashley Warlick, who was in constant contact with me in St. Thomas by E-mail.

I was and am baffled by the strength of Mae Maude's appeal, especially to women, but not only to them. She forms a bond with readers that is totally independent of me. I could not imagine Mae Maude as an adult, but there was nothing to do except send Bo to find her. While I was distracted by the postmistress of Minor, Louisiana, Mae Maude appeared. I liked her immediately. So did Bo. Only the death of Mr. Do-Boy would bring Mae Maude back to the Rocks. So both open questions were answered.

In my wheelchair with my Eyegaze computer in the Caribbean, I didn't look as much like Hemingway as I had imagined, but the book was finished. I liked the ending and I liked Mae Maude. Life is good.

Reading Group Questions and Topics for Discussion

1. Thinking that Bo has "turned him in" for his flirtations with Mae Maude, Pollo runs away when he hears sirens. When Bo realizes this, he sees for the first time the complications of their friendship. "I wanted to call out to him across the distance, wanted to take his hand and wanted to hit him at the same time, wanted to set us free, wanted to sing I went to the rock to hide my face, but the porch and the whole world fell silent. . . . And I did not then and do not now know how to set it free." Discuss Bo's mixed emotions at this moment. What emotion do you think was the strongest? Hurt? Shame? Anger?

2. Bubba Wilson rolls into town and brings with him many unpleasant realities for Bo, the most obvious being his cruel racism. But there are other reasons that Bo hates and fears Bubba. What are they?

3. What is the importance of Pollo's fascination with Kulonga in the Tarzan novels? How does this differ from his fascination with mythology? How is it similar?

4. Discuss the impact on Pollo of his discovery that the residents of the settlement at the Rocks aren't the only African Americans in the world.

5. Describe Bo's first experience attending the movies with Pollo. Explain the social significance of "Heaven" and compare this to his view of it through the eyes of a teenage boy.

6. When Mae Maude tells Bo "He raped me," Bo concludes that she means Pollo. What was your initial conclusion?

7. The cross that the Klan puts up at the end of the swimming dock symbolizes the end of the idyllic summer and the end of innocence for Bo, Pollo, and Mae Maude. When Bo tells Delphine Templeton that he had nothing to do with the cross she replies, "We all had something to do

with it." Discuss the individual culpability of Bo, Pollo, and Mae Maude for the tragic events that took place. How does Miss Templeton see herself responsible?

8. The events leading up to Pollo's (Reverend Paul Templeton) arrest depict great strength and bravery on the part of the settlement at the Rocks. But this cost Joe Douglas his life. What else did it cost the community? What did it cost Pollo personally?

9. Pollo tells Bo that Pollo has died and his new name is Paul Templeton. What else has changed about Pollo? How is he the same? Does Bo still see the same things he admired in Pollo that summer ten years earlier?

10. What is the significance of Pollo naming his youth center The Oracle? Why does he change the name?

11. "There was a saying at home that in the North, whites said to black people: 'Rise as high as you want to, but don't come any closer,' while people in the South said: 'Come as close as you want to, but don't rise any higher.'" What is your interpretation of this saying?

12. When Bo travels to Philadelphia with Pollo he feels for the first time what it's like to be treated badly because of racial stereotypes. How does this trip change his relationship with Pollo?

13. Throughout the book several "corpses" are dug up, from the first in Mae Maude's backyard, to the truth about the fire at Centennial College. Discuss the significance of some of the "smaller" truths leading up to the big discovery about Samuel DuBois.

14. Do you think that Bo and Pollo made the right decision in setting Samuel DuBois free from his secret? In the end do you think he was better off?

15. Imagine your most basic rights being taken away . . . how would you feel? How would this differ if you had grown up without these rights? What would you risk to obtain your civil rights?

16. Discuss racism today . . . how have things changed and how have they remained the same?

ABOUT THE AUTHOR

———

Joe Martin, a South Carolina native, is a former English teacher turned banker who holds a Ph.D. from Duke University. He recently collaborated with Ross Yockey on *On Any Given Day*, which described how Martin has learned to cope with ALS, Lou Gehrig's disease. He lives in Charlotte with his wife, Joan. This is his first novel.

———